RAYNA L. STINER

TAGORBI PUBLISHING, LLC

ALSO BY RAYNA L. STINER

The Broken Veil

REIGN OF SHADOW FANTASY SERIES:
The Dragon's Name
The Dragon's Eye
The Dragon's Fire

Acknowledgments

 To the anonymous man on the airplane years ago who said to me, "Never let the anxiety of failure keep you from realizing your dream": thank you. These are words I live by.

 As always, to my alpha reader, partner, mate, best friend and comic relief: I couldn't have married a better man. Thank you for your patience, support and critical eye.

 Thanks also go to my forensic nurse examiner, and sexual assault nurse examiner friend, who offered critical information to lend authenticity to the book.

 Thank you beta readers: Dan, Fran, Anthony and Danny. I'm humbled to have your thoughts, expertise and detailed feedback that pushes me to excel.

Content Warning

While *Bitsy* centers around healing and empowerment after trauma, some scenes evoke strong responses, particularly for survivors of abuse, especially child abuse.

Dear readers please prioritize your well-being and engage with this book at your own pace.

Bitsy includes themes and depictions related to:

- Sexual assault and sexual abuse (including childhood sexual abuse)

- Dissociative Identity Disorder (DID) and other trauma-related mental health challenges and symptoms

- Violence against perpetrators, including vigilante justice and revenge

- Suicide (off-page, referenced)

- Kidnapping and abuse of children

- Hospital and emergency medical settings

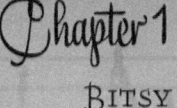

The ever-present voice in my head, or Liz as she'd come to call herself, sniggered at me. If she were in the driver seat instead of me, she wouldn't be blushing wildly at the handsome paramedic. Flustered, I ducked my head back to the task, shuffling through patient charts to see which charts I still needed to gather.

I glanced up again, eager for another glimpse. He was wheeling in some poor person on a stretcher. He and two other paramedics checked in with a triage nurse and then were pointed in the direction of an empty room. On their heels, another set of paramedics entered the double doors in a rush. They stopped in the entryway, on the other side of the nurses' station where I stood. Dr. Hurt—yes, really—was getting the rundown while simultaneously looking over the patient.

One of the paramedics held an IV bag, another administered air to the patient with a hand-held plastic pump. The room swelled with tension. Dr. Hurt squeezed his hands into blue gloves, nudged his glasses back up his nose with a wrist and looked down at the patient, his mouth a grim, flat line. I'd seen that look before. My heart dropped into my stomach for the person on the gurney.

I pulled my gaze away from Dr. Hurt and his new patient and reached for the next chart in the filing cabinet. I looked at the list scrawled out on the sticky note again to make sure I picked the right name. Movement caught my eye and I glanced up to capture sight of the cute paramedic again. He had his back to me. The view was a nice distraction from the other goings-on in the department.

"Hunky," Corey said.

My head whipped around. The emergency department's health unit coordinator, or HUC, for short, grinned at my blush.

"I'll try not to be jealous." He winked at me from behind a set of frameless glasses.

In addition to being the HUC, he was also my one and only friend. Corey turned back to his monitor, the mouse clicking away faster than I thought he could possibly track.

Without looking up, he added, "You should go talk to him, ya know. After he's done dropping off the patient."

"Uh..." I stuttered. A little problem I still had, even after years of therapy. I covered my mouth with my hand and took a small, calming breath, "I'm sure he's not interested in someone like me."

"Like you? What's that mean?" Corey didn't wait for an answer. "Listen, Bitsy, you gotta get out more, and you need more friends. I can't date you forever." He looked at me over his glasses, his gray-green eyes admonishing, before he rattled off without feeling, "Look. You're holding me back. I need some space. It's not you, it's me." He rolled his eyes at me.

"So, you're breaking up with me?" I said, in mock-hurt, clutching my hands to my heart.

"How 'bout this?" He crossed his arms over his muted-blue scrubs. "If you don't flirt with Super Sexy, I will. And you know I got skills." At this, he waved his hand down the length of his seated and scrub-attired, skinny body. "Don't even doubt me, girlfriend."

This was a joke, since I was pretty sure Corey was straight. We'd known each other for the past year, after meeting in college. I was in the orchestra and he had volunteered to assist the director with administrative-type duties. Little did I know then my music career would take such a drastic shift to being an administrative assistant myself. And in healthcare, of all places.

Corey hadn't had either a girlfriend or a boyfriend, but his eyes often scanned women's bodies with what I surmised to be appreciation. But, what did I know? Maybe he was bi.

He looked me up and down. "You could give me a run for my money, though."

My stomach squirmed at the compliment. I was tall and skinny, which was enough for most people to judge me as "pretty", but I never thought so. I lacked curves. My eyes were hazel, not some arresting color of blue or green. And my hair was a rat's nest of brown curls that almost always frizzed with the rain-drenched Portland, Oregon air.

Overhead, the intercom bonged. Corey and I paused, waiting for the announcement.

"Code Rapid Response. Oncology Unit. Fifth Floor." The woman spoke with robotic pronunciation, forming each word with care.

Corey looked toward the ceiling while the message was repeated. A woman in a white lab coat, who I recognized as our house supervisor for the day shift, and another woman in khakis and a polo—one of our doctors—with a stethoscope draped around her neck, ran past the station. Rapid Response codes were called when a patient was tanking but hadn't gone into respiratory distress—yet. A whole team of people answered these codes. And they took it seriously. If they had to run, it didn't matter if they were in their fifties, were fifty pounds overweight and sorely out of shape. Someone's life was in the balance, so they ran.

Corey went back to staring at his computer as the EMS guys rounded the desk, Dr. Hurt trotting along beside them. They took a sharp turn and headed for bay one. Trauma.

Corey jumped up, watched them wheel the patient into the room and then he plopped back down into his chair. He yanked the phone out of its cradle and pressed the intercom button. His baritone voice boomed overhead. "Code Trauma. Bay one. Emergency Department." When he ended the announcement, he looked at me, looked past me, looked back at me again and then mouthed, *Flirt. With. Him.*

I turned in the direction he was looking, over my shoulder. The hunky paramedic had delivered his patient and was heading toward the exit and subsequently toward the nurses' station.

Tucked in a corner inside my mind, Liz had been quiet, but I could feel her hunger as she eyed him. His eyes met mine. The corner of my mouth rose as Liz fixed him with that look. He started to smile, stopping for a moment in the middle of the department while people in white coats and colorful scrubs rushed past him.

His white, button-up shirt was tight on his muscled biceps, which Liz noted with no less than a lingering stare. My body, Liz's body, leaned toward the paramedic. Her control seeped into my muscles. My mind blurred with the need to go to sleep, the need to allow Liz to take over. The EMT started toward us. Liz moved us efficiently to the counter and laid an arm casually across the cool surface. She looked away from the paramedic and reached for a pen. She was all grace with our long arms and legs and all coy flirtatiousness with boys. I thought maybe it'd be best to let her do the talking, but then again, if I did that, I wouldn't get to live the experience myself. And wasn't that why we were going to counseling and working through our issues?

I wanted to live—to truly live.

I took several breaths and rubbed my arm with my hand to replace the slow-creeping numbness with feeling.

"I liked him first," I told her. Behind me, I could hear Corey typing away at his workstation.

"Oh, yeah? All right, Tiger. Go for it."

And just like that, she left me alone. Alone and facing a super-hunky guy who spoke to me, but my ears rang, and I couldn't hear a word he said.

"Huh?" I asked.

He stared at me, his blond eyebrows raised above his blue eyes and smiling mouth. I felt like an idiot. He'd said maybe three words, and I probably looked as if I couldn't understand him.

"I said, come here often?" he asked.

I laughed way too loudly. He backed away, his smile faltering. Liz laughed at me from her quiet corner. I blushed, twisting the pen in my hands.

"You ready to give in?" she asked, a smile in her voice.

"Back off."

"Fine, fine. Let me know when you want to throw in the towel. I'll be here. Like always."

"I'm Gabe," he said and extended a hand.

I hesitated while I stared at his hand. Knowing if I didn't shake, I'd really look like the weirdo I was, I held my breath and took it, noting how my hand trembled and how cold it was in his big, warm palm. The contact did what contact always did. My heart raced and throbbed, the spike of terror plunging into my chest. My breath caught. The panic stole away my peripheral vision, and the world swam. I shook his hand and felt the surge of energy from him. My nerves pulsed in rhythm to my heart. I took a slow, steadying breath, and to my surprise found his contact warming, relaxing, peaceful.

Whoa, Liz and I thought together. My panic attack stopped. My shoulders relaxed.

"Would you like to grab coffee sometime?" he asked.

The buzz of warmth tickled through me. My body melted.

"Th-that'd be nice," I said.

"Why do you always have to stutter and ruin it?" Liz pouted.

Ashamed, I let my hand slip from his. He didn't seem to notice the stutter. In fact, he was smiling at me. Thoughts flooded me, as they always did. I could never be in a relationship. Foisting my issues onto someone else would be really unfair. Plus, at what point did you reveal that there was not just one person inside you, but two? As I meandered through self-doubt, my confidence faltered.

Gabe peered down as I wrote my cell number on a hospital-branded sticky note. I tore off the sheet and handed it to him. Several of his colleagues rushed past him. He took the note, folded it into itself so the sticky part pasted the two sides together, then he carefully tucked it into his back pocket.

A short, balding man with a crazy, full mustache appeared at Gabe's elbow. He stomped to a stop and looked up at Gabe, who was still looking at me. My glance switched between the two of them. Mustache cleared his throat. Gabe reluctantly broke his gaze with me. I looked at Mustache man's uniform. The tag he had clipped to the black vest over his white shirt read *Ed Ainsworth*. Ed's eyebrows rose.

"Ready to go save some more people, kid?" Ed's voice was deeper than his height would indicate. He looked at me. "Careful of this one, sweetheart. He's a heartbreaker."

"Maybe he should be careful of me," Liz blurted before I could control the words.

Gabe grinned. Ed's small eyes widened behind a thick pair

of ancient glasses. I almost laughed. Liz was smirking. She wasn't all bad.

"Not all bad? I've kept our ass safe for a long time. Gimme a little credit."

"I don't need protecting anymore," I told her.

Her anger flared inside me. *"That's not true, and you know it."*

Ed walked away, shaking his head. Gabe saluted me and followed the older man away from the nurses' station. The glass doors to the emergency entrance opened with a soft rasp. A cool breeze momentarily lifted the medical scents of the emergency department.

"Not bad," Corey said.

I faced him, cheeks flaming.

"You even gave him your digits. I'm impressed." He stroked the length of his jawbone while he considered me. "I think this deserves a celebration. What are you doing after work?" He adjusted his glasses and flicked a stray strand of sandy hair off of his forehead.

"I d-don't know. D-do you have a suggestion?" I looked away from him and surveyed the department. The nurses' station served as the hub. Surrounding it were individual rooms, with doors of solid glass that slid from side to side. Most of the rooms' doors were left open with nothing but flimsy curtains to separate the patients from the hawk eyes of the nurses caring for them.

The trauma bays were different from the rest of the rooms. They were equipped with eye-piercing lights with wattage to mimic the sun at noon on a clear day. They were also packed with equipment and supplies. Everything had to be at the fingertips of the doctors and nurses.

I looked to bay one, the holding room for the patient the paramedics had brought in. A golden haze hung around the bed. The crowd of medical staff blocked my view of the patient. A person in another room groaned and then screamed. Someone in the waiting room was shouting at the admitting staff. An old woman, being transported by wheelchair from the lobby to an empty bay, stared at the man screaming at the poor girl at the admissions desk.

"I've been waiting for four fucking hours! When am I going to see a fucking doctor?"

"Sir, please calm down and have a seat. Someone will be with you as soon as they can. We have other patients in more critical condition—"

"I don't give a fuck what condition the other patients are in. I'm in pain, goddammit!"

Two security officers jogged into the waiting area. The energy in the room swelled with tension.

"Time to go, baby bear," Liz prodded me.

I gathered the patient paperwork I'd been sent to retrieve and propped it on a hip. Corey turned his gaze from the guy shouting at the admissions secretary. He swiveled in his chair, his long legs splayed wide. He fiddled with a pen in his hand, twisting it so it circled his thumb before catching it with his thumb and pointer finger.

"Want to head to Powell's for a bit? There's a new graphic novel I want to pick up. I'll drive."

I considered his invitation. I was itching to play my instrument, but... books.

"Sure," I said. "Meet me at my office when our shift is over?"

The screaming intensified, and the security guards closed in.

"Perfect," said Corey.

"I better get going," I said.

Corey nodded and turned back toward the ruckus in the waiting area. "See ya," he said.

On trembling legs, I walked past the trauma bay toward

the hallway that would lead me to my office. The golden light hovered above the team of doctors. One of the nurses, a female, grimaced as the sound of the heart monitor mourned in a monotone melody. The golden light expanded. I watched it, fascinated, as always, that other people in the room missed the sight.

"*Keep moving. Don't let them see you looking,*" Liz reminded me.

I knew I shouldn't watch, but I couldn't tear my eyes away.

The light shifted from golden to shimmering rainbows. A second light—the purest color of white imaginable—entered the bay from above. A crowned figure, barely visible through the intense light, wrapped up the shifting, golden rainbows then exited once again.

"Time of death, 9:08 a.m." Dr. Hurt pronounced the patient deceased, his craggy face lined with disappointment as he peered down at the body with soulful dark eyes.

Death never looked like a sad thing to me. It looked like release or maybe even rescue.

Chapter 2

After work, Corey came to my office, as promised. I was typing an email to my boss, answering her question regarding the status of the latest emergency physicians' meeting minutes, which were almost done. Not for the first time, I wondered how graduating with a music degree translated into being an administrative assistant in a local emergency department. I sighed, stuffed down the same old feeling I was living someone else's life, and finished the email.

I looked up as Corey entered. He'd changed into a forest-green sweatshirt and jeans and had a tattered backpack slung over his shoulders. Corey was a tall guy—exactly six feet, four inches, I knew, because we'd discussed it during one of our many trips to Powell's. And like most super-tall guys, he was lanky. He shuffled to the counter and dropped a chart onto my desk, which startled me.

"What's this for?" I asked.

"You know the lady they brought in when you were in the ED earlier?" he asked.

"Oh, yeah. U-um... she died, didn't she?" I asked, but I already knew. My stomach rolled uncomfortably. I'd seen it, maybe more clearly than most.

Corey nodded. He looked as if he was going to puke.

I wanted to tell him about the beauty of death, but no one could know what I saw. Or what I imagined I saw.

"You can't tell anyone," Liz reminded me.

"This needs to go to Cathy," Corey said, nodding toward the pile of papers. "Hopefully, she can help put the sick bastard away for what that poor woman went through."

I took the manila folder and raised questioning eyes to him. He backed up, half turned and pulled my office door from its stopper with one of his giant hands. It swung closed with a heavy thunk.

"Dr. Hurt told me she was completely mutilated."

"What do you mean?"

Liz perked up, and a growing, curious anger heated me from the inside. Liz might want to know, but I wasn't sure I wanted to hear what Corey was about to unload.

"I can take over," Liz said.

"No, he'll know," I argued.

"I don't think he'll care though. He knows us both," Liz pointed out. Corey had sort of become used to my "mood swings", but he hadn't guessed or questioned what caused the shifts.

"Get this. She'd been stabbed multiple times in her neck and clavicle. Then, she had three ribs broken, and her face was smashed. Dr. Hurt said the orbital structure of her eye was *gone*." Corey's gray-green eyes were feverishly bright. "And that wasn't the worst part."

"Which is why this needs to go to Cathy." I tapped the papers. My heart increased from andante to presto. My throat ached, and my ears suffered the odd, pinching pain of an anxiety attack. I breathed in slowly to stop the advance of panic.

Corey nodded. "Her—girl parts..." Corey said, a flush rising in his cheeks, proving he hadn't been working with nurses long enough to lose his sense of privacy when it came to talking about, well, everything from poop and pee to sex and "girl parts". "All her girl parts were burned. As if someone had stuck a hot poker inside her. And she was still freaking *alive* when they brought her in." His voice rose from its warm baritone and cracked. Now the flush in his cheeks was more about his anger and less about propriety.

"That's awful," I squeaked. The panic took over, and my body trembled. Liz was a flame of anger.

"He's gonna get his. Don't you worry," Liz said through my shaky voice.

"Damn straight," Corey said. "Fucker's going to a deep hole where he can rot. There's way too much evidence to keep him out of the penitentiary."

Corey followed me down the hall and waited while I clocked out. I swiped my badge over the electronic black box. It chirped and displayed my name and the time of my clock out: two-thirty. Slinging my baby-blue backpack over my shoulders, I followed behind Corey as we meandered through the hospital hallways and out into the fall day.

Corey's car was parked six blocks from the hospital.

"You might as well leave the car at home and walk to work," I joked.

"Sometimes, I envy your bus ride," he said. "No parking. What a dream."

"You too could enjoy the pleasures of public transportation," I said.

"You have a point. But here's my counterargument." Corey gestured to his cute, little, sporty blue car.

He pressed the unlock button on his key chain. The car chirped happily. I slid into the seat, relishing the new car smell.

His parents had helped him buy the car when he'd moved to Portland to go to college. The way he told it, they were ecstatic about his shift to schooling from doodling and dead-end jobs.

He plopped into the driver's seat and sighed. "Nobody else but us. No crazy crack heads or smelly homeless people. Nobody trying to start conversations when you want to be left alone. Just me, my car and my lovely passenger."

"S-stop. I'm b-blushing," I said, fighting my way through the stutter. Compliments made me edgy, but I knew from experience arguing would only invite further comments.

He started the car and quickly turned down the music. I reached for button number five. Corey had programmed it to the classical station for me.

He held up devil horns and head-banged to Mozart. I rolled my eyes.

I pulled my cell phone out of the front pouch of my backpack and sent a quick text to my roommate.

"Texting Gramma?" Corey asked. Grandma liked Corey. He'd started calling her "Gramma" immediately upon meeting her, and she'd let him.

"Just letting her know where I'm at. You know how she worries." With good reason. Me going MIA usually meant Liz had taken over and was up to no good.

"Hey, I've been good for a long stretch," Liz said.

"Yeah, we're getting better," I conceded. To Corey, I said, "So, what are we looking for today?"

"The new Sandman came out. I'm so geeked out," he said as he pulled away from the curb.

The drive to Powell's was cramped on the Portland streets, making the twenty blocks or so stretch out for fifteen minutes. Once we got within walking distance, Corey parked in a pay-for-parking lot and grumbled about the cost of city parking.

We entered through the 10th Avenue door. Inside Powell's,

dust and paper scented the air. The entrance had recently been remodeled. The big open space had full exposure to the streets outside through wall-to-wall windows. Book shelves sprang up from the linoleum floor, displaying new releases by famous authors, or staff picks.

To the left and past the checkout stands a ramp rose up to one of the many sections in the City of Books. I made a beeline for the barista, nearly skipping through the Literature and Sci-Fi/Fantasy sections. Corey was a step behind me. Not for the caffeine as much as the Graphic Novel section huddled in the corner near the coffee counter.

"You want something? My treat since you d-drove," I said.

Corey stood for a moment, facing the Romance section. "Oh, well, if you're buying," he began, "I'll take a grande caramel mocha with extra caramel and extra whip."

I raised my eyebrows. Liz seeped into the conversation. "You want sprinkles with that, too, stud?" she said.

His features smoothed; his eyes widened. "You think they have them?" he asked.

I laughed. "Don't know, but I'll check for you."

"That'd be awesome." A bright smile lit up his face. "Thanks, Bitsy."

"Go find your graphic novel," I said and turned toward the coffee bar. The black and white menu board hung from the ceiling. Near the register a set of wooden shelves boasted coffee beans and mugs to purchase. On the counter were straws, sleeves, biscotti and napkins.

I approached the girl at the counter and gave her my drink order. "U-um... do you have sprinkles?" I asked the girl at the counter.

She had a sleeve of tattoos she showed off with a black tank top. My eyes wandered over the art.

"Sprinkles?" she asked and raised bleached eyebrows high.

Her short hair was also bleached whitish-blonde. She had on a thick mask of make-up, including eyeliner that reminded me of Egyptian art. "Hm. Let me look."

She wandered over to the espresso machine and hunted through the stacks of metal milk-steaming cups and the racks of syrups. Then she gasped, snatched up something to the side of the syrup rack. She held it up, grinning, and shook it. The colorful specks rattled inside the clear plastic jar.

"Yay," I said.

She set the sprinkles down and went to work making the coffee. As I waited for it to be done, I grabbed several napkins from the dispenser on the counter, clutching one in my hand and stuffing five others into my coat pocket. The barista poured steaming milk into both cups. I noticed her dark-red nail polish was chipped most of the way off. She snatched the sprinkles from the counter and shook them onto the pile of whipped cream. She looked up at me through her eyelashes.

"Did you want sprinkles on yours, too?" she asked.

"N-no, thank you," I said. Foam was enough for me.

She handed me the coffee and looked into my eyes. Hers were a stunning, light blue-green, made more pronounced by the heavy eye make-up.

"Here ya go," she said and her thin lips twitched into a lop-sided smile.

"Th-th-thank you," I managed, blushing with embarrassment. You'd think at twenty-one I'd be used to stuttering, but the shame was still engraved on my personality. Even as an adult, I waited for someone to laugh or point or make a joke at my expense. But lots of people reacted kindly, which was always more shocking than the ones who acted embarrassed on my behalf.

"No problem," she said without a hint of bother. "My kid brother has a lisp."

I paused, both steaming-hot drinks gripped in my hands, my napkin firmly grasped between the cup and my palm. I felt myself go a little weak. Were we going to have to talk about my stutter? I racked my brain for an appropriate response. I never quite knew what to say to these types of statements. "I'm sorry" or "Is he in speech therapy" or "It might get better"?

"I'll tell you what I'd like to say," said Liz. "Sucks to be him."

Warmth flooded me. Something light and airy filled the crown of my head and rushed down the core of my body. A point in the middle of my forehead yawned in intangible opening. Somewhere in my peripheral vision, I could see rainbows. My mouth opened, and without thought, I spoke.

"Your brother. He's twelve?"

The barista stared at me. "Do you know him?" she asked. Her raccoon eyes widened as her body completely stilled.

"Bitsy, stop," admonished Liz.

But I couldn't help it. The words were coming, and all I could do was speak them.

"Evan," I said. The barista's mouth dropped open, her eyes growing in size. The name was right.

"How'd you-?" she began, but I cut her off with the information coming through me.

"Evan's light is bright. Everyone who comes in contact with him leaves a little happier. His lisp is no hindrance because the love he shares outshines what people might perceive as imperfection."

The barista visible shook. Warmth glowed in her eyes, accompanied by astonished fear and lent her sudden tears an air of reverent shock.

"Goddamit, Bitsy, you're scaring the shit out of her. Stop it!"

But, I couldn't. The words spilled out.

"Don't worry about your kid brother," I continued. "He's not damaged like I am. He doesn't even notice his lisp. It'd be best if you didn't call attention to it, but rather focus on all the beautiful things that make him awesome."

The barista's mask of make-up was ruined with messy black tracks trailing down her cheeks and chin.

"Uh... I...," she tried, but couldn't seem to form her thoughts into words.

I smiled at her quickly and backed away from the counter. Still gripping coffees and napkins, I turned and walked away.

"You fucking freak. How do you even know if any of that shit was accurate? You let your imagination take over and then spew out this stuff on people. And then they alienate us. Can't you just act normal?" Liz's anger throbbed inside me.

"I couldn't help it. The words just come in, and I can't stop them," I told her. *"They just pour out of my mouth. And Liz,"* I said.

She was silent and fuming, but listening. *"What?"* she asked after a pause.

"I didn't stutter at all through that. Did you notice?"

Her anger ebbed. *"Yes. Yes, I did,"* was all she said.

I found Corey on the floor in the second aisle of graphic novels, his long legs folded, head bent as he pored over the book in his lap. I knelt down, set my drink on the lower book-shelf, popped the lid off of his drink and waved the cup under his nose. Startled, he focused in on what was interrupting his reading experience.

"What? For real?" He grabbed the cup and looked at the colorful blobs of melting sprinkles. He looked up at me.

"Y-you're welcome," I said and sat down on the floor next to him.

He took a sip and purred. "So good."

I retrieved my coffee and took a slow drink. The mild hint of a single pump of mocha mixed with the boldness of the Americano and the froth of steamed half and half. I was in heaven.

Corey took another drink. When he lowered the cup, his upper lip and nose were covered in whipped cream. I snorted then reached into my pocket for one of my five stowed napkins.

"How is it you always have a napkin when I need one?" he asked, wiping cream from his face.

"Maybe because you a-always make a m-m-mess," I said.

His mouth dropped open. "Are you calling me a slob?"

"Well, if the bib fits, maybe you should wear it... 24/7," I said.

"Oh, really?" He scooped his finger into his drink, pulled out a glob of whipped cream and wiped it on my nose. Or at least it might have gotten my nose if I hadn't tried to dodge. Instead, he got it on my cheek and ear.

"Ugh! Sticky!"

"Now, now. Is that any way to talk about a man's cream? Heh. Heh. Heh."

"Don't be such a pervert," I said and wiped the confection from my face. "Did I get it all?"

"No, I think you missed some," he said, and then got me again with a dollop directly on my nose.

"You shit," Liz said, "Cut it out, or I'll dump this Americano all over your graphic novel."

He grasped the book and pulled away in horror. "You wouldn't dare!"

"Try me," Liz said.

"Okay, okay! Truce!" He set the book in his lap and hurried to replace the lid on his drink.

I nodded in satisfaction. "B-better," I said.

"See, that's what I love about you, Bitsy," he said.

I wiped more whipped cream off of my face.

"You go along all sweet and innocent, sometimes even stressed out, and then all of a sudden, this other you shows up

and threatens to dump her coffee all over a cherished posses-
sion and make me pay."

Liz and I perked up. "Oh, well, I..." I said, squeezing the
napkins in my hands.

"You just keep me guessing. I never know what to expect
from you," he said.

Me neither, I thought. Liz saying she'd dump her coffee
over a graphic novel was mild compared to some of the other
things she'd done when she hijacked my body. Usually those
other things she'd done were other people. Of course, then
she'd retreat and leave me with a body racked with bruises and
sometimes mutilation. There were some sick people out there.
Liz always seemed to find them. Liz was quiet, but I sensed
her shame at my train of thought. Still, she hadn't done that
since we'd graduated college this last June. It made it easier not
being around hot college guys all the time.

Corey rose from the ground, coffee in one hand and
graphic novel in the other. "C'mon, Unpredictable. Let's go
frolic through the books."

The day was shifting to evening when we left Powell's. In
the car, Corey kept the radio tuned to the classical station.
Paganini's Caprice No. 24 played. It was one of the most difficult pieces for violin. I fingered the melody on my hand, as
if I were holding my violin, working through the cascade of
thirty-second notes, imagining the bow hair flying, What I
wouldn't give to play all the time. But, after school, there were
no violin positions in Portland. Not paying ones anyway. And
I couldn't afford to leave my counselor for a position out-of-
state. We were making so much good progress with Sharon.
Grandma knew a nurse at the ED who said they were hiring an

admin. So, there I was. Biding my time until the right position came open.

"Playing violin would be better than playing secretary," said Liz.

Playing alone in my room was nice, but I missed being a part of the orchestra. Having an integral role in making music that was bigger than me gave me a sense of belonging. I loved that.

"So, what are you going to do about school?" I asked, continuing our conversation over the music that wanted to steal my attention.

Corey let out a huff. "Man, I don't know. It's crazy, Bitsy. I know logically being a nurse means making good money, it's interesting, flexible and I could be good at it."

"But..." I said.

"It's just not my passion." He illustrated passion with a shaking fist. "My passion is my art."

"Tell me again why you don't just do the art thing?"

"Money," he said. "Competition. There're a million-and-one artists out there, all vying for attention. What makes me so special?"

"Well, that's obvious, isn't it?" I asked, honing in on the violin solo ripping up those thirty-second notes with pristine precision.

"What do you mean?" he asked.

"You. You are what makes you so special. There's no other *you* like *you*," I explained.

Corey didn't answer right away, taking his time to turn a corner and maneuver around a city bus.

"Mmhmm," Liz interjected, *"One might argue the same to you, Bitsy."*

I ignored her.

"Yeah, I guess I am pretty awesome," Corey said, running

a hand through his sandy hair and winking at me through his glasses.

"Oy vey." I rolled my eyes.

Corey pulled up to an open space on the curb near the house. "Oh, speaking of my awesomeness and art, you wanna go with me to the market on Saturday? And then after, I'm taking Abigail to the movies. You want to come with us? She'd love to see you."

"As long as I don't have a date," I said and gave him a sly half smile.

"Too true. You might be getting bus-ay!" He wiggled his hips in the seat and rolled his shoulders around.

"You're a d-dork," I said and got out of the car.

"All right, Saturday. I'll text you. Say hi to Gramma for me," he yelled from the driver's seat.

I waved and turned from the car. He pulled away from the curb and was off.

The sky was periwinkle and pink and on the western horizon the sunset blazed in hot orange. The autumn breeze shifted through the neighborhood's elderly trees. Their ocher, gold and rust colored leaves rustled with a soothing "shh...". Yet, under the breeze and burning sunset, a nagging sense of danger gripped my stomach. I looked around me, but saw only the neatly lined houses and cars parked along the sidewalk.

Home was a couple of houses away. The back yard was encompassed with a well-maintained white fence, and the front yard hosted a big, beautiful oak. Nothing seemed amiss at home from where I looked at the house.

"Do you feel that?" Liz asked.

My stomach squeezed in warning. My head buzzed with an unsettling dizziness. *"No,"* I said, trying to lie my way through the odd sensations.

"You can't lie to me, darling."

I shook myself. Nothing was wrong.

The breeze was chilled in a way that seeped into my bones. My house was only steps away. I pulled my shoulders back and down, shifted my backpack on my shoulders and moved on.

My black flats scuffed against the sidewalk. I looked out at the streets and sidewalks surrounding me. My spine prickled and I turned to peer over my shoulder while still moving myself closer to home, anxious for its safety. On the eastern horizon, the bloated moon rose.

"Whoa," Liz said, "look at the moon!"

I turned to face the monstrosity of our earth's satellite, took a step backward and faltered. I yanked my head down as water splashed around my foot.

"Ack!" I said and stumbled until both feet were submerged past my ankles in yesterday's rainwater. My shoes were completely soaked through... flats, feet and all. An insistent rhythm vibrated from my legs, through my tailbone, up my spine and into my head. The vibrations rattled through me, cementing me in the puddle. My mind floundered to regain control of my body and pull myself from the water, but the more I fought the more solidly I remained frozen. Captive to the energy pulsing through me, my head tilted back centimeter by centimeter until my gaze took in only the fullness of the moon.

"I have a bad feeling, Bits," Liz said.

Her voice was distant, as the throbbing hum took over my senses. My body went rigid, the air stuck somewhere between my lips and my lungs.

"What's happening?" I asked Liz.

Panic crawled through me, igniting my heart, stealing my voice. The moon's light poured into my eyes; my mouth fell agape. The fall breeze touched my tongue and teeth; I could do nothing to stop its exploring fingers. Images flashed through my mind, too quick to grasp, too surreal to hold on to, until they swirled around me, dropping me through the light of the moon and plunged me into a foreign scene. Like a dream, I fought a dizzying wave of disorientation.

The street was gone as was the moon. My hands scooped frantically around me, smooth cool darkness sliding over my skin. I couldn't breathe. No. I was holding my breath. I shook my head, fighting the maddening slowness that halted my ability to move. I was surrounded by water. Not the puddle I'd stepped in, but a vast and foreign pool. The gray sides of the pool held engravings of women, all holding hands to form an encompassing circle. They were each slightly different and yet each appeared to have the bulge of pregnancy.

I cast my gaze up, fighting against some unseen force that dragged me downward in the endless pool. The darkness of night above the pool was interrupted by the three points of light forming a perfect triangle that wavered through the water. I tried swimming upward, but found my limbs useless. And it was then I realized my limbs were not my own.

In my hand—the hand of the person from whose perspective I looked—I held a weapon. Why was this person grasping a weapon? She should let go and swim. But, with that thought came the overwhelming connection to the thing. She could not let go, would never let him go. Him. My own mind struggled through the dreamlike state to make sense of what I was seeing and feeling and then simply gave up.

Something sucked and pulled at me. I looked below to see a man in the same struggle against whatever it was dragging us ever downward. At the bottom of the pool, I could swear it looked like a tunnel made of stars. Between me and the man, I saw a creature so unworldly I mentally recoiled from its multiple eyes and flashing canines. It thrashed against the water, but made no more progress than myself or the man below it. Realizing

the fight was useless, I calmed my body and gave in to the over-
whelming power dragging us into what I could only assume was
a watery death.

The moon burst into my vision. I gasped for air, coughing and choking against the lack of breath. A pulse exploded
through my brain, shattered my vision, and darkness consumed me.

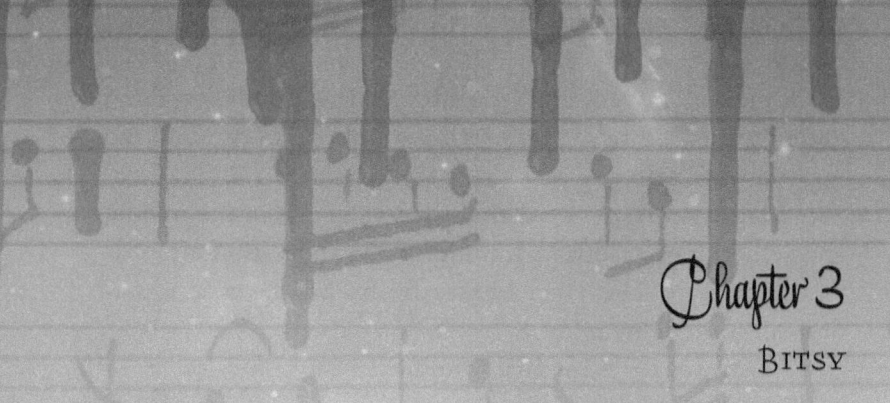

Shadows and light danced across my mind. My legs ached. My body was open and exposed. A dark figure loomed over me, pinning me down. The crush of powerlessness ignited anger. Metal glinted in the corner of my mind's eye as I raised the shiny thing with my right hand. Fire bloomed inside me.

"Elizabeth?"

The voice scratched at a throb in my brain. I pressed the heels of my hands into my eyes as the moon's glare pierced my head with new agony. A warm hand brushed over my hair. The slight smell of perfume and Ivory soap washed over me.

Slowly, I became aware of my body. I lay on the sidewalk in a puddle of dirty water, which had soaked into my khakis and muted-pink polo. There was an uncomfortable lump under my back. *Backpack*, my brain supplied the explanation.

"What happened, sweetpea?" Grandma's warm Southern drawl was tinged with worry and annoyance.

I tried my eyes, letting the light from the oversized moon spear them. Grandma looked down at me. Her bottle-auburn hair framed her olive complexion in perfect, hot-iron curls. Her dark brows were drawn down over her hazel eyes. A crystal hanging on a chain around her neck glinted off the violet sweater she wore.

I pushed myself up, splashing in the puddle, making myself wetter. Grandma rose with me, holding me around the upper arm to help me.

"I don't know. I was walking then I stepped in the puddle and something..." I looked around for an explanation for what had happened. The vivid images from—whatever it was—flashed through my mind.

"Tell her you slipped and fell," said Liz.

"I trust her," I argued.

"She'll just think you're crazy if you say something froze you and made you pass out."

"What if she can help?"

"Look. You're better now, right? It's not a big deal. If you tell her the truth, she'll make you double up on your meetings with that dreadful woman." Liz didn't like our counselor on principle.

"What time is it?" I asked. How long had I been lying unconscious on the street?

"Not that late, but you didn't come in after you texted you were on your way. I just had a feeling something was off. I called and called your cellphone. When you didn't answer, I came outside to see if I could see you coming. Scared me half to death when I saw you on the sidewalk. Did someone hurt you?" She searched me over.

"No, no. I just tripped in the puddle. When I fell I hit my head. It must have knocked me out." I hated lying.

Grandma huffed. "You klutz. Come here," she demanded and pulled me into a hug more binding than she should be capable of at fifty-nine years of age.

"You're gonna get all wet, Grandma," I told her, but I hugged her back.

At five-eight, I was much taller than her almost-five-foot-two. My lanky arms wrapped her easily. Even though I towered over her, she always made me feel safe.

"Come on, now. I was working on supper when I came out. I better get in there and check on it."

I let her lead me to the house, uncomfortable from my soaking clothes. The front porch on the century-old home opened up to us with three wide stairs. To me, it always seemed like arms outstretched, waiting to encompass me in warmth and safety, which is what the home always did.

The yard was spacious. The oak towered over the lawn, its green leaves dappled in gold peeking into the windows of the upper floor. Its bark was black with yesterday's rainfall and contrasted artfully with the colors autumn painted on it.

The paint on the house was new, a light-sage green with cream-colored trim and pillars on the front porch. I smiled as I climbed the three steps. The boards protested at my weight.

"Go get cleaned up while I finish supper," Grandma commanded.

"Okay, Grandma." I trotted up the stairs to my bedroom.

Grandma had the entire top floor remodeled. There were basically two master bedrooms and another guest bedroom. She'd considered renting the second master to help with income. That's when I'd called her to escape my mother's madness.

Liz and I hardly knew her then, except for a few happy memories of visiting her as a small child. Mom had me in Colorado at the time. She'd followed some new guy who'd said he was in the ski industry. What he'd meant was that he liked to ski and wanted someone to pay his way to the slopes. Also, he was horrible. Mom had asked for the total of our paycheck from Dairy Queen—our summer job before heading to college. Liz had apparently denied my mother's request. They had argued. I was a little fuzzy on the details, but the end result was that we were kicked out, while skier guy stayed.

She'd picked a guy over her daughter because we wouldn't give her the money we planned on using to pick up groceries.

My mother had packed me into the car, drove me in the dead of night and dropped me off at a local Denver shelter. She'd given me the name of my grandmother and told me my father would want me to stay with her. My dead father. My grandmother's son. I didn't even know what was happening until I was being dropped at the shelter.

I had had no counseling and no idea at that point that I had dissociative identity disorder. I only knew there were times when I blacked out. There were big, gaping holes in the fabric of my collective experience. My mom never believed this. She said I made it up for attention or to get away with whatever it was Liz did when I blacked out.

That didn't stop me from begging her to stay. I had a scholarship. I had a promising career at the Denver Orchestra waiting for me after I finished school. I'd even gotten a head start by getting my Associates degree in high school. I was on my way, and then Liz had come along and sabotaged everything I'd worked for.

"Bitsy, don't blame me. You know Mom was itching for a reason to get rid of us. The skiing moron wanted us out. So, we were out," Liz said.

"If you knew that, why did you push it?" I asked.

"Seriously? It's been years now. Everything turned out fine. Stop whining."

"Except I could have a job in an orchestra right now, instead of waiting for an opening."

"Uh, that was your choice, not mine. You could have had a number of jobs in other cities. You chose to stay here."

"*I know,*" I conceded. "*I didn't want to leave Grandma.*"

"*Or Sharon.*" Sharon was our counselor who had discovered our disorder and coached us through the nightmare of our situation. We had so much more work to do. I worried if I left, the tentative stability we had built would crumble. Liz continued, "*I know. You don't have to explain yourself, but don't go blaming me and looking to be the victim again.*"

She was right and Sharon would agree. Blaming Liz was the easy way out of me taking responsibility for my own actions.

When Mom had dropped me at the shelter, I had considered calling my music director from the Denver youth orchestra I'd been a part of for the previous five years. But, I was so ashamed my mother had kicked me out, and so confused as to what I'd done, I couldn't bring myself to do it. Homeless, heart broken and at an all-time low, I had pulled the crumpled piece of paper from my hand, and called the number.

Grandma had driven from Portland to Denver and had collected me. Me and nothing. My mother had not let me pack. Liz had apparently been all too happy for the spontaneous eviction and hadn't grabbed anything. The only thing my mother had the decency to bring was my violin. Its presence was one small comfort as the rest of my future dissipated in the Denver midnight air.

The people at the shelter had been so kind. They gave me a coat and shoes. I didn't even have shoes. I wondered how I'd looked to them in pajamas and gripping my violin to my chest like a lifesaver. The thought swept over me as I pulled off my clothes and dropped them into the plastic hamper. I twisted the faucet in the shower and waited, shivering, for the water to heat. After I climbed inside, I stared at my toes, thinking about how when I'd gotten inside the shelter, my feet were numb from making my way over the cold parking lot.

"*Bitch,*" Liz spat.

My heart ached. How could a mother be so cruel to her daughter?

The hot water washed away my sorrow, pulling me out of the day, the horrific images of the tortured woman, the fainting spell or whatever it had been, the memories of my mother. I let the warm glow of gratitude toward my grandmother fill me. After we'd arrived from Denver to Portland, she'd called my youth orchestra director in Denver. And the University of Denver. And Lewis and Clark College. Between the overwhelming support of my director, my grandmother and admittedly the sob story I had, I'd gotten another full-ride scholarship. I'd also nailed the audition for the final spot left for the scholarship.

It had been bad for Grandma the first year. I had lived in fear I would have a blackout and find myself being dropped at another shelter or Greyhound station.

I toweled off, flipping on the fan to pull away the steam in the bathroom. The soft rug under my toes was a luxury I still hadn't grown accustomed to. As I looked at the blurred reflection of myself in the fogged mirror and wrapped myself in the warm, clean cotton towel, the smallest part of me suffered a twinge of guilt. I didn't deserve all of these comforts. Yet here I stood, soaking in the warmth while my past still wove stories about how I didn't belong.

I combed through my long curls of dark hair with my fingers. Leaving it wet, I opened the door and tiptoed into my bedroom, skipping over the hardwood to the rugs. Rooting through an old chest of drawers, I pulled out the necessities, including a pair of flannel pajama bottoms and an oversized t-shirt. Once those were on, I tugged a gray sweatshirt from a hanger in the closet and yanked it over my wet hair.

Everything smelled like laundry soap. I hugged the sweatshirt to my scrawny body, inhaled deeply, closing my eyes and working to release the creeping guilt that stole my joy. I wanted to be happy. Who knew it'd be so much work?

I shoved my feet into a pair of soft slippers.

"Thank you, God," I whispered.

"*Yeah, okay, whatever.*" Liz didn't believe in God or Goddess or any sort of higher power.

"*How can you deny it after what we've seen?*" I asked her, not for the first time.

"*I could ask you the very same question,*" she retorted. "*Of course, you conveniently don't remember that stuff. But I do.*"

I sighed. Sometimes, connecting with my alt made for some painful arguments. Our counseling had ripped the veil between her and me. Once we were made aware of each other, we couldn't be out of each other's thoughts.

"*Yeah. Thanks, Sharon,*" Liz said to my unspoken thought.

"*We're better this way,*" I said.

"*I don't know if I believe that.*"

I didn't respond. There was no sense in continuing the debate.

I could hear the clanging of pots and pans from downstairs, so I knew Grandma was still working on dinner. Since it sounded as if I had a few minutes, I pulled out my violin and warmed up with some scales. After my fingers were nimble, I pulled the bow across the strings and worked through the solo I'd listened to in Corey's car on the way home.

The music swept me away. I closed my eyes to my room and opened my mind to the magic of music.

Fields stretched away from me in all directions. Golden grass bent against a breeze. I leaned in to take a closer look at the fruit. My hands were a deep brown and... manly. In the moment, this seemed natural, but in the background I knew these were not my hands. The fruit I held was an orangish crimson. Not quite ripe. The thought came to me, but it was not my thought. It belonged to the owner of the dark, manly hands.

I looked toward the sky with the man's eyes. The smaller, distant, dying sun glowed purplish blue just on the eastern horizon. The other sun burned brightly overhead.

Still a few more hours left in the day. Time to check on his garden. This year, Maltheron—the name came to me through the filter in my mind—had been allotted fruit and grain to contribute to the region's food exchange. But as a master grower and husband to the region's Queen Maker, he was granted the luxury of his own private garden.

He called out for someone. Another man jogged up to him through the stalks of golden plants with bobbing red fruit.

My spirit recoiled from this new man. It wasn't his odd features, a face that was a little too long and eyes a little too big to call human. There was a clinging darkness about the man that made my insides shiver.

Together, the two men made their way toward a circular stone in the field. They stood on the stone, facing each other, and Maltheron clasped his hands together to make an odd symbol. He spoke, the noise indistinguishable as words, but inside my mind, I understood his meaning: "Garden."

A flash of light, a swirl of wind, a quaking of earth and then the world adjusted itself around them. And there the two men stood in front of a patch of land laden with rows of green.

The bow on the strings faltered, screeching, then fell to my side. I shook my head from a wave of dizziness and sat on the bed. I set down the bow with a trembling hand and pressed fingers into my forehead.

"Why'd you stop? I thought that was pretty good," said Liz.

"Did you see that?" I asked her.

"See what?"

"I think I had another vision, but it was really weird. As if I was there."

"I didn't see anything. I was just listening to the music."

She sounded puzzled. We shared that sentiment. Sure, I had visions, and I saw peoples' auras and angels, and sometimes even demons, but this was something different.

"Sugar, supper's hot!" Grandma's voice filtered up through the floorboards.

I stowed my instrument and the odd vision. I turned toward the door to leave, but something caught my eye. I looked out the bedroom window. The bloated red moon dominated the sky. The sight of its fullness and orangish-red color sent a wave of emotion through me. Remembering the pool, the choking sensation of drowning, my heart thumped in triplets.

I tore my gaze from the blood moon and left my bedroom. As I headed down the stairs, I tried to shake myself from the series of visions, the emotions, the dancing moons on a pool of water. The carvings of pregnant women. Alien landscapes and foreign fruit. People who didn't look human and monsters that were definitely other-worldly. But a tingling sensation had started down my spine, and try as I might, I couldn't will it away.

Chapter 4

Liz

After the Monday we'd had yesterday, Bitsy took Tuesday off. So I was sitting in the office chair, staring at the computer screen, waiting for the system to boot up. It was a good thing she was resting. A cop outside the door sat next to a man in cuffs. Behind me, Cathy was prepping the exam room. She left the door open as she worked, setting out the contents of the forensic kit onto a silver tray. Bitsy couldn't handle this stuff. I was fascinated by it.

Cathy wandered out of the exam room and past my desk. Her profile was as grim as it always was when she did exams. Dressed in black slacks and her white lab coat, she made an impressively medical figure. She walked through the door to our office and her exam room and turned toward the cop.

"I'm all ready for him, Mike."

"Okay, let's get this show on the road," Mike said genially. Mike was in his forties and had done the whole cop thing for twenty-five years. He handled the suspect with routine authority. He stood, turned to the man at his side. I could only see Mike's left back side from my vantage point, but I could tell he stooped to lift the man out of his seat. The guy must have really let his weight fall in, because Mike faltered, righted himself, grunted. The chair feet screeched against the polished floor. Cathy took several steps back.

"Guess I'll have to have you come in with us," she noted.

"Mr. Holliday, if you resist, I'll be forced to subdue you," Mike said as kindly as if he were telling a child he'd spank them if they didn't straighten up. As if he wouldn't enjoy doling out the punishment. Maybe he wouldn't.

Mike walked through the door with a hand firmly clasped around the man's arm. His other hand rested on one of the many gadgets on his batman belt. Tazer, maybe? I salivated over the weapons. I wasn't allowed to have anything more deadly than pepper spray. I craved to hold a gun in my hands.

Mike was a tall, solid man with a head full of black hair and eyes like Elvis. He was clean-shaven, with a nice mouth and straight teeth. He was a handsome guy, made more handsome with the uniform. He was what Grams would call, "pretty".

Mr. Holliday, the man Officer Mike guided into the room, was about my height but twice as wide as I was. He had thick, muscular arms and a padded but muscular torso and chest. His lank brown hair hung down to just above his shoulders. Wide cheekbones and a rounded nose, a wide, frog-like mouth and small, dark eyes all gave the man a creep factor of two hundred plus, plus. And on that face was a collection of wicked scratches that stretched down to his neck and disappeared under the collar of his white t-shirt. Like all the men the police brought in to Cathy's office, darkness clung to him. Bitsy could see it better than I could, but everybody can sense the sort of evil that rapists ooze. Nothing special about that.

The thick, dark man flicked back his hair and turned his focus to me. I had been staring. From the note I'd read when I checked him into the electronic medical record for Cathy, this was a suspect in the case of the woman Bitsy saw die in Trauma Bay One yesterday. What he'd done to her... My own roiling hatred for a person capable of such atrocity swelled like an oncoming tsunami. And here he was, getting forensics gathered so the court could lock him up. He deserved worse than a life in jail. He deserved the same torture he'd put that woman through. Still, he got caught. And that was something. An immense satisfaction settled into me as I cheered the justice system for at least catching this guy.

"What the fuck are you looking at, bitch?" he asked.

Had I been smirking? I guess I didn't have a great poker face. I could only imagine the look I was giving him while mentally fist-pumping his expeditious capture.

"Keep your mouth shut, and get your ass in there," Mike commanded.

My body faced the computer, but my eyes were locked on Mike and the sicko. Mike grabbed the man with both hands and shoved him the last few feet into the exam room. Mike glanced at me, his pupils dilated, blue eyes wide. His nostrils flared. The energy roiled off of him, his body tensing.

The man didn't stay. I turned my body, swiveling in the chair and prepared to lunge out of the way. Cathy was inside the exam room, her eyes went wide and mouth agape as she reached out toward me, as if that would stop the man's advance. Mr. Holliday pushed Mike hard. Mike went down with a grunt, his head smacking hard against the metal filing cabinet with a muffled clang.

"Mike!" Cathy shouted while Mr. Holliday lunged at me.

Before I could think of what to do to protect myself, Mr. Holliday had swung his meaty, cuffed hands toward me. I yelped as he pushed. The scraping of the office chair wheels ended with a loud clatter. My chair toppled backward with me in it.

My nerves were on fire with adrenaline. I tried pushing myself away from my attacker, dumping myself out of the chair but slipped on the smooth floor, making no progress. From the corner of my eye, I could see Cathy reaching for the prostrate Mike to help him up. Holliday loomed over me, bringing his cuffed hands toward his shoulders. I brought my arms up to protect myself, which proved worthless.

His hands came down. I squealed in terror. My face exploded in pain. The man was on me, his knees pinning my legs to the floor. My stomach lurched as he swung again. My ribs protested against the blow. Air whooshed out of my lungs. The world was a bright vision of blinding pain.

Finally, Mike materialized over him, pulling on Holliday's massive shoulders. The man's oily, scratched face was next to mine; his cuffed hands rattled next to my ear.

"Do you want to see how I did it, sweetheart," he whispered.

I battered at him with useless fists. I could smell him, a mix of old deodorant and body odor. Bitsy would have cried. Bitsy wasn't here. I screamed and wriggled, but the man was solid as a rock. My legs were simultaneously numbing out and burning in pain where he crushed the muscles with his knees.

"Motherfucker," I whispered back. The anger swelled in me, and a dark need pulled in my brain. "You will pay for this." Something tickled in my mind. Something alien and powerful. My body turned to steel. My vision glowed on the edges.

Mike yanked at Holliday's arms, but it did no good. I pressed my slender hands into the man's chest. A disconnected strength flooded me. My body both wanted to numb out and fight back like a wild cat. The disparaging sensations warred within me. The man made a noise. As if he was turned on. The need to not be powerless won out over all of the other competing needs. I shoved and screamed, but the dizzying nothing crashed down on me.

And then, just like that, I was back again. The man was off of me. I was sitting in my chair. My legs burned and ached. The pain in my ribs made me choke on air. My hands tingled. My face throbbed, and my head harmonized to the rhythm. I rubbed my hands together to dissipate the electricity sparking at my fingertips. I looked around me. The exam door was closed. Cathy was speaking in hushed tones. Mike's voice filtered through the door.

"You need to get that poor girl a different office space. Why the hell did they set anybody up with a computer in front of the forensic nurse examiner's office?"

There was a pause, a clack of instruments against metal. Cathy finally spoke.

"I'll speak with her manager today. Stay with dude, here, and I'll get a wheelchair for when he wakes."

A plastic *fwap* snapped through the muffled air behind the door, followed by the sound of the trashcan lid opening. The water turned on.

"I'll have to get her information and a statement and ask if she wants to file charges."

"She'll file charges," Cathy said, the edge in her voice slicing through any choice I might have.

"That's up to her," Mike said.

The water turned off, followed by a rustle of dry paper.

"How the hell do you think she did that, anyway?" he went on.

I perked up. What had I done? Was it Bitsy?

"I've never seen anything like it," Cathy said. "He's three times her size. But God bless her! I've never felt so proud!"

Mike chuckled. The door opened, and Cathy emerged.

Mike peered at me from around the corner, his eyes a little wide, his black eyebrows high. Cathy shut the door on him and looked at me.

"Is he—out?" I asked.

"You *knocked* him unconscious," she stated and grinned foolishly. "Unfortunately, he'll be fine when he wakes up."

I stared at her. "I did?"

She nodded.

"Bitsy, you in there? What the hell is going on? Any ideas?"

Radio silence. The quiet was almost too much for me. I was getting used to hearing her.

"Hey, wake up! I need you."

Nothin'.

Cathy shuffled up to me and crossed her arms under her bosom. Her embroidered name on the lab coat stretched. She cocked her head to one side and looked down at me from the thick frames of her glasses. Her hair was goofy—abnormally thick, strawberry blonde and streaked with white. She wore it shoulder-length, with bangs sweeping over her forehead, just brushing the frame of her glasses. Bitsy would normally chide me for such critical thoughts against Cathy's hair, but not today. Whatever happened last night with the puddle and the moon and her subsequent visions had her all twitched out.

"Are you okay?" Cathy asked. She shook her head. "What am I asking? No, you're not okay."

She huffed and sat on the desk. I rescued a toppled—and thankfully, closed—water bottle.

"Don't worry. That guy's going to jail, and he's going to be there for a long time. I've got enough evidence to indict him seven times over."

I nodded, crossing my arms and leaning back in the wheely office chair. I winced at the pressure on my ribs and sat straighter.

"You say that, but I've seen how these things go." I raised my hand, fingers splayed in the air, and wobbled it back and forth. "Something a little funny happens in the courtroom when it's a domestic abuse case. All of a sudden, *poof!*" I made the exploding into nothing expression with my hands. "There's no case."

"You're sassy today. But that's not going to happen with this guy. These guys go away for life."

I huffed in disgust. "Right. Life." I did the little quotation thing when I said it. "As in ten years and the rest is written off for good behavior. As if good behavior in a prison is something worth being commended for."

"We're making changes, Bitsy," Cathy told me.

I ignored her use of the wrong name. She didn't know. Nobody but Grams knew... and the counselor. I thought about that for a minute. I didn't seem to be fooling Corey, either, although I don't think he really knew what he'd hit upon yesterday at Powell's.

"You'll see. He can't make this unstick."

I raised my eyebrows and swiveled in the chair, crossing my legs, biting at my nails. "Fine. We'll see." I turned away from her and back to the computer screen. I snatched up the mouse and clicked on the email program.

Cathy was still standing there, looking down at me.

"Yes, we will," she finally said. She pushed off the desk and stalked away.

Ten minutes later, Cathy and the officer had jack-wad loaded into the wheelchair. I sneered at him, no longer scared but proud I'd punched the shit out of him. He wouldn't look at me but he kept his head up, as if to say I didn't scare him.

"Bitsy, could you please check him out of the system?" Cathy asked.

"Sure thing," I said. I double-clicked the EMR icon and signed in.

Mike came back in after pushing the prisoner out the door.

"Bitsy," he started.

I looked away from the computer screen and up at him.

"I'll be back a little later and get a statement from you, okay?"

I shrugged. "Whatevs."

His only response was a pinched-mouth nod. His shoes clicked against the shiny floor as he exited. I selected the patient's chart in the electronic medical record, the only one checked into our department under Cathy, Sexual Assault Nurse Examiner. His demographics shined at me from the monitor. I stared at the pixels for a few moments and then navigated to the command that discharged him as a patient.

I went about the business of answering emails. Sometimes, it seemed as if that was all this job was—just answering emails and setting up meetings. I got a request to pull charts after an hour of mind-numbing email hell and thanked the chaos that ruled the universe. I stood from the chair and stretched, then winced. Tender bits of my legs and ribs protested. Acid thoughts churned for my attacker. My heart thumped uncomfortably.

I imagined what that poor woman had gone through. The torture she'd endured until she finally got here to the ED. My fists clenched at my sides as Corey's words from yesterday tumbled into my brain.

"Sick fuck," I said. Tears gathered in my eyes. *"Why in the world am I crying?"*

"Because it's awful. That man attacked you?"

"Welcome back." I was simultaneously grateful for her return and annoyed she'd left me alone. Silently, I replayed the reel

of what had happened, knowing Bitsy would see the memory. There was silence while she soaked in the encounter.

"*I'm sorry. I was lost. I couldn't find my way back*," she said, after the scene was done playing.

"*Didn't you hear me calling for you?*" I asked.

"*I could hear it, but it was as if I was hearing from a sound system, and I had no microphone to talk back to you.*"

"*Where did you go this time?*" I trembled with sudden, raw emotion. I sat back in the chair and wrapped my arms around my middle. Therapy sucked. Going sane, as my counselor called it, required feeling stuff. This is why we'd split in the first place, and now all the feeling was oozing up from the deep places where we'd buried it.

"*I think we should go in to see Sharon. Will you call her for us?*" Bitsy asked.

It had been a couple of years since we'd started seeing Sharon. She helped. I didn't like to admit it, but she helped. I didn't have to do this on my own anymore. The room spun around me. I realized I was breathing too hard. I gulped in a calming breath of air.

When I didn't answer her, Bitsy tried again. "*I'm really sorry I left you. I didn't mean to this time, if that counts for anything.*"

"*Yeah, well, that was scary as hell. You made me do that on my own. Not cool. I have to do all the hard stuff.*"

"*Do you want me to take over now?*" Bitsy asked.

"*Maybe just until we get to Sharon's,*" I conceded. I sat back in the chair and waited for the cool touch of escape. When it enveloped me, I sighed in relief. As the darkness folded over me, a visitor walked into the office. *Shit*, was my last conscious thought.

Chapter 5

Bitsy

I breathed in to the count of ten. Awareness and feeling seeped into the consciousness that was me. I worked to rid myself of the foreign place my mind had wandered, the alien landscape still prominently blazing on the back of my eyes. The first sensation was the throb of my cheekbone. Then I nearly gasped at the pain in my ribs. Liz quaked in the corner of my brain. As my vision cleared, I realized I was not alone in my office. My boss stood in front of me. I swallowed hard, battling against the pain.

"Taking a break?" she asked, her drawn-on eyebrows arched over small blue eyes.

Could she not see the swelling of my face? Bleached hair had been meticulously curled and stuck in place. She was short and round but in a way that looked as if she'd worked out a lot when she was younger. Her forearms were lined in less-than-feminine muscles.

I looked around me. I hadn't gotten a proper hand-off this time. I wasn't sure what it was we were doing before I took over. I looked at the screen. The internet browser was open to the hospital's intranet page. A headline about the employee wellness program's stress-reduction plan flashed at me. I pointed to it.

"I w-w-was just trying one of the techniques in this week's w-w-wellness article," I said. I smiled weakly—which hurt—hoping that would suffice.

"Bitsy, when you're here you need to be working. The company doesn't pay you to reduce your stress. Do that on your own time," she stated. "Do you have the charts I asked for?"

I had no idea.

"Liz? Do we have the charts Roxanne wanted?" I asked.

"She just called down for them two minutes ago," Liz told me. *"Tell her to get her fucking panties out of a wad and give us a damn minute. Bitch."*

I smiled at my boss. "I was just getting them. Can I bring them to your office in five minutes?" I left my eyes wide and let the soothing peace flow from me. That only worked one time out of ten with Roxanne, but it was worth a shot.

A hacking noise of disgust gurgled out of her throat. She threw her arms in the air. "I swear. No. No, just sit there and practice *breathing*. I've got the charts. When you're done de-stressing, I want yesterday's meeting minutes in my inbox. It shouldn't take you so long to do minutes, Bitsy."

She sneered at me. As if she hated me. I never understood people like that. But Sharon said Roxanne's behavior toward me was about Roxanne, not me. So it bothered me much less.

"I understand. I'll get them finished right now and email them to you," I said, bowing my head to her, hating myself for it. It was such an automatic thing. The meaner person pushed and I gave.

She shook her head and laughed in a way that didn't seem funny at all, in a way that made me the butt of her joke.

She walked out like a mini Mack truck, her dress clothes incongruous to the rest of her hard features.

"One of these days, she's going to catch my side, and I'm not going to be as nice as you are. God, Bitsy. Don't you remember what Sharon said?"

"I remember. 'Nice is a four-letter word,'" I recited.

"That woman deserves none of your subservience. No one does."

"I know," I said.

"Then why don't you say something to her? Why didn't you tell her about that psychopath who attacked me?"

Guilt boiled in my gut. I didn't even think to do that. Poor Liz had gone through that awful attack, and I hadn't even told my boss about it. And per company policy, I had to report the incident.

"I will. I'll tell her. Let me get these minutes done, and then I'll go to her office."

"You know what? Don't even bother. It doesn't matter, anyway," she said.

"Liz, don't be like that. I hate when you do that."

"I don't want to talk about it anymore."

And she was off. I wondered where she went when she wasn't with me. Were they the same places I went? Did she ever get lost, or did she always know where she ended up? She never told me. That really wasn't fair. I always told her.

I brooded while I typed the minutes. After attaching them to the email to my boss, I included a line that asked for ten minutes to report an incident that had happened this morning. I let her know I'd be reporting it through our electronic system with employee health. Without waiting for my boss to respond, I navigated to the reporting system and plugged in the information about the event. Only minutes later, the phone rang, and the employee health nurse asked me to come down.

Employee health was in the bowels of the hospital, like my office but in a different section of the sprawling campus. After wandering the windowless corridors splashed in fluorescent lights, I found the office tucked into a corner that seemed too small to house a whole department. The wooden door creaked open, and after I passed through, I accidentally banged it closed, making the blinds over the door's window clatter. I winced. The receptionist peeked over the counter at me.

"Bitsy?" she asked.

I shuffled up to the counter. "Sorry about that."

"It's not a library," she said.

Her eyes roamed my face and then widened. She stood from her rolling chair with effort and waddled to the wall of records. I wondered how all of her fit into the chair. Manila folders, blue folders and green folders lined the shelves. While they were all neatly filed, the varying colors and frayed, stickered edges disrupted the illusion of organization. I stood with an arm wrapped over my middle, grasping my other arm while I waited for her to find my chart. Every breath I took caused my ribs to ache.

Patty, the receptionist—based on the desk sign—waggled her plump fingers over the V section. She grabbed a blue chart and yanked on it. "Elizabeth A. Varret, correct?"

"Yes, ma'am," I said.

She made her slow way back to the desk. She was beautiful, really. Her face was a perfect peach complexion and her auburn hair was shiny and lay perfectly in a twist on the back of her head. Her black pants had crisp lines in the front crease and her button-up, pink dress shirt had not a wrinkle on it. She was perfectly put together, from her eyeliner to her polished nails.

I looked down at my own khaki and sweater combo. The slouchy gray sweater I wore draped around a black tank top. My black shoes were comfortable and casual. Sneakers but dressier. Near Patty, I felt severely underdressed and a bit slovenly.

Yet, beneath the layers of effort to appear she had it all

under control, I sensed Patty's deep hurt. We shared something in common, and that something was a dark thing that squirmed and clung to the core of us. I knew she added layers to herself to keep from confronting that shadow. Just like Liz handled my shadows for me.

She typed at the computer, her lovely nails clacking softly at the keys. She looked up at me with wide emerald eyes. "Nurse B. will be out to get you in just a moment."

She didn't smile until I smiled at her, halfway, tentative. Her glossy lips twitched uncertainly before I backed away and took one of the ancient, orange-upholstered waiting chairs.

I raised myself up to see over the reception counter. "Excuse me?"

Patty's hair and eyes cleared the counter.

"What does the B. stand for?"

She looked at me and blinked. "Oh." She laughed and shook her head as she slowly registered what I was asking. "Nurse. B. Ballasiotes. It's sort of a mouthful, so she goes by Nurse B."

I could see her smile because her cheeks rose, which squinted her eyes.

"What sort of name is that?" I asked.

Grandma prided herself on her knowledge of our people, and so I had become naturally curious of others' family history. Patty's eyes cut up and to her left.

"Um... Greek, I think. Yes, Greek." She turned back to her computer monitor and clicked away at the keyboard.

Nurse B. came out then. God, she was gorgeous. Heat rose in my cheeks. She was in scrubs, but that didn't hide the curve of her body, the swell of her breasts, the beautiful olive tone of her skin, the tumble of loose, chestnut curls on her shoulders. She was going to examine me? I smothered down a string of thoughts that came unbidden into my mind. Was it normal for women to feel this way about other women? *I'm such a freak,* I thought to myself.

"Elizabeth?" she asked and looked up from the chart to me. Her gaze zeroed in on the portion of my face throbbing in a dull ache.

"B-Bitsy," I managed.

She smiled. Oh wow. My heart was a runaway train.

"Come on back, Bitsy," she said and half turned, waving me toward her.

I rose from my chair, watching my feet to make sure I wouldn't trip over them. Feeling awkward and ugly compared to the Greek goddess in front of me, I followed her down a cramped hallway. The carpet was a muted gray that might have been light blue a long, long time ago. The hall reeked of age and must. We passed the scales and took a sharp right into an exam room. I found the seat in the corner and sat while Nurse B. closed the door.

"So," she started as she looked at a printed version of the report I'd made and sat down on a small stool. She placed the chart on her lap, folded her small, delicate hands together over the paper and looked at me. "Tell me what happened today."

I did. She listened while I stuttered my way through, the details blurry through Liz's memory dump of the incident.

"Man, that must have been really scary," she said.

Liz had been scared. I felt guilty for making her deal with it. "Yes, it was," I stated.

"Well, first thing we need to do is look at your bumps and bruises and make sure nothing needs to be treated," she said. "I'm going to have you get into a gown, and then I'll be back in to take a look."

She pulled open a drawer and offered a folded piece of material, white with a small blue pattern on it.

"Sounds like most of the damage is going to be on your arms and neck and ribs, so let's have you tie the open part in the front." She opened the door, and before she closed it again she looked back at me and smiled. "Be back in a minute."

Once the door was closed, I shuffled out of my clothes until I got to my bra. Was I supposed to leave it on or take it off? I went through what she said, trying to recall if she'd said what she'd wanted me to do with my undergarments. Choosing modesty, I left the black bra and cotton panties on, feeling grateful they matched, at least color wise.

The gown was scratchy against my bare skin. I looked down at my body and felt a little twinge of anxiety building... a telltale snapping in my chest. I wrapped the thin material closer around me. Pain surged through my jaw, which made my face drum away at my sore cheek. I took a slow breath, fighting to find peace in the sudden storm of the panic attack. A knock at the door made me jump. The paper on the exam table crinkled underneath me, the sound like an avalanche in my ears.

Nurse Ballasiotes slid into the room, her breasts brushing the door and making them jiggle. The swirl of desire slammed into the panic of being nearly naked with a perfect stranger. It was like a tornado in my head. I gripped the opening of the gown and prayed God would give me peace and take away the panic.

Nurse Ballasiotes turned to me, taking me in with one critical, skilled look. I felt splayed open at her gaze. She knew what I was feeling; I was sure of it. I sat with my body tightly clamped down on itself. My legs burned from the rigidity, my fingers went numb where they grasped the material. And then she smiled at me, her head cocked to one side.

"You're safe now, Bitsy. No more hurts, no more wrongs. I'm going to have you show me where it hurts. I don't even need to touch you if you don't want me to, okay?"

I was shaking. My jaw ached from gritting my teeth. I nodded, not trusting my words. With one hand, I rolled up the sleeve of the oversized gown to my collarbone. Red blossoms of what would be mighty bruises formed a handprint on my upper arm. Poor Liz!

The nurse carefully looked at my arm, then my face, then at my legs. "How is your head feeling?"

"L-like one of those melons when Gallagher gets a hold of it," I said, surprised at myself for joking.

She locked eyes with me, and I let one side of my mouth twitch in a smile. She laughed, a short, sweet sound that eased the sharpest edges of my panic.

"May I look at your ribs?" she asked.

I took a slow, deep breath and worked my fingers loose from the death grip on the gown. I looked down as I opened the gown and exposed my lanky body, wondering if she'd be disgusted by it. I glanced at her, but she was only solving a problem, fixing a hurt, not judging.

"Does it hurt when you breathe?"

I nodded, slowly, so as to not interrupt the gentle waah-waah-waah of my cheek's protest.

She leaned closer to my ribcage and hmm'ed.

"Okay, here's what I think," she started. "I don't think you're broken, but I think you're pretty banged up and bruised."

Her words struck me. Sharon, my counselor, had said something similar to me once.

"I don't think you need any X-rays, and nothing needs bandaging. However..."

She took a seat on the roll-y chair as I pulled the gown back over my bony shoulders and wrapped it around me.

"Do you have a counselor?"

I paused. I didn't tell people I went to counseling.

"You don't have to answer that," she said, waving away the

last question as she seemed to change her mind. "If you do, please schedule an appointment immediately. If you don't, here is a pamphlet on our Employee Assistance Program. You have several free visits, and they have a phone line to talk to someone. You may not need to talk today, but you should speak with someone soon." She handed me the pamphlet she'd pulled from a rack display near the sink.

"And I just want to say..." she began.

I looked up into her eyes. She wore a crooked grin on her delicate features.

"Cathy called me to give witness to what happened today. I would have paid money to see you throw that asshole off of you."

She held out a fist to me. I stared at it for a minute before I realized what she was doing. I raised my fist and bumped knuckles with her. She nodded her approval as her hand dropped into her scrub pocket.

"Go home after this and rest. Don't come in tomorrow, either. I've already called your boss to let her know."

"Okay," I said, stunned, not sure I needed the time off. Leaving today and not coming in tomorrow meant I'd be off until next week, since I didn't work Thursday or Friday, either. I'd bet Roxanne was pissed. Guilt flooded me. "Was Roxanne... upset?" A new panic rose.

"I don't know," she said. "I don't care, either. Your health and safety come first."

She winked at me, which made blood go rushing into my sore cheek. She squeezed out the door before I could stutter a thank you.

Still shaky, I dressed back into my clothes and made my way through the halls and out of the department. Back at the office, Officer Mike was waiting for me. My shoulders drooped. I didn't want to do this again.

"I don't need much, Bitsy. Just a short recount and your signature on the statement I've drawn up. Since I was there, I recounted everything already. But, I need you to look it over and make sure it's right. I know you're probably tired of talking." He stood up from the chair he'd occupied in front of my desk and placed a clipboard of papers on the counter in front of me.

I looked at them. The words were all carefully written, describing what had happened. I read them, curious about his perspective. When he described what Liz had done to get the man, prisoner Alec Holliday, off of her, I cheered her for that, while wishing silently that I could have been that strong. I signed the papers.

Mike looked at me for a long minute after I gave him back the metal clipboard.

"I don't know how you did it, but... I'm glad you did." He shook his head and smiled. "If more women could do what you did, maybe there'd be less assholes like Alec Holliday in the world."

I needed a little diversion from my sucky day. Grams was asleep, snoring loudly in the room next door. I dressed quietly, using far more concealer than I normally did. My eye was swollen, but thankfully, Grams had tended our wounds with frozen peas and colorful curses for my attacker. Grams had a great imagination, which she applied to possible punishment options for Mr. Holliday, all of which she'd gladly dole out herself.

After covering the worst of the appearing bruises, I slipped through the front door after a long pause to hear the soundness of Grams's slumber. Locking the door behind me, I skipped out into the darkness, its touch a cool tease on my exposed neck. I clutched my handbag under an arm, under a generous volume of winter coat, and headed down the street.

I met the cab two blocks away and gratefully climbed into the warmth of the vehicle. The heater whirred; soft pop music played low over the crumby speakers. The seats were clean and worn, and the air in the car smelled like fake vanilla.

"Where to?" the man asked, the whites of his eyes shining in the rearview.

"Club Tesso," I said.

He looked back at me without responding and without driving away.

"Is there a problem?" I asked, folding my arms over my middle and aiming a dark stare back into his rearview.

He shook his head and pulled away from the curb. Judgmental motherfucker.

The five-mile drive passed in silence. After he dropped me at the curb in front of the club, I paid the man and gave the smallest tip possible.

The club beckoned me. Tom, the bouncer at the door, smiled when he saw my approach.

"Liz," he hailed me.

"Hey, handsome," I said. "You workin' all night?"

He nodded. "Yeah, all work and no play for this boy." He backed into the glass door and pushed it open for me. He was a specimen of manly and not half bad in the sack. "You're lookin' very hot tonight, as usual. I'm sure you'll find someone to play with."

"Well, thank you," I said demurely, looking up at him through my eyelashes.

"Go on and get that sweet ass in there."

He spanked me as I passed by, which pushed me over the threshold and into the club. My ribs ached with even his playful pat. Tonight, I would have to embrace the pain. The door closed behind me. I descended the two short steps and made a beeline for the bar.

The bartender, Val, short for Valentina, nodded in my direction as I approached. She didn't smile. Smiles cost extra. Her dark hair was pristinely pulled back into a neat ponytail and braid. She was plump and lovely, middle-aged and strong. She was the kind of woman who took no lip but was the first to come to a person's aid when they needed it.

"Ms. Liz," she said. "It's been too long. Why have you kept your pretty face away from us?"

"Keeping busy and out of trouble," I said as I sidled up to the bar.

"That's no fun. You have fun; you live longer. It's good for you."

"*Hear that, Bitsy?*"

"*Having sex with random people is* not *good for us,*" Bitsy countered.

"*Lighten up. If you're not going to live a little, I will.*"

"What do you want to drink, mi chula?" Val asked.

I thought about it for a minute. I wanted to dull the edges, but I didn't want to be sick tomorrow. "Bourbon and Coke, please," I asked.

"Bourbon and a Coke." She slapped her hands together. "You got it. You give me your card for the tab and go put your coat away, and I'll have it ready for you when you get back."

I adored her Spanish accent. "Gracias, *mamita,*" I said. Not just anyone could get away with using Spanish phrases with her. She didn't endure fakes.

"Look at you," she said, her dark eyebrows raised over brown eyes. "You stick around me; I teach you a few things."

I winked at her and then made my way past the dance floor, down the stairs and to the shower and locker rooms. Two women were in one of the double showers together. I announced my presence with the click of my heels. There was a soft, feminine moan behind the sheer curtain. The steam rose and rolled. I took my lock out of the clutch and found an empty locker. The women in the shower whispered to each other. I could see their wet bodies touching, wrapping around each other, their faces melding as they kissed. I took my time taking off my coat, enjoying the show.

After putting the lock in place, I turned to the wall mirror.

From here, I could look at myself and see the couple behind me. The red and black corset and mini skirt accentuated the curves of my body, pushing my smallish breasts up and together. Black gloves and leather boots made my ensemble. I brushed a gloved hand across my shoulders, spread my legs a little and caressed the swell of my breasts, the hardness of the corset hugging my skinny waist and over my hip and pelvic bones. The fire brushed my insides as one of the women reached her climax, her soft cries of elation fanning the flames inside me. But I wanted more than just to watch tonight. After the woman finished, I click-clacked my way out of the bathroom and back to the bar, the flush high in my olive-skinned cheeks, my curly brown hair curlier for the exposure to the wet air.

Eager and hungry, I downed the bourbon. Its smooth kiss soothed the burn of the alcohol. I let the taste linger in my mouth and smiled. It was wonderful, finally being of age. I didn't have to sneak the alcohol. Didn't have to pretend to be someone's friend in order to get a drink. Or some of the other things I'd done. I had a job and a home and choices.

"It seems you have it all together." Not Bitsy. And the words were not really words. They were intentions that translated themselves in my mind.

I straightened. My heart did a little dance, like a puppet jerked around on a stage. No one was near me. Val was helping another customer at the other end of the bar. I took a long, slow breath then sipped my Coke through the red and white straw. Maybe I had imagined it.

Someone sidled up next to me. A woman. She was attractive in a homely sort of way.

"Hi there," she began. "Would you like to try a semi-private room with me?"

"No, thank you," I said, hardly glancing her way. I sipped my Coke.

"Sorry to have bothered you," she said, her brown eyebrows cocked high over small blue eyes. Clearly offended, she stalked away on stilettos that would break my neck if I tried walking in them. I gave her five points for skill and another five for rocking calves. In the end, she didn't come equipped with what I was looking for tonight.

I surveyed the room and waited to spot the right opportunity. When he walked in the door I turned back to the liquor-lined wall and grinned.

"Hey, Bits," I called. *"You in there? Come out, come out! There's dude perfect you like so much."*

The paramedic was hardly recognizable in street clothes, but damn was he fine. Uniforms were a bonus, but it all hit the floor when it got real, anyway. I watched him in the mirror behind the bottles. He was alone.

"Bitsy, listen. Either you come out, or I'm cumming on him by myself. You here?"

"I am here," said the foreign voice.

I froze again. What the hell? Where was Bitsy? Who was this new voice? Dude was ordering a drink. Scorned stiletto woman was eyeing him. I decided I better move, or he'd get scooped up, and I wasn't in the mood to share tonight. Resolutely ignoring the new voice, I snatched my Coke and made my way toward his table. Scorned was moving, too, but my heels weren't as high as hers, and my legs were longer. I placed my drink on the table with my back to Scorned just as she was about to close in. Behind me, she growled and stalked away, the fading clicks of her heels marking her retreat.

"Hi," I said.

Gabe eyed me up and down. Shock smoothed his features and left his eyes wide.

"Oh," he said. "Um. Hi."

I could see his blush even in the darkened bar. I bit my lip against a laugh that wanted to escape.

"You look like a kid caught with a hand in the cookie jar," I said.

"God," he said. He exhaled and smiled. "I just... I never would have guessed in a million years I'd see you in a place like this. I'm embarrassed." He raised his hands in a defeated gesture.

"Well, then you've caught me, too," I said and situated myself into the tall chair.

He looked at me, staring into my eyes. He shook his head and laughed. "It's Bitsy, isn't it?" he asked.

"You can call me Liz. Bitsy is another nickname I have," I lied.

His head cocked to one side, but he nodded anyway. The waitress came and set a drink down in front of him.

"There you go, hon'," she said.

"Can I get another bourbon?" I asked the waitress.

"Sure thing," she said. "Shot or on the rocks?"

"Shot," I said, with feeling.

"You got it, babe."

Before Gabe got done saying thank you, the waitress bounced off to the bar.

He swirled the drink in his glass. When he looked up at me he zeroed in on the left side of my face. He half rose, reached across the table and cupped my chin. I stifled a wince at the touch. The slightest movement of his hand tipped my jaw to the left. His fingers was strong and commanding without being threatening.

"What happened to you?" he asked.

I could see the scenarios in his mind. And here I thought I'd done a great job with the cover up.

"You can see it in here with all this dark?"

"I'm used to looking for these things in my line of work," he said, a little steel cutting the air.

"Oh well, speaking of work..." I explained.

"Wait, this happened at work?" Gabe asked.

"It doesn't matter," I said. He was sort of killing my buzz. I really didn't want to talk about it.

The waitress bobbed up to the table, plunked down the shot of bourbon on her way to another table. The bar area was just beginning to fill as new people trickled in, bringing with them the scent of fall and the perfume of night.

"Some douchebag Cathy needed to gather evidence from for a case."

"What? He attacked you?" He leaned forward on the round table, his hands gripping in on themselves and bunching the muscles of his forearms.

"Psha. You should see the other guy," I said.

"Man. And I thought my job was exciting," he said.

"Administrative assistants are one of the more fearsome beasts," I explained coolly. "The guy barely escaped my counterattack with his life." I raised my hands like a ninja and judo-chopped the air.

"Wow, tough chick. I like your style." He came in slow with a mock left hook.

I copied with an uppercut, which of course hit him first and threw off his left hook.

"Ahh!" He threw his body to the side and landed dramatically on the table.

Our drinks sloshed while my giggle cut the air. He lifted himself up, and a small silence filled the space between us.

"So, um..." He looked into his glass of something amber over ice. "Come here often?" he asked tentatively.

I laughed.

"You are really cute when you're nervous," I commented.

"Do *you* come here often?" I leaned over the table, clasping my shot with my elbows resting on the small, circular table.

"It's actually my first time here," he said.

I surveyed him, probing for the lie, and found none. He twirled his glass, glanced up at me through blond eyelashes, leaned back and rubbed the back of his neck.

"I gotta say, I'm a little embarrassed. I planned on calling you, so meeting you here seems really odd."

"Oh, I wouldn't call it odd at all. I'd call it fortuitous." I grinned hungrily at him.

"You would?"

"Yes, of course. Why not?"

"I don't know," he said after a thought. "I guess I thought most girls wouldn't want to date a guy they saw in a place like this."

I skipped past the obvious—that he was here to have sex with somebody. There was a part of me that said he wasn't thinking about the number Bitsy had scratched out on a post-it note. That part of me was more closely tied with Bitsy, and Bitsy had gone off again into the nether regions of our consciousness.

"Oh? So, you want to date me?" I teased him. "Well, then, this could be our first date."

He shook his head. "No, this is not a first date kinda place."

"Why not?" I asked.

"You don't have sex on a first date," he explained. His leg bounced against the barstool's footrest.

"That sounds like rules to me. Rules are great. Rules are fun to break." The word "break" snapped out of my mouth.

I tilted up my chin and dared him with my eyes. He grinned at me.

"You know," he said, "it's like you're not really the same girl I met at the hospital."

I wriggled against the truth. Bitsy would be pissed at me for this.

"We all have to maintain our professionalism at work," I explained. "And honestly"—I gave him a shy look— "you had me tongue-tied when I first saw you."

Flattery usually worked really well with most men. He shook his head as if he disagreed with my assessment and didn't think he was that hot.

"Not me. I'm just some guy." He exhaled in a big splutter. "Listen, I really like you. If we play around tonight, do you promise we can go on a real date after this?"

"He won't want to go on a real date if you allow his pleasure tonight," said the other voice. The intention formed into familiar words.

"Don't you worry," I said, *"I'm gonna get my pleasure tonight, too."* I straightened, lifted my shot glass toward him and pronounced, "To pretend dates, followed by real dates."

He giggled nervously, clinked his glass against mine, and we drank.

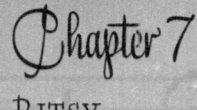

Chapter 7

BITSY

I was a Queen Maker. The title came to me as the dream pulled me into folds of disorientation. The room around me wobbled into focus. I lay on a circular mattress draped in crimson blankets. The material was shiny and specked with individual beads of gold. Just the blanket itself was rich.

I reached a hand out and found Maltheron, touching his arm in a manner that assured me of his presence. The air was chilled. I pulled the cover higher and drew my body close to my husband. Her husband.

"Are you cold, my love?" asked Maltheron.

I nodded against his warm skin, relishing how he radiated heat.

"Come here, then," he said. He rolled to his back and scooped me into his side, wrapping a strong arm around me. I nestled onto his chest and relaxed into him. But, sleep wouldn't come to me. "What is bothering you, Elada?"

I could always trust Maltheron to know my mood.

"It is my season again," I said. Not I, but the woman in the bed. El. I merely occupied her body, but she was not me, Bitsy.

Maltheron stilled beside me, his breath cinching up to shallow stitches.

"I don't want another mating. I'm tired and I'm getting old. Haven't I done my duty?" the woman said. I said.

"The law is clear," he said. His voice was resigned. He hugged me tighter into him. "Do you want me present? I will make sure the ministrations are gentle."

"No," I said, knowing how difficult it was for my husband to watch a Mating that was not with him. "I will have the Hound present. He ensures no violence."

I loved all of my children. But, the making of them was not the beautiful act between Maltheron and me. An act that was allowed to produce two children and no more. After which, he had been sterilized. All the rest of my children were spawned by men deemed as being from fine enough lineage to pass advantageous traits down through the generations. As one of few women gifted with the ability to bear children, I was required to bear as many children as my body would bear. And that so far had been twelve. Most Queen Makers bore six or seven. I felt I'd done enough.

Aside from Maltheron's children, the others were sent back to their fathers' homes. My children grew up far from me, adopted by mothers who could never bear them.

I was still fertile. I had not died in childbirth. My body had not aged out. I was strong and supple and healthy. But, my spirit ached at every forced mating. And I couldn't die from that.

I dreaded my daughter's future. She hadn't grown into a Maker yet, but I knew she would.

A mother just knows.

The phone rang, an electronic harmony so benign it slipped into my dream without notice. It rang again and again, pulling me from my deep sleep and weird dreams.

The phone rang once more. I tried to move, but my body wouldn't respond. The little success I had made my bruised ribs and black eye scream for me to lie still. Something else was slightly sore, too. Anxiety crept into my bloodstream, making my heart thud. The film of the dream wrapping around my brain broke into a quickly dissipating fog.

"*Relax, Tiger. We just had a little fun last night,*" Liz explained.

"*You seriously...?*"

"*Go back to sleep, and I swear I'll show you everything when we wake up. And turn off your phone.*"

"*Oh, my gosh! I can't believe you would do that again without my permission!*"

"*Hey, I tried calling to you. You're like on holiday lately or something. Not my fault,*" Liz said.

Angry, I rolled out of bed and snatched the phone off the bedside table. The number was the generic hospital line.

"H-hello?" My voice was garbled and raw. Liz must have been screaming during her sex-capade last night.

"*Oh, for fuck's sake. Give me a fucking break. You aren't the one who had a fucking murderer jump you!*" Liz said.

"Hi, Bitsy." A syrupy noise leaked out of the phone.

I pulled it away from my ear and then put it back again.

"Who is th-this?" I asked. I was sore in more ways than one and cranky from discovering Liz's outing for the night; plus, I'd just been woken from incomprehensible dreams that felt more like some alternate reality playing in my mind. My voice might have been a little on the annoyed side.

"It's your boss, Bitsy." Roxanne resumed her normal, angry notes.

"Oh," I said, "s-sorry, I didn't recognize you. Um, didn't the employee health n-nurse talk to you?"

"Yes, she did, but Bitsy, I really need your help," she said.

"*Is she seriously whining right now?*" Liz chimed in.

"I have a doctor's appointment today." I choked back another stutter. "I can't miss it," I explained.

"Yeah, but who's going to cover the charge nurse meeting?" Her voice rose.

I felt myself crumpling under her push.

"Don't you dare cancel on us, Bitsy," Liz said.

"I don't want to lose my job."

Liz fell silent at this. She didn't want us to lose our job, either. The money we made bought her too much freedom. Plus, I helped Grandma with the upkeep on the house and stuff. I would be such a burden to her if I weren't employed.

"I have a doctor appointment at 9:00 a.m., and then I'll be in after that," I said, determined to not cancel my appointment.

"That's fine, just fine. I'll take care of the other things since you won't be in until late." Her tone cut through the phone.

I rolled my eyes.

"We're not supposed to be in at all, you bitch," Liz pointed out, luckily in my head and not out loud.

"I'll see you later this morning," I said and hung up the phone. Did I feel guilty? Yes, I did. And I also felt annoyed at my boss for requiring me there after employee health required my leave. Annoyance in addition to guilt was progress, I decided. I thought Sharon would be proud of me.

My alarm was set for seven-thirty. The lights were still off, and the bed was still warm. And I was so tired. My head hit the pillow, and I was out.

"Elizabeth."

The voice nagged at me but I was too tired to respond.

"Elizabeth. Elizabeth Anne! Wake up, hon'. You're gonna be late for your appointment."

I grunted, unable to shake off the exhaustion weighing me down.

"Come on, sweetpea. I made us some breakfast. Up and at 'em."

A warm hand clasped my foot and shook my leg. I inhaled deeply. *Sausage.*

"*Mmm...*" purred Liz.

I sat up. Grandma looked down at me.

"Good. You're awake. Not going to lie back down, are you?"

I grunted again.

"Come on, then," she said and held out her hand.

With my non-black-eye open, I weakly gave her a hand and let her pull me from the bed. We jostled down the ancient stairs, through the foyer and into the dining area. It was situated so we could see out the front window, which faced east. The sun was rising and set the table in a glow of pink. Steam from plates of food rose like fog against the horizon.

I plopped into a high-backed chair and inhaled the smell of the food. "I don't think I'll ever get used to this," I said. It had been years. I was still overwhelmed with gratitude. "Thank you, Grandma."

"Aw, you're welcome, sweatpea," she said. She hugged my shoulders and kissed me on the head. "I'm just sorry I couldn't get to you before I did."

"I'm here now. For as long as you'll put up with me," I said.

Grandma sat in the chair next to me and placed a linen into her lap. She folded her hands in front of her plate, bowed her head and began the prayer.

"Dear Divine. We're so grateful for your kindness and generosity. We are warm and well and fed. You take us through another day with every opportunity to thrive and share Love. Please bless our food to increase our vibration and make us strong to do the jobs we were sent here to do. Amen."

She might have been born Texan, but she'd left her traditional religious ideals behind with the state.

"Amen," I repeated. I picked up my fork and cut out a bit of biscuit and sausage gravy. It was still hot. Soft biscuit melted in my mouth with hot, creamy gravy and peppery sausage. I chewed slowly, savoring the bite with relish.

"After your appointment, I thought we could go to Powell's," she said. "What do you think?"

Disappointment filled me. My fork sank to the plate. I wiped my mouth, sipped the orange juice. "I wish I could, but Roxanne called me in."

"What?" Grandma froze mid-bite. Her loaded fork fell back to the plate. "I thought the employee health nurse told you to rest."

I nodded. "She did. Roxanne called me at five o'clock this morning and asked me to come in for the charge nurse meeting."

"And there's nobody else who can do that?" Grandma asked.

"I think there is. I doubt she asked them, though," I said.

"Well, I just don't understand. How can she call you in? Doesn't employee health have the say-so?"

"I'm sure she didn't ask them," I commented. "She does what she wants to do."

"Elizabeth," she said.

Nobody else could call me that. When Grandma called me by my full name, we both listened. Liz loved her as much as I did. She was the only one with whom I felt even somewhat whole.

"Do you think it's wise to go in today?"

"I'm afraid if I say I can't come in, she'll find a way to fire me. I don't want to lose my job."

"Oh, honey, your grandmother is just fine, financially. If you have to quit and look for another job, that's okay by me."

"I don't want to be a burden. You do too much for me already. Plus, if I just quit, then I won't get a good recommendation."

"Have you checked in with the music director lately? Maybe you could give violin lessons or be an assistant music teacher somewhere," she said.

I took another bite and relished the flavors. Grandma always added a touch of nutmeg to her sausage gravy. It was amazing. Nutmeg. I didn't even know what that was before I moved in. I didn't know people could make biscuits from scratch in their own kitchen and that food could be so wonderful. Food was just something that wasn't around. And if it was, it came out of a can from the food bank, or out of a paper sack when Mom was really feeling guilty about whatever some horrible boyfriend had done to us. I could always get school breakfast and lunch, so that was something.

"Yeah, I could check in again," I said after I swallowed.

"What about checking into the Oregon Symphony Orchestra directly?"

"I'll look to see if they have any open positions," I said. "You know how they are though. Not a lot of turnover and they're so world-class I don't know if they'll take me." But, even for the chance, I'd try. I just hoped they'd get an opening soon. It had been months since graduation. I missed playing in the orchestra. I scooped another bite onto my fork.

Grandma smiled at me. "They'll take you," she said. She pulled something from the chair beside her. It was a printout of a web page. "I found this on the computer. Looks like they're hiring violinists." She beamed at me.

My fork clattered to the plate.

"Oh my god!" Liz squealed inside. *"They're hiring!"*

"S-s-seriously?" I asked, grabbing at the papers greedily. I read over the posting. Second section violin. My head wobbled in a wave of dizziness. I leafed through the other pages, listing the repertoire for the audition, along with possible sight reading materials.

Grandma had taken another bite while I'd pored over the information she'd printed for me. She finished chewing and dabbed at her mouth with a napkin.

"They say there are two positions open, and they won't be open forever. So, I scheduled you for the tryout slot three weeks from Friday at 10:00 a.m."

"Grandma! You talked to them? You scheduled an audition for me?"

"Yes, ma'am, but you're going to have to submit your CV and references by the end of this week. They're expecting it." She stuck an elbow on the table and pointed at me. "You deserve this, Elizabeth Anne. You've got talent in spades. I'm not gonna sit around here and just watch while my granddaughter wastes a divine gift. No. If you don't get this position, you need to seriously consider moving. You don't need to waste your time sticking around some old lady."

"Damn. She told you, Bits," Liz said.

A piece of me was scared to death. Another piece of me was excited beyond belief. Liz was smugly proud. I felt small compared to the opportunity looming.

"I can't be good enough for the Oregon Symphony Orchestra," I said.

"No, ma'am." Grandma slapped a hand onto the table.

I jumped. Instinct.

"You are worthy of anything this life has to offer you, missy. I will not allow you to cut yourself down. It's not the truth. You don't know the truth. You can't. But you will. You're gonna knock 'em dead!" Grandma was in a real fervor now.

I sat back, part of me just watching her passion and what drove her.

"You really think so?" I asked, the smallness of me being the biggest voice.

"Yes, I do."

She tilted her chin into the air, that look of defiance on her face.

I twisted my hands in my lap. "I'll talk to Sharon about it."

Grandma's face didn't shift. "Good," she said.

We enjoyed the rest of our breakfast in silence, me mentally plucking away at one of the pieces in the repertoire.

Grandma leaned back in her chair, her earrings swinging.

"Phoo, I'm stuffed," she said. "What time is it, sweatpea?"

I swiped at my phone. "Oh, eight o'clock already," I said.

"All right then, you go throw on some clothes, and I'll load the dishwasher."

"Thank you, Grandma."

I leaned over the table and kissed her cheek. It was soft, and she smelled good.

She giggled. "You're welcome," she said.

I hurried out of the dining area. In my room, I squeaked over the floorboards and wondered how Liz made it out last night without waking Grandma.

"Pure talent," she boasted.

I tried not to think of what she'd done.

"Oh, you so want to know what we did."

A face flashed into my mind. A beautiful face of a man I'd given my phone number to just a couple of days before.

"No!" I said aloud, not caring if Grandma heard me talking to Liz. "No, you didn't!"

Chapter 8

I wouldn't speak to her the entire trip. Grandma was silent, glancing at me out of the corner of her dark eyes every now and then. She'd heard me screaming at Liz. She'd just climbed into the car and drove when I had come down the stairs at lightning speed.

"*Bitsy, please listen to me,*" Liz started.

"I don't want to talk to you right now, Liz. You ruin everything!" I looked out the window, tears streaming down my face. "How could you do this to me?"

"*It's totally fine, Bits. Hey, we had a lot of fun—*"

"You just shut your mouth. When we get to Sharon's you tell her what happened. You tell her what you did. And how insanely cruel and uncaring you are to me."

"*It's not like that. He's going to call. You'll go on a date. It'll be fine.*"

"No, he won't! He's not going to call me now. He's already—"

I looked over at Grandma, who kept a straight face. I couldn't bear not speaking aloud though.

"He's already been with you! He won't want anything to do with me now. You blew it. You blew it, Liz. Again!" Frustration surged through me. My stomach cramped and coiled in on itself. I wanted to puke. I needed to throw up. I inhaled, but the breath I took that was meant as calming turned into a rapid succession of shallow breaths that fueled my panic.

"*Calm down, Bitsy!*" Liz commanded.

"So—" Wheeze. "So—" Wheeze. "Stupid!" I screamed. I banged my fist into the door.

"*Ow, Bitsy, stop it!*"

I banged again.

"Shut up—" Wheeze. "You slut!" I banged again.

"Stop, Elizabeth or you'll ruin yourself for the audition!" Grandmother's voice cut through the drowning panic.

I yanked my fist into my stomach, jolting forward and screamed. I covered my face with my hands and wept into them. My hand throbbed in a dull ache. Grandma was saying something to me, but her voice was drowned out in the current of madness sweeping me away.

The world went black as the panic and pain consumed me. The car stopped, but I didn't know where we were. I couldn't see past the dark edges pulling in on me.

The door yanked away from me, and a cool wind rushed against me. Its crisp blueness sparked the edges of my drowning vision. Darkness was all velvet hugs. Cold was bitter and vindictive. A sting broke across my cheek, igniting the present throb of my black eye into a bonfire of pain. I looked around for its source and saw Grandma standing over me. Sorrow, pity, anger, hurt, compassion. It was all there on her lined face. The disappointment was the worst. I hung my head and sobbed. I should leave and let her be in peace. Wet burbles of hopelessness stuttered out of me.

Grandma's warm hand was on my shoulder, and she just stood there. When my sobs slowed she finally spoke.

"Elizabeth," she said.

Liz and I both looked at her. Liz was full of regret and shame. So was I, for throwing a fit.

"I'm s—" I took a slow breath and made myself say it. "Sorry." The word yanked out of me.

"It's all right. We're gonna be okay. Come on now. We're at Sharon's."

I looked up. We'd made it to the house out of which my counselor operated. I dreaded what she was going to say to me. That I'd taken a step back or that I'd lost control and scared Grandma. That I was selfish and uncaring or weak. I undid the buckle with my left hand and climbed weakly out of the car. Grandma helped me. We made our way up the drive, past the large front yard hosting a collection of tall pines and a boulder.

When we reached the side of the house we followed a small, cobblestone path to a fenced gate. I knew there was a camera perched here that would let Sharon know we had arrived. Grandma unlatched the gate and held it open for me to walk through. I went ahead, holding the screen door for her as we entered a small, enclosed porch, where we would wait for Sharon to let us into her office. It was chilly. My face throbbed from yesterday's ordeal, and my hand hurt where I'd banged it. Panicked, I surveyed the hand. I flexed my fingers, curling them into the position of holding the bow. It was okay. I sighed in relief and turned to Grandma.

"Th-thank you," I said.

She lifted my hand and kissed it, rubbed it lightly and held it at her side.

Sharon trundled to the door, looking surprised to see Grandma.

"Carolyn?" She pushed open the door to let us inside.

I tripped over the threshold but caught myself before I fell.

"I was only expecting to see Elizabeth today."

"Liz and Bitsy had a bit of a falling out on the way over here. I thought it might be good to at least walk them to the door."

Sharon turned her dark eyes to me. She looked me up and down with a quick, analyzing glance that dissected me with the accuracy and efficiency of a surgeon's blade. My throat was clenched and clotted.

"Hmm... Elizabeth," Sharon began, as if intoning some power by using my full name.

I recoiled. Liz didn't deserve to be named.

"I will let your grandmother stay, but after she explains what happened, I need you to talk. Can you do that today?"

I wasn't sure I could. Tears slipped down my cheeks.

Chapter 9

I didn't go to work. Roxanne was furious. Grandma drove us home from Sharon's office. I'd just hung up with Roxanne when a text flashed on the screen. The car jostled along down the city streets of Hillsdale. Our house was on the opposite end of town in Alameda.

COREY:

Hey, Bitsy-Bits. You okay? Roxanne was just down and said you weren't coming in. She was pissed.

I'm fine. You know the lady on Monday who was raped and tortured?

Yeah?

The guy who did it was brought in yesterday for Cathy to get forensics. He attacked me.

OH MY GOD! Are you okay???

> A little banged up but not too bad.

I wasn't going to tell him about the damage Liz had done. I couldn't explain that one without getting into the details of my state of being.

COREY:

> That's crazy! I can't believe you were attacked! Damn. They gotta get you a new office.

> Yeah, that's what I keep hearing.

> So, you're really okay? You didn't get hurt or anything? What did he do? Like, how did he attack you?

> He was walking past my desk toward the exam room. Mike, the cop, was with him. I guess I was sort of smirking at him.

> Uh oh.

> Yeah, he didn't like that. So he jumped on top of me, knocked me to the ground and smashed his hands into my face. I have a bit of a black eye. Wanna see?

> Yes, pic!

I snapped a selfie. I looked awful. Not only was my shiner there, it was worse than yesterday, due in part to the amount of crying I'd done this morning. My body ached all over. My ribs screamed in pain, my face throbbed, my back was sore and rug-burned and my girl parts were tender. I couldn't even not think about what Liz had done because she'd done it so roughly I had to feel the aftermath. But at least she'd stopped trying to talk to me. Trying to rationalize what she'd done.

I sent the pic.

COREY:

OMG! I can't fucking believe that!

I know.

So, not to be insensitive, but does this mean no market on Saturday?

Sharon and I had discussed Saturday's plans. She had recommended by Saturday I would be stable and should most definitely get out of the house and be around other people.

Nah, I'm all about Saturday market.
And seeing Abigail. 😊

COREY:

Yay!! Hurry up, weekend!

The weekend didn't hurry. Without the distraction of Liz, my mind wandered, wading through odd images and strange-looking people. Sleep was only a venue for the dreams. Thursday's slumber was no exception.

I floated in a cloud of warmth. The ankles of women skittered by at eye level. Their bare feet slapped softly against the floor. The smell of flowers and spices filled my nose. One of the women entered the room from a curtained doorway, carrying a large copper-colored pitcher. She knelt in front and above me. I looked around to find the warm cloud that enveloped me was a bath filled with hot water. The bath was large enough to submerge my whole body and stretch my legs out.

The woman tipped the pitcher and a golden liquid fell from the spout and into my bath. I pushed my body away from the dark gray edge and toward the water where the woman had poured the golden liquid. I stretched my starkly white arms wide and scooped the water toward me. My hands met an oily substance that slid over my skin like silk.

I already knew I wasn't me again in this dream, but the look of my naked body confirmed it all the more. While it was still humanoid, the limbs were overly long, my skin white and strange dark dots lined the side of arms. My stomach was soft and my hips were much wider than my own body. The hair floating on the water's surface was the color of honey in the afternoon sun.

A young girl flew through the curtained entrance, dropping to her knees at the bath's edge. Her face was the same shape of the woman whose body I wore in the dream, with the same strange dots lining the sides of the nose and over the eyebrows. Her deep blue eyes were wide and beautiful, glittering excitedly.

"Mother, Father says I can take the hound to the fields today!" she said.

"Did he?" I asked, my voice coming out with a certain disconnectedness since it was not my voice. I sat as a silent audience in a theater of a body. Elada sensed something was off.

"Well. I mean, he said if I have your permission," the girl amended.

"Aerylia, do you know what today is?" I asked and a little

steel cut into the patient question. Something niggled at the side of my preoccupation with the day's event for which I prepared—for which Elada prepared. My daughter and I shared an empathetic bond and through it I glimpsed an untruth. Not only an untruth, but a small fear the girl held. Still, children were prone to tell white lies on occasion and to be afraid every now and then.

The girl looked up and around, seeming to notice the other women in the room for the first time. A hint of shame covered her face.

"It's Mating Day, isn't it?" she asked, hanging her head. It wasn't just shame that made her hang her head. She regretted not being able to take the Hound with her.

"Yes, it is. And both you and your father should remember the Hound watches over me during Mating Day." I could feel Elada's anger, not at her daughter, but at her husband who seemed to have forgotten the day his wife had dreaded for weeks. Disappointment filled me, and a sorrow at not being more carefully considered. That was not usual of her husband.

"Yes, Mother. I'm sorry I forgot Mating Day was today."

"Go play, my love," I said to my daughter. "And Aerylia, do not go to the places where you're frightened. You must listen to your inner voice."

The girl nodded and turned away, her childish sadness for not getting to play with the Hound evident in the frown on her alien face.

Elada stood in a room with a roof but surrounded by open walls. The warmth and breeze from the outside wafted over my naked body. The women who had tended her bath buzzed around the room. *The cool touch of material caressed her skin. I looked down with her eyes to find a crimson robe covering her nakedness. A wide violet belt went around her waist two times and the larger end was ceremoniously tucked above and below the layers.*

Three women led her to a low-backed chair and lowered Elada into it. The cushions wrapped her body in a welcoming softness. One of the girls pulled Elada's hair back and began braiding, the gentle tug sending prickling sensations into my scalp. I was offered food; the tray was spread with an assortment of unrecognizable items. She took a small creamy yellow square and placed it in a large leaf, then topped it with several small red fruits. She rolled the leaf up and nibbled at what I surmised to be an alien sandwich.

When her hair was complete, the young women gathered in front of her. They were all varying degrees of beautiful. Each wore a short white dress with long legs exposed. One had white hair, another the same honey color as Elada, and the third was a sweet shade of bubblegum. Their eyes were equally unique colors of violet, green and blue.

"Is he here?" I asked. The three nodded. "I will call the Hound and then you will show him in. Understand?" Again, they nodded, but their eyes grew at the mention of the Hound. "The Hound will not harm you. Do not worry, my sweets. Thank you for your service." She bowed her head in respect to her servants, but she sounded so weary.

The women scuttled away, casting concerned glances over their shoulders to their Queen. When they'd disappeared out a curtained entrance, Elada looked out through one of the openings in the room, where the outside bled into the inside. She paused, inhaled deeply, cupped her long fingers around her mouth and let out three, long and distinct notes. The sound carried like a struck bell over the open country side.

Elada stood from the chair as a growing dark spot on the

horizon began to take shape. The Hound slowed as he entered the room and approached me. My breath hitched at the sight of the creature and as my anxiety began to spread, I woke.

My eyes sprang open as my heart beat wildly, my breath heaving. I pushed myself up from the tangle of pillows and blankets and cupped my hands to my face.

Groggy and disoriented, I pulled myself out of bed and got ready to meet Corey. Flashes of the bear-dog-like alien creature popped and faded in and out of my mind's eye. The thought of it nagged me to the point I wished I could somehow get it out of my thoughts. And then, I had a great idea. Smiling, I pulled my clothes on, yanked my hair back into a pony and headed down for breakfast before leaving for Saturday Market.

We had decided to meet by the fountain, near the trolley tracks. I perched on the lip of the fountain and pulled out my cell phone. The market opened at 10:00 a.m., and the crowds were less intense first thing in the morning. Corey was always late, so I told him I'd meet him at 9:30, which meant I'd see him at 9:50.

The day was a typical, dreary, Portland fall day. November meant chilly weather, cloud cover and probable rain. I had on my rain boots and rain jacket after listening to the forecast for the day. Vendors on one side of the fountain were finalizing set up of their tents and tables, busily spreading merchandise over tablecloths or hanging art and photos from hooks on display walls.

The air smelled like still-wet pavement and chlorine from the fountain water. Past this small section between where I sat at Skidmoore Fountain and Naito Parkway, the market spanned several blocks. Then it sprawled north in a city of tents to occupy the underside of Burnside Bridge.

The Max train trundled up from the south. People heading toward the market skipped over the tracks to get out of the way. A mom with two small children grabbed their tiny hands and trotted over the rails. The girl—I guessed she was about six—watched the train roll past them, her eyes wide.

I looked for Corey among the oncoming crowd but didn't see him. I did see a bleached-blond man in a highlighter pink fishnet shirt and shorts headed toward the fountain. He carried a boom box. It was vintage, you could say. Something that hailed from 1982, maybe. I wondered if he'd play Thriller from a cassette tape.

The man in pink marched with purpose, once-white Velcro sneakers sported duct tape over the toes of the left shoe. His skin was orange-ish tan, wrinkled and lined. He set his boom box onto the ledge of the fountain and flicked back his hair. He jogged in place, kicking up his worn sneakers so the heels touched his pink shorts. Then he moved into a series of stretches. He caught my eye as I gaped at him, not even aware I'd been staring, and winked. I flushed and looked away.

"God, I love Portland."

I jumped, my heart slamming into overdrive from the proximity of the voice. I twisted around and Corey grinned at me.

"Jumpy much?" he teased.

"You startled me," I confessed. He wore a navy jacket over jeans and sneakers. As always, he carried his tattered backpack.

"That's what happens when you stare too long at the locals. You lose brain cells," he said.

"How was parking?"

He shrugged. "Not so bad. I think the weather might keep a lot of folks away today."

"If you can't do it in the rain, you can't do it in the

Northwest," I quoted the popular saying amongst hardcore locals. Getting a little wet never bothered me. But shopping in the rain wasn't for everybody. "Where do you want to start today?"

"Wherever. I just need to get my people-watching fix in."

"And satiate your inner art geek," I said.

"Yes, but let's face it; geek boy's appetite for art is never sated," he said.

He looked... embarrassed? Angry? Flustered? He was bothered by his artist identity. Uncomfortable with this piece of him he wanted to let out yet stifled from the pressure of his parents. The battle waged on. I looked at him, trying to decide how best to soothe his mood about art.

Deep within me, something vibrated like a struck tuning fork and resonated until I couldn't keep it quiet. If he continued on this path, he would grow dark and bitter. The art mattered that much to him. I wanted to help him. Help him stand up to his parents or help his parents to see.

"What have you been drawing lately?" I asked.

His eyes lit up behind his glasses. He jerked his body to sitting on the fountain, pulling the backpack from his arms and unzipping.

"I've been working on something for Abigail," he said.

He pulled a sketchpad from the largest pouch, the one that sat flush against his back and didn't crumple. He flipped through the pages while I looked on, trying to capture the images he ignored in his quest.

"Here it is." He turned the pad to me.

An angel stared back. My mouth fell open. My hands shook and a quiver started in my gut.

It wasn't your typical angel. I hadn't seen anyone render them the way I saw them. But here one was, staring back at me. As if Corey had transferred my visions to paper. My heart propelled into overtime. Could he see them too? Maybe I wasn't the only one. Excitement thundered through me.

Corey fidgeted. "Well...?" he asked. Uncertainty and a sense of guarded vulnerability thrummed in the one word.

I tore my gaze from the crowned figure, robed in stars, eyes like gaping windows to the universe. Its robes flowed away behind it, stretched out and wing-like, and in them Corey had sketched an abstract pattern of hearts. I met his gaze. His eyes were wide, eyebrows pitched up and causing a vertical crease in the middle of his forehead.

"Are you kidding me? It's so beautiful," I said. I took the pad from his hands, sat beside him and stared at the being. "I've never seen an angel drawn quite like this. What inspired you?"

"An angel. Hm. I didn't realize that's what I was drawing," he said.

I looked up at him, my stomach clenching. Was I giving away my little secret?

"Oh, well, I guess that's the way I interpreted it. What did you intend it to be?"

He shrugged, sticking out his bottom lip as he frowned. "No idea. It came to me, ya know. They all just show up in my head, and then I have to draw them."

"They?" I asked.

"Yeah, this isn't the first being I've drawn," Corey said and gently pulled away the notepad.

He flipped through the pages, gaze roaming over the images. Then he turned the notepad toward me again, and sure enough, there was another angel. This one he'd colored with pencils. She was golden. She reached out, as if her hand would transcend the plane of paper and pencil and enter into our world. There was a great longing love captured in her star-fire eyes. An overwhelming need motivated by utter compassion. Compassion so strong it couldn't be swayed by a little thing like unworthiness. Behind her, Corey had filled the page with a beautiful purplish blue and then had added stars that seemed to twinkle and spark.

"You know what else," he said. "I didn't start seeing these beings until I met you."

I stared at the angel on the page, unable to speak. I saw angels. Corey met me, and then he'd started drawing angels. What did that mean? Could I possibly tell someone about what I saw? I'd never spoken of it. Only Liz knew. And she knew, having witnessed from the corner of my mind. Corey wouldn't believe me, would he?

"R-really?" I asked. "I wonder why." I really did.

"I don't know for sure, but, Bitsy, I think there's more to you than what you let on. I know these angels are showing up because of you."

I half looked up at him. He was pointing at me, eyebrows raised. He lowered his long, skinny hand to his thigh.

"W-what if I told you..."

"What are you doing?" Liz said, finally coming out of the silence in which she'd kept herself the last three days.

Even her worried words soothed my anxiety of missing her. And yet, even as she announced her presence, the flames of my anger toward her fanned higher. I quieted my emotions.

"I'm being vulnerable," I said, *"like Sharon suggested."*

"I don't care what Sharon suggested; don't do it," Liz said.

"Told me what?" Corey asked. He leaned forward, his eyes wide.

"That I see them," I said, leaning toward him, whispering the words and feeling my heart jam into my throat. Liz sprang to the fore front of my mind.

"You idiot! He's going to think you're cuckoo. You just can't tell people this shit. You just gotta keep a lid on it, Bits."

I waited for his response while anxiety drove my heart rate

to jogging standards. Corey nodded, slowly at first then more emphatically.

"That makes sense to me," he finally said. "I've heard about people who channel angels, but I've never known anyone. So what do you think? Is it accurate? Did I get them right?" He fidgeted on his seat and pointed to the golden angel. "This one has a name. And get this! It's Abigail, same as my sister. So I'm giving it to her today when we see her."

I took a slow, calming breath and allowed the anxiety to dissipate.

"You were wrong again," I said to Liz. *"Maybe you ought to listen to me every once in a while. Maybe I don't need protecting like you think I do."*

"He'll burn you in the end for this. You'll see. He'll betray your trust. He'll tell others, and they'll think you're crazy. They'll shun you."

"I'm so done with you," I said, and I forced her out of my mind with a shove.

The lingering frustration with Liz twisted at Corey's excitement. I let the flow of his bubbly energy overwhelm the nasty argument with Liz. "Th-th-that's perfect. She'll love it. I can't wait to see her face."

"So?" he asked, nearly jumping up and down and looking at me.

"What?" I asked.

"Did I get them right? Is this the way they look?"

He grabbed my arm and gently shook it. I sucked in air. He pulled his hands away and put them in his lap.

"Ooo! I'm sorry," he said.

"It's ok-kay. It's just sore from the jerk who attacked me." The bruises in my arm throbbed and burned. "Anyway, yes. These are s-s-so right," I said, still astonished. "It's like you pulled the image right out of my head and put it onto paper."

"Oh my god. Really? That's amazing," he said.

"It really is," I agreed. I flipped back to the first angel he'd shown me and pointed to it. "This one has no gender. They don't always. And this is the one I saw the other day with the tortured woman. It took her spirit when her body died." It felt like a million pounds being lifted out of my heart and throat. The secrets I kept that could lighten others' lives sometimes burned in me like sin.

I looked up at Corey, smiling, stunned to find tears standing in his eyes.

"You saw her spirit be escorted to heaven?" He clutched his heart. "My god. I bet that was beautiful."

"Yes. It is," I agreed. "Most especially after hearing what she'd been through."

He swiped at his face to hide the escaped tear. "Wow. God, you're making me cry, Bitsy."

I decided to change the topic. "Hey, listen, though. I need a favor."

He looked relieved. "Anything for my lovely friend-of-angels. What's the favor?"

I ignored the angel comment. The cat was out of the bag with Corey, but it didn't mean I was comfortable with talking about it.

"I had a dream about this dog creature. I thought maybe you could draw it for me."

"Oh, hell yes," he said.

"C'mon," I said, "let's walk and talk."

We meandered through the booths, window shopping while I described the creature from my latest dream.

Corey listened intently, his eyes scanning the vendors, but showing no intention of stopping at them. "That sounds freaking awesome! I can't wait to sketch it out. I'll work on it, and when you come back to work you can look at it. It'll be a welcome-back present."

He paused in the street, looking over at an artist selling prints. I led him over to the stall, a silent way of giving him permission to look. He flipped through the box of prints. I stood next to him under the vendor's tent. It had started raining.

"So, when will you be back to work?"

"The c—" I stopped myself. I'd almost said counselor. A mistake I rarely made. I was really letting my guard down with Corey. "D-doctor said it's best I don't return next week."

"Wow, that's a long time," Corey noted, half-looking up at me before continuing to pore over the art.

"Yeah, I'm sure Roxanne is pissed," I said, feeling the truth of my statement.

"Oh, she is," Corey said, not even bothering to look up from a print he'd pulled from the box.

My heart jigged in my chest.

"I just love to see her angry. She's like a tiny thunderstorm."

"You l-love to see her scary-mad?" I asked. "You are so bizarre."

"Well, I don't love to see her mad at me, but if she's mad at someone else, it's kinda like a free show."

"Hey," I said, "but I'm the target. It's not funny when it's me, either." I thumped him on his arm.

"Ow. Meany," he protested.

"I think you'll be f-f-fine," I said.

Corey turned to the artist. "Hi, I'd like to buy this one, please."

I turned around, looking to see which vendors we might hit next. There was a jewelry shop across the aisle and at the end of this row of vendors there was a bamboo clothing shop. I needed a few t-shirts. I made a mental note to visit the stall.

Something caught in my peripheral vision. The shadow came and went, but there was a flash of color that arrested my attention. I turned to get a full look at whatever it was.

At the end of the row, where we'd come in, a massive dog sniffed the air. Not just a dog. A dog that looked more like an alien mash-up of dog and bear. I stared, unable to even breathe. If it stood on its hind legs, it could lick the water collecting on the tent near it.

I looked around. No one else seemed to notice it. Yet, it was too massive to just not see. The creature was a tawny blond color with a ruff of black that seemed to shift from brown to gray depending on which way it turned. It was the exact creature from my dream.

The thing glanced over its shoulder with two sets of eyes, narrowed to glowing blue slits. It shifted, and seemed to be looking for something. Its slender tongue lolled from its mouth, blackish-purple and revealing yellow canines so large they overhung the lower jaw. Nostrils that slit the animal's snout up along each side flared and revealed a soft purplish flesh inside. The rain picked up.

The monster of an animal, so alien in the Portland market, sneezed on the wetness, and yet, not a sound issued from it. He shook his head silently. It was as if I was watching a holographic movie. I peered more closely at the apparition and realized the dog beast was a shadow, a greater cloak on a smaller, more normal dog. By contrast, the Shiba Inu was blondish white and oh-so-cute with its curled tail and black button nose.

The beast attached to the Shiba Inu swiveled toward me, its nose pulling in what I could only guess was my scent. It locked eyes with me, its four to my two, and whined. The noise rang in my head but not my ears. I clapped a hand to my temple. Something intangible jostled around in the confines of my body—something foreign and angry. I took several steps toward the beast and fixed it with my gaze. I opened my mouth and heard two words come out.

"Find him."

The creature whined again, as if to say, *I'm trying.*

Dizzying blackness swirled with the images of my surroundings. I fought against the current pulling me under, but the undertow was too swift and insistent. With one final gasp, I fell into the waiting arms of unconsciousness.

Elada was perched in her chair with the Hound lying at her side. The creature was so large, she could reach the top of his head to stroke the soft, black fur. Occasionally, the Hound reached up and licked at Elada's fingers with its purple tongue. I caressed the length of its nose with one of Elada's slender fingers.

The alien man was shown into the Mating room by the maid whose hair was bubblegum pink. She cast a wide-eyed glance at the Hound, then a soft, encouraging look toward me before she pulled the curtains closed. I took it as a signal that she approved of this Mate.

The sky outside the bedroom was tinged in pinks and purples of a late afternoon under the growing season's sun. I needed this to be done and over, yet my body yearned for the coupling of the Mating. The magic within me that made it possible to make children thrummed with a need all its own. My sense of divorced acceptance of my role and my duty fought against the urges, wanting not to share them with this stranger, but with my husband.

But, the law was clear, as my husband had stated.

Resigned, I watched this new Mate slowly approach, raking me over, surmising my beauty with nothing less than reverent awe. That was an improvement from most. At least I would be met with worship rather than sheer lust. Legends still lived that Mating with a Queen Maker was more pleasurable than making love with a woman who couldn't bear children. I hated that sentiment. My sisters were as worthy of worship as I was.

"Queen Maker," he began, "I am Selus and I have come to

offer myself to ensure our existence in future generations." It was the standard line he had to say as part of the ritual.

Selus was handsome. His body was fit under his ceremonial red Mating robes. His features were almost royal with sharp cheekbones and a long, slanting nose. His eyes were a unique orange color and set against pale, almost bluish, skin, they demanded my attention. I couldn't help but surmise the absolute beauty of the child we would make together. She would be lovely.

At this premonition, a tickling sensation ran down my spine and settled in the pit of my stomach like molten rock. A future denied? Something about the thought of a daughter brought a stab of panic. In my peripheral vision, I saw my aura shift from tranquil blue to a subtle bluish green.

"Well met, Selus. I am Elada, Queen Maker of twelve children, the most in five generations, and I am at peace to welcome your contribution. As a Queen Maker you will understand I have the power to unmake as well as make. Should you seek to harm me during the Mating, I will not hesitate to use this power against you." The words flew over my mouth with something between curiosity and annoyance. My body wanted to Mate. My mind wanted to be left alone. My spirit was giving me a warning I couldn't decipher. Beside me, the Hound's ears twitched at the tone of my voice. I wrangled my emotions while Selus swallowed against my warning. It was a standard statement among Queen Makers, but one only Mated with a Queen Maker once. "Join me for wine so that we may get to know one another."

My servants brought in the pitcher and two crystal glasses. Selus situated himself on a large pillow in the center of the room, still twenty feet from me and the Hound. The bravest of my maids brought my wine to me, visibly steeling herself as she gained proximity to my furry protector.

I took a sip of the proffered drink and let the alcohol soothe my edgy mood. I opened my mouth to ask a question and begin the conversation, but stopped as pain and panic stole my breath.

My daughter.

Not a daughter to be. Aerylia. The crystal glass slipped from my hand, shattering into hundreds of fine shards and splashes of red liquid against the floor. I stood from the chair as my child's pain swept over me through our empathetic connection. The Hound stood at my side, black hackles rising as a growl erupted from his clenched jaws.

At once, regret boiled inside of me. She'd asked for the Hound today and now she was in danger. My stomach trembled, my body shook as my daughter's fear resonated through me. Pain sliced at my stomach, my chest, my face as if I were being ripped apart. I screamed and fell, glass puncturing the soft skin of my hands and knees. Rolling waves of nausea overtook me and at last I vomited while my ears rang with the far-off sound of Aerylia's screams. I looked up at my Hound, willing the vision to be only a warning and not reality. He met my gaze with his four vivid blue eyes, hackles on end, muscles bunched and ready to spring into action.

"Find Aerylia!" I shouted.

The Hound bayed, the note filling my ears, my room with such strength I cowered against its power. And then, my faithful protector and guardian of the next Queen Maker of the region flew away from me, padded feet carrying his large body over the threshold of my bedroom in a bolt of speed.

As soon as the creature was out of sight, Maltheron burst through the curtains. He rushed past Selus, who'd scrambled to his feet, crystal glass still gripped in his hand.

"It's Aerylia. I can't find her."

Chapter 10

"Bitsy, what happened?" Corey cradled my shoulders.

He looked down at me, and I looked up into his face. Past his face, the clouded sky brooded. I rubbed my forehead at a pulsing point of pain. I stifled a cry at the insistent throbbing of my bruised ribs.

"What?" I asked, the question grating through my gritted teeth.

I'd been standing in the artist's tent with Corey, and now I was looking up into his face. I felt around. Gritty bits of rain-soaked concrete scraped the tips of my searching fingers. Corey's wiry arm supported my shoulders in a surprisingly strong grip. His gray-green eyes were concerned and kind.

There was too much of him in way too much of my personal space. Ignoring the god-awful pain in my ribs, I wriggled and squirmed until he let me go, and with an awkward jostling of limbs, I finally shoved myself into a standing position while Corey helped pull me into place. He held my hand and shoulder to steady me. Everything in me wanted to melt into the earth and out of sight of the crowd that had gathered around us.

"Are you okay?" Corey asked.

"Uh-uh-uh... Yeah. Sorry," I said. "I'm f-f-fine, everyone. Just fine, thank you."

Corey looked at me with more concern but waved away the crowd.

"Nothin' to see here, folks," he said, "She just needs a little grub, and she'll be fine."

A middle-aged woman with graying hair and a vivid purple raincoat approached me.

"Are you sure you're okay, hon'?" She reached out to me.

I pulled away my arm before she could latch a concerned hand over my raincoat.

"I didn't eat breakfast. I'll just go grab something to eat, and I'll be good to go."

"Okay," she said, shuffling away. "Well. I'm sure that'll do it." She half smiled and then turned and meandered down the aisle, past the bamboo clothing stall and around the corner.

"All right, let's go get you something to eat," Corey said. "What are you feeling today? Empanadas? Gyro? Pizza? Thai?"

"Food sounds disgusting, actually," I said. I brushed myself off from where I'd been lying in rain and muck. "Let's just keep shopping. I feel fine right now."

"But you just said—"

"I just wanted her to leave me alone. C'mon. I need to shake it off," I said.

Eventually, we did give in to the lunch hour. I ordered an empanada and pecked it enough to make it seem as if I'd eaten. Corey scarfed down two of them and then looked at the partially eaten meat pie in my lap. I handed it over to him and watched his enthusiasm with his meal—and mine. The rain had stopped, but the clouds clung to the Portland sky. My head throbbed behind the center point on my forehead. I rubbed the spot between my eyes for a moment to relieve the ache.

I tried to recall what had happened before I blacked out but came up with nothing. I thought about asking Liz. Maybe something had triggered her to come out. But I wasn't in the mood to talk to her. From our perch on the picnic table bench, while Corey finished the empanada, we watched the thin crowd of people pass by.

Corey wadded up the empty food wrappings and tossed it into a trashcan near our table, lobbing it in like a basketball through a hoop. After that, he knuckled his glasses up his nose and looked at his wristwatch. "Well, I think we saw the best parts of the market. You ready to head out to Gresham with me?"

"The best part was the man in pink by the fountain," I said and then I held up my bag of new t-shirts. "And these."

He held up his canvas bag of new art prints. "Definitely loving my new art. But the best part is hanging with my best-y." He shouldered my shoulder and grinned at me.

"S-so true," I said and nudged him back. Maybe if I just kept touching him, I'd eventually get used to the contact. Part of it felt good sometimes. On the other side of panic. Maybe my body just needed to see touch wasn't the enemy.

Gresham is a nearby town to Portland. The suburb sprawled and spread. Some pockets of the city were nice, new, or old and well-maintained. Other parts of the city were the kind you wouldn't want to be walking alone. The kind of neighborhoods I grew up in.

Corey pulled into a nice neighborhood. A neighborhood I might have daydreamed about when I was a kid. Such places weren't a part of my reality—too good to be true and too good for me. The house Corey grew up in was nice. His parents were nice. His childhood had been nice. It was all lovely and good and happy.

Except for the tragedy of his sister's accident.

We parked in the drive next to the van and made our way up the ramp. I looked down at my clothes, aware I probably looked shabby and not dressed enough for his parents. But I found my clothes were fine. My knee-jerk reaction was to assume I wouldn't fit in.

"Bitsy, we can never fit in with people like this. They just haven't seen the dirty side of life like we have," Liz said.

"Everybody has tragedies, Liz," I said, rolling my eyes at her negativity.

"Not like us," she said.

I inhaled deeply and let it out with an effort to calm myself.

Corey lightly knocked and then without waiting, went into the house. The living room was sunken down from the entry-way and opened up to the dining room, farthest from the front door. Soft, beige couches complemented the light-green carpet and decorative rug. The TV was mounted on the wall opposite the couches, and flanking it were wooden shelves housing a collection of movies and video games.

Corey's dad, Jon, had a college football game going on the TV. When he saw us come in, he jumped up from the couch. "Hey, son, good to see you," he said.

He was a tall, lanky man with a small belly. It was easy to see where Corey had gotten his looks from. He was basically a younger, slightly skinnier, less-bald version of his dad. Jon wrapped Corey in a giant hug, clapping his back with affection. I watched their interchange with only a little envy. I wondered if my father would have been as affectionate had he not died when I was a child.

"Hey, Dad. How are you?" Corey asked as he pulled away and adjusted his glasses.

"Can't complain," Jon said. Even though it was Saturday, he was dressed well. He wore jeans and a button-up shirt tucked in. His skin shone with that just-out-of-the-shower glow.

He turned to me when he was done with his son. I braced myself for the typical Jon greeting and was not surprised when his heavy hand landed on my shoulder and gently squeezed. I fought against the terror that rose automatically.

"Bitsy. Glad you could come over with Corey. How's work?"

"U-u—" I wriggled to free myself of his grip, trying not to wince at the pain.

He caught the hint and pulled away his hand. As for the question, work was pretty crazy—and I had the bruises to show for it. Did he really want to hear that? Probably not, I decided.

"J-just fine, thank you. You?" Best to let others talk.

"Real good. Real good," he said, looking at me like I was a puzzle rather than a person.

Corey scowled up at his dad. Jon looked down at his son, smiling before he realized his son was mean-mugging him. His smile slipped from his face, and his mouth stretched into an O.

"Oh, gosh, Bitsy. Sorry. I forgot." He held his hands up in surrender.

"F-forgot?" I asked.

I looked at Corey, who pressed fingers into his forehead and shook his head.

"Dad," he said, "you have no subtlety."

"What?" his dad said, obviously really confused now. "Bitsy, you have to forgive me. I'm a touchy-feely guy. Corey told me you were banged up from some guy jumping you at work?"

I looked at Corey. So he'd tried warning his father. That was really sweet.

"Y-yeah," I said. I clasped my hand over my middle and held onto my other arm. I turned to Corey and smiled. "Thanks for trying."

His cheeks flushed. "I'm so sorry for my family," he said.

"Hey," Jon said, "I'm standing right here, son."

Corey rolled his eyes and stepped down into the living area with the comfort of someone who'd lived in a place their whole life.

Jon laughed. "I'm just glad you're here," he said to me.

He perched his hands on his hips, which looked like a means of restraining himself from hugging me. I smiled back at him before scuttling around him toward Corey. Jon went back to the couch and his football game.

Abigail was in her wheelchair. Papers covered the dining table in front of her, along with pencils and crayons.

"Hey, Abi-girl," Corey said and gave her a hug.

She wrapped her arms around his shoulders. Corey plopped himself into the high-backed chair next to his sister, dumping his backpack to the floor between his feet. Abigail picked up a crayon and went back to working.

"What are you doing? Is this homework?"

She looked up at her brother. Her hair was vibrant golden blonde and wavy. "Yeah," she said, sighing. "It's kind of silly, though. We have to color pumpkins for math since Halloween is coming."

"And this displeases you?" Corey asked, perching his chin on his hand and propping his elbow onto the table.

"It's just too easy," she said.

"Most children enjoy coloring," Corey pointed out.

"Coloring is okay. But I like math," Abigail said.

Corey blinked at her, slow and long. "Mom," he said, stretching the name out, "are you sure Abigail and I are really related?"

To my surprise, his mom actually answered.

Her voice floated through the kitchen and into the dining room, accompanied by soft footsteps. "I was hoping to drop the news in a more private setting, but since you asked the question... no, Corey. You're adopted." She walked up behind her son and wrapped an arm around his shoulders.

Corey's mom was round, bright and cheerful. Her hair wisped here and there, partly blonde, partly whitish grey. She caressed her bangs away from her forehead and grinned wickedly down at Corey with sage-green eyes.

Corey stared up at her, mouth gaping, then snapped his jaws shut, lowered his head and shook it mournfully. "I always knew I was different."

Gina giggled and squeezed him, bending over and kissing his forehead.

"There's way too much sarcasm between you two to deny familial bonds," I noted.

Gina laughed. "Too true. How are ya, Bitsy?"

"G-good," I said.

"Don't let her lie to you, Mom. Bitsy was attacked by some psycho at work and has to take two weeks off," Corey said.

Heat rose in my cheeks. The full disclosure this family had was almost unbearable. I wasn't used to so much honesty.

"P.S. She has bruised ribs, among other things, so don't hug her," Corey told her.

He cast an accusing look over his shoulder toward his dad, who continued staring at the screen.

"Oh my god," Gina shouted.

I jumped, startled at the volume of her shock. My body shook with the rush of adrenaline.

"Are you okay? Did he hurt you?"

"N-n-no," I managed. "I mean—yes. Some." I stood and slipped my arm out of the sweater to show her the purple bruises of a hand grip around my upper arm. "And of course, my eye." I leaned my face closer to her.

"Your dark skin helps cover the bruising," Gina said.

I nodded. She inhaled as her gaze roamed the rest of me and landed on my neck and shoulder. "Oh, he got you there too." She pointed. "And your ribs?"

"Y-yes. They hurt the worst," I explained but didn't offer to raise my shirt to show her the bruising.

"Wow," she said.

"What happened, Bitsy?" Abigail asked, looking up from her work.

"Oh, it's okay now. Just some guy at work."

"Did he hit you or something?"

"Yes, he did," I said. "But the police got him."

"So, what are you guys going to see today?" Gina asked.

"You know that animal movie that's out?" Corey asked.

"Sure," she said.

"That one," Corey said.

"Can Michelle come with us?" Abigail asked.

"Who's Michelle?" Corey asked.

"My friend from school. She's really nice and pretty and she's black."

"African American, sweetheart," her mom said.

"Huh? Michelle is too black. Black and beautiful. Can she come?"

My sight hazed out as a vision slammed into my mind's eye. *A little girl with ebony skin whispered to another girl. The bus jostled. The smell of old upholstery and exhaust filled my senses.* I shook myself from the intrusive image.

Corey glanced at his mom. A look passed between them, their faces sharing some secret they didn't want to bring up with Abigail. I caught Corey's gaze. He held up a finger then pulled his phone out of his sweatshirt pocket.

Gina answered her daughter. "Honey, remember, we asked already, and they're busy this weekend."

My phone vibrated in my jeans pocket. I pulled it out

while Corey gave me a pointed look. I glanced down at the new text on my phone.

COREY:

> A girl went missing in the area earlier this week. Aidan, someone from the school Abigail goes to. Everybody's a little nervous lately. They haven't found her yet.

> Omg. That's awful. Do they have a suspect or anything?

> Nope. Nobody. All they know is that she was at the playground during recess. Nobody remembers seeing her after that.

My stomach sank at the thought. What that poor mother had to be going through. I didn't even want to think about the girl and what she might be enduring. If she was still alive. The school bus vision played again in my head. I shook myself, trying to rid my mind of the eerie feeling. I could still smell the bus. My head throbbed against the scent.

"Oh, yeah, I forgot," Abigail said. "Bummer."

"Bummer," Corey and I agreed in stereo.

I wondered if Michelle was the girl in the vision. There was no way to know if what I saw was prophetic or just my imagination, and the latter made way more sense.

"Oh, but hey," Corey said. He yanked his backpack toward him. Unzipping the large pouch, he pulled out his sketch pad, flipped through the pages and carefully ripped the angel from its hiding place among other art.

Gina's features stilled as she looked at the being on the paper. Abigail took the drawing.

"Is this for me?" she asked.

Corey nodded. "This is an angel. And guess what?"

"What?" Abigail asked.

Gina was looking at her son with what I thought was an expression of disappointment.

As if Corey could feel his mother's gaze boring into him, he looked up at her and his excitement faltered.

Unwilling to let the beauty of his art be swallowed by his mother's expectations, I spoke up. "Her name is the same as yours," I told Abigail. "She's an angel of healing. She was kind enough to show herself to your brother and allowed him to capture her essence in the drawing."

"Bitsy, you never stutter when you talk about angels," Liz said.

"So," Gina started, "how's the schoolwork going, Corey?"

Abigail's eyes were wide as she stared at the angel. "She's beautiful. Mom, can we hang her on my wall? I want her to look over me when I sleep."

Corey ignored his mom's question and beamed at his little sister. He stood from the chair, squeezed past his mother, who stepped away from the table, jaws gritted closed. Corey went behind Abigail's wheelchair and began pulling her from the table. "Heck, yeah, we can. Come on, I'll help you put it up."

Chapter 11

Almost two weeks passed before I was healed enough to return to work.

During my time away, I practiced my violin as if there was no other reason for being. The intense hours at the bow and strings forced me back into the steady rhythm of playing I'd built since I was a child. My constant grooming with lessons, practice and then performing with the elementary, high school, and youth orchestras and then the college orchestra made the few months I'd neglected my craft melt into non-existence. The music soothed away the hurts and offered a temporary respite from the inner battle waging between me and Liz.

While I dealt with all the lingering effects of the violent event and Liz's actions afterward, the odd dreams, disjointed nightmares and sudden visions continued without interruption. Perhaps it was another symptom of dealing with the trauma.

And I couldn't talk to Liz about the foreign landscapes, the ever-present aliens, Maltheron and Elada—and their daughter. The dreams nagged at me. I'd had so many of them now, I could write a small book on the story that was being pieced together. It was as if every vision, every nightmare, was a scene in a movie. Or an episode in a show. Or more disconcerting was the feeling I was experiencing the memories of these fictional people. The more dreams I had the more the me I knew melted away and into the existence of these strangers.

Snippets of last night's dreams played in my mind's eye as I sat at my workstation, willing the computer to boot up faster.

This time, I was the Hound.

The girl was special to me. I lay on the fragrant ground and soaked in the scent of the growing season. My nose tickled with the scent of flowers. The girl hummed while she weaved another bloom into what was rapidly becoming a ring of flowers. I nudged her hand, eager for a pat. She obliged, speaking softly to me. The words washed around me without meaning. Between the lull of her words and the gentle stroke of her small hand over my fur, I drifted back into a comfortable slumber.

Her hand left my head and where her caress had warmed, the chill of a breeze accentuated the lack of her touch. I opened two of my eyes to look at her. She weaved another flower into the crown. I sniffed at it, then sneezed. She giggled and that made me smile, my tongue lolling out and soaking in her happy scent.

Another smell wafted toward me. I swung my head in its direction. While he was well out of sight, the touch of his intention reached out like inky tendrils, ready to ensnare the girl. My hackles rose. My belly tightened as a growl erupted from me. He was out there, hiding in the tall grasses and watching my Aerylia. It was the man who'd come to help Maltheron during the growing season. I knew his scent and I did not like him.

When my growl didn't cut off the hungry stare, I stood, situated myself between Aerylia and the man and barked. I could

feel Aerylia against my back, making herself small enough that
my large body would hide her.

After another nightly episode with the same cast of characters, I woke up thinking about Liz. I missed her. I missed speaking with her. I also needed her, I realized. The dreams were getting weirder and weirder, and yet, there was something naggingly realistic about them.

Sharon's message was also sinking in. I needed to be compassionate with Liz, even if she didn't want my sympathy, at first. I needed to listen to her and understand why she made the choice to have casual sex with a guy I was interested in. Thinking about what she'd done still grated on me. But that was an improvement over wanting to hurt her for her choices.

I sighed and opened myself up to the idea of dropping the wall. That was enough for today. I still needed to get through the piles of work and emails waiting for me. It would have been overwhelming if I'd had the energy to be overwhelmed. Instead, I forged ahead with steady efficiency.

A commotion outside the door drew me out of the trance of staring at the email program, wishing there were one hundred fewer messages. Peering over the black monitor, I saw Cathy's back first, her white lab coat wrinkled and smudged.

"All right, right this way," she said and motioned someone in the door.

I tensed. Liz might not be speaking yet, but inside, she roused to witness another forensic exam, in some way eager to experience their pain with them. Cathy brought a woman, who half carried a young woman—a girl, really. The girl was maybe thirteen or fourteen. She paused next to my desk, waiting until the duo cleared the chairs. The older woman had a horrible haircut of flat, dark hair that parted directly down the middle and feathered to both sides of her head. The rest of the hair was short, almost like a style you'd see on a boy. She wore a tacky, navy-blue sweatshirt with an unfamiliar logo on the chest, jeans and cheap tennis shoes.

Her face was manly, but even though her nose was too big and kinda crooked and she hardly had any lips, there was something really beautiful about her. Something that shone from underneath the stocky body and lack of fashion. This was a woman who loved fiercely and who would move heaven and Earth and even hell for the girl at her side.

Maybe that was why the shame and failure were so readable on her face. That heart-breaking love, so bent on protecting, had failed.

The set of her jaw was stern, and her smallish eyes shined. She gripped the girl at her side with strong yet gentle hands, and I thought how similarly Grandma handled me. The girl was nearly as tall as the woman and, in appearance, her polar opposite. She had auburn hair and peach cheeks that were flushed and tear-stained. She had a purpling eye. I touched my eye, which was nearly all healed now. Her full and deep-red lips couldn't hide her overbite. She had blood around her mouth. And bruises.

The girl clawed at the woman, clutching her navy sweatshirt, sobbing into her collarbone. She was wearing those blah-blue hospital socks, and she walked on her tiptoes as she cried and jerked forward in halting steps. Liz supplied me with the sensation from our past that compared accurately with what the girl was feeling. Along with the sensation, the uncomfortable horror for the girl ballooned in me. I looked at my computer screen as the girl cried with every step. She stopped when she reached the counter, and I wished I could disappear, could stop being, that I could become invisible to the girl in her moment of anguish.

"It hurts," she sobbed, her words muffled against the woman's neck.

The woman wrapped the girl into an embrace, tears slipping down her craggy face. She swallowed hard. Anger tickled at my stomach. My heart thumped in my ears.

"I know, babes. Hey, Auntie Mel is here. We're gonna get tru dis. We're gonna get tru it togetha." Her Brooklyn accent was heavy but no heavier than the emotions that filled the room.

They walked past me, never looking at me.

Cathy snatched the bag of personal belongings from Auntie Mel and plopped it on my desk. I stared at it. Past the bag, a small trail of blood on the lanoleum marked their path into the exam room. The door shut behind me. I stared at the smeared crimson. The room swam, my breath wheezed, my heart plunging double-time until I got my wish and everything went away in a whirling blur of darkness.

Maltheron approached Elada. Her back was to him. One sun was setting on the horizon, and the other hung, small and ineffectual, just above it. The large sun shone with a white-blue light while the second smaller sun burned like an old ember.

The field Maltheron and the woman stood in was wide open and bare. Nothing grew there. This seemed odd to me. Maltheron was a grower of things. Why an empty field? And then I remembered hearing somewhere that often farmers leave a field to rest for a season. Fallow. That was the word. The field was left fallow in order to let it get fertile again.

The woman stood in front of a pile of wood that reached the height of her chest. Stones circled the wood pile in a precise oval.

As I watched through Maltheron's eyes, and he approached his wife, the white object atop the wood came into focus. It was person shaped. And then I realized, as Maltheron's stomach caved and sorrow overwhelmed me, the white shape was his daughter, dressed in death linens. Elada's empathic experience had been the last moments of her daughter's life.

Elada had an odd, bluish glow radiating from her center. The color throbbed and wavered. There were other attendees surrounding the pyre, too. Other alien-looking people of varying ages, of both genders, but all wearing a striking shade of true blue. A woman detached herself from the crowd of onlookers and began to sing. The words were foreign, but their meaning was so heart-wrenching and obvious I had no need for the translation. The lilt of the song, the key of the notes, dripped in sorrow. And yet, the music was so hauntingly beautiful, I hung onto each note, storing them all away for when next I played.

When the woman's voice fell away, a man walked forward, a small bowl holding a tiny flame cupped in his hands. He knelt near the head of the girl wrapped in white and gently placed the bowl next to the base of the wood pile. They must have put some sort of ignition fuel on the wood, or maybe the wood was extremely dry—I couldn't be sure—but the wood caught fast and bloomed quickly. When the first flames caught on the girl's funeral wrappings, Elada erupted into screaming sobs. My heart ached for her. She'd experienced her child's death. She'd even had the nagging premonition that could have prevented her daughter's death. What an awful way to lose a child.

Maltheron put a hand on her shoulder as Elada fell to her knees. The setting sun glowed, casting purples and blues on the sky. The girl's body burned. As the flames licked away at her, Elada's throbbing inner light shifted from light blue to violet, and then to an angry crimson.

"We must find who has done this," she said to me—Maltheron. "We must find the person, and they must pay for their crime."

"It is your right as a Queen Maker to ensure the perpetrator can no longer harm another living."

Elada looked up into the night sky as three moons crested the horizon. "Tonight, we will hunt," she said. "Bring the Hound."

Maltheron nodded. "It shall be as you wish, my queen."

Chapter 12

LIZ

"*I can help her,*" said the foreign voice.

I woke with the new voice's intentions ringing in my head. My breath came in shallow huffs. As my vision cleared, I soaked in my surroundings. Work. We were at work. Bitsy was gone. I'd been watching as Cathy had escorted the latest patient. I heard the soft sobbing on the other side of the exam door.

Plastic crinkled, and Cathy's voice punctuated the noises. Bitsy always left me for these parts of our job.

"Hold still for just a minute," Cathy said.

Feet shuffled, followed by the clink of glass tubes on the counter.

"Now, I'm going to take pictures of the damage. This is so we have evidence of what's been done when we go to court." There was that edge in her voice, anger meant for the perpetrator.

The girl sobbed again as the camera *snick-snick-snicked.*

I had to agree with Sharon. Working in this environment was no good for either of us. Of course, asking for a move meant Bitsy would have to stand up to Mack-Truck-Roxanne, and Bitsy wouldn't do that. I'd told her to let me at 'er. She wouldn't do that, either. So, here we were, listening to some poor girl whimper as Cathy gathered the evidence of a rape and assault.

The computer screen went black. I shook the mouse to wake it. And I was supposed to sit here calmly and work, while listening to some of the most horrific moments of a person's life. *Yeah, okay.* Anger boiled in me. Not for the situation I was in but for the girl. They were lucky to at least get medical attention. My throat squeezed in on itself. I swallowed back my own horror story. These people would never be the same again. They would be scarred. Like Bitsy and me.

What I wouldn't do if I could catch these guys. I fantasized about justice for a moment, since we lacked it in our current system. People could rape children and get away with it. Or, if they did serve time, they only got a few years. A slap on the hand. While I received a lifetime spent in therapy and battling my demons. Bitsy and I got a big, gaping scar down the middle of us that left us broken in pieces.

"Listen to me," said the new voice, her intentions filtering through as words.

I sighed. I guessed I couldn't keep ignoring her. She'd been talking to me off and on the whole two weeks since the attack. I had a pang of guilt that I hadn't told Sharon. Or Bitsy.

"You're not just going to go away, are you?" I asked.

A long pause followed my question.

"I wish I could. I wish I could return home. I think I am stuck here," she finally answered.

"Who are you? What are you doing in my head?" I asked.

"For the first question, I am Elada. I am a Queen Maker. As for what I am doing here in your head, I do not know. My husband, Maltheron, and I were hunting our child's murderer. My Hound had scouted his scent. I was on his heels, certain my next step would bring me close enough to bring vengeance and peace to my daughter's restless

soul. *The murderer dove into a pool of water. My Hound dove, and then I did, too. When I woke up I was here. If you call this being awake. I do not understand my surroundings. I do not have my own body. This is not even my own planet. I am lost."*

Ain't that some shit. I shook my head. Oh, dear god. I was truly going crazy now. Fingers poised over the keyboard, I flicked my nails against my thumb as I thought. I reached for the phone. I needed to call Sharon. This was insane, and I was insane.

"Wait, before you do that, I can prove this," Elada said.

Elada. What kind of name was that?

"Oh, yeah?" I asked her.

"Go to your backpack," she said.

I pulled the lavender thing from its cozy spot in the empty file cabinet to my left. It was heavy. I heaved it into my lap and waited.

"In the middle section, at the very bottom."

That was all she said, so I unzipped the bag, feeling my eyebrows in my hairline and wondering how fucking insane I was to be following orders from a voice in my head. This had to be a third alt we'd uncovered from the trigger of the latest trauma. I slipped my hand between the cool, slick material of the inner pocket. My fingertips brushed something cool and hard; tiny ridges scraped my skin. My heart pounded. That was nothing that felt familiar. I reached in deeper and curled my fingers over something that slid so perfectly into my hand it was as if it had been made just for me.

"What the fuck is this?" I began to pull it out.

"Not all the way!" Elada warned.

I halted as the object caught the light of the overhead fluorescents and before it was all the way out of the bag. A nurse walked past my office, shoes squeaking against the highly polished linoleum floors. I smiled as he looked in. The man saluted with two fingers to his surgical cap as he lumbered past.

I pulled the thing out enough to see it without it being visible to any passersby.

The thing whispered to me. A distinct male voice leaked from the device, which looked like a weapon, although unlike any weapon I'd ever seen. It had a handle that was formed from some deeply coppery-black metal, and what looked like a scabbard, of sorts. I knew scabbards were for blades, but the shape was so odd I didn't identify it as a dagger at first.

Peeking over my shoulder, I pulled the knife from the bag, aware that someone could walk into the office and find me sitting at my desk with a weapon. Definitely a no-no in a hospital. I gripped the case, which slid under my fingers like leather. With my hands in my lap, hiding the dagger under the desk, I pulled the blade from its casing. My breath hitched.

Colors in the blade sparkled, swayed under a nearly opaque blackness. Like the color of Apache tear stones held to the light, the dark, black-green shifted with the blues of star fire and bloomed with sunlight, swayed like the sea, swirled like purple thunderclouds.

"It's beautiful," I said.

I swear to god, I thought the thing politely said thank you. Although I could not understand the words, the meaning came through to me.

"Liz, please handle my husband carefully."

"Your...?"

"Yes, this is my husband. We performed a powerful spell to exact our revenge on our child's murderer. Everything that is him is molded into this blade."

"No wonder it's heavy," I said, grinning to myself.

Elada didn't seem to have much of a sense of humor.

She shifted, a sensation like a shadow in the corner of my

brain, shrinking away from the light. I covered the blade with its case and slipped the dagger back into my backpack. Thank god our hospital had no metal detectors.

"That girl in there. She's been... raped."

"Ding, ding, ding! For an alien ghost in my head, you sure catch on quickly, don't ya?" I said.

"I can help her. I have the power to heal her wounds. To ease her memories." Her voice was deep and warm, the kind of voice that could seduce a man in one moment and soothe a child to sleep in the next. I pushed the backpack into the empty filing cabinet and put my hands in my lap.

"All right, El," I said, *"I'll bite. What do you mean?"*

"My name is Elada," she said.

"Yeah, well, that's kind of a mouthful, so I'm gonna call you El."

She paused. Maybe they didn't have nicknames on her home planet.

"Very well," she finally said.

"So, then... tell me about this power you have," I prompted.

"In my world, a woman is a sacred gift. Only a few are born with the ability to conceive and bring life. We are elevated to high positions. To wrong a woman is to pose a threat to our very existence, and this cannot be tolerated. Such a person is executed. A Queen Maker, like me, performs such executions. The ritual ends the cycle the attacker started by ridding the world of their presence and by severing the energy cord that binds the victim to the horror of the crime."

"Well, as you've noticed," I said dryly, *"things work a little differently here on Earth."*

"We can change that," said El. A bright need dawned in me. A need to make right all the wrongs I saw people suffer at the hands of others. *"Take something of the girl's. We will hunt down the one who has done this to her."*

Hunt him down. I let the idea swirl in my mind. I imagined coming upon a child rapist in the dead of night and making him quiver with fear, as I had done. What if we could turn the tables...?

"We have laws to take care of this sort of thing." I said the words, but it was a half-hearted statement.

In the other room, the girl was talking. I eased my way out of the chair and tiptoed to the door.

"He's my older cousin."

"He's in town visiting." This from the woman, her East-coast accent strong. "He's always liked kids. On the quiet side, but otherwise, I never would have guessed..." The woman's words trailed off.

"How old is he?" Cathy asked.

"Twenty-three," the woman said.

"Okay, now, Kaitlyn, I'm going to need you to tell me everything that happened. From the very beginning. I'm going to record your statement, okay?" Cathy said. "Don't leave out any details. I know this is hard, but I need you to tell me every-thing now, while the memories are still fresh."

I quietly kneeled on the floor, settled in and listened as the girl described how the cousin had always been kind to her. He'd brought her a gift this time. He'd done things to her before. Small things. He'd told her it was normal to do these things. When he came back, even though he'd told her it was normal, she didn't want to do those things again. No one had been in the house except for the two of them. When she told him no he'd grown violent, and in the end, he'd backhanded her, forced her over the foot of the bed. He couldn't get it in, at first. And that had made him angry. She'd fought back, but he overpowered her and without much of a fight, he'd won. It had hurt so badly, all the way into her insides. After he was done, he'd pushed her to the floor, yelled at her for getting blood all over his clothes, threatened to kill her if she told anyone, and then he'd peeled out in his pick-up truck.

El and I were taking notes and letting the disgust and horror fill us up.

"You called the police before you came here?" asked Cathy.

"No. I found her curled in a ball and bleeding. I didn't even know what had happened until we were on the way here. Nobody knows yet," said the woman.

The girl began to sob. "Please don't tell anyone. Please, please," she cried.

My head sank to my knees. I knew exactly what she was thinking. She was probably thirteen, maybe fourteen. If people found out, they'd think she'd wanted him, and then they'd call her a slut. She was probably feeling dirty and wrong right now. As if what had happened was her fault.

"But, honey, he's done a bad, bad thing. He can't get away with that," the woman said.

Cathy remained silent.

"No one will believe me. They'll think I made it up."

"That's why I'm here," Cathy said. "I've gathered the evidence. In a court of law, we can prove what happened."

"My aunt is going to side with him. I live with her. We can't tell anyone," the girl said.

"We can't hide this from Juney," said the woman. "You and me, we'll move out together. I'll take care of you. It's unthinkable, what he's done. He has to be punished, sweetheart."

"*Yes, he does,*" I said. I slowly eased myself up from the door and went to my desk. "*Okay, what do we do?*"

El seemed to nod in satisfaction, and a hunger that was not all her own swelled within us. Fear throbbed around the edges of the hunger.

"*You will see. This is best. Take something that belongs to the girl.*"

Chapter 13

LIZ

I woke in the dead of night, my internal alarm ringing loudly. I slipped from the warmth of the bed and let the cool, dark air cloak me in its chill. Gooseflesh rose on my arms and legs. I dressed quickly, strapped the backpack over my shoulders and slipped down the stairs.

Once we were out the door, El spoke up. *"Take the thing that is the girl's."*

I shrugged out of the backpack, lowered it to the front porch and pulled the bracelet from the small front pouch. I held the little piece of jewelry in my hand. It was one of those rubber-band bracelets kids make. It looked as if she was a Seahawks fan; the colors were navy and lime green. I reached back into the backpack and pulled out the dagger, gripping it in my right hand. Then, I carefully pulled the backpack back onto my shoulders.

"You remember what the girl looks like?" El asked.

I pulled at Bitsy's memories, carefully, so as not to wake her, and produced the image of the girl she'd seen this morning.

"Focus on her as much as you can," El instructed.

"Man, we couldn't do this inside? It's cold out here."

"*Quit complaining,*" El chided. "*Let your mind slide into the nether and focus only on the girl.*"

"*Should I be doing this while standing?*" I could see myself falling to the porch, alerting Grams I was out here in the dead of night.

I actually think El huffed.

"*Do whatever makes you most comfortable, but it's important not to get too comfortable. I cannot have you falling asleep on me.*"

"*All right then, I'll stand,*" I said. I widened my stance to keep myself from swaying and let the cool air wash around and over me, focusing on not feeling it.

So... falling into the nether. What did that mean? I quieted myself, searching for the place where the nether might be. In my mind, I walked down an empty corridor. It was dark, and the concrete underneath me echoed with the thump of my boot heels. Every ten paces or so, the glint of metal shone against the darkness. I reached for the first light and paused, realizing these were doorknobs. All of them. The hallway was lined with doors. This door, this wasn't the right door. I didn't know why, but it wasn't. I moved on. I held my hands halfway out, waiting for the right one to make itself known. Was I feeling for something? I wasn't sure, but listening with my fingers stretched toward the doors just made sense.

The hallway sloped away, and I walked downhill. Soon, the dark ceiling of the hall disappeared, and the doors stood without framing to support them. The floor turned from cement to grass, and my feet were suddenly bare. My steps whispered down the corridor of doors. The grass pricked softly on the soles of my feet, its touch cool and comforting. Its fresh, green perfume wafted to my nose, filling me with peaceful energy.

My pace slowed. My breath grew more even. I was no

longer searching for the right door; I was simply walking. All around me, the world in my mind shifted from pure darkness with doorknobs for lights to the subtle twinkling of far-away pinpricks of light. The grass faded away, and I no longer walked but drifted over nothing. A never-ending sea of stars spilled out above and below and in all directions.

The doors shrank, spread out farther away from each other, and yet I still followed a path, of sorts.

"Where are we?" I asked El.

She drifted next to me. She looked like a human in most ways but not all. Her honey-colored hair hung down her back, pulled away from her slightly elongated face. Her blue and hazel eyes were larger than most humans' eyes. There was also a strange set of dots lining either side of her nose and then extending up and over the arch of her eyebrows. She wore a robe that looked as if it was ripped from the night sky. The galaxy blue twinkled and shimmered, a reflection of the place around us. Underneath the robe, a light permeated from the middle of her being. It glowed crimson, like the coals of a long-burning campfire.

"Why are you glowing? Am I glowing?" I asked.

"No, but you do have colors and light. They are not quite like mine, but your spirit is beautiful."

In this place, I let the compliment slide over me, neither rejecting nor embracing it.

"Is this the nether?" I asked her. *"I thought the nether would be behind one of these doors."*

"We are looking for a door. It is a door that will lead us to the girl's attacker. Are you holding the bracelet?"

"I am," I told her.

"Do you have the dagger in your other hand?"

I nodded.

"Are you thinking of the girl? You must focus on her in order to find the door. You must see the way she was when we saw her today at the medical house. See the girl and her pain."

My breathing was a function left somewhere in a plane I no longer had access to, and yet something in my chest where the breath and the blood intertwined gave a sharp stab. Only a panic attack, I told myself... nothing I wasn't used to. I opened my soul to the prospect that the panic held no sway over me. A miraculous thing happened then. The panic actually held no sway over me.

I imagined the girl's face, her pain as she'd cried and walked to the exam room past Bitsy. I pulled out the details of her walking on tiptoe. The way she leaned into her aunt, her shoulders and body rounded forward. Her pain was palpable to me until I wasn't sure if it was her pain or mine that I felt. Crimson blood dotted the floor behind her hospital-sock-covered feet. Her slender, teenage body shuddered with horror. Her nose was slightly snotty, and her blondish-red eyelashes were dotted in tears. Her cheeks were ruddy from crying and made the light freckles blaze into existence.

I gripped the blade of the dagger as the swelling anger for her assailant infused me with purpose. The stars around me shuddered, danced, swayed in the endless night sky. The doors bulged. Next to me, El's scarlet light blazed.

A single door shimmered to life in front of us. It was black and cracked and seeped shadows. The knob was old and rusty copper. It was a cheap door. El reached for it, turned the knob and pushed the door inward.

There he was.

He slept on a crusty bed, the sheets and thin blanket wrapped around his waist, his arms splayed to his sides. A leg protruded from the tangle of bedding. He wore a white t-shirt and a pair of striped boxers. There was no light in the room, but from somewhere, a bluish glow spilled into the wide window; it captured the man like a comic frame.

"Are you ready?" El asked me.

Did I have what it took to do this? Could I? I let the question tumble around in the big space my mind occupied. How long could we allow ourselves to be victims? We women were abusers' prey. And it was time the hunter became the hunted.

The feel of the blade in my hands was a comforting power. Maybe the young girl from the ED today couldn't stand up for herself. And probably the justice system would fail her. Her family might abandon her, or at least part of her family might. Her friends would misunderstand her from now on. She would be scarred and broken and alone. I would not let that happen, given the ability to help.

I stepped over the threshold and into the motel room.

And I was there. I breathed in the stale air, my feet firmly planted on aging carpet, its color lost to the blue glow. The backpack was slung over my arms and rested against my back, the bracelet clutched in one hand and the dagger in the other. I looked behind me, but there was nothing but a paneled wall. My heart *tick-tick-ticked* away, a pulse in my brain indicating my fear.

"Whoa," I breathed. *"We're here. I mean, we just like teleported or omething. Did you mean for us to do that?"*

"Yes," El said quizzically, as if this were a mundane task performed daily. Maybe it was, where she came from.

"Well, it's a lot quicker than taking the bus, that's for sure. What do we do now?" I was afraid to move but suddenly aware the muscles in my shoulders ached from the weight of my backpack. I shoved the little bracelet into my pocket and lowered my backpack centimeter by centimeter until it hushed to the floor behind me.

The man in the bed twitched. In the blue light, I could see the familial resemblance, and somehow, that made me being here all the more delightful.

"Wake him and let me take over."

"How do I do that?" I asked. I knew how to handle a handoff to Bitsy. I knew she could take control when she wanted to, if she asserted herself. El was a different story. I didn't know if I could voluntarily submit to her conscience.

An awkward silence passed between us. I tried to retreat to the safe corner where I went when Bitsy took over, but I was too afraid that would call Bitsy, and this was something she would definitely not want to know about.

"What if I just..." El shifted in my head, but she didn't come through.

My mind was firmly in control of my body.

"Listen, I think you're just gonna have to walk me through this."

Gritted teeth muffled a wail of frustration that pinged around in my head and then receded. It sounded as if El was throwing herself against the walls of her confinement in me. I let her sob for a moment, understanding the frustration of sharing a body and imagining how difficult it would be to have no control, ever. To find yourself in a foreign place inside a species you never knew existed. The dagger in my hand vibrated, and the sorrow rolled over me.

"I'm really sorry," I told them. *"I don't know why you've come to be here or what will get you home. Do you want to leave now? Do you want to not do this?"*

"No!" they said in unison, the dagger speaking with a voice of muted emotion rather than with words.

"We must do this. We must help someone if we cannot help our daughter. She is lost, but this girl is not lost," El said.

El seemed to pull herself together in a long moment that felt like a deep inhale. The man in front of us twitched some more. A car door slammed outside. I froze. An engine revved to life. I wanted to squeak.

"Shit!" I said to El.

Headlights cut through the blue glow hanging in the room. The man in the bed shifted, rolled toward the window, flinging a hand to the side of the bed.

That's when the lamp snicked on.

Chapter 14

Frozen, I gripped the blade's handle. The man with reddish hair and reddish stubble patching a pointy chin and hollow cheeks stared back at me. His eyes were bloodshot chips of sea captured under feathering eyelashes. His skin was a peachy shade, similar to that of his cousin. Their similarity made me squirm. Sure, I'd been raped as a girl, but the man had been a guy my mom knew. Not my kin. How could a family member endeavor to cause so much suffering?

"He's damaged," El said.

"Who the fuck cares?"

"He does. He is broken. If, somewhere along the way, a Maker had been alerted to the crime against him, this cycle would not have continued. It could have broken with the generation before him."

I paused, dagger still gripped in my hand, the swirling, foreign, unearthly shapes pinching into the softness of hands.

"There is a pity in our work tonight. A compassion for his lack of compassion. And not just compassion for him and for the girl, but for the future generations."

I looked at the guy and pictured the girl tiptoeing across my office floor with blood dripping and pain scrawled across her face. Where I was coming from, I couldn't fathom feeling sorry for him. "*I'll leave the compassionate feelings up to you on this one.*"

"*Very well,*" El said. "*Before he grabs that gun in the dresser drawer, it'd be best to lunge at him now.*"

"*Wait, what?*" Air caught in my throat, sticking the dry tissue together.

The man dove across the mattress, his body stretched toward the bedside table. I lurched, an animal-like scream ripping from my lungs. My legs sprang me forward, toward the foot of the bed. I pushed off the jumble of covers and blankets, launching myself into the air. Right arm raised, I pounced on him, knees landing squarely on his legs. He made a noise somewhere between a groan and an exhale. He twisted to scramble out from underneath me, freeing an arm.

He pulled back a fist and punched my face with biting knuckles. The sting blossomed across my cheekbone and woke the hungry anger in me that craved greater exposure. I snarled as I turned my head back toward him. I grabbed a shoulder and shoved him back into the pillows. The movement caused his leg muscles to squish under my knees. A kneecap popped out of place. He yelped. I pushed my knees into his hipbones.

"Stop squirming," I growled.

Up close, his eyebrows knitted over his reddened blue eyes. He gritted a set of big, yellowing teeth. Teeth that would be beautiful if he took care of them.

"Who the fuck are you, and how did you get in my room?" His voice grated out of him through his struggle against me.

It was a good question, and I couldn't answer it entirely.

"I clicked my heels three times," I said.

He jiggled around, but I had the advantage of being on top and being fully energized by my anger.

"What do you want?" His eyes flicked to the blade in my hand, sudden realization and fear dawning on him.

"*Run your thumb up from the middle of his nose to his hairline and say what I say,*" Liz interjected before I could open my mouth.

I resituated my body and did as she instructed. A sensation like the shock of lightning ran down the crown of my head, along my spin and through my arm, hand and thumb. He jolted against the bed, the headboard banging against the wall, then froze, his muscle rigid.

"*It is not what I want but what you want,*" El said.

"It's not what I want but what you want," I said, my head tilting as I listened. Curiosity swelled in me as a companion to the excitement.

His breath wheezed. I could smell him—a mix of fresh sweat, stale clothing and halitosis.

"*You want a release from your guilt,*" El continued.

I repeated the intention, translated as words.

"You remember every time you've hurt a little girl."

His eyes began to widen, his jaw going slack. He almost seemed to quit breathing. I leaned closer and whispered the words El fed me.

"Every defenseless child who has suffered at your hands weeps inside your mind. You can name every one of them. You recall their faces, the age they were when you hurt them, what their favorite color was and the things that made them the happiest. You are no longer the predator but the prey. You understand their confusion with each wrong touch. You are the fear you caused them. There is nothing in you now except for their pain."

The man sobbed. I had zoned out while repeating El's words, drifting off to the memories that lurked like shadows in my mind. I was numb. Snot drained from his left nostril, tears poured down his cheeks, and his peachy complexion grew angry red and blotched. He gritted his teeth so much I could see all of his puffy red gums. His muscles underneath me hardened as his sorrow turned him to stone. He rocked his head back and forth and mumbled unintelligibly.

"Can you see the energy cords that connect him to his victims?"

I looked down at him. "What am I looking for here?"

"At his heart, there are threads pulsing like dark shadows. There are several. If you look closely, you can see them running along the center of his soul."

I peered closely as the man went on wagging his head and moaning. Just as I was about to give up, I saw them. Black shadows stretched like ropes from his throat all the way down his torso. They squirmed against invisible anchors. "I see them!"

"Those are the energy cords tying himself to his victims. We will sever. You may release him," El said.

"What? But don't you want me to...?" I asked.

"Release him. You will see."

I shuffled off the man. I expected him to bolt or lunge at me, but no. He used his newly freed hands to cover his eyes. A guttural scream built into a crescendo. I looked out the window, sure someone would wonder what was going on and come to check, but the parking lot remained dark except for the blue fluorescent sign indicating the motel had vacancies.

"Lay my husband next to the man."

I obeyed, not sure what would happen next, but at this point in the night, it hardly seemed worth it to argue.

"Now, ask him this: What do you want now?"

I did as El instructed.

"Please. I want it to be done. I want death. I want it to end. I want the suffering to end. I'm so, so sorry!" More sobs jolted out of his body. He spasmed, tossed, rolled... and then his hand touched the blade. He inhaled sharply, as if he'd just broken the surface of a lake in which he'd been drowning. He held his breath as his fingers curled around the hilt. Slowly he exhaled, spit fluttering from his cracked lips. He sat up, his eyes staring out into some other reality. Gripping the blade in his hand, he pushed off the bed. His lanky legs carried him around the bed and into the bathroom. He turned on the light. It flickered before obeying his command, buzzing an insistent, whining complaint.

He turned slowly toward the tub and pushed aside the flimsy curtain. I stayed where I was. The view was fine from here. He stepped in, his head tilted forward and down, the blank look covering his sorrow-sodden face. He sat down in the tub where I could see him, the opposite side of the water spout.

"Get over there! There is one more piece we must do!"

I ran until the toes of my sneakers teetered on the threshold to the bathroom. He raised the knife.

"He must hold the thing that belonged to the girl!"

"I have to go in there?"

"You must! Or else this will be for nothing!"

He raised the blade and rested its dark and multicolored edge to his throat. My rising horror gave way to a curious lust. I was eager to see him end himself.

"Hurry!"

His forearm turned ropy as he began to pull the blade. I launched myself forward, falling to my knees and skidding to the edge of the tub. I shoved my hand into my pocket and pulled out the small green and blue bracelet. I reached forward, snatched his empty hand and shoved the bracelet into it. Warm wetness splattered my face. I flinched, my gaze jumping up to the man. He stared at me, gurgled, and then his eyes went blank. The wide arc across his neck spilled blood and painted his white t-shirt in a curtain of crimson.

"Say, blood for blood, be free of your suffering."

I said the words, my voice quivering.

"Look," El said, *"the cords are severed."*

I fought against the wave of nausea and focused on the man's chest area, past the blood-soaked t-shirt. The squirming shadow cords limply fell aside from the cut at his neck where they faded and dissipated like smoke on the wind.

There was a wild sense of accomplishment that started in my gut and went thrilling up through my heart. Yet, mixed in with the awful satisfaction was disgust. I couldn't say where the disgust was aimed: the girl's cousin who lay dead in the tub, the alien in my head who'd talked me into this, the person who was a dagger that aided the suicide, or myself. I shook as I stood, and the world went all swimmy in the clash of emotions within me.

"*Do not leave my husband,*" El commanded.

The thrum of his energy reverberated around the bathroom. I reached over the dead man, my pulse ratcheting away. The bitter copper of blood prickled my nose. Oh, dear god, warmth from his body still emanated from him. My heartbeat throbbed in my ears. The air sawed in and out of my lungs. A jagged pain jammed into the ribs covering my heart.

The dagger was still in his hand. I turned. I didn't mean to, but I did. His eyes stared past me. His face was ghostly white. His mouth hung slack in a look of surprise. I squeezed my eyes closed and turned back to the dagger. Tears slipped down my cheeks as I uncurled his limp but warm fingers and removed El's husband, carefully touching only the handle. I snatched the dagger away and pushed back from the tub in one movement.

I was in the midst of a full-blown panic attack now. I couldn't breathe. I was trying. The air was moving in and out, but it wasn't soaking into my lungs. The edges of my vision bled away into white light.

"*You are light. You are love,*" El said, her voice soft and caring. "*You are the universe; its vastness is in you. This small thing you feel you are is not so. You are an amazing and strong woman, and you just helped to end a cycle that would not have stopped with the girl in your work today."*

"Is that true?" But I knew it was. Why would he stop? He'd run from this last victim, and the girl didn't want to press charges. He would get away, scot-free. I gripped the handle of the dagger. It was practically singing in my hand. My breath slowed. "Is the girl... she won't remember now?"

"She'll have no recollection of the event."

"Well, what about the aunt who was with her?" I asked.

"Her memory of the event is also clean."

"And Cathy?"

"She is a keeper of memories, but without anyone to press charges she will have nothing to do with the memory."

"So, they're going to mourn this jackass?" I asked.

"Yes, he has paid for his crime," she said. She seemed matter-of-fact. As if she'd just witnessed someone paying off their car loan instead killing themselves over the grief of a lifetime of perpetrating child molestation and rape.

I breathed in deeply, still staring at the mess of a man in the bathtub. I looked around. Had I left any markings of my presence here? I took a towel from the rack and wiped down the edge of the tub where I'd gripped it. When I looked, the man had a blade in his hand.

"Wait, how...?" I asked El.

"It is like a memory. The magic leaves him with a copy of what he imagined he used to kill himself."

"For real?" I gripped the towel and looked around. What else had I touched? Anything? I wiped down the bathroom counter, but I was pretty sure I hadn't touched it. Next time, I would wear gloves.

"You will do it again?" she asked.

I stepped out of the bathroom, leaving the overhead light

humming its monochrome, fluorescent song. I looked over the bed, but it just looked as if someone had tossed and turned in it. I hadn't touched anything else in there.

"*That depends.*" I had been thinking about this all day. I wasn't sure I could be fixed. Unlike the girl today, I was damaged from multiple incidents, which I guess was pretty standard, from what Cathy told me about the statistics. "*Could the ritual work for me?*"

El paused before responding. "*I am not sure. The ritual was never performed for someone with multiple crimes against them and with such time having passed after those crimes.*"

Something fragile and small broke inside me. I dropped my head, looking at my skinny body. I picked up the backpack and slung it over my shoulders and fought back an oncoming flood of tears.

"*We can try, if you choose. Do you know who your assailants were?*" El asked.

A small swell of hope rose inside me. "*No. But Grams does.*"

"*I will help you try this thing. And then will you help me find my child's spirit?*" she asked.

"*Is that possible? I thought she was in another world or something.*"

"*I think she might be here, like we are here. And I think her murderer has made it here, too, since we followed him.*"

I stood in the weak lamplight at the foot of the bed, where I'd arrived. My nerves were raw, and exhaustion seeped into my bones. I was covered in somebody else's blood, and there was most certainly an ache in my cheekbone that would be another black eye. I touched the sensitive side of my face, wondering what I'd look like in the morning and what I would say to Grams when she asked.

"*Can we go home now? Maybe we can talk about this later?*" The need to leave overwhelmed me.

"*Very well,*" El said, but she didn't sound happy about it. "*We will go back the way we came. When we step into the nether, I will heal your hurts."

"*No shit?*" I asked, excited to be rid of the need to fabricate some lame excuse about falling or something.

"*No shit,*" El promised.

Days off were the best but also meant counselor appoint-
ments, which were work. Sometimes, I craved a day of
selfish luxury or longed to go someplace new, or wished I could
just hide in my room and play music all day. I headed down
the stairs and contemplated cancelling my appointment while
a new tune cascaded through my inner hearing. I thumped
down the stairs in time to the song teasing its way out of me
through a quiet hum.

I stepped down from the last stair, slipped and fell backward. Images flashed across my mind. The living room washed
away as my vision splintered into some unreal reality.

*I was on a bus. I could feel the jostling of the wheels against
a pothole-riddled road. The smell of exhaust and upholstery
oiled with WD-40 filled my sense of smell. I laughed. Not me.
It wasn't me laughing. I was head-to-head with the girl next to
me. She was my best friend. Her dark hair bounced with every
bump in the road.*

*She whispered in my ear. "He said we get a special treat since
we're the last stop!" And she giggled with her hands covering her
mouth and the two front adult teeth that dominated her smile.*

I wiggled in the seat next to her, dancing, pointing my fingers into the air and shaking them.

"Oh," she said, suddenly serious.

She tapped my shoulder, and I leaned in for another whisper.

"We can't tell anyone, though. It's a secret." She covered her mouth with a single pointer finger and said, "Shhh..."

I nodded, crossed my heart and hoped to die.

Grandma's hands were on my shoulders. The wrongness of the words from the vision registered in me. The real me. Not the me in the vision who wasn't me at all, who was someone I'd never known. I gulped air as tears stung my eyes. Those girls. They were in danger. Why did I see these things? What could I do for them? Something foreign and big stirred inside me. Like a sleeping animal, waking. An animal so powerful I shied away from the bigness of it.

"Honey, are you okay?"

I blinked furiously at the burning fear and at that other power that wanted a way out.

"I..." I shook my head. Liz's memories of our childhood trauma smashed into the vision. I gripped my head in my hands and closed my eyes. *It'll be our little secret.* The words that had been whispered to Liz so long ago trumpeted in my mind, leaving the residue of the consequences of those words coating my soul.

"Elizabeth?" Grandma asked.

I waved her away, unable to speak. "C-c—" I tried and shook my head, crawling up the stairs and away from her caring touch. I needed to be left alone.

She straightened, holding her hands together, as if she wanted so much to embrace me but knew it would hurt me. I sat on the steps and breathed. It was the only thing I could focus on.

"Ask her," Liz prodded.

I shook my head again and rocked against the awful flashes playing like a movie in my mind.

"Ask her!"

I sobbed, wrapping my arms over my stomach.

"Who," Liz began, not even looking at my grandmother, "was it?"

She got the words out, despite my willing her to not say them. Did a piece of me also want to know?

"Who was who?" Grandma asked.

Liz burst fully onto the scene. "You know damn well who. The one who did this to us."

I looked at my grandmother, curiosity overwhelming the other need to not know anything about what Liz asked. I dissected my grandmother as she thought about the question. Her jaw clenched, her head tilted up, her eyes sparked behind the darkness of their warm brown. We'd never asked before.

"The one who did this to you? That's a complicated question. There've been lots of hands responsible for the horror you went through."

And although she didn't supply a name, I got the feeling she knew more than I'd ever guessed, which scared the hell out of me.

"Liz, I don't want to know. I don't think I can have a name or see a face. I mean, what does it matter? The damage is done."

"I want to know, Bits," Liz insisted.

There was an awful need in her. A need that would lead to what? I couldn't say, but it made my soul squirm.

"I'm not ready," I said. "I'm not ready," I added out loud. I pulled my hands apart and held one up to Grandma before she could divulge anything else. I said once more, as if repeating it would give me the power I needed to stop Liz's curiosity, "I'm not ready. Not yet. Maybe not ever."

Liz boiled in anger, frustration and most of all, a deep sorrow and desperation. She wailed as she dropped away from consciousness.

I gripped my knobby knees, working to calm myself. When I was through the turmoil, I looked up at Grandma. She extended a hand. I took it but pushed myself up, rather than relying on her strength. She dropped her hands to her side as she looked up at me. Something crossed her thoughts. I could almost catch it behind the deepness of her eyes and the set to her grim mouth.

But I let it go.

"Is there anything for breakfast?" I asked.

She smiled, still keeping her distance from me, as if I were a fire that seared your face when you stood too close.

"Sure there is, sugar. Want me to make you something?"

"Nah," I said. "We got any cereal?"

"I think there's some raisin bran in there," she answered.

I wolfed down a bowl while Grandma sipped her coffee and watched the morning news. Some poor motel maid had found a suicide victim in the bathtub of one of the rooms. Suicide was on the rise, the newscaster announced, and then he went on to talk about a local walk to raise awareness.

There was something naggingly familiar about the victim's photo that shot across the screen. I shrugged. Maybe I'd seen him at the ED or something.

"All right, I gotta head out, Grandma," I said.

"You want me to drive you?" she asked, looking at me from her old recliner. She muted the TV with the remote and set it on the coffee table perched next to her favorite sitting place.

"It's okay. I can take the bus," I said. I needed the time alone to think about everything. There was too much in my head. Visions and memories so intertwined I could barely keep them apart.

"All right, hon," she said, "be careful out there, okay?"

"I will," I promised.

I sat on the couch with my legs folded underneath me to one side. My shoes sat tidily on the floral rug in front of the couch. I curled my hands into the long sleeves of the oversized sweatshirt I wore. Liz was showing me a lot of new things lately. A lot.

"How many times are you purging in a day?" Sharon asked me.

I looked at my covered hands. Sharon looked, too.

"Six or seven," I whispered.

"That's a big change in the last couple of weeks," she noted.

"I'm sorry," I said.

"Don't be sorry to me, Bitsy," she said, her voice firm and yet caring. "So, talk to me about work. What's going on there?"

"Liz is there a lot. I stay away from the actual ED when I can so I don't have to see... him." I swallowed down my mortification.

"And have you talked to Liz about this yet?" Sharon asked.

"No," I said, my voice raised. I pulled the sweatshirt sleeves down and curled my fingers into the folds of the wristbands. I pursed my lips, my breath wheezing.

"Bitsy, I understand you're upset with Liz, but like I've told you before, it's important to work through this with her."

"Why is it important? I f-forget."

Sharon regarded me. I stared back. Something tickled my face. I brushed back the fine new hairs curling around my forehead with a sweatshirt-covered fist.

"It's important because Liz is a part of you, and you pushing her away will only rip you further into two. If you are two, you'll continue to take actions to harm yourself with reckless choices."

I blinked at her. How could I tell her again? I twitched; my legs wriggled.

"Liz is not me," I said vehemently. "She just happens to live in the same body as me."

Sharon didn't flinch. She didn't move. She took a slow breath and folded her hands into themselves and over the notebook she used to record our sessions.

"You don't think Liz is a piece of your personality? You used to believe that."

"No. I just told you that. She isn't me. I would never be so cruel as to sleep with a man I was interested in."

"Now, that's hardly fair, Bitsy. Liz has done so many things for you."

"Oh, yeah? Like what?" I crossed my arms over my waist and waited while my stomach squeezed on me. I wanted to throw up. I needed to vomit. Trouble was, I didn't think I had anything in my stomach to throw up, having emptied my raisin bran on the way out of the house. Plus, I was right here with Sharon. If I left to go throw up, I'd draw attention to it. I didn't think she'd take well to me puking in her bathroom during a session.

"Liz has protected you from the horror of your childhood," she stated.

"Not all of it," I snarled. "I remember some stuff." The whispers remembered this morning needled into my brain. *It'll be our secret.*

I wriggled in my seat. She had a look, and she was giving it to me. With her shock of short white hair and her square jaw, she was a force to be reckoned with.

"Okay, she protected me," I conceded.

"Yes, she did. How do you feel about that?"

I squirmed. And huffed. "I'm grateful she did it. It means a lot to me that she kept so much safe from me." I pulled my topmost leg over the other one and kicked my socked foot into the air. "But why is she sharing all this stuff with me now?" Frustration surged through me. I'd done just fine not knowing... not hearing the awful things my body went through while Liz bore the agony of those experiences. It was enough for one of us to know, wasn't it?

"Bitsy, where is all that compassion you have for others? Does Liz not deserve your kindness, too?" she asked.

I turned away from her, but I could still feel her analytical gaze on me.

"Bitsy, what makes you so special that you think you deserve extra amounts of punishment? Why do you think you deserve less love than anyone else in your life?"

"I don't know," I said, feeling small.

"Do you think you're different because you went through more than other people?"

"No," I said, although a piece of me felt that statement was true. I had gone through more than most people.

"You're not alone in your experiences," she said.

I looked at her.

"Do you know the statistic? An estimated one in every three girls is sexually abused," she told me.

I wiggled my shoulders. I hated when she started spouting statistics.

"One in three. One third. Every third woman you meet will have been sexually abused or raped. You are not alone."

I wiggled my foot, gripped my arms.

"I d-don't believe that many people had to go through it over and over... and over again," I said, raising my arm and circling it to signify the endlessness of the abuse in my childhood. "Every kind of abuse. Every day. Some-someth-thing.

Rape, molestation, neglect, physical abuse, emotional abuse. People d-d-don't go through the hell I've gone through. Sorry, Doc. You can say that stuff to me, but I know better. People just don't have to deal with what I've dealt with."

"I see. You've got it worse than others. You really are special."

"Yeah, I am," I said, and I felt the weight of my words hanging on me. My throat constricted, turning to a lump.

She raised her eyebrows over her glasses. "You're sounding a lot like Liz this morning."

I recoiled. It was as if she'd slapped me in the face with a frozen washrag. Stunned, I stared at her, unable to speak.

She waited while the silence between us dragged out, uncomfortable and palpable. When it was apparent I wasn't going to say anything, she continued. "If it's true you have it worse than most, then that means you're even more deserving of your own compassion. You. Meaning the girl who has guarded you from the painful memories of your youth. Because Liz is part of you."

"But she hurt me!" I said, unable to keep the whine from my voice.

"Yes, that's true. But she was also hurting. You left her to deal with the hard stuff again. Why is it that Liz has to do all the dirty work? Do you really think that's fair?"

Liz woke and shoved me aside. "Don't talk to Bitsy like that. Bitsy's softer and kinder than me. I can handle the hard stuff."

"Hello, Liz," Sharon said. "Is that true? You've got all of this under control?"

Liz nodded. "Yup. Sure do."

"Ladies, this is not good. Instead of working together, like you should, you've pushed each other away again," Sharon said.

"*I got this, Bits,*" she told me. I retreated into my safe place, not wanting to talk with Liz, and certainly not with Sharon any longer.

Liz

I unfolded myself. Bitsy was always trying to make herself smaller. I pulled my hands from the sweatshirt and looked down at myself. Man. She'd even taken off her shoes. "*God, Bits, what are we wearing?*"

"*It was comfortable.*" She defended her choice of wardrobe.

I pulled the black and white sneakers back on my feet. We were completely devoid of color today. Somehow, I felt that was a bad sign.

"We're here for each other. We might beat each other up on occasion, but we're still a team. Right, Bitsy?"

She didn't respond.

"Look, I'm sorry for what I did. How many times do I have to tell you? It was wrong of me. I should have stayed away from him. But maybe you're making a big deal about something that isn't."

"He'll never want to date me now!" Bitsy shouted, surprising me by using my voice and not just speaking in my head. And speaking without a hint of a stutter.

"You don't know that. Why don't you try and see?" I reasoned with her.

She quieted for a minute.

"It doesn't matter, anyway," she said. "No one will ever want someone so broken." She sobbed.

I took a steadying breath, fighting back the hurt she was sharing with me.

"Yeah," I said. "Maybe you're right. Maybe we're unlovable."

"That is not true, ladies," Sharon interjected. "You are well loved by your grandmother and your friend, Corey."

"Grams doesn't count," I said. "Grams loves us because that's who *she* is, not because of who we are."

"That's a big, fat lie," Sharon said. "Your grandmother has been through other relationships and ended them because there was no worth in them. She hasn't quit on you because you are worthy of love."

I shrugged and crossed my arms. "You know, I think I'm done for the day," I said. I stood from the couch. "Thanks for the time."

"That's just fine," Sharon said, an edge to her voice.

I walked out the door.

"Don't forget the backpack," Bitsy said.

I backed up, totally ruining my exit, snatched the lavender backpack sitting just inside the door and walked out again.

Once I was outside, I walked down to the nearest bus stop and checked the schedule. We had a whole thirty minutes before the next bus.

"You really think he might be interested?" Bitsy asked.

I nodded. *"Yeah, Bits, yeah, I do."*

She paused. Someone shuffled up next to us and sat down on the bench.

"Do you like him, too?" she asked.

There were two people. A man and a woman. The man said something to the woman that involved a few f-bombs. I shifted down to the end of the bench to give them their space.

"He's a nice guy," I confirmed.

The man got to his feet to stand in front of the woman, who still perched on the bench. Their clothes were tattered and worn. I watched the two out of the corner of my eye, my senses tingling. I got ready to stand.

"You think he'd be good for us? You think we'd be good for him?"

The man's voice rose. The woman shrank back.

Distracted, I answered Bitsy.

"*I dunno. You can't tell that from being with someone once. You have to get to know them. It's worth a date, though, yeah?*" Bitsy wouldn't know about relationships and how it worked after sex. She was a virgin. Of course, I wouldn't know anything past the sex part either. That thought was sort of sobering, but I let it go, not wanting to consider what that might mean.

"*Yeah,*" she said.

"*Go to sleep, Bits. You've worked hard to keep it together. Let me take a turn.*"

"*Okay,*" she said, "*a rest sounds nice.*"

When I was sure she was asleep, I left the arguing couple at the bus stop and started walking. I pulled the phone out of the raincoat pocket and texted Grams.

> Grams. It's Liz. I'm grabbing some coffee and maybe shop a little before heading home. Need anything?

She texted back after I'd made it to the end of the block. She must have had the phone nearby.

GRAMS:

> Okay, sweetheart. Grab me some dark chocolate while you're out, would ya? Chicken and dumplings tonight.

"Oh, sweet southern cooking. How did I ever survive your absence?" I salivated at the thought of dinner.

> You got it! Dark chocolate coming up. Can't wait for dinner. Xoxox

Thinking about dinner caused me to notice another sensation: I was starving. Maybe even literally. I took stock of my body. I was skinnier, for sure. Damn. We needed a few Liz days to get some meat on our bones. I checked my phone. 11:32 a.m. Plenty of time for lunch before dinner. I texted Corey.

> Hey, hey. What are you up to?

COREY:

Well, hey, grrrrlll. I'm working on your creature thing. Nearly done.

I had no idea what he was talking about.

> Sweet! Wanna grab some lunch? My treat. I'm SSSTTTAAAARRRRVVED!

COREY:

You're paying? Man. How'd I get such an awesome friend? Where do you want to meet?

I checked my surroundings and gauged my food cravings. I ditched the idea of riding the bus and decided on finding something within walking distance.

> I need some burgers and beer. You feel me?

COREY:

This is why we're best friends.

> Brunch Box?

Hell, yeah!

I'm not far. Meet you in 20 minutes.

Cool.

The main Brunch Box location was a small establishment. The walls were lined with framed poster photos of the various sandwiches they were known for making. The order counter was manned by a beefy guy with dark hair and dark stubble. Above him, backlit menu boards dominated the front of the store. The wall to our left was old brick and mortar. It was cozy. And it smelled amazing: like greasy fried meat and potatoes.

I inhaled deeply and salivated over the aroma. "Mmm..."

Corey and I stared at the menu board.

"I know, right?" Corey said. "What are you getting?"

There was really no question about it. "Trial by fire, baby."

"You and your spicy," Corey said.

"What about you?" I asked.

Corey sighed. "They're all so yummy. Can I have one of each?"

"Sure you can, buddy," the guy at the counter said. "We wouldn't mind that at all."

He winked at me while Corey continued staring at the board. I grinned at him and winked back, wondering if I should give him my number. He'd already checked out the goods and appeared to approve. Although, I thought I was a little on the scrawny side, thanks to the starvation methods

Bitsy was implementing. She was probably ruining our teeth with purging, too. Disgusting. Why would you eat good food just to throw it up again?

"Okay, I think I've decided," Corey said, sounding as if he'd just chosen the fate of the world rather than his lunch. "I'm going with the Burgermeister." He turned to me. "You want to split some loaded fries?"

I thought about if I really wanted to share. I shrugged. "I guess we can start with one and see how it goes."

"Girl can eat," the cashier said, his thick, dark eyebrows pitched toward his hairline, "I like it."

"We're going to need some beers, too," I said.

"You got it," Cashier said, seeming more joyful with every consumption choice I made.

We paid, collected our beers and took a seat by the window.

Corey dumped his backpack onto the bench beside him and fiddled with one of the pouches. I sipped my IPA and watched his hands. They were artist's hands, long and slender. They handled things with care. I wondered if he was good with his hands, sexually. He wasn't my type, but I was still curious. I looked over at the cashier while Corey flipped through the pages of his sketchpad.

I caught the cashier looking at me. I perked up, straightening my back and smiling at him shyly. Guys really liked that. Even if "shy" was not a personality trait I had. I could pretend to be shy. I could pretend to be a lot of things.

He grinned, looked away and continued wiping down the counter.

"Okay," Corey said, "how'd I do?"

I turned toward him. He held up a sketchpad with a beast on it so scary I jumped.

"Oh my god, what is that thing?" I said.

"You don't recognize it? I really did that bad of a job?"

I breathed through a sincere panic attack as I clutched my speeding heart. "Why would I recognize it?" I blurted.

"Because you told me to draw it," he said, looking like a puppy that'd been kicked.

"That is my Hound," El said. The last word's translation was rough.

"Hound? As in, dog? As in, I have cynophobia?" I said. And clearly, I needed to hide this fact from Corey.

"Oh, god. Sorry. I—um—forgot all about asking you," I said, trying to recover.

I looked away from the sketchpad to get a break from staring at something that looked spawned from nightmares. Or hell, maybe. Yes, hell was better. A group of five had come in and were chatting as they approached the counter, filling the air with a warm, excited buzz.

"I'm sorry, Bits. I must have really messed it up," he said.

"The artist has done a commendable job. That is exactly what the Hound looks like," El said.

"Why the hell is our artist friend drawing a beast from your planet?" I asked.

"It is here with us," she said.

I whirled around, waiting to see the thing right next to me, longish jaw gaping and weird, slitted nostrils capturing my scent. My body was poised to run. Instead, the dude from the counter stood next to me with a tray of our food. I yelped and backed away. In return, he took a step back.

"Bitsy, are you okay?" Corey asked.

"Uh—didn't mean to startle you," the cashier said. "Here's your burger."

"Wow. I'm super jumpy. Sorry," I said.

The guy set the food on the table, eyeing me warily, while I recovered from my freak-out. Corey pushed the sketchpad aside and unloaded the burgers and fries in front of each of us.

"What do you mean 'it is here with us'?" I asked El.

"The Hound was hunting my child's murderer. It chased him. The man dove into the pool of our ancestors. The Hound dove. I dove. I had Maltheron in my hand. We've all ended up here. The Hound still hunts the murderer. Bitsy saw the Hound in the market."

"Aw, hell," I said, "you mean that thing is running loose around Portland?"

"Do not worry. Just as I am inside you, the Hound is inside of another of its kind. A much smaller and gentler beast. Still. They must be one in purpose enough to have become attached. As you and I are one in purpose."

"So, Bitsy saw this thing and then asked Corey to draw it?" I asked.

"She dreamed about it," El said.

And then I came along and totally blew my cover. Shit. Time to repair.

"Here, let me see that thing again," I said.

Corey nudged the pad toward me, not even looking at his food. He was staring at me hard. Dissecting me with his cool gray-green eyes. "I'm sorry. It was a rough morning, and to tell you the truth, I'd totally forgotten about this guy." I held up the pad and glanced at the image then to a white space in the corner, not able to stare fully at the thing for more than a moment.

"Wow," I said. "I mean, really wow." I gripped both sides of the tablet and pushed it out in front of me. Corey couldn't see my face, but it looked as if I was staring at the image. "This is amazingly accurate. Just like what I saw in my dream. How do you do that?"

I peered out at Corey from behind the sketch, meanwhile flipping the pages over to the cover. Corey looked at me as if he was trying to decide if I was lying or not.

"Are you sure? Because you didn't recognize it at first."

"No, no," I said, "it's—awesome. I was just distracted.

Sorry." I handed him back the pad and sighed in relief as he put it away.

"*So, this dog thing is out there looking for your daughter's murderer. Can't it just find him and kill him?*" I asked El.

"*Given the size of the animal the Hound is occupying I think that is highly unlikely.*"

"*But how will we know if it finds him?*" I asked.

"*Bitsy is now connected to the animal, as I am connected to the Hound. One physical connection and one spiritual connection. The Hound will work through the dog to find Bitsy.*" That meant, at some point, I was probably going to be in close proximity with the Hound and a dog.

"*Oh, god. I hate dogs.*"

Chapter 16

BITSY

Work was its own sort of relief. I arrived early and let the mundane busyness sweep me away. I tried not to think of our appointment with Sharon. Or the audition for the orchestra, which was in two weeks. I would need to practice every day to make sure I was sharp. Liz disagreed with this. She was certain if I walked on stage and just played, they'd beg me to stay.

I also tried not to think of Gabe or the memory of being with him, which Liz wanted to share with me. I would eventually need to see the memory, but the thought of doing so had me twisted in knots.

Answering emails, scheduling meetings, ordering office supplies, reviewing timecards... I could do those things. The tasks gobbled away at the day until a soft rap at the door pulled my attention from the computer screen. Nurse Ballasiotes stood in the doorway.

"Hi," I said. "Um. C-can I help?" I forgot the "you" in the statement. So dumb.

She had on regular work clothes and no lab coat today. The plum-y-colored crocheted sweater hugged her curves and displayed just a touch of her neckline. She was gorgeous.

"Hey, Bitsy," she said. "I was on my way back from new employee orientation and thought I'd make a house call. How are you doing?"

She looked around the office, a little wide-eyed. Cathy was out for the day, so it was just me there. Luckily, no cases had come in.

"Pretty g-good," I said. I held up my arm to her. "Bruises are turning yellow, so getting better." I smiled at her. "Thank you for taking care of me."

"That's what I'm here for," she said.

There was a moment's pause, during which I tried and failed to think of things to say.

"How do you like working here? I mean, in this space." She cocked her head to one side and waited for a response.

"What, is she kidding?" Liz chimed in.

I looked around the room.

"Maybe she's going to put in a good word to have us moved out of here," I pointed out to Liz. I didn't want Nurse B. to think I was being negative, but I did want her to know I'd rather work somewhere else.

"U-um..." I stuttered. I took a deep breath and tried again. "It's close to everything. And I like being next to Cathy."

I paused and watched her.

Her eyebrows furrowed. "But...?" she said.

I could sense her rising anger. "But, you know, what happened last week was—" I cut my sentence short and took a breath.

"It was terrifying, actually. Kind of like being in our childhood again," Liz supplied the answer.

I hadn't lived the experience, so I really couldn't say. "Scary," I finished, toning down Liz's dramatic words.

Nurse Ballasiotes frowned, leaned against the doorjamb and crossed her arms under her big breasts. I tried really hard to not stare at them, but my eyes flicked down and back up to her face. Luckily, she was looking around the room and not at me.

Liz laughed at me.

"Here's what I'm thinking," Nurse B. began, looking back at me with steely eyes. "I'm thinking no one should be in this office. It's unsafe. So, I'll be drawing up some paperwork and sending it through."

"Oh, good. In three months, something might get done," Liz said.

"Wow. Really?" Even I could hear the hope in my voice. "I— That w-would be s-so awesome."

Nurse B. unfolded herself and propped a tiny hand on the fullness of her round hip. "Yeah, I think so, too. Let's see if we can't get you out of this environment."

"I appreciate it."

She nodded and winked. My heart fluttered, and I was sure my cheeks burned crimson. Nurse B. flashed me a fuller smile of white teeth.

"I'll be in touch soon, Elizabeth."

The sound of my full name in her voice sent a little buzz through my head. Nurse B. walked away while I recovered my racing heart.

But there was no time for that. My next visitor ramped it up to full speed.

"Nurse B. To what do we owe the pleasure?" My boss's voice floated around the corner.

I wiggled the mouse to wake it from the black screen of stars and checked all the tasks she'd sent me. Had I done them all?

"Just checking in on Bitsy."

My ears perked up. She'd used my full name to me but just my preferred name to my boss.

"Out of respect," Liz said. *"Roxanne doesn't deserve your full name."*

"Do you think she knows about us?" I asked Liz, fear wriggling in my stomach.

"Hmm... well, I don't know why she would. They ask about depression and anxiety but not dissociative identity disorder. Go figure."

"I understand from HR that you called Bitsy in to work the day after her incident."

"Whoa! Nurse B. knows how to lay down some crucial conversations. Damn."

It was good to have Liz back and talking to me. I smiled a little, hidden behind my monitor where no one could see.

"I did call her, but of course, I *offered* her the option to come in to work," Roxanne said without a hint of remorse or regret and stressing the word, "option".

"Blech! That woman. She basically guilt-tripped you into coming in."

"My recommendation for Bitsy's health and wellbeing was for her to stay home. What could have been so important for you to call her in?" Nurse B's voice snapped like a whip.

"Holy crap! I've never heard anyone get into it like this. Bitsy, scoot closer to the door."

"We can hear just fine from here," I said.

"We had a very important meeting, at which Bitsy was required to take minutes. I fail to see why it's such a big deal. I asked if she was okay to come in, and she said she would come in."

"Your administrative assistant is emotionally fragile in the first place," Nurse B. whispered.

"Um, what?" Liz said.

My stomach clamped down on itself as my head buzzed.

Ballasiotes continued. "Then she was jumped by a man and threatened with rape and murder. And you. You have the audacity to call her in the day after such an incident and make her work in the same office where she sustained both mental and physical injury."

I stood from the chair, limbs shaking.

"For the sole purpose of taking minutes?" Nurse B. continued.

The words "emotionally fragile" sawed away at my insides. My heartbeat pulsed on my eardrums. I moved without thought, as if I was a puppet, and only my sheer horror was the master.

I walked past the desk, the waiting chairs and through the doorframe. Nurse B. had her back to me and was blocking Roxanne's view of me. I rounded the nurse and looked into her face. She was flushed, her lips pulled back over her white teeth, her eyes a little too big and her small nostrils flared. If I weren't mortified, I'd have thought she was terribly cute.

"Excuse me," I squeaked. My limbs were rigid with rage.

Nurse B. and Roxanne barely looked at me.

"I had every right to call her in and give her the option to work," Roxanne said, holding up a hand to me to silence me.

To silence me! Anger exploded within me, sending a shockwave of red up to my vision. The steady hum-hum-hum of my elevated heart rate echoed in my ears. A nurse in pink and black scrubs skirted around the trio of us, wide eyes glancing our direction as she hurried down the hall.

"Excuse me," I yelled and stomped my foot for good measure. The nurse down the hall rounded the corner with a final, mortified but curious glance.

Roxanne and Nurse B. whipped their gazes to me, but Roxanne's hand stayed resolutely in the air.

"Put your damn hand down," Liz said.

I wrestled control back while Roxanne's mouth dropped open, but her hand fell to her side.

"*Back off, Liz.*" I warned.

Another employee in navy blue scrubs jogged past us,

his basket of phlebotomy tools clanking. I watched until he was past.

"I..." I took a slow, deep breath, looked first into Roxanne's eyes and then into Nurse Ballasiotes's eyes. "I would appreciate it if you would keep my 'emotional fragility'"—I put the words in quotes with my fingers, my head snapping from side to side, my voice rising— "*out* of the hallways!" I finished in a roar.

Nurse B. flushed, dropped her gaze to the floor and then shifted to look at the wall. After a moment, she glanced at me through her eyelashes. "I'm so very sorry. You're right. I shouldn't have said anything out here." She paused, swallowed and then looked at Roxanne, who was still gaping. "Roxanne, I'll be in touch with you soon."

Nurse B. pushed off the wall, rounded me and headed off down the hallway.

I left Roxanne in the hall and went back to my desk, my muscles trembling.

"*Good for you, Bitsy,*" Liz said.

"*What did I just do?*" Fear pushed its way into my heart. "*What did you just do? You cursed at our boss.*"

Sure enough, Roxanne stomped through the door, then yanked at the handle. The door pulled away from the magnetic stop with a stubborn *thunk* then groaned to a close. It snicked into the jam as Roxanne faced off with me. She stared down, gripped the edge of the counter on the front of my desk. I looked up at her from my chair, feeling my position of submission.

She pointed at me. "This is fair warning. Talk to me like that again and you'll be out of a job. I will write you up now. Come by my office after you clock out to sign the papers."

My throat resolutely stuck shut.

"*That bitch! She's writing us up?*" Liz said.

"*Why did you have to use language with her?*" I moaned to Liz.

I swallowed and nodded to Roxanne, while tears pricked at my eyes. I was due for a performance review. Getting written up meant no raise.

"It doesn't matter, Bits. You're going to get that job at the orchestra soon, anyway."

"That's not a for-sure thing, Liz. I don't even know if I'm in the same league as those people."

"Stop worrying. You have an amazing CV, glowing recommendations and amazing talent. It's in the bag," Liz said.

"I think you're underestimating the caliber of people the Oregon Symphony Orchestra hires."

Roxanne pushed off the counter, eyed me with contempt and then stalked away. There was a jiggle at the door and as Roxanne reached for the knob, the door flew open, a harassed-looking Cathy behind it. She pushed the door open with a shoulder since her arms were full of charts.

"Oh, hey, Roxanne," Cathy said and clanged the door back to its magnetic stopper, looking up at it to make sure it actually stuck.

"Hey," Roxanne said perfunctorily, and without offering to help Cathy with her burden, exited the room.

I was glad to see her go. Hunched over, Cathy made her way to the small office area through the doorway on the wall opposite my desk and dumped the charts on a not-so-cleared-off space on her desk.

She raised a hand and wiped her brow. "Phew," she said.

"W-wh—?" I gave up.

Cathy cocked her head to one side and eyed me. "What happened?" she asked. Then she shuffled forward and peeked around the corner, clearly looking to see if Roxanne was still in the room. She yanked a chair from the waiting area and pulled it close to me. Then she sat down in front of me, leaned forward and motioned with her hand.

I opened my mouth, but my words wouldn't work. I frowned. The computer screen blanked out to the screensaver. I pointed to the screen. Cathy looked puzzled for a moment then nodded in understanding.

"Oh! Good idea. You type. I'll read. God, you're so smart." She pulled the chair closer to the monitor and nudged her thick glasses back up her nose... adjusted again with a pull of her face.

I pulled open an empty Word document, zoomed in on the magnification to make it easier for her to read and began to type. When I got to the part where I (meaning Liz) accidently cussed at Roxanne, she whistled under her breath. I finished the story and turned to her.

"Oh, Bitsy, I'm so sorry. It's not as if she doesn't deserve every curse word and fifty times more."

She did not pat my arm, but I felt she wanted to, and I both appreciated her desire and that she chose not to touch me while I felt so raw and vulnerable.

"I would have never thought Ballasiotes would be so inappropriate." She shifted in her seat. "But then she apologized for saying what she said?"

I nodded and felt the tears stream down my cheeks. My body shook. Frustrated with myself, I pushed away the tears with the heel of my hand. Liz was boiling inside. Not about Nurse B. or Roxanne but about all the people who'd scarred us so badly, making us into a split mess.

Part of us crying... part of us raging.

Liz was angry about the wounds that gaped and oozed and bled, leaving us debilitated. Unable to accept the warm touch of a friend who cared. Unable to speak in moments of stress. Being called fragile. Having our weaknesses exploited by people in power. Unable to listen to certain songs for fear they'd trigger memories of abuse. Panic attacks. Mood swings.

And none of these things was our fault. We were left to deal with the aftermath of others' bad choices.

Just day-to-day living was overwhelming.

Cathy cooed. "I'm so sorry, hon'. I know this is hard. You are so brave for doing what you do."

I shook my head to argue, to say I was not brave, that I was the worst sort of human. Liz didn't argue.

"It takes guts to get up every day and face the world after you've seen so much of its ugliness."

I looked up at her. If anyone saw the world's ugliness, Cathy did.

She smiled at me and extended an open hand. I hesitated and then placed my fingers into her palm. At first, the touch was a shock. A pain squeezed my chest; my heart thumped uncomfortably, my stomach turned. But then she squeezed my fingers and nothing more. She would not use the touch to hurt.

"Most people get up in the morning and the worst thing they have to face are things like not getting to work on time or having their coffee order wrong. Or maybe a jam in the printer." She laughed and shook her head. "Every day when you get up, you have to focus on being a better you than what circumstances have given you. But the bravest thing of all is that you do. You do! You give the world joy by being in it, Bitsy."

I hung my head. That couldn't be true. To give joy to the world by being a mess? What did I have that could bring joy to the world.

Your music, for one thing, Liz said.

"I know it doesn't make sense, or maybe it just hasn't sunk in quite yet. It took me until I was in my thirties to develop a healthy view of me and of my life. So just be patient with yourself. All this crap you've been through, you shouldn't have had to go through, but you have a choice to let it serve a higher purpose. And I know. I know. You will stand on it, rather than let it stand on you." She squeezed my hand.

I lifted my eyes, searching for the lie in her words. The trouble was, I felt nothing but truth. I had strength and goodness, and I had something to contribute to the rest of the world.

I nodded.

She let go of my hand. "Good. When you're ready I could use your help, but not before you're ready. Okay?"

I nodded again and rose from my chair. I needed fresh air to get my voice back.

I spent the afternoon filing charts of information on sexual assault victims. I ached for every name I put away. I wished Corey was here. Someone to chat with to divert my attention. Until it got to be too much and Liz tagged in to take over.

I sighed in relief when Bitsy went to sleep and let me take over. She'd stayed strong for a long time. I took the charts still left to file and held them on my knees. The locking file cabinet was open. Four drawers of charts with little room left for more hulked over me. And these were just from the last five years. Anything older than that, we sent to a storage facility. I stared at the testament to the darkness people suffered at the hands of others. Almost all of these victims were women or girls. A much smaller percentage of these charts contained information on victims who were boys.

"Your patriarchal society is broken," El chimed in. Her anger boiled. The cut of her words would slice through hearts if spoken aloud.

"You're tellin' me, sister," I replied. *"So. Where do you want to start?"*

We'd seen rape, incest, molestation and torture, so far. How could you pick one perpetrator over another? They were all awful. Some so much worse than what I'd been through.

"Let us start with someone recent."

That was easy, since Bitsy had been filing the recent ones. I pulled the file with information about a little girl. There was a companion file with the same last name. A brother and sister. My gaze roamed over the report. The contents were pretty typical. Single mom who had to work relied on the goodwill of a "nice guy" she'd met. "Nice guy" turned out to be child molester. Several days ago, Cathy had collected the evidence and that meant it would be stored in her office. She would take collected kits to the police station on her weekly visit.

I went to Cathy's office and found the box of envelopes on her desk. They were all lined up with the all-caps title facing toward me: "SEXUAL ASSAULT EVIDENCE COLLECTION KIT". I sifted through them until I found the two kits with the same last name. Lucky, lucky. They'd each left a piece of clothing for testing. I pulled the smaller garment envelopes from the larger kit, reclosing the kit and filing it back alphabetically.

I scuttled back to my workstation, my adrenaline singing like a warning bell. I stuffed the envelopes into the deep parts of the backpack and hurried back to the filing cabinet.

"Memorize the names of the children and the name of the perpetrator," El instructed me.

The photos were school photos, I guessed. Pictures taken before their horror story started. I read the names and looked at the pictures, memorizing the lines of their faces, the gap where an adult tooth would grow in, the color of their eyes and tilt to their smile. And I had no trouble committing the pedophile's name to memory.

I put away all of the charts, carefully reading through the names to access them later. The room was all mine. Cathy had a forensic case and was busy gathering evidence from an accused off-site. My boss was holed up, probably gleefully writing my disciplinary report. I'd closed the door to keep people from seeing my snooping, but if anyone walked in, all I needed to do was close the file and keep putting them away. No worries. No problem.

The charts were color coded with orange for deceased victims. Since we were also a pediatric hospital, we kept the charts of pediatric patients marked in pink. One of the files had an orange tab that accompanied a pink tab. My insides quaked. How could they?

The papers shushed in the quiet of the office as I tenderly opened the folder. A sixteen-year-old named Keysha. She hadn't come home from a sleepover. Concerned, her parents had searched and found her on the street near a house her friends reported they'd been at the night before, at a party. The house had belonged to a known drug dealer. She was alive when they found her, but she'd been beaten and gang-raped after being drugged. She'd suffered from internal bleeding and drug overdose, and because none of the partygoers had called the cops she'd died the next day in the ICU. The report included the address where she'd been found. I looked at the date. Last week.

"This one, too," El said.

I could see her point. We could get several at one time. It was sort of a wonderfully efficient thought process.

"But, hey, Princess, how are we going to take on a gang of drug dealers who probably have guns? Or do you not know what guns are?"

"I have been watching and listening. I have seen these guns in your television and newspapers," she said curtly. *"I have a few tricks*

up my sleeve. *Things we do easily and naturally on my world.*" She sounded smug.

"*Like what?*" I asked.

"*I will show you.*"

I shrugged and rolled my chair toward the desk. I yanked a sticky from its dispenser and wrote down the address. After shoving the sticky into the backpack, I went back to work on the filing.

I had to admit, the steady rhythm and monotony of putting away the records couldn't tamp down the rising hunger for the hunt.

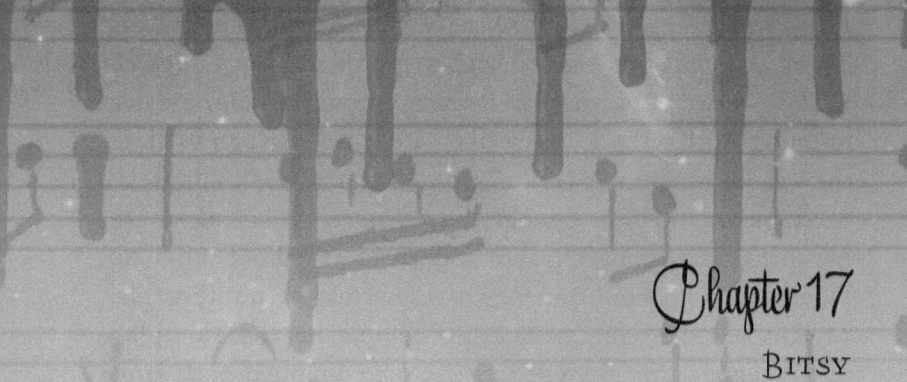

Chapter 17

BITSY

"Is it time for the meeting with Roxanne?" Bitsy asked.

I stuffed away all the thoughts of the upcoming night.

"*Just about. Don't worry, I've got this.*" I was looking forward to it, actually. I grinned.

"*No. I'm taking over. I don't want you getting us fired.*"

"*No trust!*" I whined.

But Bitsy was climbing out of the mental room she kept herself in, and I was going to sleep without a say in the matter.

"*Bitsy, wait, I can handle Roxanne. You don't need to do this.*"

"*No,*" she said again, and she said it firmly.

Surprised, I was hardly able to fight the fog pulling me into silence.

"*I want to handle this,*" Bitsy said. "*I won't let Grandma down by losing our job and being unable to help with the bills.*"

I tried to say Grams had plenty of money stored away in that savings account of hers. I knew; I'd seen the statements. But Bitsy took over fully and completely, and darkness wrapped me up just after the shock of her strength became real to me.

I breathed deeply and looked at the pile of records in my lap. There were only two left. I hustled to put them away. The clock read two-thirty; Roxanne would expect me within the next five minutes. Rolling back to my desk, I clicked through to close the various programs I had open and restarted the computer.

I pulled the file cabinet drawer open and yanked the backpack from its hiding spot and then dashed out the door. Unfortunately for me, someone had been just on the other side. My face smashed into a sweatshirt's zipper, my toes stomping on someone's toes. I yelped as the man wrapped both arms around me to keep me upright. My arms yanked into a guard position, and I turned my head away. Adrenaline flooded through me, making my heart trip into double-time and washing away my peripheral vision in a blur of white light. My skin writhed with prickles of electricity; my muscles turned to steel.

"Oh, god! Sorry, Bitsy. I totally scared the crap out of you," Corey said.

He backed away, holding my elbows to steady me, his face a surprised mask of concern. His hands trembled on my arms. Flashes of white pulsed in my vision. Shaking, I took a breath that sounded like a drowning person breaking the water's surface. Embarrassed, I backed away from him and labored to calm myself. Corey let go of me and adjusted his glasses with the back of his hand.

"Are you okay?" he asked.

"S-sorry," I started. "You j-just startled me." I laughed, but it sounded more like hysteria than humor. I straightened and made an attempt to gather myself. "You were at the door. Did you need something?"

"I was just stopping by to say hello to my most favoritest administrative assistant," Corey said. He looped his thumbs through the straps of his backpack and rocked back on his heels. "How's it goin'?"

"Actually, not so good," I said.

"Why? What's up?" He cocked his head to one side as he regarded me.

"Oh, well, I might have m-m-mouthed off to our mutual boss, and she might be firing me in the next moments of my employment," I explained.

"Whoa," he said, holding up a hand. "Back up. You mouthed off to Roxanne?" He looked down at me, mouth agape. "And I missed this?"

I groaned. "Did you not hear the part where she might fire me?"

"She can't fire you. Are you kidding me? Nobody gets fired in this place. Not without at least a six-month, drawn-out process, complete with all levels of retribution and punishment. You'll get a verbal warning, and that'll be that."

"Maybe if I worked for Cathy or Charlie in ICU, but this is Roxanne we're talking about. Rox. Anne!"

He cupped his chin in his hand and stroked his face. "You could have a point."

"I gotta go," I explained.

"Want me to wait around for you? I've made more progress on the dog-slash-bear thing." He said it as if he was tempting me with chocolate. He wiggled his eyebrows suggestively, which made his glasses slip down his nose, which caused him to nudge them back into place with a knuckle.

"T-t-tempting, but I need to get home and practice," I said.

"Oh, that's right. Hey, when is the tryout anyway?" he asked.

"It's an audition. And it's one week from today. I have one week to finalize preparations. Hopef-f-fully..." I trailed off, suddenly fearful saying my hope would lead to its destruction.

"When are you going to let me listen?" he asked.

I had been thinking about this. I hadn't played for an audience in several months. Maybe playing for Corey could be its own sort of practice.

"Well, I'm off after today until next week. I can play for you anytime, really," I said. I had the pieces down. I was just perfecting the finer points of executing them.

He gave a celebratory air punch. "Yes. Okay. Can you come over to the family's house this Saturday?"

"Oh," I said, "so, not only do I have to play for you, but I have to entertain the whole family?" I paused while he looked on with baited breath. "What if Abbey doesn't like it?" I asked.

Corey threw back his head and let out a bark of laughter. "I love you, Bitsy. I mean it. You're not worried about the adults. You're worried about the third-grader. You're so freaking awesome."

I shrugged. "Well, Awesome has to go get awesomely written up now. Let's see how awesome I feel after that."

I slipped past Corey and out into the hallway.

"Good luck with that," he said and turned toward the exit.

I waved and headed down the sloping hallway, deeper into the earth, farther into the hospital's underbelly and into Roxanne's office.

Roxanne had papers on her desk. Lots of papers. And folders, books, charts, pens, highlighters and other various office supplies. The things were scattered in some places, piled in others. She saw me enter and put down a piece of paper into an open box of hanging file folders. She was wearing reading glasses. She turned toward her monitor without addressing me. She shoved a pile away from her mouse so she could maneuver the thing and clicked away. I wasn't sure what to do. So I stood in front of her desk and waited. Her breathing was loud.

The desk printer behind her whirred to life, ch-chunking away until three pieces of paper had pushed each other out of the tray and landed with a whispery *fwap* onto the carpeted floor. Roxanne groaned, rolled over to the printer and bent to pick up the fallen paperwork.

"I'm going to need you to sign these." She put them in order, stapled the upper left corner, signed herself and then put down the pen and went on looking at her monitor as if I weren't there.

I tiptoed forward and picked up the pen, leaning over to sign the document. My backpack slid, bumping into my elbow.

"Don't sign that yet," Liz said.

I held the pen poised over the "Employee Signature" line.

"Read it first."

I picked up the document by the stapled corner and flipped to page one. The title was, *Performance Improvement Plan, Level II.*

"Liz, it's a level II. Can she do that? I've never been written up before."

"I don't think so. What's it say?"

The gist of the document talked about needing improved performance and outlined the issue, as typed up by the manager, and then the expected outcome. It also detailed all the things I was ineligible for, including a raise, for ninety days. Knowing Roxanne, she'd use this as an opportunity to skip my annual increase for good for the year. It also meant I was ineligible for transfer, and if I left the organization, I would not be able to cash out my paid time off.

"Do I even have a choice to not sign it?" I asked.

Liz was quiet. She didn't know. I flipped to the last page and began reading. Roxanne cleared her throat.

"Is there a problem?"

"Well," I began, "you said in here, 'employee's disregard for leadership caused major disruption to the productivity of the department.'"

"Yes?"

"I d-don't understand," I squeaked. Fingers of ice plunged into my chest and neck.

She stared at me for a moment over the rim of her reading glasses. She took them off and stood up from her chair. It didn't really help. I was much taller than she was. She never seemed to notice that, though.

"Bitsy, what is your problem? Just sign the paper."

"But," I said and fought back the need to just sign and run away from the confrontation. My stomach roiled.

"*C'mon. You got this,*" Liz said.

"I don't think I was a disruption to the department."

"Bitsy. You"—Roxanne jabbed her finger at me, her head wobbling with the effort— "were a disruption to me." And then she yanked her thumb into her own chest. "And I am the head of the department; therefore, you were a disruption to the department."

I fidgeted, gripping the paper by its staple. I couldn't sign this. This was unfair and unjust. Liz was coiling back for a major strike. I fought against her rage.

"*That stupid bitch! She's going to write us up because of her own ego! This is ridiculous! The only reason she's doing this is because she's pissed you owned the situation.*"

"You don't have a choice, Bitsy. Sign the document."

She yanked the papers from my hands. The jagged points of the staple dug into my finger tip and sliced through the tender flesh. I inhaled through my teeth, awareness sharpened by the jolt of adrenaline. Blood welled up from exposed capillaries. It was my left-hand pointer finger—a crucial finger to a violinist.

Roxanne flipped through the pages and slapped it onto the pile of papers that was the most stable and upright. She pointed to the employee signature line. My finger stung, and a cold anger swept over me. Roxanne had now caused a hindrance to my ability to play.

I held up my finger as blood welled at the cut and dribbled over the next knuckle. I turned my hand toward Roxanne, showing her the cut she'd just given me.

"It's a little cut. Oh, my gosh! You gonna run to Employee Health again?"

A silence seethed between us. She didn't know I played violin and I wasn't going to tell her. I let my hand fall to my side, gripping the knuckles into my palm. The wetness from the blood spread between my fingers. She leaned back as if she'd won.

"Now, sign the damn paper!" she shouted at me. Shouted. And then she laughed as if I was a joke to her.

Liz's anger sang right along with mine. We were one in that moment. The pen in my hand crunched then snapped. Carefully, I lifted the pieces and gently placed them on the papers. Ink ran onto the document, smearing into her signature. Roxanne gaped.

I turned away, my ears ringing, my shoes like cement blocks as I took careful steps out of her office.

"Bitsy! Get back here and sign these." She was scrambling, fighting her way around the clutter of boxes and medical supplies.

Hearing her coming after me released the weight from my feet, and I bolted down the hall, not running but walking faster than I've ever walked. Her feet slapped against the linoleum behind me. Chancing a look, I peered over my shoulder. She was out of sight, thanks to a bend in the hallway. I took a left after five feet, not the way she'd expect. Quietly, I pulled open a stairwell door and jogged up the stairs before the door could close with a clang. Two flights up, I swung through another door, narrowly missing a surgeon entering the stairwell.

He grumbled an insincere, "Excuse me."

A quick right brought me face-to-face with glass doors. I pushed through both sets and was outside on the street under a steady fall of cold rain. The air tasted like wet cement and traffic, the sunlight weakened by the thick down of storm clouds. The percussion of the rain followed me as I dashed up the sidewalk. A bus roared past me. I looked behind me, but no one was there. The bus stopped—thank god it stopped! I climbed the rubber-lined steps and looked around. After feeding the meter two dollars from my pants pocket, I sank into a seat as the bus pulled away from the curb.

I closed my eyes and caught my breath. My hair was wet from my sprint through the rain. The hard plastic chair felt like heaven, and not because it was comfortable but because the gentle rumbling through it meant I was being taken away from that place and that woman. I exhaled and opened my eyes. I pulled a napkin I'd stowed in my pocket and wrapped it around my bleeding finger. I was just settling in for the ride when someone tapped me on the shoulder. I turned.

"Hi," Gabe said.

Could I possibly handle one more surprise today? I inhaled the shock and it stuck in my throat.

Chapter 18

"Um... hi," I said. I straightened in my seat and immediately patted my wet hair. I hadn't even pulled the coat from my backpack. My navy shirt was soaked. I prayed it wasn't evident how cold I was from the rain. Self-consciously, I threw my arms over my chest. "You ride the bus often? I don't think I've ever seen you here."

At the sight of him, Liz began playing a reel of Gabe movies in my head. I unzipped my backpack and yanked my coat from the large pocket, slipping it around me while Gabe's honey-sweet voice chatted away.

"Sometimes." Gabe said. "I'm surprised I haven't seen you. You live on the southeast side of Portland?"

"What?" I said and remembered I hadn't even looked at the bus number; I'd just jumped on board. The digital sign over the seats read Route 20—Burnside/Stark. I groaned. "Oh my gosh." I pressed my fingers into my forehead. My route was 15. I was going south instead of north.

Liz was practically jumping up and down. *"I'm so glad I didn't tell you we were getting on the wrong bus!"*

Gabe tilted his head. He was still wearing his navy EMS garb, and beside him he had a small black duffel bag.

"What's the matter?" he asked.

Squirming with embarrassment, I looked up through my fingers and said, "I got on the wrong bus."

He laughed, warm and throaty and sincere. The sound of his laughter sent a thrill through me.

"Tell ya what. When we get to my stop, get off with me, and I'll give you a ride home."

"Doesn't that defeat the purpose of taking the bus?" I said.

"It's not a problem. I have to head back that direction, anyway." He was lying, of course. But he was lying so he could give me a ride.

Look at you. Catching on pretty quickly, Ms. Bits.

"You wouldn't mind?"

He shook his head.

"Well, thanks. That'd be great." I pulled a stray strand of hair off my face and tucked it behind an ear.

He smiled at me with one corner of his mouth.

"What?" I asked.

"Huh?"

"You were just smiling at me," I pointed out.

"Oh," he said and smiled again, rubbing the back of his neck while his face flushed a pretty shade of red. "Yeah, sorry. I was just—"

"Hahaha! Thinking of having sex with me." Liz laughed.

I couldn't stand her ego. Her bloated sense of accomplishment over having sex with perfect strangers. I reached up and pulled the cord. The rumbling of the bus slowed as it shifted gears.

"On second thought, I need to get home."

"What? Why?" Liz cried.

"I changed my mind. I don't want to do this," I told Liz.

"Oh," he said, looking up at me with angelic blue eyes.

I almost changed my mind again, but the bus was stopping, and I didn't want to turn back from what I'd said.

"You still have my number?" I said. I stood up and pulled the backpack onto my shoulders.

"Bitsy, you don't want to do this, but I do. Let me take over."

"No," I told her flatly. *"I'm not letting you take over and have sex with this guy without knowing him."*

"It's my body, too, Bitsy. How can you deny me this?" Her want surged through me.

"You've had your fun, and you've gotten us in enough trouble for the day."

"Don't blame me for your boss's actions!" Liz said.

"I don't blame you for Roxanne, but if you hadn't interjected, I would have handled the situation without infuriating her off to the point that we might lose so much! You don't think before you act."

"And you think too much," she said.

"I have to practice. I have to get out of that job," I said, desperate for her to agree with me on at least this one point.

She fumed.

"Yeah, I have your number," he said.

Gripping a steel bar, I looked down at him. "You didn't call after the last time I saw you, so I figured you weren't interested in anything but casual sex," I spat.

I pointed out the truth. Weeks had passed. No call. Liz didn't argue.

He looked away from me. The bus stopped, and I shuffled out and onto the street. When the bus pulled away I took out my cell and called Grandma.

We didn't get home until late. My nerves were raw and my finger hurt. I ate the food Grandma had made, helped clean up the kitchen, kissed her on the cheek and retreated to my room. I found a small, round bandage for my finger and carefully placed it over the cut, which had stopped bleeding. If I tried to play with it uncovered, I was sure it'd get blood on my strings.

My violin case was propped in the corner near my nightstand. I pulled it from its cozy resting place and set it on the bed. I pulled the hair tie from around the broken clasp and popped open the other one that was intact. I touched the strings with one hand and grasped the rosin with the other. The bow pulled from the case with soft resistance. As I slid the rosin block over the bowhair, I mentally prepared for the piece I needed to practice.

Outside the window, the darkness of night reigned while rain pattered against the roof. Bow rosined, I lifted the instrument from its case and recalled the first time I held it. I was in grade school. There was a program for underserved kids to get instruments for a discounted price or free. We were so poor; I didn't have to pay a thing. The man had even given it to me without my having to tell my mother first.

The violin was so beautiful to me. The man who brought the instruments, the orchestra teacher and the aide had played a piece of music for the group. I was hooked from that moment on. They brought many stringed instruments into the music room and let us look at all of them, playing them so we could hear what they sounded like at a master's touch, letting us play with them, pluck at the strings, hold them. They wanted me to play cello.

"You have such long arms and legs. You will be perfect for the instrument," the instrument man had told me.

Nothing could do it for me except the violin, though. The complexity of the pieces played, the melody, the violin was for me and me for it.

At first, I didn't think my mother would let me keep it, so I'd hidden it and only played while she was out of the house. I was so often alone; it hadn't been hard to find the time. Or to sneak out in the morning to the bus stop with the instrument. Eventually, my secret was discovered. Luckily, I had practiced so much... I had worked past most of the awkward squeaks and mismatched notes. I couldn't play complex music for a long time, but the sound was more music than racket.

It had been a cold and gray afternoon. I'd finished my homework, and Mom wasn't home yet. I didn't even know where she went. I'd pulled my violin out from under the bed and had set the sheets of music on the small mattress. Most of the kids were still playing the first year music, but I'd advanced so quickly the music teacher had given me the second and third-year books as a Christmas present. Looking back, I realized I owed her a lot for her kindness.

Music had saved me.

That day, I had started playing a song from the third-year book. It was slow and pretty with long notes that made the violin sing. Something magical happens when I play. I am transported from whatever room my body is in to a place of moonlight and stars. I hadn't heard Mother come in. I'd finished the song and was ready to move on to the next one when I heard a shuffle behind me. Turning, I found my mother standing in the doorway, her hazel eyes wide with awe. Not angry, not apathetic, not annoyed. Her face was so soft in that moment. She didn't get everything wrong.

"Oh, baby, that's so beautiful!" She crossed the room.

I stiffened, but she threw her arms around me, even though I flinched. Her hot tears soaked into my hair. She smelled like pot and liquor. When she pulled away she held my shoulders and peered into my eyes, her reddened-hazel eyes wide with admiration. Nothing could have shocked me more. She could have slapped me or pushed me or cut some remark about being a pain in her ass, but admiration? In that moment, I'm not sure I even understood what the look had really meant.

"Can you play it again for me?" she'd asked.

The softness in her voice and the sweetness of her smile had made my heart bloat with love. I'd do anything for her. Anything to make her look that way. I hurriedly flipped the page back and let the notes rise and fall around us.

"That's just lovely, sweetheart," she'd said. "When did you get this?"

"The people at sc-school gave it to me."

I quickly pulled the note from my violin case, the one that certified the instrument was mine. She would think I'd stolen it without the note. She looked over the paper and then handed it back to me.

"I want you to keep playing. Every day and whenever you want. I'll find some way to get you lessons, too. I'll bet there are programs to help. You're gifted, Elizabeth." She'd smiled and then she'd left the room.

Throughout the years, the men came and went, some complaining about the noise, but Mom never abided it. So much other ugliness pervaded my youth, but for the music, she allowed my full participation and gave her full protection.

I touched the bow to the strings in remembrance of her kindness in this one thing. Grateful, I let the music swell inside me. Liz came forward, a light melody on her lips. She sang as I played, our minds melding. Its bright sound washed away the veil between us.

But when another someone tickled on the edges of my consciousness I faltered.

I stopped playing. Liz popped back into the place she always occupied. I listened, looking around as if I would see some other person standing in my room.

"What's the matter, Bits?" Liz asked.

"It's just... It felt as if there was someone else with us."

Liz froze. I could feel her alarm.

"Don't worry. It could have been my imagination."

I wasn't sure that was really true, but now that I'd stopped playing the sensation was gone. I began to play again, feeling tentative, at first, mentally looking around for the other presence that had whispered through us moments before, but soon the music took us over again. Liz relaxed, and we fell into the music. Its touch released us, issuing our escape to that other place of stars and moons and planets... like a dark field of lights. The rush was heaven, the notes transporting us entirely. We were nothing but music, and music was the universe, its secrets open to us, willing their way to us, drawn by the beauty of the notes.

The images flooded through me. Beings of light drifted through the everywhere and the nowhere that enveloped us in the tender notes we played. The angels gathered to listen; to dance and shine. The love emanating from them filled us, making me play faster, harder, more urgently, more passionately. I was a vessel for the light, and it was spilling out of me through the bow and strings. My body was distant and yet prickled with the knowing of light, weak from humility and strong with purpose.

This is what I was made for. Getting lost between the notes and the beyond. This is what I was meant to share with the world. My sense of self and sense of the love that spread through the field of stars and pulsed in the beings of light merged into one, until I knew my integral place in the universe. I knew how my thread tied to my grandmother's, how my mother's choices helped me fulfill my higher purpose. I could have pity and compassion toward her when I was bathed in the light of un-discriminatory love. No being could not be loved. All life was treasured and honored.

At this realization, Liz's awareness yanked away from mine.

The notes faltered and fell. I dropped the bow to the hardwood with a clatter. The room spun in the lamp-lit glow. I sat on the edge of the bed, placing the instrument carefully in the center of the bedspread to avoid it getting damaged. Something dripped from my chin. I swiped at my face and realized I'd been crying. My lungs labored, as though it had been minutes since I'd taken a full breath.

Liz glowered in a dark corner but was otherwise unresponsive. The image of the light beings swam in my mind. The memory of the love was so real; I could hardly bare the weight of it. I clutched at my sweatshirt, wiped away the tears on my face. This new comprehension of the value of life vibrated through me.

A soft knock at the door startled me.

"Come in," I said. I picked up the instrument and stowed it in its case.

Grandma poked her head in, a smile on her face making the apples in her cheeks bob to the surface. Her hair had been done that day, the auburn color fresh and vibrant. She pushed the door open all the way and stood framed in the doorway. She was dressed in slacks and a soft teal and royal blue sweater. Her beaded earrings, which looked like peacocks, swung on her earlobes. Her dark eyes were so bright she looked ten years younger, which was really saying something because she looked good for a woman in her sixties.

"Sugar," she said. "That was the most gorgeous thing I've ever heard in all my life."

I had one week to get myself prepared. Hopefully, I could postpone getting fired until I knew what was happening with the orchestra. Although, after today, I wasn't sure I'd have a job to go back to after my days off.

Liz was grateful for the time away, too, but I sensed her perspective on our days off came with a lurking darkness I couldn't name but knotted my guts with worry.

"Liz, what's going on?"

She resolutely didn't answer me.

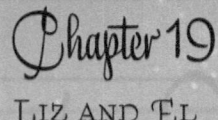

Chapter 19

LIZ AND EL

"*Wake up.*"

The voice was a whisper in a throbbing barrage of dark images. I thrashed in the blankets until I couldn't take the fear pulsing through the nightmare any longer. I jerked upright. Sweat made my nightshirt cling to my back. I covered my face and shoved away the tears.

If only my nightmares were products of imagination.

The center of me caved in to a hollow ache produced by the flashbacks.

"*These things happened to you?*" El asked.

My legs and arms ached and that wasn't all that hurt. True story: remembering the trauma often made my body re-feel the physical pain in all the places on my body that had suffered. Sometimes, I wished I could be Bitsy and not remember.

"*Yes. These things happened,*" I answered El, embarrassed to have shown some other somebody the reality of my past. "*God, you watched that shit? Can't you—like—turn away or something?*"

"*It would not seem so,*" El said. Her voice was raw and full of pity. "*I am so sorry this happened to you.*"

"*Don't be. Let's go help some other poor kid who's going through this,*" I said. There was certainly nothing I could do to ease my own pain, what with Grams holding out on information. I pulled the cover off, slipped quietly out of bed and started getting dressed.

"You remember the faces of the ones we will protect tonight?" El asked.

"Yes, ma'am," I said, pulling the image of the children up in the forefront of my mind.

"Very good," El said.

"But I don't understand, why are you doing this? Why not just search for the guy who killed your daughter?" I asked.

"I think the Hound is trying." She paused, seemingly in thought. *"I was drawn to you because we are alike in purpose. The Hound was drawn to the dog for the same reason,"* she said.

"So, you think the murderer might have taken up residence with a child rapist on this planet." I finished her train of thought.

"I do. Which means the scent is gone. All that remains is our energy. If we continue hunting child rapists who have murdered their victims or might, perhaps we will come closer to the one we seek."

It made sense to start there. And to start with people in our small corner of the world. El, Maltheron and the Hound had showed up in Portland. Aerylia's murderer must be close as well. Still: there could be hundreds of men to fit the bill—which was a bone-chilling thought. The task seemed like looking for a needle in a haystack, but it was all we had. The only upshot was that we could dispatch these monsters who hurt innocents while we hunted for El's bad guy.

After hurriedly throwing on warm, dark clothes, I tiptoed out of the house. On the porch, I faced the night sky. *"Okay,"* I said to El, *"it said in the report the brother and sister were released back to the mom. They're on the southeast end of Portland, closer to Gresham."*

El never actually spoke English. She spoke something foreign, but it somehow made sense in my head. *"We are looking for a different address. Last time we found the red-haired man with a focus on your anger for what you personally witnessed. Since we do not have that experience to draw from, we will need help.*"

"Help?" I asked.

Inside my mind, I saw El cup a slender hand around her mouth, draw in air—which really seemed odd to me since this was her soul I was looking at and not her body—and sing three long, sweet notes. The bell-like quality of her voice in my head sent shivers down my neck. I opened my mouth to ask what she was doing but was interrupted by a shift in the darkness down the house-lined street. Four bluish lights dislodged from the twinkling of rain against the streetlights, swiveled and bounded toward us.

When the Hound was within throwing distance and wasn't stopping, I tried to scream. Instead, I found my hand covering my throat and all the sound lodged between my chest and my mouth. I gave up on voicing my fear. El looked at the Hound, flicked a hand his direction, one word yanking out of my throat. The Hound stopped and sat on his haunches, his eyes fixed on me.

OhgodOhgodOhgodOhgod... My heart hammered against my ribs.

He looked like no dog I'd ever seen. "*That thing is scary as hell,*" I said to El. There was a dog in there. Under the shadow of the creature that had attached itself to it. A little Shiba Inu with light fur. If I could think of dogs as cute and not with gleaming canines ready to rip into my flesh and tear at my skin, this dog would be a cute dog.

But not the creature. El had been right. Corey had drawn the thing so accurately; I understood now why I had been frightened at the sight of a mere sketch. What I couldn't see from the sketch was the odd coloration of the Hound. The slits of nostrils stretched up the side of the elongated snout and revealed purplish flesh that flared in my general direction, catching my scent. Its long, slender tongue lolled from its mouth, the same purplish hue as the nostril flesh. Its fur was blondish except for the large ruff, which shifted from black to brown to gray.

"The Hound is a fierce creature, bred for its loyalty to its family. I should have listened to my daughter. She'd asked to take the Hound with her into the fields." Her voice halted and I could hear the gut-wrenching regret drip from her voice when she continued. *"I told her no because I needed the Hound for myself."*

I suffered an overdose of empathy for this mother who'd lost her child. Of course she would blame herself. It's what most moms did when some horror happened upon their children.

"Hey, listen, now. You didn't know. If you'd have known, of course you would have sent the Hound. Nobody can ever guess a person could do something so awful to another living being. You couldn't have known that."

The little Shiba Inu wagged at me and shuffled back a step.

El was quiet, but I sensed all her sorrow staining the silence, her guilt palpable in my mind. No matter what I said, she would always wonder if she had done things a little differently, would her daughter be alive now.

"Thank you for your kindness. No matter how you look at it, I failed to protect my daughter. I won't fail her again in the afterlife. I will see her murderer put down for his crimes."

Without further notice, El pushed me toward the Hound, lifting one of my hands to stroke its shadowy fur. I squealed and pulled away. She allowed my hand to retract, even while the Hound stretched its snout toward me.

"Perhaps I brought this on her with my thoughts as well," she began, rubbing my hands together as they fought to stay away from the creature standing in front of me. *"She would have been a Queen Maker. I dreaded that future for her."*

"Why?" I asked. "Aren't you elevated above other women? I mean, you're royalty, right? Pampered."

"It's true my duties afford me a life of financial ease, free of those stresses, but it does not mean I do not know pain and sorrow. See for yourself."

The street in front of me spun, dropping away to a world of bluish light. I was lost, caught up in a whirlwind of pictures, colors, scents, sensations that were not mine, and yet, somehow they were.

El was young when her mother died, and she was alone with a father who neither cared for her nor valued her. Not until she began to bleed. She hid the blood of her cycle for several moons, afraid all the stories were true, and she'd have to face them. She imagined what it would be like, and her fear grew. And then her father discovered what she was and that she'd been hiding it from him. He'd hit her. Not just once, but he was careful to avoid her face and stayed his hand so as not to damage her when he presented her to the priests and priestesses of Life-Giving.

She was only fifteen. I shuddered as she showed me the scene. During the full of her moon and the full of her cycle, the priestesses dressed her ceremonially in scarlet robes and a wide violet belt and presented her to the priest of the full moon. There was a priest for every stage of the moon. The Full Moon was a young man but still years older than she was. A decade, maybe more. He had hurt her. He had hurt her so badly. And the initiation was only the beginning. After the full of her cycle, he came to her again, and again and again until she conceived. Her first child was sacrificed to the temple. He would grow up to become a priest. Like his father. Oh, certainly, she was elevated, pampered, protected.

"Prisoner," El said.

The single word snapped through my nervous system as the rape scenes and forced matings closed in my mind.

"Do not think that because a person has a different station than you that they are excluded from suffering," she told me, her voice a soft snap of retribution.

"I'm sorry," I said, after the last of the images faded away. *"I didn't know."*

"That's just it," she said. *"You cannot know another person's journey. But you can most assuredly assume they've suffered in some way. That is a part of life. That is a part of existing and part of what brings us together as sentient beings. And that is why we must dispatch this evil with compassion. With reverence for the idea these who have done the most heinous crimes against children have also suffered. And that the kindest thing to do for all of life is to end the cycle of violence in order to perpetuate love."*

"Sure, sure," I said, not totally convinced she made perfect sense. *"So, what's the plan with the big, scary dog thing?"*

The dog thing, it turned out, could sniff out the predator from the sample we'd stolen from the assault kit. I pulled the backpack from my shoulders and set it softly on the wooden slats of the front porch. Kneeling down, I dug to the bottom of the inner pocket and pulled out the evidence envelopes. Somewhere in the distance, a siren sounded. I ripped the tops of both envelopes at once.

The Hound was already sampling the air intently. The Shiba Inu scrabbled up one of the porch stairs to get closer. I pushed myself away from the dog, grateful for the backpack impeding its path toward me. My arms yanked into my body in a defensive posture. A hot poker stabbed down my left arm. My vision wobbled.

"Calm yourself, Liz," El said.

With her words came some deeper power that reverberated through my body.

Her command had the same effect on me as a shot of bourbon. The warmth of the reassurance relaxed my anxiety. My heart rate dropped to normal again. The pain in my chest and arm subsided.

"*Breathe, my friend,*" she said.

I obeyed her command, inhaling and exhaling the crisp night air. Once I stopped shaking, I leaned forward again and held out the envelopes to the dog and the larger beast. The Hound seemed to expand as it sniffed the packages. Once it was done smelling, it locked eyes with me.

"*He is ready,*" El said. "*We will access the location of the perpetrator through the hall of doors. Please take us into the nether, Liz.*"

I dropped into it more easily this time, ready to distance myself from the dog. I wasn't prepared for the dog and Hound coming with me. But in the vastness of the universe surrounding us, my fear was intangible, if it existed at all.

In this place, the four entities occupying two bodies were separated as individuals. The Shiba Inu looked more like a white wolf than just a dog. The Hound remained the same, its bear-like body as large as in the real world, with a ruff of dark shifting shadow, four blue eyes, elongated snout and lolling, slender tongue.

The doors misted into existence on either side of the four of us. The Hound lumbered along the corridor, occasionally pausing at a door to smell it more thoroughly.

"Liz, you have armed yourself with Maltheron?" Beside me, El only had eyes for the hunting Hound, her honey-colored hair and alien features more beautiful than I'd noticed before. The reddish glow emanating from her center throbbed like a heartbeat.

"Uh—" I began. In fact, my hand still clasped the evidence envelopes.

Maltheron was in the backpack.

"It is okay," she said, "you will simply need to split your consciousness and reach for the dagger."

"Oh, sure, yeah, just split my consciousness. No problem," I complained.

Around me, stars blazed, planets twirled, comets whizzed by. The hall of doors streamed past us, led by the ever-hunting snout of the Hound.

"You can do this," she said and took my hand in hers. "I will keep you tethered here. With your other hand, feel the envelopes, place them back into the backpack and reach for Maltheron."

Back in the world, I brought awareness to my hand. The sensation of being half in the ether and half in reality caused an uneasy moment of vertigo. I clasped El tighter with one hand as I reached the other into the folds of the backpack. My eyes were still locked onto the ether. I had the odd sensation my hand was the only thing existing in the real world. I pictured a hand reaching out of nothing and plunging into the backpack. The slick material grazed my searching fingers as I dropped the envelopes and reached for Maltheron.

I curled my fingers around the hilt and was rewarded with the soft hum of Maltheron's greeting. El pulled at my hand, and with a soft pop, I was fully in the ether once again, one hand in El's and the other gripping the blade.

The corridor stopped moving as the Hound sat on its haunches at one of the many doors. He turned his odd, huge head toward us and growled. The Shiba Inu at the Hound's side yipped at the door.

"We are here," El said.

She let go of my hand as we turned to the door. I gripped Maltheron more tightly. The door was one of those pressboard things—flimsy and dark with a brass knob. The molding framing the door was the same color of wood but had been scratched at by an animal. As I reached for the handle, another entity appeared at my feet, which now stood in thick carpet, muddled in browns and beiges.

The orange tabby cat hissed at the door. I bent and stroked its fur. It looked up at me with sage-green eyes, pleading, then turned back to the door and growled, deep in its throat. On the other side of the door, a soft whimper barely permeated the thin wood.

Real rage ignited an instant bonfire inside me. El's throbbing red light expanded to consume all of her being. She stepped into me as I turned the knob and opened up to a child's nightmare.

The worst part was seeing the abuse happen real-time. The best part was catching the perpetrator in the act.

The room was small but sweet. Toys were neatly put away in bins on one wall. A dresser was on the other. Pink flower stickers decorated the upper third of the walls against a background of light purple. But this was all a blur to what was happening on the white and purple bedspread.

I knew from the chart the girl was eight. She was sitting on the edge of the bed. He was standing in front of her with one knee resting on the mattress, so he half-straddled her legs. I could smell his sex and her unearned shame. I heard his voice, gasping with pleasure, and saw the silent tears slide down her cheeks. At least she was crying. At least she hadn't gone numb yet.

He didn't even turn at the door opening. Not until I shoved it fully open and it banged against the doorstop with a wobbling thunk. The girl pulled away, eyes wide and red, and scuttled into the corner of her bed. The man turned, the drowse of pleasure and control quickly evaporating from his eyes. His underwear was shoved down to his hips. His penis was out. I looked at it. It still glistened with wetness.

The girl stared at us, wiping at her mouth and trembling.

"Close your eyes. Plug your ears and sing a song," I told the girl.

The cat dashed past me, leaped onto the bed and into the girl's lap, looked at the man and hissed, growled and spat at him.

At this point, several things happened simultaneously. The man yelled and lurched.

"Who the fuck are you?" he said. He was a slight man. Small and wiry. His hair was a nondescript color of brown, and his eyes seemed to match, although lost under the thickness of the glasses through which he looked at us. And then looked past us, seeing a swirling, endless expanse of stars outside the bedroom door. His mouth gaped as real, confused fear crossed his face.

There was a gray, button-up shirt slung over the edge of the bed that had an embroidered nametag on it. It matched the name in the charts that accused the man of his crime. Yet, here Chad was, molesting this poor kid once again.

For her, the nightmare would end now.

No more. It was as if every victim the worldwide cried out to me to do something about this. To assert some justice for all of the injustice heaped upon innocent women and children. To stand, rather than cower in fear. And I would. I gladly would.

The girl squeezed her eyes tightly as she shoved fingers into her ears. "Amazing grace. How sweet the sound," she sang.

The cat hissed again. The Hound squeezed into the room beside me. I reached behind and pushed the door closed. The man looked at the dog and flinched in fear. Could he see the Hound?

I gripped Maltheron as the hunger rose inside me. Maltheron's music joined the girl's music in an odd harmony that gave the religious tune a steel edge. El began to chant, and the words no longer only echoed in my mind but found their way into the girl's tiny room.

"See the pain. Feel the pain. Be the pain. See the pain. Feel the pain. Be the pain." The words cut a steady rhythm to the haunting harmony and sweet notes of Amazing Grace.

The man clapped his hands around his throat as his eyes went out of focus. A bright spot between his eyes blazed orange. Farther down on his chest, a golden light gradually glowed brighter, illuminating the cords that bound him to his victims. They squirmed like black worms. The man fell to his knees as the rhythm and tune gained momentum.

"I once was lost, but now I'm found," the girl sang. Her voice trembled and broke.

Chad sobbed. He was seeing the pain he'd inflicted. As if called forward by his memory, images ghosted into the room to stand around the child molester. When the crowd of children was close to two dozen and the room was thick with the energy of past victims, I opened my hand to Maltheron. My guts caved at the sheer number of children the man had assaulted.

"Please," Chad moaned, "make it end. Make it stop. I'm so sorry."

I stopped chanting. Maltheron's song droned on and on, gaining in volume as the girl's singing rose to a crescendo.

"Was blind, but now, I see."

Chad lifted a hand toward us in supplication. Maltheron flew from my hand to Chad's. Chad regarded the dagger as if it were the answer to every prayer he'd ever uttered. Maybe it was. The ghosts of his past victims looked on with apathy, their faces drawn and tired and scarred. Relief washed over Chad's face, a smile lighting his haunted features as he plunged the knife deeply and firmly into his own carotid artery, cutting through the many strands of dark energy he'd woven with his acts.

"Wish granted," I said and watched with growing

fascination as the blood leaped from his body and soaked into the multicolored carpet.

Chad went down with a crash. The girl on the bed jumped, screamed and then slumped. The Hound threw back his head and howled.

"*This was not the man who killed my child,*" El said, a little sadly.

"Oh my god," I said. "Is the girl okay?"

"*She is stunned. She will be out for a while. When she wakes the memories will only be faint,*" El said.

"Only faint?" I said. "I thought they would be gone."

"*Given the circumstances, she will not be able to avoid remembering some of it.*"

"Why the hell not?" I asked.

"*The horror of a man killing himself in her room is one that must be explained by way of his guilt.*"

"Why didn't you tell me this beforehand?" I asked. "I could have moved him or something."

"*That would have been best, but we had no time for such shifts in the plan.*"

"This wasn't part of the deal," I said, heating up. "The deal was: bad guy dies; good guy-slash-girl gets the break."

"*And she will, but not completely, as with the last victim.*"

"Goddammit, El. Next time, why don't you read me the fine print before I sign my name to a contract?"

I looked at the girl on the bed. The cat was still curled in her lap and had taken up purring loudly. I looked at the dead guy on the ground. There was so much blood in the carpet.

"*I am sorry it happened this way,*" El said, "*but, surely you are happy there is one less molester to perpetuate his crime.*"

"I'm happy. I'm fucking ecstatic. I just thought this would be a clean slate for her and her brother."

"*It is mostly clean,*" El said.

I gave up. "Fine," I started. I would have finished my

thought with a question. Something that went like, what do we do with this body to keep the girl from waking up to yet another horror scene, but I heard a sound somewhere down the hall.

"Cammie? Sweetie? Are you having nightmares again?"

The voice grew louder, footsteps sounded off down the carpeted hall. Stupid woman. How could she bring her daughter back into the house of a monster? For a fleeting moment, I considered if the mother was as guilty as Chad.

"*We must go,*" El said.

I grabbed Maltheron from the blood-soaked carpet, fascinated as a false knife appeared in Chad's grasp, complete with blood.

I leaped past the Hound and faced the closed door. The footsteps were close. I had mere seconds before I would be caught. I focused intently and urgently on the ether. A hush against the door signaled the woman's hand resting on the pressboard. I clutched the knob and twisted. When I opened the door there was no woman, only the vastness of eternity. I stepped into the stars. The Hound and Shiba Inu darted past me across the threshold as I closed the door behind me.

As if from a great distance, a woman's scream reverberated on the other side of the door.

Chapter 20

BITSY, TWO DAYS LATER

I'd had a glorious three days away from work, and I still had two more to go. I woke up with sunshine spilling in through the little window. It was late. The digital clock shone dully in the full light of day, reading 11:00 a.m. I lifted the cover and winced. My arms burned from the effort. I rose from the bed, feeling muscles in my stomach and back I didn't know existed.

"*Liz, did you work out again last night?*" I asked. Wasn't two days in a row enough? I was tired of waking up sore.

"*Sorry, Bits. I couldn't sleep. I had to get out the energy,*" she told me.

Something about her words nagged at me. If she were using our voice, it would be hoarse.

"*Are you okay?*" I asked, thinking she sounded rattled. I poked around, feeling for her memories, and came up with nothing—not even her supposed workout. "*Liz, did you go to that club again?*"

"*No. I didn't,*" she said tersely. "*Listen, while you were sleeping soundly, I was having nightmares. So if you don't mind, I'm tapping out.*"

And she was gone.

I stumbled down the stairs and was greeted by the smell

of coffee. Grandma rounded the corner out of the kitchen and came into the dining room.

"You're up. I thought you were going to sleep the day away. I switched over the laundry you had in the washer," she told me.

Problem was, I hadn't put anything into the washer.

"Thanks, Grandma," I said. So, Liz was up late, working out and doing laundry?

"You want to go into town today? I need to go to the library," she asked.

"Sounds awesome," I said.

"Grab some breakfast, then, and get dressed and we'll get going."

Grandma had made sausage links and pumpkin waffles. The cinnamon and nutmeg still hung in the air, pairing with the warm, rich scent of sausage. She'd left the food on the stove. I loaded my plate and sat at the dining table while Grandma filled her coffee cup then joined me. I plopped my phone on the table next to my plate. The light was blinking orange, indicating I had a text message. It was probably Corey, making sure I was coming over tonight for my performance.

I shoveled a bit of waffle into my mouth and chewed. Man, my throat was even sore. I went into the kitchen, grabbed a glass of orange juice and returned to the table. Grandma had the morning paper on the table.

"What's news?" I asked, peering across the table to the front page she read from.

"Well," she said, after scanning the page for a minute. "The last two weeks there's been a string of suicides. Can't say I feel too bad for them. Every last one of them was suspected of rape or child molestation." She looked up at me, watching me for a reaction.

My stomach squeezed then squirmed. "Uh... that's odd," I said.

"Today, they're saying the profiles of the suicide victims and the manner of their suicides are all too similar."

Liz crept into my consciousness, listening and watching.

"So they're thinking these might be murders made to look like suicides. Now everyone is going out of their minds." She chuckled. "Lots of people are writing in, saying they hope if it is murder, the vigilante keeps on going. 'Course the cops disagree."

She kept reading while my eardrums throbbed.

"Liz, why do I suddenly feel guilty?" I asked.

"Probably because you agree with the people writing in. You know the world is better off without these sickos," she said.

"But killing to make something right?" I asked. *"Can you imagine having all that blood on your hands?"*

"But it's not on your hands. So just enjoy the fact that the monsters are dying."

Happy and with new books, I unloaded my burden onto the bed and checked my texts. Corey had messaged again.

COREY:

You ready?

I typed out a quick response.

Yup. Just gathering my violin. Um...
should I dress up or something?

COREY:

Lol! No. Just be comfortable.

I glanced down at myself and decided I looked fine. Actually, I'd sort of dressed up today. I wore leggings and a nice purple sweater. Even Grandma had commented that I looked good. And a guy had winked at me in the library.

I grabbed my violin and headed down the stairs.

Corey beat me. He was in the door and greeting Grandma with a long-armed hug. "Hey, Gramma. When are you going to invite me over for more chicken-fried steak?"

Grandma giggled. "Well, now I know that you've been craving it, why don't we make it next week?" She really was a sucker for anyone who loved her cooking. Which was everyone because she was an amazing cook.

"Yes," Corey said in triumph. "It's a date."

"Oh, Bitsy," Grandma said as I made my way to them. "Corey's been invited for dinner next week for chicken-fried steak. Maybe we could schedule it for after your audition."

"Sounds amazing. Do we get g-gr-gravy, too?" It's not as if she splurged on fried foods all the time. And gravy was a treat.

"Of course, darlin'. It wouldn't be chicken-fried steak without gravy," she said. "Okay, now, y'all get going. I don't want your mama waiting for you to serve supper."

"Yes, ma'am," Corey said. He hugged Grandma again and kissed her on the forehead. "Gramma, you smell so good."

"Well, thank you, sugar," she said as she pulled away, giggling.

"Quit sweet-talking Grandma. She already promised you chicken-fried steak. What else do you want?" I asked.

He leaned toward me, covered his mouth with one hand and whispered loudly. "I was going for the apricot pies for dessert."

"Now, don't press your luck," Grandma said, shaking a finger admonishingly toward him. "But if Elizabeth gets the open chair for the orchestra, there just might be something sweet to celebrate." She winked at him.

Corey's jaw dropped, his eyes threatening to pop out of his head. He gasped in air. "Don't you tease me, Gramma. You mean it?"

"Well, we'll just have to see, won't we?"

He turned to me. "Bitsy. This is serious. The fate of my sweet tooth hangs in the balance of your performance. You must get that position."

"G-g-grandma. Didn't I tell you? He'll just keep coming around if you keep feeding him."

Grandma laughed. "All right, now, y'all shoo. Go have fun. Play something nice for them, Bitsy."

I gave her a squeeze and we were out the door.

Dinner at Corey's family's house was a fun affair. His mom wasn't a bad cook; the salmon on cedar plank was moist and flavorful with just the right amount of dill and lemon.

Gina sipped her wine and looked at Corey. "How's school going?"

Corey cleared his throat and wiped his mouth with a napkin before answering. "Uh, well, English went really well. And my elective art course is going great. Anatomy and physiology are a little more torture than I'd planned."

Jon propped an elbow on the table and looked at his son. "Aw, that's all right kiddo. Just keep plugging away. You'll get it." Jon was a bottle deep, but he was such a sweet guy, his buzz made him funny.

Corey had his hands under the table. His shoulders squeezed into his chest, folding down and making himself smaller. "Well, maybe," he said quietly.

His mom had a steely green gaze that she'd locked on her son since he'd started speaking. She set down her wineglass and glanced at me, then at Abigail, who still nibbled at her Brussel sprouts. Strangest kid I'd ever seen. She liked math and Brussel sprouts. I was pretty sure that was an algorithm for determining if a child was an alien.

"I'm sensing some reluctance on your courses," Gina said.

"Honey, he's fine," Jon said. "Just let him work it out. He'll be okay. Right, Corey?"

I felt I'd wandered into an awkward conversation for a friend to be witnessing. And yet, I knew Corey needed to change his major to what he loved and not what would make the paycheck. I thought for a moment while Corey struggled.

"The thing is..." Corey began. "You know, I'm just not a hundred percent sure... I mean I don't know if..."

His mom's eyebrows had reached the point of no return, having retreated halfway up her forehead. Her green eyes popped with color against her pale skin.

"Hon," Jon said, "let it go. We'll talk about it later." He reached over and put his giant hand onto his wife's.

She swiveled her gaze to him, and he withered, pulling his hand away as if her skin burned him.

"I just don't know if I'm cut out to be a nurse," Corey blurted.

He'd spoken while his mom's gaze was diverted, no doubt the only way he could work up the courage to tell them the truth.

My jaw dropped. I quickly snapped it closed again and tried disappearing. It didn't work.

"*Go, Corey,*" Liz said. "*I thought it'd take him another year to say that.*"

"*Show's not over yet,*" I said.

"Well, then, do something about it," Liz urged.

Gina inhaled around an oncoming barrage of reasons why Corey needed to stay true to his original course, but before the assault could fire a single shot, I spoke up.

"Oh, g-g-gosh," I said. I made sure I really emphasized my voice and clanked my phone on the table to capture everyone's attention. "Is it really 7:30 already? Abigail, when's your bedtime?"

"Eight," she said, but her eyes still volleyed between her mother and her big brother.

Her mother looked at me, then at Abigail.

"Would you guys mind if I went ahead and played now? I'd hate for Abigail to miss it because she has to get ready for bed," I said.

"Yeah, I want to hear Bitsy play," Abigail said.

"Oh, sure," Jon said, throwing his hands into the air as if in celebration. "Yeah, we'd hate for Abi to miss out. Let's go into the living room. Hon', I'll do the dishes after Corey and Bitsy leave."

Gina crossed her arms and leveled her husband with that wicked gaze she had.

"Gotta give it to him; he's not even flinching," Liz said.

Gina looked over at me, and I smiled as brightly as I knew how, hoping it wasn't obviously fake. Corey was gripping the edge of the table and looking between me and his mother, like a deer caught in the headlights.

Gina exhaled, long and loud. "That's a good point, Bitsy." She smiled at me, but I felt only most of it was sincere.

"Please. We'd hate for Abigail to miss the performance," Gina added.

Corey slumped, obviously relieved. Gina stood and turned toward the wine rack in the kitchen to refill her glass. While her back was turned, Jon caught my eye, mimed wiping sweat from his brow then grinned and winked at me. I winked back, stifling a giggle.

"All right, my dear, may I escort you to the auditorium for this evening's entertainment?" Jon offered a hand to his daughter.

She grabbed it and pulled on him.

He pulled out of the chair with a groan. "Good golly, you're strong."

Abigail giggled.

He pulled the wheelchair from the table and eased it backward down the ramp and into the sunken living room. He wheeled her close to a recliner and leaned over. "You want to sit in the chair or the recliner?"

"Recliner, please," she said.

"All righty. You know the routine. Hug my neck," Jon said as he knelt in front of the chair and leaned into his daughter. This was easy now. What would it be like in ten years when she was grown? Would she take after her dad in height?

Jon set her down gently into the recliner and moved the wheelchair out of the way. Gina came into the living room with two glasses of wine. I sat at the edge of the sunken living room and opened my violin case. I pulled out the bow and rosined it while everyone got settled. Corey took the recliner next to his sister, away from his parents, who occupied the couch.

I plucked at the violin strings and tuned it. Then I warmed to some scales. Abigail gasped, covering her mouth with her hands and looking at Corey with glee in her eyes. I laughed.

"That's just a scale, Abigail," Corey said.

"But it's so pretty," she said.

"You've never heard a violin before?" Corey asked.

"Not in real life," she exclaimed.

"Your first concert?" I asked.

She nodded.

"I am honored for the privilege to play for you." It was true. I was honored.

Once I was satisfied with the sound the violin made, I stood on the edge of the living room, tucked the instrument under my chin and pulled the bow across the strings. At first, the music seemed too loud for the little living room. And I was too small to stand so tall in front of these people. But the music always had its way with me. Before the second stanza, it took me over.

I had a habit of closing my eyes when this happened. I didn't watch the audience. I didn't consider if they would like the music. I didn't worry about rejection. I just played. Everything in my being was perfectly attuned to the process of playing music. My arms were strong, my ears were keen, my fingers were nimble. There could be no self-doubt, because self had nothing to do with what happened between me and the music. I was simply its instrument.

When I pulled the bow through the last notes and let them linger in the air, I finally opened my eyes.

Gina had a smile that looked like it'd last for days.

Abigail clapped and squealed. "Bavo!" she said.

Corey had a hand over his heart while his mouth hung open.

Jon wiped a tear from his eye. "What piece was that?" Jon asked.

"Oh," I said, "sorry, I should have introduced it first. Um... performing Moonlight, by Elizabeth Varret, performed by Elizabeth Varret." I smiled at them.

"That was so pretty," Abigail said, still clapping lightly.

I stowed my violin quickly and ran to her recliner. I knelt down next to the armrest and leaned over to her.

"Was it okay for your first concert?" I asked.

She threw her arms around me, startling me with her strength,

"It was perfect in every way," she said, her words muffled against my neck. Stunned, I sat there for a moment until the appropriate response came to me, and I wrapped my arm around her. She was warm, and I could feel her heartbeat. In that moment, I would do anything to protect this tiny thing. At this proximity, I could sense her innocence and emotions. What she'd been through had been so trying, had been so difficult. I wished I could take it all away for her.

"Bitsy! That was the most beautiful performance. I mean it. You have nothing to worry about. You'll get the job," Gina said, still smiling with eyes lit and gleaming.

"You are magical," said a voice but it wasn't Liz's.

"Who is this?" I asked as ice snaked down my spine.

"I said, you're magical, Bits. It's freaking amazing," Liz said.

Relieved, I let the paranoia slip away from me. *"Man, I thought that was another voice for a second there."*

"Nope. Just me," Liz said.

Jon opened his mouth to say something else, but as if in chorus, four digital alarms rang from various points in the house. I looked toward the dining room table at the source for two of them. I patted Abigail's back and slid from her embrace. Walking to the table seemed like walking through sludge. I moved in slow motion. I picked up my phone from the dining table as Corey reached for his. The phones screamed at us, out of sync, creating a wild cacophony that set my nerves on edge. A prickling sensation throbbed around the crown of my head, sending a wave of dizziness through me.

From behind me, I heard Gina's voice read the words flashing on my screen.

"Oh, god. It's an Amber alert. From Gresham. Again." She gasped. "Jon, look."

I swiveled, looking at the couple, and quickly swiped my

phone to turn off the alarm. Jon's eyes went wide. He still had tear tracks on his cheeks.

"Michelle Clarke. Age eight. African American. Black hair. Brown eyes. Emma Johnson, Age nine. Caucasian. Blond hair. Blue eyes. Last seen at school yesterday. Yesterday? Why did they wait to call the alert?"

"Michelle and Emma? Like from my class?" Abigail asked. "Mom, is that Michelle and Emma from my class? What's an Amber alert?"

Nobody answered her. I lowered myself to a dining room chair and tried to dispel the sense of panic spreading through me. It wasn't as if I knew the girls. Why was I feeling so much from this? The room grew claustrophobic. The warmth and light all pressed down on me.

"Excuse me," I said, "I j-j-just need some fresh air."

I pulled myself out of the chair and crossed the living room. Behind me, I could hear Gina starting a conversation with Abigail. An explanation. Corey went to his little sister, scooping her into his lap and settling in the recliner with her.

"Honey, it sounds like your friends may be missing. Did you see them at school yesterday?"

"Missing?" Abigail squeaked. "Like, kidnapped?"

"They don't know for sure, hon," Jon said. "But maybe if you can remember anything, it could help the police find them."

"I—" Abigail said.

I opened the door. Gina's phone rang, and she answered it.

"She was in class. I think I saw them getting on the bus together after school," Abigail said.

"Hello?" Gina said into her phone.

I walked onto the front porch and closed the door behind me. The air was cold and slapped awareness back into the drowse threatening to take me over.

"Bits. What do you see?" Liz asked.

I gulped in air, gripped the railing on the porch, and closed my eyes to concentrate. As if on command, the images flashed through my mind's eye.

"*A bus. I see a bus,*" I said. "*And there's this dog. It keeps crossing my mind's vision.*" The dog was important. I'd seen it before, but I couldn't place where or when.

Liz got quiet. There was a silent wrestling match in my mind as some other something tried to rise to the surface. Liz's awareness swelled within me, and the other something slipped away from me.

"Queen Maker," I said, formally. *Maltheron said. Tonight I was the man Maltheron. The room opened up to the outside world. Aerylia lounged in a corner of the room with the Hound, absently patting the dark, multicolored ruff of fur as she watched me approach her mother with a stranger in tow.*

The man at my side walked more slowly as we approached our Queen Maker, his blue eyes wide in apparent fear. He knew what was coming.

"This is Golen, this year's grower of green vegetables," I said.

Elada looked at the man with dissecting eyes, the blue aura that floated around her drawing close to her body as she read the man to discover his crime. I recognized the behavior of her aura after years of serving her. I was humbled to be her husband.

Golen was here because there was a rumor he was growing fruit in a portion of his fields instead of vegetables. Elada tilted her head up and looked at Golen down the length of her nose.

"You know it is unlawful to grow anything in your fields that has not been assigned to you. Why did you grow the fruit?" So it had been true.

"Queen Maker," Golen began, "please forgive me. My wife. She loves the fruit. It's only a small plant. Nothing more than that." Again, Elada regarded Golen, reading if what he said was true.

"He's telling the truth, Mother," Aerylia said from the corner.

"Child," Elada said patiently, "I asked you to stay silent. If you cannot obey me, you must leave."

"I'll be quiet," Aerylia said through tight lips. "But, he's still telling the truth."

Elada sent a reproachful look at Aerylia and then turned back to Golen. "Please approach me."

I put a hand against Golen's back and pushed him forward to meet my wife. Elada reached forward with a slender white hand, her long fingers extended toward the man's forehead.

"You must understand why it is important for us to abide by the law," she said and stroked the man's forehead with an outstretched finger.

Golen gasped and fell to his knees, his blue eyes no doubt searching through a truth that my wife had opened inside his mind.

Everyone had a role to fill in our region in order to ensure there was enough of each type of food we needed. To ignore the year's assignment was to put the region in jeopardy. Perhaps it was just one plant. But, if the Queen Maker did not strictly enforce the law, one plant would become two and two would become a garden and then there would not be enough food to share at harvest.

"I understand now, Queen Maker." Golen bowed his head, shaking it slowly.

"Very well," Elada said. "You know what you must do. Pull the plant, but harvest the fruit first so you do not waste it."

"Yes, Queen Maker," Golen said.

I helped Golen to his feet and started to back away, my hand held firmly under Golen's arm.

"And Golen," Elada said. He looked up at her. "Whenever your wife wants the fruit, you may come to Maltheron. He will supply you with a small portion from our private garden."

Golen's face softened and then he smiled. "Queen Maker. You are too generous. My wife and I thank you for your grace."

Annoyance was the mood for the evening. I shucked the pajamas Bitsy had put on and dressed in black clothes and gloves, hat, scarf, the whole outdoors outfit. I slipped out of the house with no more noise than a squeaky stair. Grandma went on snoring while I closed the front door and locked it behind me. Slipping the backpack over my shoulders, I called on El. I was getting good at this.

"What the hell was that about tonight?" I asked once El had surfaced.

The night air was wet and cold. The moon was hidden behind a perfectly solid layer of gray clouds. I rubbed my hands together, feeling the warmth through the fabric.

"Bitsy saw the dog. The dog is hunting Aerylia's murderer. The two must be related. I think Bitsy can help us."

"Whoa, whoa, whoa. Absolutely not! Bitsy would never go for this."

"That is the very reason I would think she would 'go for this.'"

"No, things are too clear-cut good and evil for Bitsy. She wouldn't see what we're doing as a means to accomplish a positive end. Only murder." Ohhh... I didn't like saying that word. It sat wrong in my guts, made them squirm. Was I a murderer?

"This is not murder. This is ending cycles that have gone on for too long."

"Whatever, lady. Just tell me what we're doing now, and please don't ever bring Bitsy into this. She will not see it like you and I do."

"Very well." She paused, as if gathering her thoughts. *"Let us call the Hound and see if we can connect the missing girls with the images in Bitsy's vision."*

"That makes sense to me," I said and waited.

El did that strange call, an eerie set of three notes that rang out like a struck bell. I braced myself for the appearance of the Hound. It had gotten easier the last few nights, but it still scared the bejesus out of me when it made sudden movements. I watched up the street for it to appear, the little Shiba Inu trotting along in the massive shadow of the wolfish-bearish beast.

We waited for five minutes, but the dog and creature never arrived.

"What gives? Where's the Hound?" I asked.

"I-I do not know. I can feel its presence out there somewhere, but it will not obey my call."

"Call it again," I suggested.

She did. We waited. Nothing.

"Well, now what?" I asked.

El's emotions of frustration and impatience bled over into mine.

"I wonder if he is trapped," El mused. *"Perhaps he or the dog have been captured or detained in some way."*

"So, what do we do?" I asked again.

"Since you will not allow me to speak with your Bitsy, I do not know where the Hound is, and he will not answer my call. I think we should continue our own hunt. Perhaps we will stumble onto the location."

"All right," I said, not totally convinced that would work, but what other option did we have? *"Are we going after Keysha's gang tonight?"*

From the depths of the backpack, Maltheron sang his hunting song.

"*Maltheron believes this is a good plan. And we have the address, so we will not need the Hound to find the perpetrators.*"

"Okee doke," I said. "Let's do this."

"*Please take us there,*" she said.

I stood on the porch in the dark and looked out at the empty, rain-filled streets stretching out in front of me. The only punctuation to the night was occasional streetlights that cast a yellow glow into the expanding puddles. Did she mean for me to get there on my own? Like, no instant transport through the hall of doors?

"*I must reserve my energy for when we have found the criminals,*" she said.

I huffed, pulled the backpack off my shoulders and retrieved the cell phone from the small front pocket. Like I had a bunch of money to blow on a taxi ride. Bitsy would see it gone. She watched the bank account like a hawk.

I started walking before pulling up the number for the taxi. The hood on my coat kept my head dry, but the backpack would be soaked in minutes. It took twenty minutes to walk to where I'd asked to be picked up, then another ten for the taxi to arrive. After that, the trip took a good fifteen minutes.

At 2:00 a.m., I had the taxi drop us several blocks from the address scrawled on the yellow sticky note. My nerves were singing by the time I paid the driver and exited the car. In addition to the thrum-thrum-thrum of my anxious heart, a sound was emanating from the backpack, and I knew it wasn't my phone.

"*Why is your husband making all that racket?*" I asked El.

I looked around me. This couldn't be the right place. Even in the dark, I could tell this was an *über* nice neighborhood. The yards were manicured, trees trimmed, cars clean in their driveways. Kind of like the neighborhood I lived in with Grams. Respectable. I checked the address on the yellow sticky again then turned to find the nearest address and street sign. The house on my left—with a fancy brick flowerbed lining the front porch—boasted 1347 in proud numbers. The street sign two houses down read *Massachusetts Ave.* The sticky read *1426 Massachusetts Ave.* I shrugged and started walking. Maybe the neighborhood took a turn for the worse after the next block.

El finally answered my question. *"He is eager for the hunt. He was forged for vengeance. It is what feeds him."*

A little thrill ran through me, and I wondered if it fed me, too.

I stopped in the middle of the manicured sidewalk to get my excitement under control. The rain had slowed but still dripped from my coat hood. Raindrops glittered as they fell through streetlights, and in my amped attitude, I thought they seemed to spark like little fireworks. The neighborhood was nice enough that I could smell the trees rather than exhaust and restaurants. I breathed in, letting the rain-drenched air fill my lungs and soothe away my anxiety.

And then we walked. I was quiet and kept to the shadows. As my steps drew me nearer to the address, I thought about the young woman who'd lost her life. The article I found said she'd gone to a friend's house, and the two of them had come to the house I approached for a party. Of course, there were drugs and alcohol there. The friend had left the party with a boy. In the story, she said Keysha, the deceased, had said she'd get a taxi back to her friend's. They'd meet up before dawn. No big deal. I wondered if that's how the conversation had really gone. The rest of the article described the party as getting out of control and other partygoers as saying the hosts became aggressive.

Somewhere along the way, Keysha had been taken or led to a bedroom. The labs showed she'd been given the date-rape drug. Cathy noted in her report that Keysha had endured a broken femur and collarbone, and a fractured supraorbital foramen—the eyebrow bone. Her pubis had been broken, too.

I shuddered. They raped her so hard they broke her. And yet, they made bail to await trial. The boiling anger I'd felt before, for myself and for Bitsy and for the girls led through Cathy's door for one more torture in the ordeal, came roiling back through me. And so many of the people inflicting this hurt would just walk away. I thought about my own bad guy. How I'd been shushed and quieted. Quieted over and over again, until I split and broke and all the little pieces of me skittered away into a darkness I had to search through to uncover my own truth.

"No one will believe you," and "Please, if you say anything, he'll have to go away," and "He didn't really mean it that way." She'd said all those things and more. My own mother had protected him instead of me. And his words were mine to bear. Ugly words that stained me but kept Bitsy safe. I straightened, wiggling my shoulders under the weight of the burden. If I could keep Bitsy safe, maybe I could keep other girls safe, too.

The house was one door away. I paused on the sidewalk, pulled the backpack from my shoulders and reached in for Maltheron. A soft hum reverberated through my hand as I clasped the handle. I tried not to think about the idea that I was grabbing a person imprisoned in a blade, but his intention sang through me. A high of anger, a need for vengeance filled me up, making my body light and powerful.

The power radiated off me in waves of energy that shuddered and shifted in a halo of reds and oranges and blacks. If I were transforming, it would be into a dragon, and I relished every moment of the change. I was pure and indestructible strength. I was justice personified. Those who harmed the innocents would pay for their crimes.

El's emotions mirrored mine. We three were one in purpose and commitment. The house number, 1426, was visible under a dull porch light that barely cut through the misty rain. The house directly to my right was dark, peaceful looking under the constant patter of rain. In the darkness, the trees towered, silent and nonpartisan observers to the world around them.

As I approached the hedge surrounding 1426, a car drove past me. I froze. A man jumped out of an old—what did they call that color? Cashmere gold?—Toyota and trotted up to the front door of the house. I ducked into the arbor of the house next door and watched through a diamond-shaped slot in the lattice. The murmur of their voices drifted over to me, but I couldn't make out the words. The man at the door was getting rained on. He gestured, waving his hand in the air.

He was my age. Probably in college. His clothes and well-trimmed hair suggested he came from money. He handed the person at the door—who was concealed from my view—something, turned and looked around him while the door closed on him. He rocked from his heels to his toes and rubbed the back of his neck. The door opened again, and the man was handed a small package that he swiftly stuck in a coat pocket. He trotted down the stairs, jumped into his Toyota and backed out of the drive. I ducked down so his headlights wouldn't find me until he passed, and it was just me again, alone in the night.

Well, me, an alien woman in my head and her husband in the knife I held in my hand.

I peeked around the hedge and looked at the house again.

"Okay, now how are we going to do this?" I asked El, peering at the illuminated white front door, which seemed out of the question for an entry point.

"Why?" asked El.

"What?"

"Why would the front door not be an option?" El elaborated.

"*I dunno. Seems like they might have it locked.*"

"*Hmm... maybe. Is there another door?*"

I tiptoed my way back onto the sidewalk and rounded the yard.

"*Look there,*" El said.

Sure enough, at the back of the house was a door with a little window on the top. By the way it was all fogged up, it looked as if it might be the laundry room. Huh. Drug dealers do laundry? Weird.

A skinny patch of grass that was sorely in need of trimming separated the two houses. I waded through the Portland-rain-thickened swatch of green and found myself face-to-face with a chain-link fenced gate. And a lock.

And a dog.

A dog whose head came up to my ribcage. Its growl ripped through the night and rain and rumbled through my chest. Its eyes caught the light from the back door and glinted. Glowing against its black and brown fur was a set of wickedly white canines. I backed away from the gate and nearly fell over the short fence marking the edge of the neighbor's territory. I caught myself on a fence post, banging my arm in the process. That was going to purple beautifully tomorrow.

"*Back to the front door then,*" I told El. "*Can you deal with that?*"

"*Yes. We can do this.*"

I bounded back through the tall grass, but the damn monster dog was onto me and chased me along the perimeter, barking madly.

"*Better be able to do it quick, Princess. You're going to have one shot at this.*" I rounded the hedge, beat a path down the sidewalk, my sneakers slapping through the gathering rain. My face was soaked. The backpack jostled and shifted on my back. I skidded around the bend in the concrete, raced up the path to the front door, thanking my lucky stars the back yard was the only residence for the dog. They would be alerted to my presence, though.

There were three short steps leading to the front door. And just as I figured, the door opened, and a face peered through. I bounded up one stair, skipping the others. My body tingled as El's excitement rose. My hand burned from the thrumming of Maltheron. Without thinking, I raised my right leg and kicked the door into a face with wide brown eyes and a mop of greasy hair.

The door flung back, pushing the man into the wall behind him. His head hit a piece of wood with a row of hooks on it. Keys and leashes rained around the man as he slid to the floor.

"How do we know who did it?" I asked, frantically looking around and waiting for others to come flooding toward me.

"The girl shows us. This one is innocent of her blood. Leave him."

"What girl?" I asked.

"The one we avenge. I see her. Her spirit calls out to us to avenge her. Look out!"

From my right, a man rushed toward me. I caught a glimpse of a white t-shirt, black sweatshirt and a baseball cap twisted to the side. He was about my height and probably my age too. He opened his mouth.

"What the—?" he started to say.

"Him!" El proclaimed.

My arm raised, led by Maltheron. I took in the details of his face in a split second. The man's blue eyes went wide. Full lips were wet and partly open with a slight sneer. I even saw the blackheads on his nose and the stubble of an unshaven blond beard. And then Maltheron struck true, dragging my body with him. I saw the blade run through the man's neck. It yanked at the muscle and bone of the windpipe. I saw my hand gripping the blade, and yet I felt unattached to it.

The man never had time to raise the gun he held in his

hand. The weapon dropped to the floor with a heavy clunk. There was a moment's pause, during which everything went still and silent. My hand was still raised, Maltheron humming, clutched in my fingers. The man tried to swallow, his eyes wide, and then in a sudden burst, blood sprayed across my face. The man fell to his knees, looked up at me. At me. Not at the knife, not at the weapon but at the wielder.

"Rapist." The word ripped from my mouth.

The man gurgled. I kicked him over with a small shove of a sneakered toe. Falling to the ground, he tried to make a noise and failed as scarlet spread around his head and shoulders. There was no opening of his sight this time. No moment of realization of his wrongs. A certain dissatisfaction ranged through me. They needed to know.

"There was no time. He would have killed you," El told me.

I stepped over the corpse and pressed my body against the wall, listening.

"How do you know?" I asked.

"Derek?" The voice came from the other side of the wall.

"Have you not figured it out?" El said.

"Figured what out?"

"Why my soul came to be with you. With the other one. The one you call Bitsy."

Shuffling sounds echoed around the wall I pressed my shoulder into. This was once a nice house. I found myself wondering who owned it. The drug dealer? Or was this a rental? There was a framed print on the wall. A depiction of a queen, knighting a medieval soldier. The picture hung crooked. In the reflection of the glass, a tall man in a hoody hulked.

"I don't know what you mean," I told El, but a tickling realization ached to be known. *"Maybe let's chat about this later? When we're not right in the middle of something?"*

I pushed the thought aside and listened, working to

breathe without sound, sure my heartbeat could be heard by the man on the other side of the wall.

"Hey, bro'?" the man asked.

"There are two more," El told me.

I shoved away from the wall and spun around to face the man. He was ginormous. I craned my neck to look into his face. A flash of fear spasmed through me. Not my fear. Over the man's right shoulder, a circle of light burst then faded.

"What was that?" I asked, startled.

"Liz?"

Oh, damn. Bitsy. Not now!

"Where are we?"

"Bits, go back to sleep," I pleaded.

"Who the fuck are you?" the man asked.

He wasn't afraid. Not a bit. I wouldn't be, either, if I were six-and-a-half feet tall and as muscled and solid as he was.

"Well, shit," I said. "Looks like it's a party now."

"What are we doing here?" Bitsy screamed at me, sounding as if she was close to tears. *"Are you here for more of your stupid sexcapades?"*

I didn't turn around. She hadn't seen the dead guy or the guy knocked out and slumped against the wall.

"Wait. What are you holding?"

"Bitsy, this is a really bad time for you to try to be in charge."

"Why? What is happening?"

I fought her as she grappled for control. My body leaned to the left as I wrestled with Bitsy.

"I don't remember scheduling a party. But you're here. And I'm here. So what the hell. Maybe you'd like my friends to join in, too," said the giant.

Fire blossomed through me. "Is that what you told Keysha?" I asked.

"He is one of the three." El said.

216

"*Who is that?*" Bitsy asked.

Her questions and confusion built into a flood. I fought to hold her back. Maltheron wanted to be bathed in the giant's blood.

"Who's Keysha?" Mr. Giant asked. Even his voice was big and deep.

I gripped the blade, the patterns carved into the dark metal biting into my gloved hands.

"What is that on your face," he asked. "Is that...?"

"A little bit of Derek," I said and launched myself onto him, my arm raised, a warrior yell ripping from my throat.

An audible hum reverberated from Maltheron. Finally, Mr. Giant looked a little startled. Not too bright, I guessed.

El fed me a whopping dose of strength. Her cry was my cry.

Somewhere in the corner of our mind, Bitsy was screaming. "*No!*"

Ignoring her, I gripped the man's meaty shoulder. My knees planted into his stomach. I looked into his eyes.

"*Say the words, El.*"

I held Maltheron back from a killing stroke he aimed at the man's carotid artery.

"*He deserves to suffer more than just death.*"

El used my voice. It was so weird. So wrong and right. She changed the way the vocal chords worked, and the sound was foreign to my ears.

"Know the pain of your victims," she said.

But she didn't just say it. Each word evoked a tone that rang in the room. A note that stretched and twisted. The man's hazel eyes grew wide, his mouth growing with each note that layered upon the previous, until a cacophony filled the room, and chaos broke him. He screamed, a vein in his forehead pulsing beneath the skin. I smiled down as his agony overtook him.

And then he gripped my waist. The air in my lungs was squeezed out. Organs in my abdomen protested. Surely they would burst. He heaved me above his head like a rag doll while I kicked and fought to breathe and lashed out with Maltheron. My head dipped. I saw the hood of his gray sweatshirt, the curl of his dark hair at his neckline. He launched me. A moment of free-fall ended when my body slammed into the framed art-work. Glass shattered around me, biting into the skin of my exposed face.

"Liz, what the hell are you trying to do to him?"

Bitsy's hysteria was hardly controllable with the lack of air in my lungs. Glass crunched beneath my arm and shoulder, as I lay crumpled on the linoleum of the entryway. I fought the feeling of dying, and finally my abs let go. I sucked in air as stars burst into my vision.

"We need to get out! Run, Liz! He's coming!"

"I can't run, Bits. We can't run anymore." I pushed my shaking body off the floor. I was still on my hands and knees. *"C'mon, body. Work with me."* Oh, man, was I going to be sore tomorrow.

Footsteps rocked into the floor; vibrations shivered through my hands. I whipped my head to the side in time to see Gray Sweatshirt aim a heavy work boot in my direction.

"Move it," El shouted.

I dove. Somehow, impossibly, I missed receiving the full force of his kick. His boot caught on my sneaker. My forward momentum pulled his foot. His legs tangled with mine, and he landed on top of me. His other foot kicked my head in the process, pulling away the stocking cap. My hair flew out in a cloud of brown curls.

I yanked myself to my feet. He gripped his head as if it would explode. He growled. Then sobbed. He rocked from side to side.

"*Where is Maltheron?*" El shouted.

I glanced around and saw the blade lying inches from the man's head.

"*What is Maltheron? Who are you?*" Bitsy shouted and fought me with all her might. "*We have to get out of here. This place. Liz. You have to believe me. There's so much evil here.*"

I tried to take a step toward the oversized dagger, but Bitsy was heading for the door. We froze as the internal battle waged.

"*Yes, there's tons of evil here, Bits. That's what we're trying to do. We're trying to stop it!*"

Bitsy yanked my head, making me look toward the corpse in the entryway.

"*Please don't tell me you—*" she started.

"*No one else is going to do anything. You know what they did to her? To Keysha? An innocent girl?*"

"*Liz, you didn't kill someone, did you?*"

One carpet-softened footstep drew my attention behind me. A man in a Seahawks jersey sneered, raised a hand and the world went dark.

Chapter 22

BITSY

I was tied to a chair. Every inch of my body ached. Liz was asleep after the blow we took from the second man. My head suffered a series of tiny explosions. One small inhale drove a dagger of pain through my left side. I was in the living room, alone, situated next to a glass coffee table and in front of a television playing a basketball game. A raggedy blue couch was behind me, and a tan love seat was to my right and in front of a sliding glass door. When I craned my neck far enough, I could see a small kitchen behind the blue couch.

The carpet was ruined, splattered in oil and animal stains. There were splotches of bleach spots and what looked like ink. It was impossible to tell the original color of the carpet. The coffee table was littered with drug paraphernalia.

I peered over my left shoulder and saw the broken glass from the framed art Liz had been thrown into. All else seemed clear. The light leaking in from outside was weak and tinged with pink. A clock on the wall above a stand of DVDs read five thirty.

Why had Liz come here? I remembered the corpse. She hadn't really killed someone, had she? Guilt and fear twisted through my stomach like a bad meal.

"Hello?" The voice issued from inside me like a ghost wrapped in mist.

Did I even really hear anything?

"My name is Elada," said the voice, more clearly this time.

"Elada? You're the woman from my dreams. You're real?" This was just too bizarre. And couldn't be a coincidence. I was manifesting a third personality. And she happened to be an alien spirit who'd had her daughter raped and killed. I hung my head.

"I know what you are thinking. That I am another one of your identities. But this is not so."

I shook my head as tears rolled down my cheeks. This just couldn't be. Another identity meant another memory bank that could be opened up and shared with me. Could I bare such a thing? My stomach hardened on the thought of being shown more horror and violence. Wasn't Liz enough? Weren't the dreams enough?

Clips of Liz's memories flashed through my mind's eye. Words floated up to me. Images rolled, one after another. My heart raced, my body ached, and fear pushed through me. I closed my eyes to the world around me. I was supposed to listen. I needed to share in the memories with her. To be patient and compassionate with Liz, who was another part of me. But being tied to a chair, all I wanted to do was get free and escape.

I wriggled against the zip-tie binding my wrists. The plastic dug into my skin, but my hands moved. I looked down at my feet and was relieved to find my feet and ankles were free. My arms were wrapped over the back of the chair at an awkward angle that pulled at my shoulders. My tailbone ached, along with the rest of me. How long had I been sitting in this chair?

"Bitsy," Liz said, and her voice was a mixture of pleading and understanding. *"We can't not do anything. Not when we have the ability."*

I squished my hands in on themselves to make them skinny and worked the zip-tie back and forth down my hands.

"*Is killing people your idea of doing something?*" I said as horror filled me.

"*Bitsy,*" Liz started, her tone taking on a note of patronizing patience, "*these people drugged a girl, beat her and raped her. She died from her injuries. They need to be taken out.*"

"*Two wrongs don't make a right,*" I told her. "*You can't just go around killing all the bad guys in the world.*"

"*You think Keysha, the girl they killed, was the first or that she'll be the last?*"

I paused and worked through my thoughts. The zip-tie was at my knuckles and wasn't budging. I widened my hands and pulled, grunting with gritted teeth. "*No, I'm sure she wasn't. But now you've put blood on our hands. You can't answer evil with evil. Killing is evil.*"

"*So we just stand around and let the bad guy get away? I'm so sick of the bad guy winning.*"

"*And we have done so much to help those who have suffered at the hands of evil.*" The woman with the foreign voice spoke up.

I ignored her.

"*Liz. You've been talked into this way of thinking by this new alt. This course of action isn't for us.*"

"*I am not one of your personalities,*" Elada said.

I rolled my eyes. "*Yeah. You're an alien. A Queen Maker, right? A woman of rank and power, albeit power in a position forced upon you. Listen, I've seen enough of your story. This isn't about freeing the children who've suffered. This is about your thirst for vengeance. Your daughter was murdered and you want the man responsible to pay. And to get to him, you're what? Going to hack through enough bad guys until you get to the right one?*"

"*You know El?,*" Liz asked. "*How?*"

"*I've been having a lot of dreams lately,*" I said.

"Why didn't you tell me?"

"I wanted to, but you were apparently too busy playing vigilante," I said, my anger boiling in my gut. My head was reeling. *"How many times have you done this? This killing thing you're doing?"*

"Bitsy, don't freak out. Every one of them deserved to be ended. And the death means the victim has less memory of the awful event they went through. We help wipe their memories, Bits," Liz explained.

I paused at that. They undid the memories of the abuse. Things were starting to come clear. *"Let me guess. Elada promised to help you wipe your memories in exchange for finding her daughter's murderer."*

"Yes," Liz said. *"Is that such a bad thing? We could be whole, Bitsy."*

"Maybe if we knew everyone who harmed us," I said, *"which we don't."*

"But, Grams knows."

"I don't think so. Too much happened after we left Portland when we were little. She doesn't know those people."

Liz squirmed and fought my logic. *"She would have known the first one. She was there. She found out who it was. I remember."*

"But, Liz," I said, pushing as much kindness into my words as possible, *"maybe she knows the first one, but she doesn't know all the ones after that. And do you remember who they are? You have their names and their whereabouts? Do you even remember what they look like?"*

Liz sobbed. *"I just don't want to do this anymore! I'm so tired of reliving the nightmare!"*

A low, murmuring noise interrupted our conversation.

"What was that?" I asked.

Liz seemingly wiped away tears and stowed her hurt. *"It's Maltheron. I think he's saying something to us."*

Maltheron. That name. I knew it too. I jerked my head around the room, looking for the man from my series of dreams.

"On the table."

"What?" Utterly confused, I cast a glance at the paraphernalia scattered across the glass table. And then my eyes lit on a dagger. It was both beautiful and dark, something that made me want to look away and stare at the same time. Staring won out. Especially since, as I stared, a hum of words echoed across the room to me. I could almost make out its intention. It was saying something to me. The emotion was urgent and... eager.

Liz and El went quiet. The knife began to vibrate, slowly, at first, and then clattered so much it jumped and rattled around the glass table. A hypodermic needle bounced its way over the edge and fell to the stained carpet. A spoon and lighter joined in. The clattering of the different items on the table made a harmony that layered on top of the low hum, like a bass or cello holding a note. I froze, mesmerized by the sounds and the dagger's emotion filling the room.

"Hello, Maltheron," I said to the dagger.

He hummed, but the notes took a dive toward warning.

And then I saw her.

She hung in the air in front of me and looked as if she was made out of watercolors. She moved closer, ghosting through the air on nothing. Her mouth stretched too wide to be humanly possible. Her hair floated, as if a wind beneath her blew it upward. She writhed and jerked. Her shirt was ripped, her shoulder pushed down and away at an awkward angle, her head snapped to one side. Shadows converged on her, and I watched in horror as she was raped and beaten. I closed my eyes, but the scene just kept playing behind my lids.

"Please, no! Stop! I can't take it."

But I received no mercy. The ghost just kept showing me. Tears rolled down my cheeks, hot and salty. She was strangled, her windpipe crushed. Her pelvic bone broken. I could feel the pain. The fire of the injury exploded through my lower half. I screamed with her as one shadow pummeled her with heavy fists and broke her face.

"Bitsy!"

I was lost in the pain. I screamed over and over.

"What's going on?" Liz shouted.

"Keysha has appeared to Bitsy and is showing Bitsy the death she suffered," El said.

I heard them, but it was as if they were speaking in a tunnel, the words filtering through the roar of passing cars that echoed off cement walls.

And then it stopped. It all stopped.

My mind pulsed with a new image. A man on top of me. A dagger in my hand. Red. Everything bathed in red.

Footsteps echoed somewhere to my left, getting louder. I yanked on the zip tie, and choked back a sob of relief when it pulled from my hands. I grabbed at the dagger instinctively. My body vibrated with the rush of adrenaline. Pushing out of the chair, I dashed out of the living room.

"Hey!" a man shouted.

I cried out and sprinted toward the broken picture. There was no corpse in the entryway, but the floor was smeared with blood and littered with towels that were half white and half reds and pinks. I reached for the door, but I knew already what would happen.

My hair yanked; my head snapped back. He dragged me. I fought to keep my feet underneath me. A dark hall swallowed us as the man pulled me. He took a hard left. My shoulder whacked into the doorframe as he whirled me around. My feet were off balance, so when he shoved me I fell. Something soft caught me, and a resulting bounce and squeak gave away the fact I'd been thrown onto a bed.

I rolled onto my back and scrambled to hide the dagger, while the man turned from me and closed the door. Shadows leaked from under the baseboards lining the small room. He flipped a switch, and a dull light flickered to life in a perturbed way.

He was short and wide and muscled. Like a bulldog. He had black buzzed hair, an egg-shaped head and a face scarred from severe acne. His skin was a dark tan. His eyes were dark pools that matched the spirits swarming around him. I gagged on the fear. The shadows lengthened as the man undid his belt then his pants. One step brought him to the bed, where he clasped my legs in a solid un-giving and practiced grip. He whipped the belt from his jeans, and before I could react, he lashed out at me. The leather caught my face. I screamed at the pain.

"Motherfucker!" Liz screeched.

The shadows bulged, black hunger strengthening them. They pawed at me as tendrils of fear closed over my throat and arms, making me weak. The man grinned at me as I clasped my fingers to my cheek. He cracked the belt again, and it caught my neck and chest. I didn't cry out this time. My mind spiraled. I was losing it, going away to the bliss of dark quiet where I didn't have to remember.

"It's okay, Bitsy. I can take this." Liz's voice trembled in fear.

"No," I squeaked, fighting against the fog.

"Don't forget your power," El said. *"Don't forget your friends in the spirit realm."*

It was really hard to concentrate on her words as I watched the man stroke himself as he geared up for another lashing.

Then I heard the music. Maltheron was singing Moonlight. The notes woke me, shook me from the sleepy mist that threatened to envelope me in impuissance. Music tripped through my mind. The feel of violin strings against my fingers pricked at my nerves. The melody rang in my ears as it pulled me into some other place of being. My vision flashed. I was in the universe, surrounded by a comforting darkness that was unlike the sleepy down I experienced when I went away. I was more awake here than any other place I could be.

Elada stood to my left. I turned to see her. Somehow, time paused in this place. She was lovely in an alien sort of way; just the way I recalled seeing her in my dreams. She shone with a crimson light that emanated from her middle. Her heart-shaped face and crescent eyes were rimmed in markings much like tattoos. She turned to me and inclined her head.

"Listen. I have been drawn here because you have power you do not realize. You are powerful," El said.

My head swam with the intricate fabrication of stories in my mind from this new personality. This was a true realization of insanity. Her words stunned me. *Not me,* I wanted to argue. *I'm just crazy. Not powerful.* Liz stood next to me then, grasping my hand.

"We're in this together," she said.

I turned to my other personality. The one I'd known for so long now. The one I'd grown close to yet pushed away when the stories she told got to be too much. Because, selfishly, I didn't want to allow her reality to hurt me.

"I've left you so often," I said. The realization brought real pain to my soul. I'd pushed all the sorrow and pain onto her.

She bowed her head and nodded slightly, the emotions of past hurts washing over her features. My features. She had done so much for me. Protected me for years, saved me from completely and utterly breaking. Instead, we were here. Together.

I turned toward her and clasped her other hand in mine. *"I'm not going to leave you anymore."*

She wept. I took her in my arms, holding her close to me. She was so familiar, this separate part of me. Not like El, who was alien in every way.

The image of Liz flashed, and I found myself holding a

little girl in my arms. My heart broke at this picture of a smaller me. I hurt for her as she showed me her sorrow and pain.

And at last, she had someone she could rely on.

I had someone to rely on.

They came to me then. White and golden beings floated through the infinity, drawing closer to the music. They were so beautiful, but more importantly, the love they radiated filled me up with light. When I opened my eyes to reality, the beings of light stayed with me, filling the room behind me.

The shadows behind my attacker grew teeth, hissed. The room was split—half darkness, half light. The man grunted as he jerked the belt toward me, his knees knocking against mine where he straddled me. I raised an arm and caught the belt. His eyes widened. I yanked. He let go, and the belt buckle smacked me in the mouth. Something cracked, and a piece of my tooth fell onto my tongue. Fire bloomed. I fought back against the pain while I spit out the piece of tooth.

"Fine. Playtime's over," he said, his voice laden with a Spanish accent.

The beings of light behind me brandished swords, and with a tone like an unearthly trumpet, they went to war against the shadows. The man grabbed at the waist of my pants and yanked, pulling my hips toward him. My body was bare from the waist to my shins. He moaned.

"That's a fine pussy."

He fumbled with my sneakers. I kneed him in the face while he was bent over. He acted as if it was no big deal, just put a meaty hand on both my knees and yanked my shoes from my feet, which felt as if they'd go with my shoes, he used such force. My pants were gone in a millisecond and then, horribly, he was on top of me. He pushed against my legs as I fought him, kicking and screaming and punching. Meanwhile, the light glinted and shone with each slash of heavenly swords.

The shadows bit and clawed at the angels, who only glittered more brightly in the battle.

Finally, the man got close enough. Too close. My fingers wrapped around the handle of the dagger, the design pressing into my skin while Maltheron's rendition of my piece crawled up a crescendo. My muscles were strong. My body set on its purpose. The visions from the last few weeks flashed through me, and everything made sense.

I pulled Maltheron from the covers and buried the blade into my attacker's chest, my voice ripping out of my throat in a warrior cry. He almost didn't stop. The vulnerable pieces of my womanhood were brushed against his vile weapon. I screamed as I pulled back the blade, fighting to keep him from entering me, and then I plunged the dagger into another part of his chest. His face was next to mine. His breath was on my swelling cheek as he turned to meet my eyes.

"I will not be your victim," I whispered.

Maltheron's song filled the room and not just my mind. The angels battling overhead swelled while the shadows were cut away with flashing swords the color of summer lightning. Warm wetness dripped on my chest. My attacker looked up, watching as the shadows fled from the angels.

The man swallowed and gasped as his body slumped onto me. I yanked the blade from his chest and more blood spilled onto me. I shoved him. His body thumped to the narrow floor space next to the bed. He labored to breathe as the angels gathered over him. I pushed myself off the bed, scrambling to pull my clothes back on.

When I was dressed again I stood amid the angels and peered down at the man, gripping Maltheron in my hand. His past flashed at me. I stumbled back as his memories floated around him. An angel the height of a giant wrapped a robed arm around me.

"Compassion," it said, *"has no judgment."*

"Maybe not," I said.

I could feel Liz standing strong with me, closer than we'd ever stood.

"But even you fight against the darkness when it threatens to overwhelm the light," I told him.

The angel nodded as if in satisfaction. *"Find the right way to fight,"* it said.

A golden angel that sparkled in a rainbow of colors reached a hand toward the dying man. His spirit pulled from his body. The angel took the man by his hand.

I asked, "So what happens to him?"

The giant angel turned toward me, his eyes lost in the light spilling off him. Or her. Or it. The being seemed without gender.

"He must try again."

"Reincarnation, huh? No shit?" Liz asked, completely without regard that she spoke to a highly intelligent being of light.

But the being didn't seem to mind. It simply nodded, its crown of light tilting forward and back.

"Just as you have been through many other cycles. This spirit will go through more cycles until he has evolved, as you have."

"As I have?" I asked. *"Wait, I've been through other cycles?"*

The angel nodded. *"You are almost ready,"* it said and turned from me. *"Almost."*

"What's that mean?" Liz and I asked together.

Without answering, the angels gathered their charge and began escorting the spirit of the man away. He turned to me as the beings and spirit grew watery and insubstantial, and whispered, *"I'm so sorry."*

And then they were gone.

Chapter 23

I gathered Maltheron and searched the house for the back-pack Liz had brought. I found it in the hallway, propped near a half-open door to another room. My nerves tingled. There had been two other men in the house. I tiptoed across the carpet and leaned in to grab the backpack. A groan echoed from the room. My heartbeat tripped into overtime.

"*It is okay,*" El said. "*His mind is lost.*"

Tentatively, I peered around the corner of the room. One man was on the floor, unmoving. The giant man who had thrown Liz into the art was stretched out on a small bed—too small for his height. The light was on, but the man's eyes were closed.

"*What happened to him?*" I asked.

"*I opened his spiritual eyes, and when I did, his mind couldn't take it.*"

"*Is he one of the people who killed that girl?*" I asked. The horror of the torture she'd endured flashed through me, but it didn't touch me the same way as watching it had. I wondered if her spirit was at rest. If she found peace in knowing her murderers would never murder again.

"*Yes,*" Liz said. Her voice throbbed in my head. "*I'm sorry you had to see Keysha's torture.*"

"*I needed to see it. I need to remember what we've been through, even if I can't recall all the details. Turning a blind eye isn't going to help anyone.*"

Turning a blind eye had pushed Liz to seek a way to make a change in the world. She'd been brave enough to stand up against the bad guy. And she'd done it without me because she'd assumed—no, she'd *known*—I wouldn't go for it. I had been so closed to everything she represented I had alienated her. So she had taken matters into her own hands. But this way was not the way for us.

I looked at the man tossing and turning, eyes squished hard against themselves. He deserved what he got. Maybe somewhere along the way, he'd serve the sentence El had passed to him and live again. Or maybe he, like his friends, would cycle through again to evolve. It wasn't up to me, thank goodness. There was a higher power to answer to. One day, his angels would come for him, too, as they did for us all.

I placed Maltheron into the depths of the backpack, checked that everything Liz had brought was still there, and then pulled it onto my shoulders.

"*What about prints and stuff? I'm pretty sure we've left some sort of evidence behind,*" Liz noted.

"*We just took out three drug dealers and rapists. I don't think there's going to be much of an investigation,*" I said.

"*Do not worry,*" El said, "*while I am with you there is a veil around us that keeps us protected from leaving any trace of our presence.*"

"*How's that work?*" Liz asked, her voice dripping with sarcasm.

"*I have power you do not have in this world.*"

"*But it's not your body, so how do you have any power?*" I asked.

"*Power lies in the soul,*" she said.

I thought it was creepy this other soul was inside me, and that it had somehow surrounded us with its essence to serve as a barrier between this world and us, but I kept those thoughts to myself, grateful our tracks were covered in what had transpired in the last several hours.

I tiptoed my way down the hall, a little anxious there might be someone left in the house I hadn't seen yet.

"There is no one left," El said.

I straightened.

"Are you reading my thoughts?" I asked, realizing how dumb that sounded since when I spoke with her it was with my mind.

"No, just your actions and body language. If you do not mean to think it to me, I do not hear it."

I sighed in relief. Bad enough finding out there was some other spirit inside you—having them be able to read your thoughts would be unbearable.

"But you are covered in blood. You should find a bathroom and try to clean yourself," El said.

I glanced down at myself. She was right. A little farther down the hall there was a bathroom. I went inside it, hating having to be in the house any longer. Looking in the mirror was a mistake. I looked like the victim of a horror movie. I ran the water in the filthy sink until it was warm and washed my face and neck, wincing at the pain of my swelling cheekbone. I wondered if it was broken.

"There's an extra sweatshirt and a plastic bag in the backpack," Liz said.

"You were prepared to get bloody?" Premeditated was the word that came to mind.

"It happens," Liz said.

I was so horrified, I didn't respond.

I pulled the blood-soaked black shirt from my body and set it on the toilet lid. After I pulled the plastic bag out of the backpack and deposited my dirty clothes, I paused. *"So, that's why you've been doing laundry in the middle of the night."* The dirtiness of the deeds she'd been performing coated me. *"How long has this been going on?"*

"A few weeks," Liz answered.

I huffed and pulled a towel off the rack. I ran it under the water and scrubbed it with soap then washed down my face, neck and torso. Once I'd dried myself, I pulled the sweatshirt out of the backpack and put it on, reveling in the warm comfort of dry clothing.

"Liz," I started, *"I promise to listen, but you have to promise to share, too. We can't heal if there are secrets between us."* I could feel Liz hang her head in shame. I grabbed the backpack and headed out of the house.

I exited the front door and stood on the porch, glancing around. The dawn was still approaching, and there was a heavy cover of gray. Mist rolled down the street, clung to the air above the wet ground. The gray was nothing compared to the heaviness inside me.

I had killed a man. No. It was more than that. I wobbled down the stairs on numb feet, my body protesting every movement. I glanced around to make sure there was no one watching as I took a left at the edge of the sidewalk and retreated from the house. I didn't turn around to look back. But I chewed on the events. I had not just killed someone. I had protected myself.

The man had tried to rape us, and he had beaten us. I'd stood up for us. Me. Bitsy. The small one who always ran in fear and hid when the world got to be too much. I straightened my back under the weight of the backpack and allowed myself the moment to be proud of standing up for myself.

The bus ride was a silent affair, but Grandma sure wasn't silent when we got home.

"You had me worried sick!" she shouted as I crossed the threshold.

"I'm so sorry, Grandma."

I walked up to her outstretched arms and pulled her into a tight hug.

"Couldn't Liz at least leave a note or something?" she griped and cried and squeezed me all at once.

Liz squirmed. *That would have been an interesting note. 'Dear Grams, I've gone out to kill some bad guys. Be back before dawn,'* Liz said.

"It's not all Liz's fault," I told my grandmother. "She only chose to do what she did last night because I pushed her away. But it's not going to happen again."

"Please, Bitsy," El began, *"I still must find my daughter's murderer. You must help me."*

"It's not going to happen again," I repeated.

El fell silent. Liz was indifferent.

Grandma pulled away from me finally and gasped. "What happened to you, sweetheart?"

She was looking at my face, which took turns throbbing and burning. I touched it with my fingertips.

"I think we have another personality," I told her.

Her eyes widened and her mouth fell open. Then she closed her mouth, gripped my hand and led me to the kitchen table, where a steaming cup of coffee sat waiting for her. She pushed it aside as she sat down. She looked at me with her soulful brown eyes, clutched the neckline of her burgundy robe and urged me to speak. And I did.

Liz had to talk first because she was the one who'd started the evening. She and I seemed to be of the same mind. Grandma had to know. She was the only one who would know. And she would know everything. Liz and I held nothing back.

Grandma only stopped us to ask clarifying questions. When I told her about the angels that came to the call of the music she rubbed her arms.

"I've got goose bumps all over!" she told me.

After I told her the part about killing the man who'd tried to rape us, she gripped my hands in hers while tears streamed down her finely lined face.

"Oh my god, Elizabeth," she said, "that must have been terrifying!"

I nodded, crying for the first time since I'd woken in a drug house. The light of morning had slowly filled the dining room through the gray haze of mist and clouds.

"I'm a murderer," Liz said, our voice clotted with her emotion.

Grandma turned her head to one side. "How's that?" she asked.

"What do you mean? I killed that guy."

Grandma shook her head as she frowned. "What'd you call that knife thing?"

"Maltheron," I said.

I reached into the backpack at my feet and rummaged through it until my hands fell onto the oddly wide handle of the blade. I pulled it from the bag and placed it on the dining room table. Grandma eyed it suspiciously.

"He's the one who killed the man," she said and pointed to the blade.

"Grandma, you don't think I'm crazy?" I asked.

She chuckled. The sound was warm and wise and full of humor, and it set me at ease.

"Well, we're all a little crazy, but, sweetheart, you've got the proof of your story right here. Even if I were having a hard time believing you—which I'm not—I'd have to believe you after looking at this blade. It's not like anything I've ever seen."

She touched the handle with arthritis-stricken fingers, drawing close to it to inspect the odd carvings and strange metal.

Maltheron greeted her with a faint hum, which rattled into the oak of the table and then went silent.

Grandma jerked her head back, her eyes gone wide. She looked up at me.

"No, sweetpea, I'd definitely say you're not crazy. And now, what about this El you mentioned?"

"Talk to Grandma, El," I urged her. I relaxed and focused on letting my voice be used. I didn't want to go away; I just wanted El to speak.

As she came forward, in my mind's eye she approached a microphone. I saw her as I had seen her when the angels came. As a separate being, features foreign, face markings distinct, clothing unfamiliar.

"Hello," El said. "My name is really Elada." She pronounced her name as El-lah-dah, with the emphasis on the El.

"How did you come to be here?" my grandmother asked. She'd gone all stern and still, sitting straight in her high-back oak chair.

Uneasiness snaked down my spine.

"My daughter was raped and murdered, and her soul cannot rest."

As El spoke, her emotions expanded and spilled into me. Horror and sorrow reverberated through me until I gasped for air. All of the dreams I'd been having tumbled into my mind. The Hound and Maltheron had found his daughter in the field behind their dwelling. I gagged against the sight.

"What's wrong, hon'?"

Grandma was gripping my shoulders and pushing me back upright in my chair. The room swam around me.

"I can see it. I can feel it," I said. "She was a Maker and sacred."

The history of their planet passed over me like a file being downloaded into a computer. I heaved against the overload of information, which overlapped the countless dreams. The room around me tilted. I gripped the table with both hands and willed the world to stay still.

"My husband and I hunted her murderer to a place of old worship," El told Grandma.

In my mind's eyes, I saw the field. Long yellow grasses bathed in the light of three moons that were perfectly aligned in the shape of a triangle. One moon was light golden, the other red and the third a brilliant blue. The energy in the atmosphere palpitated, eager and agitated. I wriggled against the overwhelming anger. I could feel the grass whispering against my robes. No, they were El's robes.

I watched the memory as she turned to her husband, sang an incantation with the light of the moons pouring over her. It was not a pretty sight. He had screamed in pain, his body ripped and crushed and molded into something that contained all the elements that made him human—or whatever it was they were—but in the form of a weapon. Maltheron hummed at the touch of the memory, taking a sort of pride in the fact that his suffering had formed him into what he was now. It was a pride I could not understand. To be changed from a person gifted with the ability to grow life and food—because that's what he'd done before his daughter's death—into a weapon meant only for death.

El spoke again. "The murderer dove into the pool of water that was once used by the Makers to perform sacred rituals. The Hound dove after him. I dove after the Hound with Maltheron in the form he wears now. And when I woke, I was residing in this body. The Hound is out there, too, inhabiting a smaller creature you call a *dog*. I can only presume my daughter's murderer is here on this world, as well."

"So you're looking for him in order to avenge your daughter?" asked Grandma.

"I wish my daughter's spirit rest. She is haunted by her death, twisted into something dark and un-whole."

A tickling sensation ran through me, and then an explosion of light burst through my vision. I was rocked back in my chair, arms blasted to the sides of me where they were held rigidly in place.

"Elizabeth!" my grandmother screamed, her voice muffled through the buzzing in my ears.

For the third time in several weeks, I saw the spirit of someone's past rise up in front of me. Teeth gritted together, cheeks like iron, I was splayed open and made to watch this alien child's murder.

She had been playing in one of her father's fields. The plants were foreign but bore what looked like a spherical orange bloom. She carried one. The girl was tall and lanky, all awkward long bones and overgrown hands and feet. She had the same somewhat elongated face and fine honey-colored hair as her mother. On either side of her nose, near her eyes, were black spots that followed up along her nose and over her eyebrows.

"Raston," Aerylia said, startled. She shook slightly, her mouth hanging and eyes wide. She took a step back away from the man who'd appeared in front of her.

"He was the man Maltheron hired to help with the growing season," El explained, her thoughts a rough cut against the scene playing against my eyes. And even with their intensity, her thoughts were a quiet corner mouse in an IMAX theater.

The girl stopped and peered around her, looking through the tall plants, maybe in hope there was someone else close by.

"Aerylia had been afraid of something. I didn't know what and I couldn't be bothered," El said, her self-loathing leaking into her

words. *"If I'd have just let her take the Hound, she would have been protected. If I had just listened to her."* I remembered the dream in which Aerylia had asked for the Hound.

I would have said something to calm her self-doubt, but I could not speak as the movie played on.

"The Hound is close by. Mom said I could take him with me whenever I wanted," Aerylia said, backing away.

"Oh?" Raston said. He looked out over the fields and then back to Aerylia, his eyes dark and hungry. I gagged against the awful evil of the man's intentions which rolled toward Aerylia in waves. "I don't see him anywhere. I think you're really alone." He took a long step toward her. Something glinted at his side.

Aerylia turned on her heel and ran, her eyes wide with fear. Golden stalks the height of the girl whipped around my vision, orange blossoms batting at my head. No, at her head. She burst through the last row of vegetation, the house in sight far off in the distance, but somehow he'd circled around her. He met her face to face. With a knife to her chest.

Not a knife like any I'd ever seen, but it certainly did the job of cutting down the poor girl. She gasped as she looked down at the sharp instrument in her gut and the purple blood spreading into the white material of her clothes. Then she looked up at him. His face was an awful mask of ugly triumph.

He smiled like a dog with rabies. The dark, almost orang- ish skin of his hands contrasted so totally with the girl's white- ness that he seemed dirty.

"That is the color of our skin when we spend too much time under our suns."

I choked as he twisted the knife, and the girl gurgled, so shocked she couldn't scream. He laid her gently on the ground with the instrument still in her belly. She was still alive, still trying desperately to die when he raped her.

"Please!" I managed through muscles too taut to work properly. "No more!"

I tasted salt and felt the wetness on my face. My head swam from barely being able to breathe through my horror.

The scene cut out, and a new picture took its place. There was no man in the field. Only the bloody bits of a broken girl bathed in the light from three moons. I couldn't even say it was a body. There were too many pieces. The orange blooms on the foreign plants cast their faces to the heavens, to the moonlight, as if in supplication to a goddess who could avenge the girl's death.

The Hound found the remains first. His howl filled the air, deep and mournful, so loud it shook the blooms on the plants. Maltheron ran toward the Hound, guided by his ceaseless howl. When El's face came into view and her scream ripped the night air, and her body fell hard to the ground, I screamed with her, and then there was nothing.

I panted in the darkness that enveloped me until the lights began to sparkle. I was in that place again. The universe, I guessed it was.

"He's going to do it again," said a voice.

Flashes of the girl's memory echoed around me, no longer ravaging me with the feelings and tastes and sounds. Here, it was impersonal.

"How do I stop him?" I asked. I searched around the forever, looking for the owner of the voice that had spoken to me. "Are you there? What do I do to keep it from happening? Hello?"

I turned, and a golden orb of light flew like a laser from another universe, moving fast from a long distance. It sparkled and shimmered and tinkled in my ears. And then it stopped so close to me, all I could make out was her face. Startled, I backed up. She was frowning, her face a ruin of slashes and holes. I didn't want to look at her body. I couldn't.

I fought against the wave of panic and spoke to the girl. *"You're showing me this so we can stop him from hurting other girls."*

The spirit writhed in pain then snapped back to a still picture of her mutilated body. She nodded.

"Don't let him do it!"

"But who is he? If he's on your planet, there's nothing I can do!"

She flew into my face again, twitching against her wounds that oozed and gaped. *"Here. He is here with us. I will show you."*

My body lurched forward, arms banging against the dining table. I heaved, and the air burned in my lungs. I gasped and choked, coughing against the need to breathe and fighting to not vomit. My body shook, almost convulsing with the speed from the adrenaline dump. Grandma's hands rested on my arm, her flesh so warm and soft against my frigid skin.

I lifted my head to look at her, but her eyes were squeezed shut, and she was mumbling. I guessed she was praying.

"And we sure as hell could use some extra prayers right now," said Liz.

Grandma opened her eyes and squeezed my arm. "Are you okay now?" she asked.

I shook my head. No, I was not okay.

"Tell me what you saw." She kept hold of my arm.

I told her everything, every detail. She nodded slightly from time to time to show me she understood but never interrupted me. When I was done she stood up from the table, taking my hand and leading me to the sitting room. It had a modest, flat screen TV, a recliner, an overstuffed armchair and an ottoman. And there were books in shelves lining all the walls.

She sat me in the overstuffed chair and sat herself on the ottoman.

"How long have angels talked to you?" she asked.

"Forever," I answered back. "Since I was a little girl. They led me to the music room where I found out about the violin, they sang to me in my sleep, watched me, showed me what happened in our childhood was abominable."

"And how about the other spirits? How long have you seen them?"

I thought about it. That hadn't been forever; that had been more recently.

"Since after I moved out here?" I asked myself.

"No, you've always seen them too, Bits. It's just that there were usually only dark ones hanging around."

"Liz says forever. She says we only saw demons when I was a child because of what we were surrounded by. As if they were drawing the negative spirits to us."

Grandma nodded knowingly.

"There's always been a war waging around you," she told me.

My body prickled at her words.

"Would you be pulled to the darkness or the light? Would you be broken for good, or would you learn to mend?" She squeezed my hands in hers and smiled at me. "You're mending. You know how I know?" Her dark-gray eyebrows arched into her bottle-auburn hairline.

"No," I squeaked, feeling dizzy and sleepy.

"Because your purpose is becoming clear. Oh, maybe it's not one hundred percent crystal yet, but it's taking shape. Will you be pulled to the darkness or to the light?" she repeated.

"It doesn't feel so clear cut," I said, "all this light and dark. Taking a life to save others—is that light or dark? Good or evil?"

"Maybe there's another way for you to beat back the darkness. I mean, when you think about it, how do you conquer darkness?" she asked.

I looked at her, waiting for her to answer the question,

thinking she'd meant it rhetorically. When she didn't answer right away I was forced to think.

Her warm hands were still steadily gripping mine as I puzzled her question. I thought about dark places. At first, I thought about bad memories and hard times. Those thoughts led me to illustrate the idea with a physical thing—darkness. I imagined a room with no windows and no lights. How do you conquer darkness? The only way you can battle darkness is to...

"Turn on the light," I finished my thought out loud.

Grandma smiled. And then she nodded, slowly and steadily and proudly. "That's right. You have to shine a light. And as long as the light is shining, the darkness can't come in."

"So, what are you saying, Grams?" Liz asked out loud.

My head tilted to the side while I listened.

"I'm telling you"—she squeezed my hands harder, surprising me with her strength—"to shine!"

I swayed at her words. Maybe because I'd had zero sleep. Maybe because of the trauma of getting beaten and then nearly raped. Maybe because I'd seen two girls get mutilated in spirit form within the last twelve hours—both Keysha and Aerylia. Maybe the idea of shining was so foreign, I didn't know what to do with it. Whatever Grandma meant, her idea just wasn't sinking in.

"I don't know how to shine," I told her. "I don't think my shine makes much of a difference."

El huffed into the corner of my mind. Liz didn't respond, just sat quietly and waited for me to not be contradicted.

Grandma said, "I understand what you're saying. I know why you're saying it. Just as much as I know how untrue it is. Let me ask you something, sweetheart. Do you think seeing angels and speaking to spirits is normal?"

Oh god. Here it comes. She's going to tell me how bonkers

I am and have me committed. I tried to connect that with shining and felt stupidly lost. "No. No, I think it's crazy."

"Oh, now. Not crazy. Saner than most folks, in fact. Although the crazy ones won't understand your gift, and you shouldn't expect them to, either. They have to evolve on their terms."

The word "evolve" struck me. The angel had said the spirit he collected had to evolve.

"Hey, it's kinda like Grams knows what she's talking about. Weird," Liz said sarcastically.

"You, my dear, are powerful. And you are meant to use your power to great ends. This little spirit girl has told you there is something you need to prevent, and by the divine power that makes order out of chaos, you should make sure you let that happen. Your music tickles the fancy of heavenly throngs!" she said triumphantly. "By all the love in the universe, you should make sure to share that with the world. Shine, Bitsy! You've got so much light in you. Don't let the demons of your past tell you what you can and can't do. Just shine."

I didn't have a response. The only emotion roaming through me after everything was a blissful numbness that coated my throat with the inability to speak. So I nodded, instead. Grandma stood up, releasing my hands. I thought she was done and would go and sit in her chair with a good book. She went to one of her many bookshelves, the wooden floor creaking along with her footsteps.

I moved to get up and put myself to bed, but she came back to me with a pile of books in her arms. She dumped them onto the ottoman. Some of them slipped and fell to the floor. I reached down and started picking them up. Liz eyed the covers.

"*Psychic Development?*" she read. "*Clairvoyance? How to Speak to Your Angels? Medical Seers?*"

Grandma nodded as she put her hands on her hips. "You know you're not alone when there're this many books out there on the stuff you see and do every day."

"Grandma, why do you have these? Are you psychic?"

"Baby girl, we're all psychic, to one degree or another. But I didn't get these books for me. They're for you," she explained.

"I don't understand," I said.

"When you were four years old and your mama was still here in Portland, I had the privilege of watching you regularly. I was your daycare. And wouldn't you know the sort of stories you told me then are the same things you've told me now—about beings of light and angels and spirits that had passed and talked to you."

"I don't remember any of this," I said.

"That's not surprising," said Liz.

"One day, you told me a man we saw in the grocery store was bad. He was so bad, your stomach hurt, and you wouldn't let me finish shopping. We had to leave the store. The next morning, the man's picture was in the newspaper. He'd held up the grocer, and when the man couldn't unlock the safe he'd shot and killed the store owner and two other shoppers. This happened minutes after we'd left the store.

"Two weeks before you left, you kept saying you'd be leaving soon. And you told me about the place you were going to live next. It was a small place, you'd said, with brown carpet and white walls and a skinny staircase with bars on it.

"After that, when your mama came to pick you up one day, you hugged my neck so tight and begged me to let you stay with me. You said bad things were going to happen if you left the house that night." She started to cry, the tears slipping from her brown eyes and her voice shaking with emotion. "And what could I do? I asked your mama for you to sleep over, but she refused. She dragged you kicking and screaming from the house, and I didn't see you again until you were seventeen. The only thing I got from your mama was one picture. Just one."

She rummaged through the pile until she found a particularly old book. The cover was dusty blue and yellow. It was titled, *The Truth of Angels*. She pulled something from the inner pages and extended it toward me. It was a photo of a little girl, half-smiling, perched on a staircase and looking out between wooden slats. The walls were white; the carpet was brown.

"Holy shit, I remember that place, too," said Liz.

"Language, Liz," Grandma scolded.

"Sorry, Grams."

"So you see, I have known you were special for a long, long time. And nothing has changed between then and now."

She smiled at me as everything sank in... well, not sank in, really... more like floated on the surface. I figured it'd take a good six months to process the events and revelations of the last few weeks.

Grandma gathered up the books and put them back on the shelves. She pointed to them. "These are here when you're ready to start reading."

"Thank you, Grandma," I said. "I think I'll go to bed now."

Grandma nodded as she wrapped me in a hug. "It's been a long day. Go get some sleep."

She pecked me on the cheek and turned to her chair and settled in with a remote in her hand. The TV snicked to life as I turned and gathered the backpack. I couldn't wait to get into the shower. Even though I'd washed off most of the blood, I still felt dirty.

In my right pocket, my phone vibrated. I pulled it out. The burble of words spilled from the news station. I walked toward the stairs on stiff and heavy legs. I took two steps up the stairs before I looked at my phone. It was Corey.

Did you see the news? They're finally talking about the girls missing from Abigail's school.

It's on right now.

They have a suspect! Yes!

I turned toward the TV to listen to what the newscaster had to say.

"Gone missing from the Gresham area elementary school in the last week. The three girls are reported to live in the same neighborhood."

I half-fell back down the stairs and dragged my exhausted body to stand in front of the TV. The female reporter's beautiful ebony face and stylish, short hair disappeared, and three photos of girls of various ages filled the TV screen.

A circle of light popped into my vision. Aerylia's face flashed then faded.

Chapter 24

"Thank you, Charlene," another woman said.

The TV screen flashed to an equally beautiful woman with blonde hair and blue eyes. She sat behind a desk next to a man in a suit whose hair was perfection.

"The suspect currently under investigation is the girls' school bus driver, Cecil Tate, who is also missing from his residence in Gresham. If you see this man, please call the Gresham police department."

A picture of a man filled the screen. I was sure if a person had never been molested or raped as a child, they'd think he looked like a kind, middle-aged guy who was good with kids. But to me, it was like the word "Pedophile" was written across his forehead. I marveled how people could miss it.

"It's him!" El said.

"How can you know?" Liz asked.

I gripped Grandma's chair as a wave of exhaustion and emotion overwhelmed me. My heart stuttered. I fought to catch my breath. Images flashed through my mind's eye.

The bed was made with a pink and green quilt. Past a tripod, a mirror hung on a wall. In the mirror, I saw a girl's face, her wide eyes filled with fear. A man stood at a closed door. A shadow lurked in the corner.

"Honey, are you okay?" asked Grandma as she craned her neck around to look up at me.

I shook my head. She pushed herself from the recliner and guided me into the oversized chair. I fell into it as I continued to stare at the TV. The words Gresham Police Department and a phone number dominated the screen.

"My daughter is showing me," El said.

"The flash of light," Liz said. *"That was her daughter."*

The news reporter promised to share more information as it became available in this breaking news story. And then they moved on to report on the weather. I stared at the screen. Sweat prickled my hairline and down my spine. Grandma sat on the ottoman and gripped my shoulders. My stomach rolled and bucked. The room swam around me. Grandma's face pitched sideways. No, *I* pitched sideways. I groaned as the encroaching blackness overwhelmed me.

My dreams were dark and disturbed, flashed through with angry reds and the screams of children. But my body was too exhausted to fight and too overwhelmed to wake.

When I finally did open my eyes the moon peeked through my window. My window. I was in bed. I wondered how Grandma had gotten me there but not for long. I hurtled from the bed and into my bathroom. The clock on the bathroom counter read 11:10 p.m. After relieving my overfull bladder, I turned on the shower, stripped myself down and climbed in.

I had intended to dally, to soak in the hot water and let it wash away the stains of the night before. But Aerylia appeared in front of me. She was whole but misty through the fog of the steam.

"*She'll die soon,*" she said. And then she was gone.

"*Fuck!*" Liz said.

Weariness still weighed me down, as if my marrow was made of iron. My face pulsed an angry beat of pain. The hot water hitting my body found all the bruises from the night before.

I scrubbed myself anyway, half-relishing the pain of my injuries since they served to shock me into wakefulness. I pulled myself from the shower, dried and wrapped my wet hair in the towel. Rushing from the bathroom, I found a clean pair of jeans, a long-sleeved t-shirt and a sweatshirt. After throwing on socks and hiking boots, I finger-combed my curly hair and yanked it into a wet ponytail. I was going to freeze out there. But there was no time.

Maltheron was still in the backpack, and I wanted to leave him there, but he begged me to take him along. This was his daughter's killer, was it not? The whole reason he'd been made was to avenge his daughter's spirit. Not even all my ideals could deny that.

Having him close gave me an uncomfortable assurance of protection. Uncomfortable because it would be someone else's life over mine. But if that someone else was raping little girls, maybe I could stop them.

My heart beat too many times with a palpitation of anxiety. Liz rose up, a fiery anger seething inside me.

"*Oh, hell yeah, we're bringing Maltheron,*" she said.

The pictures of the little girls flashed through my mind.

"*How'm I going to find them?*" Panic rose in me.

Aerylia's voice echoed back to me... "*She'll be dead soon.*"

Footsteps whispered down the hall. Grandma cracked the door. "Bitsy?"

I froze.

"Dang. Caught!" said Liz.

"Yeah?" I said tentatively.

"Good, you're up." She pushed inside. She was fully dressed in black pants and a black dress shirt, including hair, make-up and swingy earrings. Her black shoes were on, and she was clutching her nice leather handbag. She clasped her hands in front of her and looked expectantly at me. I stared back.

"Are you ready?"

"Ready?" Liz asked.

Grandma straightened, tilting up her chin and looking down her nose at us. "We have to find those girls, and by god, you're not going by yourselves. I'm driving." Regally, she turned away from me and headed out of the room.

Stunned, I picked up my backpack and followed.

"We know where I get my spunk from, don't we?" said Liz.

"This isn't safe for the old one. What if she gets hurt?" El asked.

"Um, you want to try to stop her?" I asked.

El was silent for a moment as we followed Grandma down the stairs. When she set her feet on the landing, she pulled the keys from her purse and turned to us.

"C'mon, c'mon, c'mon." She rushed us, motioning me out the door, keys jingling.

Wide-eyed, I obediently stepped out onto the porch. Chilled fingers pressed through my wet hair and dug into my scalp. My skin prickled down my neck. I pulled my sweatshirt hood closer to my ears while I waited for Grandma to lock the door.

"I have no idea what we're doing." I finally said what I'd been thinking since I woke. "I don't know where to go, and once we get there, I don't know what to do."

Grandma led the way down the porch stairs toward the drive where the car sat in darkness.

"Come on," Grandma told me. "Let's get in the car, and we'll figure it out."

I shrugged and rounded the front of the car, climbing into the passenger side.

Grandma slid into the driver's seat, fumbled with the keys and put them in the ignition without starting it. She turned to me from behind the wheel and put her hand on mine, which rested on my knee.

"As to where we're going, that's really easy. We ask the girl's spirit to guide us."

Immediately, Aerylia materialized in front of the car, like some oversized hood ornament. The air in the car grew chilly.

"And as to what we do when we get there, even easier. We call the cops."

"And tell them what, Grams? We say we know where he is, they'll ask how. What do we say then?" Liz said.

"Well, you just tell them we were in the neighborhood and happened to see him."

"What if it turns out he's not there when we are?" Liz asked.

"Then we'll say we saw him earlier in the day," Grandma said.

"That's messy. They'll see through our story," I said, joining the conversation.

"We will kill the man. You must let us take out our revenge on him," El chimed in, using my voice, which croaked against her force.

"No," I said, my voice firm against her. "Murder is not the way for us. You're ladling darkness into our soul. We don't want to be darkness. We've seen enough of that already. No. We'll call the cops, like Grandma said. They'll arrest him, and he'll go to jail for the rest of his life."

"What if he doesn't?" asked Liz. "What if he gets off on insanity or some other bullshit? And then they let him out for good behavior after a couple of years, and then he goes after some other girls!"

"My daughter's spirit won't rest until he's dead!" shouted El.

"Stop it!" I yelled. "That just can't be true. It makes no sense. You can't murder and expect it to add any light into the universe. It doesn't work that way."

There was a long silence in both the car and my head. The girl's spirit floated above the car. I looked at her.

"What will give you peace?" I asked.

She began to glow, to shimmer, to sway. Her voice rose to a crescendo, an unearthly scream that ratcheted first in my mind and then swelled into the here and now and burst into the audible reality. Grandma clapped her hands over her ears, staring with her dark doe eyes over the hood of the car. Aerylia's spirit shifted—first whole, then mangled, then dark, then light—and as she did, she came closer to the windshield, and the screams raged. Grandma was panting through gritted teeth.

"Stop!" I screamed.

The girl disappeared. One moment a screeching mass, the next, nothing. Grandma loosened her grip on her ears, looking around in bewilderment.

"Was that her, Bitsy?" she asked. "Honey, what's wrong with her?" My Grandma. So brave.

I waited, eyes fixed on the front of the car. Knowing, listening, watching. And then she was in the car with us, the cold touch of her spirit caressing my skin like the bite of winter. The keys dangling in the ignition turned. The engine roared to life, headlights clinking on. Grandma grabbed for my hand, which I took without hesitation.

"Save them," she said. The quietest whisper but so loud it could start an avalanche. Quiet so substantial it could move a mountain.

With those soft words, the gentle splash of images washed through my mind. My head tilted back; air caught in my throat as the vision flooded through me.

I traveled, my mind and spirit yanked street by street, led by the haunting shadow of the Hound, the headlights of the car casting white circles into the darkness of the road. Road signs flashed at me. Hemlock then Aspen then 31st. A house came into view. A normal-looking house with a normal chain-link fence and a normal front door. But she didn't lead me there. She led me down along the cramped side of the house, over a trail of gravel and rock, the windows at my eye level. The back of the house was just as plain as the front of the house, with a big back yard and a small, blonde Shiba Inu that wagged its tail at us as we passed.

She yanked my attention from the back yard, from the innocuous swing set and pristinely mowed grass and well-pruned Japanese maple. I was staring at a shed. A building no bigger than one of those found in many back yards, where homeowners stored their lawnmower and maybe one of those big chest freezers.

I snapped open my eyes as the images faded. My breath wheezed into me. Had I been holding it the whole time? Once I could breathe properly, I said, "I know where to go."

Chapter 25

Grandma backed the car out of the drive as I told her to head toward east Portland. It wasn't far. Not far at all and way too soon, we were edging toward the house, riding along the side of the road with the lights off. Grandma stopped when we were close.

"I'm your getaway, sweetpea. I've got my phone ready."

I looked down at the phone she held awkwardly in her hand. She waved the happy, lit-up screen at me and raised her eyebrows. As if it would save us from all the problems we faced. I leaned over the console and kissed her cheek.

I got out of the car before I could regret the display of affection. Maltheron was stowed in the backpack slung over my shoulders, and my cell phone was neatly tucked into the pouch of my sweatshirt. I pulled the hood up over my still-wet hair and followed the memory of the vision. The road jogged left, and before I could freeze to death or get so scared I turned around and headed back to the car, the house was there in front of me.

"This house?" Liz asked. "Are you sure?"

I knew why she asked. The place seemed so benign. Before

I could answer, Aerylia appeared in front of me and scared the crap out of us all.

"We got it," Liz hissed. "We don't need you to spook us out at every left-hand turn."

But the alien girl's spirit was drifting toward the door.

"Not the door," I thought, remembering the night before. I rubbed at the bruises on my body.

"Trust her," El said.

"Yes, but in the vision, she showed me the back yard and the shed. Now she's showing the front door. What does it mean?" I asked.

"Maybe something changed," Liz offered. *"You know, between the vision and now."*

I walked across the blacktop, sliding on an icy spot. The full moon was out, a golden globe hanging above the horizon. The sky was lead gray and black that shifted and swayed. The air was still, pregnant with the silence of winter. There were no lights on at the blue house, except for El's girl, who hung like a lamp on the small front porch.

Problem was, the front porch was just past the chain-link fence. I had no idea how I was going to get in there.

"Why don't you just try the gate?" Liz said sarcastically.

I followed the edge of the road along a ditch and then passed over the earthen driveway and up to the gate. I pushed up the metal U. It was unlocked.

"See? Easy peasy," Liz said.

I tentatively pushed open the gate. It squeaked in protest. I tried to quiet it by shh-ing at it.

But that was okay, because the sound of the gate was getting drowned out by a new sound.

"Oh, god!" Liz cried out. "Not a dog!" She yanked on the gate, but it was already pushed open, and pulling it was harder than pushing it.

Growling snarls accompanied the jingle of a dog tag and the scuff of claws in the dirt. The dog burst through the gate. I had just enough sway over her to stifle her scream as she fell backward. The Shiba Inu that bound through the gate was awfully familiar. But it wasn't the dog coming toward me that startled me as much as the creature enveloping it like a shadow.

El burst forward as the dog lunged onto us. Pushing off the ground then setting herself in a wide stance, she opened up her arms and raised them.

She shout-whispered, "Hound, stop!"

The dog skidded to a halt two feet in front of us.

Both the dog inside the creature as well as the creature, wagged their tails at me as I took the reins from El. I held out a hand, which the dog nuzzled with a wet black nose, then it butted its head into my fingers for a scratch. The creature seemed to lick at my face with its extremely long, purple tongue. I imagined if that had been anything other than a spirit tongue, I would have sputtered and batted the thing away. Liz recoiled from the dog, but she'd stopped freaking out, which was new. When did this change happen?

"Good girl! Who's a good puppy? You are. Yes. You're a good dog," I crooned in a whisper as I took a closer look at the house.

"The Hound will get jealous if you do not show it affection, as well," El said.

"And who's a good boy," I said.

The Hound ducked its nose and repetitively made a huff-huff-huff noise, digging his shadowy paws into the earth and then shaking his dark, multi-colored ruff.

"That means he likes you," Liz said.

"And you know this how?" I asked.

"The Hound hunted with us," Liz said, her voice small and terse.

"You let a creature from another planet that's ten times as terrifying as a dog get this close to you?" I asked.

"Well," Liz said and paused to work out the explanation. "When we hunted, it was in the ether, and things just aren't that scary there."

I reached a hand toward the Hound, fascinated with its four electric blue eyes and nose slits up the length of its long snout. He pressed his cheek into my outstretched hand. The sensation was like when you try to push two magnets together with the same poles facing. There was an invisible tension in the air between us. I ran my hand down the length of its face and reached for its ruff. The Hound lowered its head for me to caress fur that was an echo of an animal from another planet.

If we freed them. If somehow the host of spirits from another realm could get back to their own place of existing, would it be with a body they'd left for weeks? Would they be ghosts forever more?

A pang of pity spread through me.

"I'm sorry you've gone through all of this, Elada," I said. "And I'm sorry I didn't believe you at first."

"It is understandable why you reacted the way you did," she said. "But let us move on and discover if this is the residence of Aerylia's killer. I am anxious for the reunion."

Maltheron chimed in with a resonating hum of agreement. And then I wondered if being stuck as spirits would be their karma for pursuing murder instead of some other form of justice. But I kept that thought to myself.

I dropped my hand from the Hound and turned my attention to the house.

The place crawled with shadows. Their dark touch reached out to me, and I swayed. The dog whined. I leaned over and pulled the tag from her collar. *Bella*, it read. So, she was a girl. I'd been right.

"Hi, Bella," I said.

The dog cocked her head to one side at the sound of her name.

"You have to be going crazy with all those shadows in there."

She cocked her head to the other side and made a noise somewhere between a growl and whine.

"I hear ya. Can't say I'm going to like going in there."

"Save them!" The alien girl's spirit reappeared on the covered front porch.

I looked down the driveway. There was a closed carport. The windows were all covered. No telling if the owner actually used the carport for its purpose and not just for storing junk.

"Lead the way, girl," I said, my voice shaky even to me.

The Hound and Bella turned away from me and trotted into the yard. The grass was thick and green and well-tended. Enough so that I worried at my footprint indentations in its lushness. The porch boasted a little hammock swing. The house was small but seemed in good repair. By all accounts, this homeowner cared about his belongings and abode.

Bella trotted up to the porch, climbed the few small steps on the side of the house and paused to look back at me. Once I moved forward, she dodged away, nose low to the porch boards, then sat down proudly beside a garden of empty flowerpots. They were stacked neatly and void of anything that should be in flowerpots.

I glanced around for the hundredth time before half-crawling up the stairs. On my knees, I shuffled under the length of the front window that glowed mutely under the cover of heavy curtains. A small breeze snaked through the corridor of the porch, catching against my exposed face and damp hair. The moon over my right shoulder rose big and yellow. It was a cloudless night, a rare treat for the Pacific Northwest.

The towers of pots were located just past the welcome mat in front of the door. I scuffed along, being careful I raised my feet enough that they didn't go clunking into the wooden boards. Bella whined at me, as if to tell me to hurry it up. A noise from inside the house froze me in place. A faraway door opened. Footsteps reverberated. A light turned on, further deepening the glow from the front window. The footsteps grew louder. A shadow clung to the curtain.

"*Shit! Run, Bits!*" Liz screamed at me.

I couldn't move. My hands and knees were glued to the porch. Absently, I wondered why I hadn't pulled Maltheron out of the backpack. The Hound peered up at the window, then to the door and back to the window again. What was I going to do if he came out the front door?

"*Do not be afraid,*" said El. "*I will protect you.*"

Her voice splashed me with wakefulness.

"*You'll run Maltheron through him, is what you'll do. More blood-shed.*" The disgust was plain in my voice.

"*It is nothing more than he deserves.*"

"*Maybe so,*" I said, "*but you've taken the matter of judgment not only into your own hands but into Liz's, as well. I won't let you do that with me. There will be another way.*"

El's anger boiled away. The shadow and footsteps retreated and then disappeared. I let go of a breath I hadn't realized I was holding. The cold night air burned through my lungs. Bella lay down by the front door, resting her head on her paws. The Hound watched me closely.

"*I think we're supposed to go inside,*" I said.

"*Are you sure?*" Liz asked, her fear evident with the quaking of her voice.

Aerylia appeared in the window and pointed to the door. After she disappeared, there was a soft snick at the door. Heart hammering wildly, I looked at the window again, expecting to see the shadow of the man standing there, but none came. I closed a hand around the knob, inhaled deeply and twisted.

I peered through the crack in the door. The room was abandoned. A single lamp lit the small area with a yellow glow. An ancient arm chair sat in one corner facing a small tube TV. I opened the door an inch further and listened. Footsteps sounded in some unseen room. I looked around. I knew the girls weren't in here. They were in that shed, I was sure of it. So, why was I here? Aerylia ghosted past to the right of me. I turned my head to see where she went and caught the glint of metal on the wall next to the door.

Keys.

There were keys pinned to paneling on the walls. I would need a key to get into the shed. Problem was, there were several sets of keys. With my stomach clenched and body trembling, I stepped into the house, turned my back to the living room, and surveyed the collection. My skin crawled. Unseen fingers of fear tickled down my vertebrae. My lungs ached as I tried to not breathe. Cold air flowed into the house and skirted around my ankles.

"Oh my god," Liz said, "thank you, Jesus! They're labeled!"

I was just about to sigh in relief when fast footsteps bounded through the house, growing louder with each step. I snatched the silver key with appropriate label and jetted out of the door, not bothering to close it behind me. Bella sprang back from the doorway and into a pile of flower pots towering near the door.

"Run!" Liz said.

Before I could let my fear freeze me, she took over. Liz took off with speed and grace, covering the length of the porch and tripping down the stairs. Rounding the house, we squeezed up against the side wall, breathing hard and heavy. Light flooded the porch and front yard.

And that's when the shadows started swirling. They crept down the porch stairs, oozing like molasses toward me. Liz didn't have to tell me this time. I bolted away.

"Hey! Who's out there?"

"Oh, my god! Did he see us?" I asked the other two residing in my head. I dodged around the back of the house, hopping over a small yard decoration shaped like a colorful mushroom. I skidded into the grass near the other end of the house then crawled around the hulking shape of a covered barbeque. Bella's bark sounded off around the front side of the house.

"Just you," said the man, his voice pitching into a different tone. Was he annoyed? Disgusted?

Bella whined. Muffled footsteps retreated over the front porch then paused.

"It's him!" El said. *"I can't believe it, but it really is him!"*

Maltheron started in with the low moan that throbbed in the small confines of my tiny backpack. Broken crockery shifted. I opened my hand and saw the key glinting back at me. A thrill of fear zipped up my spine. He was going to see this was missing.

I turned in the grass and saw the shed. Like the rest of the house and property, from all appearances it looked as normal as any other homeowner's shed. It promised nothing more disturbing or exciting than tools to trim the hedge and extra paint for the upstairs bathroom. Then why were my arms and neck covered in gooseflesh? And why was Aerylia hovering in front of the small door?

"Hurry! He's coming back here!" Liz said.

I stopped thinking and listened. Sure enough, more footsteps echoed on the boards of the porch. I lurched from a crouched position and sprinted to the shed.

"But Grandma! We need to text her and tell her to call the cops! We can just give them the key!" I said, even as I made it to the door

and stared in hesitation. I looked around. If I ran now, could I make it back to the fence and climb it? Was that a possibility?

"He's coming now! Just get in there, and then we'll figure out what to do next!" Liz yelled at me.

I shoved the key into the hole but it wouldn't go. Nearly drowning in panic, I turned the key the opposite direction as the sound of crunching gravel echoed toward us. Dancing from foot to foot, I twisted the lock, turned the knob and threw myself into the shed.

Chapter 26

I slammed the door behind me and locked it. If he had another key, that was going to be useless. I blinked. I was in one hundred percent darkness. I leaned against the door and listened, hoping the hammering of my heart wasn't as audible as it felt. The crunching gravel stopped. Silence stretched away while the darkness consumed me like an ethereal beast.

The doorknob digging into my back muscles moved.

I nearly squealed in fear, but El clamped my hand over my mouth and nose.

The doorknob jiggled harder. I splayed out my legs and braced against the wood that separated me from the predator. The barrier jolted as Cecil Tate, bus driver and kidnapper, threw his weight against it. I pulled out my phone, touched the button for the flashlight. A shadow scurried from the circle of light. The door shivered again.

"Hello?" I whispered. "Is someone in here?"

Bam! Cecil growled like an animal.

The banging stopped. Still leaning against the door, I cast the flashlight slowly around the room. Two girls huddled on a small bed in the corner of the room. I blinked and looked again. Yes. It was a bed.

"It's going to be okay," I told the girls, my stomach turning to steel. Where was the third girl? Was I too late?

Hoping beyond hope the man didn't have another key, I pulled away from the door and shined my phone on the walls and ceiling. The black skeleton of a tripod passed through the light. My stomach dropped. What they'd had to endure... the memories floating in the small room tripped through my mind, a parade of unwelcome images, smells and sounds. Tears rolled down my cheeks.

The light switch was next to the door. I switched it on and took a slow breath before turning around. The girls sat on the bed, wrapped in a thick pink and green blanket and clutching each other. One was a blonde and pale, and the other had black hair and ebony skin. They both looked about eight or nine years old. I was that age once. By then, I'd already been raped and molested by three different people. It was as if I had been marked. They knew where to find me and how to get to me, and my mother had done nothing to keep them from coming. I closed my eyes against the awful memories triggered by the energy soaked into this little shed of horrors. But I wouldn't ignore them anymore.

"I'm so sorry you had to go through that, Liz," I told her.

She cried silently. The memories were separated from my feeling them the way you watch a movie and see someone go through something awful. Like a camera had recorded the events, and the film was playing now, showing me what happened rather than me experiencing it first person. I knew Liz was the one in the film. Liz had borne the awfulness of our childhood, protected me from it. Would these girls suffer the same fate? Did they each now have a Liz of their own?

"Better to have a Liz than to be dead," said El.

Liz snarled at her. *"What do you know, Princess,"* she spat. *"You don't! You don't know what it's like to live every day with a fucked-up view of reality. To be so scarred you're split into two pieces instead of a whole person. To constantly base your relationships on the idea you're either not worthy of what love you might get or too worthy of the shit they're bound to toss at you. That's better, huh?"*

I rubbed at my wrists. I hadn't always thought life was better. Only Grandma had taught me I could be loved unconditionally. Maybe if these girls had someone to love them like that, they'd have a chance. Maybe this could be an isolated experience, and they'd be supported to heal and learn to thrive again.

"And maybe you're stronger because of what you've been through."

Liz didn't have to butt in on this one; I had this covered.

"That's such a cliché. It's tired and old and it doesn't work. I'm not stronger because of what we went through. I'm stronger because I want something, and I won't let the past hold me back from getting it." I said.

"What is it that you want?" El asked.

I could feel Liz wondering, too. I thought about the way the music felt inside me when I played. How notes transferred me to another place of light and love. I thought about how the moon looked lovely in the night sky and how wind played against my skin and how I loved the smell of fresh-cut grass and long, lazy summer afternoons spent with Grandma, watching TV. I thought about the sense of accomplishment I got from finishing a busy day at work and the feel of my muscles after a long walk. The taste of ice cream and hot fudge. The scent of clean laundry. A good long cry at a great movie. The feel of Grandma's strong hug.

"It's true; there's a lot of ugliness in life. We've seen our fair share. But there's so much to love about it, too. So much to treasure. I want happiness, so I can enjoy all of those things. I think, after everything we've been through—that's been done to us—we deserve that goodness. So that's what I fight for. That's why I'm strong. Not because bad things happened. Because I want the good things."

Liz and El didn't speak.

"We have some work, ladies. Let's get to it," I said.

"My name is Bitsy," I whispered to the girls and waited.

The girls from my vision of the school bus stared, their eyes wide as saucers. The fear owned them. I took a slow, deep breath and prayed. *My Mother and My Father: please shine your light on us. Please send your angels to help these girls and me escape. And take down the one who has caused so much damage and pain.* I took out my phone and sent a text message to Grandma.

> I found two of them. Call the police.
> We're in the shed behind the house.

I waited for the reply. And I waited. A shrill fear burst into my chest and neck. I pressed the phone app and dialed 9-1-1.

"9-1-1. Please state your emergency," said a warm voice on the other end of the line.

"I found those th-three m-missing girls," I said, so panicked my stutter was a challenge to work around. "Well, I found two of them. I don't know where the third one is yet."

As I said that last part, the dark-haired girl jerked her skinny arm from the blanket and pointed.

"Aidan's over there," she said. Aidan must be the name of the girl that had gone missing weeks ago.

"Where are you, and what is your name?" asked the dispatcher.

I could hear her typing furiously on the other end of the line.

I spoke as I walked toward where the girl was pointing. "I'm at 1928 31st Ave E. My name is Elizabeth Varret. My grandmother and I were driving together when I saw the guy in his yard. So I went in to check it out. And I found them in the shed."

The two girls followed me with their eyes. A throbbing pain began in my forehead and spread into my sinuses. The farther I moved, the more focused the pain became, settling into the spot between my eyebrows.

"Aidan, you're my special girl." A disembodied voice thrummed through my mind.

I lurched as fear gripped me, turning my stomach to stone, setting my heart on a race. His face burst in my vision then cut out like a bad connection to a TV station. I fell to my knees as the room tilted around me, and the next memory gripped me in vicious claws. I will not describe it. It was too horrific.

The voice on the other side of the phone was talking. "I want you to stay on the line with me, Miss. I am sending help right now."

I crawled across the dusty boards of the shed, the light overhead casting my shadow under and in front of me. The corner I crawled toward held another mattress but no bedframe. It was one of those foam mattresses. It was easy to see why I'd missed her. She was curled in a ball, hidden under a heap of blankets, and the mattress had sunk in under her tiny frame. I didn't want to even touch the bed. My mind went foggy. I fought to regain control.

My voice would hardly work. I swallowed against the terror and pain I felt from this little girl.

"I found the third one," I whispered into the phone. "I don't know if she's alive. She's under a pile of blankets." My voice squeaked. I wondered if the woman could even hear me. There was such a long pause of silence I thought I'd accidently cut off the connection.

"Okay, it's up to you, darlin'. You can uncover her and see if she's alive, or you can leave her. The ambulance is already on its way. If you uncover her, I can tell the paramedics what to expect, and they might be able to respond quicker." She stopped talking.

I stood there.

"Bits, you gotta look at her. You gotta see if she's alive."

My hands shook as I reached for the covers. As if they were a Band-Aid, I pulled them back quickly. It didn't help. The onslaught of Aidan's memories buckled me. I screamed out loud. An explosion of sound interrupted my horror. I yanked my gaze toward the door. The man on the other side grunted, and then a shiny sliver of something peeked through the wood. The girls screamed.

"What's going on in there?" asked the dispatcher. "Tell me what's happening."

Another blow and more of the shiny thing appeared in the door.

"Jesus Christ!" Liz screamed. "He's got a fucking axe!"

I turned back to the little girl. She wasn't moving. She wore a white smock over her olive skin. Her body was emaciated. I watched her as the next blow from the axe splintered more of the wood, the night outside becoming visible through the widening hole.

"She's breathing!" I told the woman. And then I saw all the blood on the sheets and nearly puked. But there was just no time for that. "I think she's really badly hurt." I sobbed.

The smell was awful, and the blood was old and brown. I crawled over the mattress, no longer caring about the inundation of images and feelings. The girl's eyes were closed, and dark circles surrounded them. Her cheeks were gaunt. She had to be on the verge of death. How long had she been missing? How long had she lain here in awful pain to the point of passing out and not waking?

Her stomach was distended, and her lower body was a solid pattern of bruises. "I think she has internal bleeding." My brain was going numb, but my mouth was still speaking. "She's got bruises all over her legs and butt; there's old blood here, and she's burning up. Her belly is distended. She looks really emaciated," I told the dispatcher over the deafening hacks of the axe against the door.

An animal anger rose within me while I surveyed the girl and conveyed the information to the dispatcher. I could see what he'd done to her. Over and over again.

"Okay, I've sent the message over to the ambulance. Is there somewhere you can hide? Is there a way out of the building? The police are only a couple of minutes away."

"I'm sorry; I can't chat anymore. I need both hands if I'm going to protect us." I hung up the phone and shoved it into my sweatshirt pocket. Pulling off my backpack, I motioned to the two girls on the bed. "You two come here and get behind me. I want you together, so he can't go after any of you."

The girls obeyed, miraculously. I figured they'd be too shell-shocked and afraid, but they lurched off the tiny bed and ran to me. I pushed them behind me.

"Be careful you don't bump her, okay? She's in really bad shape."

"He's a bad, bad man!" screamed the little black girl. "He hurt her really bad. He was going to hurt us next."

She shook behind me as I pulled Maltheron from the backpack. I wouldn't kill anyone if I didn't have to, but I wouldn't let these children get hurt any more than they'd already been hurt. The other girl didn't speak. I could understand that.

The hole in the door was enough for him to get his arm through. Bits of his face peeked through the hole while he searched for the lock. He was middle-aged, white, balding. There was sweat on his wide forehead. His teeth gritted together as he fought to reach the doorknob. He growled against the few inches keeping him from his goal. He adjusted his stance against the door, which pushed his searching fingers close enough to touch the shiny brass of the knob. I stood up and widened my stance, trying to ready myself for whatever physical action I would have to take against the man. I quaked at my lack of confidence. Physical prowess was not my strong suit. Outside the shed, Bella's barks sounded off like a car alarm's panic button. In my mind, the Hound joined in with growling so deep it reverberated inside my skull. Silently, I prayed for the cops to hurry up.

"*I am here. I will help you if you will let me,*" El said.

"*Can I trust you not to just kill him?*" I asked.

The man's fingers were on the small button of the lock. Each of my heartbeats tripped over the next.

"*If I do not have to kill the man, then I give you my word, I will not. The children matter more than my vengeance.*"

The man grunted and pushed the lock the last centimeter to unlock the door.

And then I heard a maniacal female cry from outside.

"Grandma!" I screamed.

The man yelped. His arm yanked out of the hole in the door. "Get off me!" he shouted.

A loud thump shook the door as something heavy was thrown against it but not high enough to be seen through the axed hole. I rushed to the door and pulled it open. Grandma fell in. The axe fell. Grandma screamed. I shouted and lurched at the same time.

His face wasn't what disturbed me the most—it was the multicolored shadow vibrating around him. A mix of unearthly shades of reds and gray and muddy brown. The axe was buried in Grandma's knee. He still had his hands on the handle. I raised Maltheron as I lurched toward him, stepping over my grandmother. He had time to pull the axe from Grandma's knee. She screamed at the pain. I launched myself onto him.

The man and I tumbled to the ground, and before my knees could find purchase to pin him to the well-manicured lawn, he kicked out. His foot found my gut, and he pushed. My body flew through the air and landed with a solid thump.

I gasped and drew air back into my lungs but was left in a wash of white light and dancing stars. Grandma screamed again. The bus driver clambered to his feet, axe in hand.

"El, help!" Liz screamed.

I was no longer gripping Maltheron, but my hands were disconnected with my consciousness. I sat back as an observer as El rose from the ground. She opened my right hand, and Maltheron flew neatly into it. Aerylia ghosted up behind the man, and caught off guard, he swung wildly with the axe. His next aimed blow at my grandmother missed. The axe fell and stuck blade first into the rain-softened soil.

El moved my body with lightning speed. She caught the man around the shoulders. The shadow surrounding him expanded, shifted and burned with murky reds. There was a crimson shimmer in the corner of my vision. That was El. And her husband glinted in metallic greens and golds.

"Tell me, foe. Speak your name," El said, her voice not mine but her own, deep and rich like sorghum.

A laugh like darkness itself rumbled through the man.

"You also came. And here we are to merry meet again. Even the daughter Aerylia is present with us."

"She has uncovered you and brought us to you. Speak your name."

"You think I'm a fool."

"I do," El said. "You're a fool to think you can keep it from me. I am a Maker. Do not forget."

Maltheron whistled into the man's throat.

"Speak," she said.

A humming energy coiled out from El's scarlet aura,

slithered down my arm, wrapped around Maltheron and leaked into the little cut that exposed the man's life blood. The energy glowed and sparkled with El's intention. A spasm went through the man, starting at his head and traveling—like fire touched to gasoline—toward his feet. He grunted; his teeth ground against each other. The shadow that pooled outside him shifted, twisted and pulsed against El's will. And then the name came.

"Raston." The voice was distorted, deep.

El's shrill of triumph was covered in her lust for the man's blood. She made the minutest motion with my arm. A movement that meant to slice the man's throat open and spill his blood in a sacrifice for revenge. But before she could finish the movement, Aerylia appeared behind Raston, arm outstretched, and she spoke a single word.

"*No!*"

The voice was loud enough to send a shiver of fear through me, and yet it was disembodied and surreal. El held Maltheron to the man's throat but stopped her movement to cut him down. My breath wheezed in and out of me, my heart banging away in frustration. El's confusion and bloodlust raged through me. I felt it for her, but it was not mine to feel.

"Why?" El croaked. "Does your soul not require this to find peace?"

"*Maker, I am whole in this form. Another death will only stain you. But I will not abide that others suffer at his hands,*" Aerylia said.

"Then we will kill him and end his cycle of hurting others," El said.

Maltheron thrummed in my hand, as if to champion this idea.

"*Do not kill him. Let us return home and awaken his awareness to his crimes,*" said Aerylia.

Her ghostly voice made the hairs on my arms and neck

spring to life. The moon, in perfect, full brightness, slid out from behind a curtain of grey clouds. El, Maltheron, Aerylia and Raston all gasped at the same moment. El and Raston's gazes flew toward the heavens. The moon was so big, so exactly centered in the night sky, but in the middle of such an awesome struggle, I couldn't see why they were drawn to stare at it.

Maltheron was still positioned at the bus driver's throat, and a slow trickle of blood slid down his neck. Aerylia appeared to my left, reaching out one hand to her mother and the other to her killer. Bella and The Hound trotted up to the small group and closed the gap across from Aerylia. Sirens whined in the distance. Aerylia's eyes clapped onto me, and though Elada's focus was purely on the moon, I was able to look back at her daughter.

"*Thank you,*" she said.

The world around me vibrated. My hearing muffled. The light of the moon grew, and as it did, a prickling chill crept into my toes. The chill continued up my legs, leaving my feet warm and light. The sensation crawled up my body, trading the cold for warmth. I looked up, my vision distorted by the red aura of Elada. In front of me, the bus driver swayed against the knife as a shadow lifted up and away from his body, moving toward the moon in El's and Aerylia's firm grip and flanked by the hulking presence of the Hound.

"*Wait,*" Liz cried. "*What about our ritual?*"

"*What are you talking about, Liz?*" I asked.

Elada looked down at us, compassion easing across her face. "*If you still want it, the dagger will work. It still maintains its power,*" she said.

"*Liz, what is she talking about?*" I asked.

The spirit rising out of the blade was manlike and handsome. He was all too familiar from the series of dreams I'd had. Elada, Maltheron and Aerylia tucked the dark form of the fourth person into a tight circle as they continued their journey toward the moon. I sucked in air and fell away from the bus driver, who took one look up before his eyes rolled back in his head, and he fell to the ground.

I held the dagger, empty of the spirit of Maltheron, hoping desperately that since his purpose was fulfilled he would return to his previous form. One that gave him the ability to grow things and nurture life.

"It still has its power?" I asked Liz.

"If we wanted, we could still find the person who split us, kill them and be freed of all of our issues."

I held the dagger in my hand as I considered the possibility again.

"But there's more than one," I said.

"True, but what if we started with the first one. Maybe that would be enough to heal the break between us."

"We don't even know who the first one was."

"Also true. But Grams does," said Liz.

Above me, the dark spirit of Aerylia's killer struggled against the forced embrace of the four. But he was going nowhere. Nowhere except up into a swirling circle formed in the light of the moon. As they drew closer to that light, El looked down at me. She didn't speak, but she smiled... as if to express her thanks.

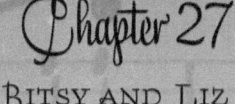
A muffled groan dragged my attention from the dissipating, swirling circle that had swallowed the four spirits. I turned to see Grandma fighting to sit upright and holding a hand over a gaping wound in her leg. I stuffed the dagger into my sweatshirt pocket and rushed over to her and added pressure to the slippery mess of her thigh. She gasped and then fell back against the shed.

"Oh, my god!" I screamed. "Grandma!"

But my horrific screams were drowned by the whine of the sirens. A different kind of fear swelled within me. My hands were red with her blood. The skidding of tires in gravel was a welcome sound, but they couldn't get here fast enough.

"Over here!" I shouted, hoping they could hear me through the cracking sobs and wavering of my voice.

I shouted again and heard an echo of my words from an oncoming paramedic. The white of his shirt glowed in the night.

"Oh, god, dear goddess and all your angels, please come to me. Please bless my grandma and keep her safe. Help these people to save her life, so I can keep her with me. Please, please, please. I don't think I can do this by myself. I can't. I know we can't. We need her."

Paramedics gathered around us. Gut-wrenching sobs ripped out of my mouth and throat. My face was wet and snotty, and I could hardly see through the tears pouring from my eyes. Someone jostled me, and I nearly lost the grip I had on the wound. Someone spoke to me, and I looked up to see five men and women circled around Grandma and me.

"All right, we're going to take good care of her. Is this your grandmother?"

"Yes, this is my grandma," I said to the man beside me, and with a start, I realized who he was.

He looked at Grandma, but when he looked up at me his face relaxed with shock.

"Liz?" he asked. "What happened here?"

I was pleased that the story we'd practiced came so fluidly from me. "Grandma and I were driving and we saw the guy from the news on this front porch. So we stopped. I shouldn't have, but I came into the yard and looked around to see if I could find the missing girls. I found them in the shed. But then the guy came out and tried to k-kill me. Grandma stopped him, but then he got her, too."

I glanced behind me, relieved to see a small gang of police turning the man to his stomach and cuffing him while he mumbled groggily. One large cop was reading him his rights.

"Listen, we're going to take over with your grandma. Don't worry. I'm going to take really good care of her, okay?"

I nodded but didn't move. I was afraid if I moved my hands, Grandma would bleed out and die right there. My stomach twisted at the thought.

"Someone should go into the shed. The one girl is..." I nearly couldn't say anything else. What she'd been through... "She needs help right away."

Gabe looked behind him toward the shed.

"A woman should see to her, if you have someone," I added.

He nodded grimly. His blue eyes looked tired and old, but his aura was a beautiful green that shone and sparkled around him in a soothing pattern.

Liz spoke up. Not in the smartass way she usually did but sounding wise and sort of resigned. *"You really should try to open up to him. What's the worst that can happen? He won't like you? You already think that, anyway, so there wouldn't be any surprise if that were true. You have nothing to lose."*

She had a point. But now was really not the time to think about relationships.

Gabe yelled out to a new gaggle of paramedics arriving in the back yard. Someone had positioned an ambulance to shine its headlights into the yard. The oncoming figures looked like black pillars against the artificial light. They rushed past us, slowing at the entrance to the shed and calling out to the girls inside.

Small, cool hands covered in gloves touched mine. I looked up. A woman with long, curly black hair pulled into a ponytail, and brilliantly green eyes, caught my stare.

"Let me take your place now, sweetheart. You did a good job here. We've got her now."

I sobbed but slowly pulled my hands away. The wound had stopped leaking so much blood. The woman paramedic's gentle and practiced hands kept carefully close while she surveyed the wound and reported what she saw to her on-looking colleagues, who took turns chiming in with what was best to do to stabilize her. I pushed myself out of the circle and let them take over, but I was no idle observer for long. A hand touched my shoulder.

"Bitsy?"

I turned to the police officer.

"Y-yes," I stuttered. "Oh, hi, Officer Mike. I'm seeing all

kinds of familiar faces tonight." I swayed in place. God, my body was so sore and so tired. I blinked heavily.

"I heard the call over the radio that you'd found the missing girls from Gresham. Couldn't believe I heard your name."

I took a deep breath and launched into my explanation again.

"Whoa, whoa, let me take some notes."

He pulled a pencil and notepad from his front pocket and scribbled away while I talked.

Behind Officer Mike, paramedics were hauling out a small stretcher with a tiny figure lying on it. The EMTs' faces were grim, alight with righteous anger... and something else. Stunned with loss. As if they weren't carrying a live girl out of the shed but a corpse. But I knew she was still alive. She wasn't in a body bag. She was on a stretcher.

What sort of life would she have after what she'd endured? Once her body was healed, what would be left of her spirit and mind? Liz and I shuddered at the torture I'd seen. Maybe El had a point, after all.

"What is it?" asked Mike, clearly seeing the pain cross my face.

"I was just thinking of what sort of survival the girl is going to have after she's been through all—" I gestured toward the shed, toward the horror. "All this."

He nodded and sighed. "Yeah, sometimes I wish there was a magic pill to make people forget the awful things I've seen them have to go through."

I was quiet, thinking about how Liz had given that to some. How would that girl's life change without all that crap in her head? What would it be like if Liz and I couldn't remember what we'd been through? To have the slate wiped clean and to be given a fresh start without the deep scars and hardened places of hurt. Mike started talking again.

"But what would she trade for that?"

"Sorry?" I asked.

"Well," he began, rubbing at the back of his neck, "seems as if people don't grow without opposition. You think about people who are pampered. They're shallow. They've never had to dig deep to keep their hold on sanity. They've never had to fight to find joy."

Liz cut in. I could feel her boiling anger. How could I respond to his thoughts when she had always borne the worst of our trials?

"Right. Your trials make you stronger. Trials like what this girl has been through can just break them. I've seen it," Liz said.

He nodded while Liz quivered inside.

"It takes a long time to get back around to thriving after you've barely learned to survive. It takes a whole lot of work."

He knows. He's not just guessing, I told Liz. I could see the shining scars in his soul, the hurts inflicted on him that had stopped bleeding and healed with remnants of what he'd endured. It somehow lit his eyes with a deepness, casting shadows in the corners most others couldn't see.

"Listen, this girl will have the very best help available to her. I've met her family. It isn't like the ones you and I grew up in, if I'm guessing right at what you had to go through in your family. She'll have people like your grandmother over there—willing to take an axe to the knee to keep her safe. And she's been shown love and kindness. That will continue after this horror is over."

He shifted toward me. I thought he would grab my shoulder, and I flinched away.

"Sorry," he said, "I should have known better." He moved a little slower back to his original position and grabbed his neck, rubbing it as he cast a glance toward the shed.

"There are two others in there," I said.

He nodded and slowly turned to look at the shed again.

"Right. There's going to be some happy parents when I call them." He started to move away. "I'll be in touch if we have any further questions for you. Looks as if they've got your grandmother loaded up now. Go on ahead and follow her to the hospital."

I nodded woodenly and watched him go and headed for the shed to grab my backpack. The room was crowded with paramedics hovering over the two girls in the corner.

Michelle saw me when I walked in, pulled away from the woman holding her arm and rushed toward me. She ran across the little shed, tiny bare feet slapping over the boards. As she reached me, she jumped. I could do nothing but open my arms up to catch the catapult of her body. I wrapped her up, my body barely able to hold her against the exhaustion and bruising.

I sank to my knees with her in my arms. Her small hand reached up and patted my still-damp hair. Her body quivered against me, and hot, wet tears dripped down my neck. I crumpled against her, my own tears giving way under the pressure of so much emotion. Her spirit wrapped around me, a golden glow like what I'd seen in the beings of light. I closed my eyes against the sorrow and joy. Another pair of small arms wrapped around me, and a warm, soft cheek pressed into the hollow of my neck and shoulder. I pulled my arm out and wrapped the other little girl, Emma, into the hug.

"It's going to be okay now, girls," Liz and I told them.

Liz softened at the touch of the girls. Michelle pulled away from me, still sobbing, and pressed my face between her hands.

"You rescued us," she said brokenly. "He was going to do the same things to us, but you beat him."

Emma stayed where she was, not speaking. I didn't think

she'd be speaking for a while. But Michelle was a little spark of energy. I could see why Abigail liked her. That thought reminded me.

"Do you know Abigail, in your class?"

Michelle nodded emphatically, her hair bouncing around her round face.

"Well, she's a friend of mine, too. She's going to be happy when I tell her you're safe."

There was a shuffle of feet around us. I blinked through the tears and looked up to see a crowd of police and paramedics crammed in around the three of us. One by one they kneeled, and scooching in, wrapped their arms around the growing group hug. Claustrophobic in the best way, ever, I let these perfect strangers join me in a soggy embrace.

One woman pulled away first, and with tears in her eyes said, "Good job."

A rough-looking, red-haired man with a walrus moustache pulled away next.

"Thank you," he said, his green eyes shining.

After that, the crush of people eased, each taking a turn to thank me or comment on a job well done or call me a heroine. Which was really weird. The paramedics walked the little girls out of the shed and into the yard. They would be taken to the hospital for further evaluation and would meet their parents there. In the emptiness of the shed, I ignored the camera on the tripod and the mess of small mattresses and rumpled sheets and blankets and the ugly mirror hanging on the wall. I pulled my mind away from the stain of the awful things that had happened in the room.

After transferring the knife from my sweatshirt into the backpack, I zipped it up, pulled it onto my shoulders and walked out of the shed, a little heavier and a little lighter, too. I pulled my phone from my pocket once I was back on the grass, under the full moon's awesome light. I texted Corey, despite it being near midnight.

> You can tell your sister Michelle and Emma are safe. I don't know if it'll hit the news right away.

COREY:

> What? How do you know that?

I thought about that. How much did I want to tell Corey? He knew about my ability to see angels. Maybe I could trust him with all of it.

"*I know I've told you to keep your mouth shut, but, I think I was wrong about that with Corey. You can trust him.*" Liz said.

Relief washed over me, and I realized I was dying to tell him about us. That's what friends do, don't they? I decided it was, and that it was time for me to really invest in this friendship.

> Well, it's a really long story. But listen, Grandma is hurt, and I need to get to the hospital. Want to meet me there?

COREY:

> Gramma is hurt??? I'm on my way.

Corey beat me to the hospital, mostly due to my rusty driving skills causing me to creep along the Portland roads to get there. Grandma got checked in and was rushed to the operating room once the on-call orthopedic surgeon arrived. While she was in surgery, I talked. And I talked. Corey listened. There was a lot of revelation, including the introduction of Liz as Liz, my alt and not just an odd mood I had from time to time. While he could have been upset I'd kept so much from him, he wasn't. He understood.

We sat in the emergency department's family room waiting area while I divulged all of my secrets. Codes were called now and then. The department was familiar, but being on this end instead of bustling through to get my job done was surreal.

"So, you're not mad at me?" I asked for the second time. "I've kept a lot from you."

"Bitsy, this kind of stuff is hard to share. I wouldn't expect you to tell me so much when we were first getting to know each other. I get it. I really do."

I nodded before I changed topics. "Did you call your parents."

"Yeah," he said. "Abigail asked if her friends were okay."

"It's tough to say. I don't know how 'okay' the one girl will be. Emma and Michelle should recover pretty quickly."

"I told her the other girl was in bad shape, and she should pray for her," Corey said. "You know what she told me?" He smiled, looking at the floor over his crossed arms. He kicked the carpet and then looked into my eyes. "She said she'd ask the angel Abigail to go heal her. 'That's why you drew her for me,' she said. 'Because I needed to call on her.' Damn, that girl's the most selfless person I know." His voice cracked; his body twitched as he sobbed. He wiped at his face, jostling his glasses.

I couldn't help the tears falling as I knew with surety the angel Abigail was with the girl and ministering healing to her broken body and spirit.

"And do you know what else?" he said. "You've inspired me."

"What do you mean?" I asked.

"I've been watching since I first met you. It's like you're coming out. You're pulling off these wrappings and showing the world who you are. And it's inspiring," Corey said. He smiled at me. "You inspire me to be who I want to be."

I waited for what I knew he would say next, excitement building inside me.

"So, I'm changing my major," he said.

"What about your mom?" I asked.

He exhaled, his eyebrows rising over his frameless glasses. "It's not going to be pretty. Who knows, she might even pull her financial support."

"What will you do then?" I asked.

"Well, I'll keep working here as a HUC until I find another job in the art industry. And there's always student loans. It'll be all right. I'll figure it out."

"Wow. Are you sure?" I asked.

"Certain," he said. "Your angels helped me see that."

"They're not my angels," I said. "They're just angels."

"Well, they seem to like you," he said.

I shrugged. "Seems as if they like you, too," I noted.

He paused, looking at me steadily with his gray-green eyes.

"Huh," he said, "I guess I didn't think of that."

"You're welcome," I said and winked.

Chapter 28

BITSY, MOVING ON

Despite the fact I worked in a hospital, being in one as a patient's visitor set my nerves on edge. In addition, I had to work today, and the audition was scheduled for that evening.

All in all, I was a wreck.

Luckily, Grandma was recovering well. She had been dubbed the nursing staff's favorite. So it was no surprise when the venipuncturist tiptoed in and smiled in my direction. She was a squat woman with round everything. She looked to be in her fifties, with graying hair and kindly eyes. When she smiled she showed a gold cap on a lower tooth near the back of her mouth that glinted. And her forearm revealed a tattoo of a sugar skull. Hard but sweet. I liked her. Liz approved, as well.

Rosa whispered, "Is she still sleeping?"

I nodded. Grandma was perched in the bed, its head at a slight incline. Her leg was casted and propped in a sling that attached to the ceiling.

Cecil Tate had done a number on her. She'd gone through three different surgeries in the span of a week to replace the shattered knee—she argued she'd needed one, anyway—to sew back tendons and to pin the broken shinbone into the right formation for everything to heal correctly. She'd endured all this with a smile on her face, only becoming demanding when she needed to be. Which turned out to be not at all while I was there. Word had circulated of how Grandma had received her wounds, including the part where we had saved the lives of three little girls who'd been kidnapped by the child rapist.

We were heroines.

"I'll come back later then. She needs her rest," said the venipuncturist.

I nodded in appreciation, and as she squeaked out of the room on high-performance walking shoes, I checked the clock. I needed to leave in ten minutes to get to work—my first day back after the last encounter with my boss. I wasn't sure what to expect. And Lord knew I'd need my job to help Grandma with the hospital bills.

I was going to have to kiss butt and grovel. And the part that was Liz, who vehemently hated that idea, was becoming a part of me, too. The last thing I wanted was to bow to a bully. I sighed and looked out the window. It was raining. Pouring, as a matter of fact. But the evergreens were thick on the horizon, rain-drenched and bright green. I loved the sound of the rain. The pattering soothed away the nerves of the day to come.

I let it wash over me until my ten minutes had run out, and Grandma was still sleeping. I rose from the uncomfortable chair. I squeezed Grandma's hand and kissed her on the cheek, above the oxygen hose hovering over her face. She stirred but didn't wake. It was just as well. If she woke now, I'd probably be late. That would do me no favors in trying to salvage the situation with my job. I blew out a huff of frustration and left Grandma to be tended by the radiant spray of bouquets and potted plants and get-well balloons from her adoring fans.

I shuffled out of the room, hitching my backpack into place and gripping my violin case. The audition was imme-diately after work; I wouldn't have time to go home for it, and leaving it in the car unattended was my version of leaving a child or adored pet locked inside. No way.

The walk to the office was long. I swear, everyone wanted to stop me to commend me, to grip my hand or give me a hug. Which was super uncomfortable. I declined hugs and went for the awkward side embrace, instead. Eesh. No respect for personal space.

Cathy wouldn't take a side hug, though. She tackled me like a linebacker when I entered the office.

She sobbed for a good two minutes, which felt more like twenty, before she pulled away, gripped me by the shoulders, and with snot running down her face and her eyes red and swollen, she said, "Elizabeth! You sure did make us proud! I told you, you brave girl. You are something special. Now, tell me all about it."

My stomach twisted. I was so tired of telling people "all about it". But if anyone deserved to hear this story, it was Cathy.

"You know. Just happened to be at the right place at the right time," I said, for the millionth time.

"But what you did! Standing up to him when he threatened to kill you. Omigod! That must have been terrifying! And then seeing your grandmother hacked up when she tried to save you." She fanned herself. "You two have to be the bravest souls on Earth!" Then she stopped and looked seriously at me.

"What?"

"I examined her," she said.

The deadly chill in her voice was enough for me to know who she meant by "her". Aidan. Poor Aidan. I looked away. I didn't need to know what she'd found. I'd seen it. I'd seen it all with a crystal clarity I wished I could forget.

"It was awful," I said.

"You know? But how?"

"I just do," I said, my voice hoarse with force.

She stared at me for a while, probably considering whether or not to push me further. Instead, she said, "He'll serve the rest of his life in jail. That's for certain."

I nodded.

"Good," I said.

She hugged me again, and when she pulled away she looked down at my violin case. She whipped her stare up to me.

"Is today the day?" she asked.

"Yeah. At four. I gotta leave straight from here."

"You nervous?"

I exhaled in a whoosh and nodded emphatically. "I've never done anything like this. The closest was trying out for chair placement and the occasional solo during a concert."

"Don't worry. You're going to be awesome. I just know it." She smiled at me, her small green eyes glittering behind her hopelessly outdated glasses.

"I hope so. Roxanne could be here any moment to fire me. I'm surprised I made it all the way to the office."

"Why?" Cathy asked.

"I refused to sign a write-up," I said.

"In dramatic fashion, too," Liz piped up.

I cleared my throat, as if I could *a-hem* away the change in tone and personality. Cathy didn't seem to notice, though. Her eyes got big, and her mouth flopped open.

"Oh, my gawd! What happened?" She steered me over to my desk. "Put your stuff down first, though. That backpack and violin look heavy."

I set the violin case on the long file cabinet behind the desk and then shrugged out of my backpack. Liz took over for me.

"She wanted to write me up for standing up for myself, basically."

I took over then. "But not just a written or verbal warning, even though we've never been written up before." I plowed on, hoping Cathy didn't notice the plural pronoun I'd used. "She wanted to give me a second warning. So I refused to sign it."

Cathy slowly shook her head while she looked at me, her jaw set forward. "That. Woman!"

"Thing is... I was pretty strong in my refusal. I think she might just fire me because she's angry," I said.

"She can't do that," Cathy said and perched a fist on her hip. "So don't worry. Do you know how difficult it is to fire people around here?" She raised her eyebrows above the rims of her ancient glasses and looked down her nose at me. "Takes an act of congress. It's easier to lay someone off than out-and-out fire them. Even when they deserve it."

"My luck, she'd find a way," Liz chimed in.

"Now," Cathy said, tilting her head to the side. She reached out and rubbed my shoulder. Her lab coat made soft, crinkling noises. It looked as if she'd finally gotten it cleaned and pressed. "Think positive, Bitsy. There's just no way she's going to fire the heroine who saved those three little girls. It's not going to happen." Cathy shook her head to emphasize her point.

"I don't think she gives two shits about those little girls," Liz said.

But I felt the untruth in that statement. Roxanne might be cruel in some aspects, but she'd gotten into healthcare because somewhere in that hardness, she cared for people. Unfortunately, she only cared for the ones who were sick, injured or dying. The healthy ones? Not so much.

"Oh, well. I don't know about that," Cathy said. "In any case, there'd be too much pressure from others to treat you well."

I nodded. "Good point," I said.

A soft knock pulled our attention from the conversation. Cathy looked at the door.

"Is it locked?" she muttered. And then she spoke louder. "Enter."

I smiled and sat at my desk. The monitor was blank, and the computer was turned off. I clicked the button and waited for the machine to make its way through the sluggish start-up process.

"Hey, Cathy."

I looked up at the warm voice. It was Corey. I smiled at him over the counter. He looked at the violin case.

"Today's the day," he said. He knew this. He wasn't asking. "You going straight after work?"

I nodded.

He grinned and winked at me. "You feel good? Confident?"

"J-just nervous," I said.

"C'mon, girl. You got this," he said.

"That's what I said," Cathy told him.

"You heard her play yet?"

Cathy crossed her arms under her breasts. "No," she said, reluctantly. "You?"

"Well, I don't want to brag, but my family might have gotten a private performance by the one and only Elizabeth Varret." Corey made a show of brushing invisible lint off of his scrub-clad shoulder.

Cathy gaped. "What?" She turned an accusing look at me. "And you didn't invite me?"

I hid my face behind my hands. "Sorry," I mumbled.

She swatted me playfully and grinned. "I forgive you. I'll come see you when you're in the orchestra."

Corey turned to Cathy, getting serious and back to business again. "We've got a patient for you."

"You have the details?" Cathy asked.

Corey handed Cathy a chart.

"Great. Break it down for me," Cathy said.

Corey filled Cathy in on a fourteen-year-old boy who had been beaten by what appeared to be a group of people.

Someone had choked the kid until he almost died. Cathy was an expert on strangulation. She'd gather the evidence, prepare it and submit it as testimony in court. Cathy listened to the full report, her face going stern. I'd seen this look before. It was the look she gave when she went into problem-solving mode.

"All righty. I'll grab my camera and be right down there," Cathy said.

The patient couldn't be moved, and since it wasn't a sexual assault there was no need for the privacy of the exam room in our office.

"Thanks," Corey said.

Cathy turned to go, her lab coat flapping wildly about her in the windstorm of her movement. And in a rush, she and Corey were out the door, Corey leading the way to the teenage boy. After a few seconds, Corey popped back in the doorway.

"Hey. You got this. I mean it," he said and pointed at me, daring me to argue.

I spent the entire day peeking over the counter at every approaching set of footsteps, thinking it was Roxanne come to fire me. I fretted until lunch, visited Grandma, fretted all the way back and then fretted some more until three o'clock was approaching, and I had to fret about my audition.

Cathy was charting in her little alcove of an office. It was ten 'til three. I started closing up shop early. The audition wasn't until four. There was plenty of time. But I was so nervous I'd get lost or wouldn't be able to find parking, I'd resolved to leave as quickly as possible. Cathy spied me out of the corner of her eye and turned to me.

"Getting ready?" she asked.

"Yeah, I'm going to be so early it'll be ridiculous, but I'm nervous."

"You mind doing me a favor on your way out?" she asked as she stacked another folder onto a pile of charts and fussed with their neatness.

"Sure," I said, feeling more anxious than I could let on.

"*Relax, girl. Plenty of time to run an errand for Cathy,*" Liz said.

I closed down my computer while Cathy stood and hefted the pile of blue folders.

"I've got to run to a meeting, and these charts need to get over to the child abuse department."

Inwardly, I sighed in relief.

"Oh, I'm parked in Lot C. The child abuse department is on my way. No problem." I smiled at her.

"Let the ladies at the reception desk know you need to deliver them to Harley. She's the social worker for these cases. Don't leave them with the receptionist. I made that mistake before. They sat on the counter for a week." She pinched her mouth in a look of frustration.

Most people I worked with in the Emergency Department were not keen on people who didn't expedite their job tasks. Emergency Department employees tended to forget not everything was an absolute emergency. But I wasn't going to remind them.

I pulled my backpack over my shoulders and grabbed my violin case from the file cabinet, then opened up my other arm for the charts. Cathy plopped them onto my forearm.

"Thanks, sweetheart. You're a dear. Hey, I'm praying for you."

I nodded. "Thanks," I muttered.

"All right, off you go." She went and opened the door for me to pass through. "See you tomorrow. I can't wait to hear how it went."

I turned and smiled then went on my way.

Those charts got heavy by the time I reached the child abuse department, which was located in a separate brick building, detached from the main part of the hospital. There was a buffer of rose gardens and small trees.

It was chilly out, but the sunshine was trying really hard to make an appearance through the gray overcast. I followed the winding path through the stunted rose garden; the roses had been dead-headed in preparation for winter. I had never been inside this particular department before, and my heart squeezed at the thought of where I was. I had to set down my violin case to open the door, hold it with my foot, grab my violin case and then awkwardly push myself, violin case, stack of blue charts and backpack through the door. My violin case clacked against the doorframe, and the sound echoed through the office. I looked around and found two small faces peering at me from an open lobby area.

"Sorry," I said lamely.

The girl behind the counter was my age or maybe even a little younger. She looked up at me from the computer screen she'd been staring at.

"Hi." She paused long enough to check out my full arms and disheveled hair. "Can I help you?"

She was one of those girls who looked perfect. And kind, too. Her hair was the color of honey. She had flawless skin and nice clothes and matching jewelry. I looked down at myself. I was wearing leggings and flats. Okay, they were pretty cute flats... two years ago when I'd gotten them. Now, they were a little on the tattered side. My sweater was pretty plain... and the color of rain clouds. My curly hair was frayed out around my face from the humidity in the air, much of it having escaped from the haphazard bun I'd yanked it into this morning.

I shuffled up to the reception desk. "Hi. I work in the ED."
I pointed to my badge. "I need to see Harley. Is she around?"

The receptionist smiled. "Yeah, I think so. Oh. Um. Hold
on. I'm not sure which office she's in." She looked up at me as
she stood from her chair.

Dang. Even her body was perfect and slender and athletic
looking.

"Why don't you have a seat in the lobby while I go find her."

I nodded and turned toward the lobby.

Petrified, I shuffled to the nearest tan-and-blue-
upholstered chair and lowered myself into it, perching on
the edge of the seat since I still had my backpack on. I sat my
violin case on the blue carpet and situated the pile of charts
onto my lap. All under the silent gaze of the two children. The
boy had dark hair and big dark eyes. The girl was equally dark-
haired, but her eyes were a steely gray. It was apparent she was
the older child.

An older woman with short, gray hair and wearing a bright
Hawaiian shirt sat in another chair and peered up from the
magazine on her crossed legs. She nodded and smiled and
went back to her magazine. I tried to ignore the fact that I was
being stared at by two small children who, frankly, scared me.
I knew why they were here. I could read it all over them, the
information like a shadow clinging to them.

They were little innocent reminders of my youth. But even
so, my heart went out to them. They were playing behind a
table. They'd moved it away from a window and had created
a little cave in which to play. The little girl, who was, I'd guess,
six or seven, pointed to the violin case.

"What's in there?" she asked, not like a curious little girl
who was sweet. Like a little girl demanding information. The
pushiness of her tone was off-putting. I could see Liz in her.

"*Thanks,*" Liz said sarcastically.

"That's a violin," I told the girl.

She was the protector. She had been raped and beaten, but when her abuser had decided to hurt her little brother, she'd run away with him. I wondered if what I sensed was true.

"Play it," she said.

The older woman looked from me to the little girl.

"Ana, that is no way to ask a perfect stranger," she said.

I took a deep breath of relief but had hardly exhaled before she continued.

"Say *please*," the woman said, drawing out the word "please".

Ana looked at the woman and then back at me, and without so much as tilting a corner of her mouth in a smile, she tried again.

"Please play it," she said.

I got the feeling this whole kindness thing was new to her. The idea of asking versus demanding really didn't sink in. She'd simply modified the demand with the required word. The fact still remained she'd asked me to play. I wanted to make some excuse. I glanced around me, but no one else was in the lobby or the reception area. When I looked back, Ana had stood from behind the table, her brother with her, and she'd wrapped one arm around his small shoulders. She pushed her long lank of hair out of her face and stared at me with those cutting gray eyes.

"Man. She seems like she means business," said Liz. *"You better play for her."*

"Jesse likes music. Please play it." She looked down her nose at me, challenging me.

"Jesse is your brother?" I asked.

She nodded.

"Do you like music?"

She shrugged. I glanced over at the woman, whose brows were raised. She clearly expected me to play.

"Well then. Guess I can't refuse since you said 'please,'" I surmised.

Only then did one corner of her mouth shift into something that might be a broken piece of a smile. I wondered if she was telling the truth—if her brother was the one who liked music and not her.

I set the pile of charts onto the little table beside me and shrugged out of my backpack, allowing it to slump back in the chair. I unwrapped the hair tie from the broken clasp and clicked the other one open. I pulled the violin from its red-velvet casing. Jesse and Ana stared, not moving.

Nothing came more naturally to me than holding my instrument. I propped it on my knee, pulled the bow from the case, made sure it had plenty of rosin, closed the case and replaced it on the floor. Jesse shifted and sank down behind the table, so all I could see of him were his eyes, forehead and hair. Ana looked down at him and then settled next to her brother, leaving her purple-clad shoulders and head above the table.

"Hmm..." I said and cast my eyes to the corners of my mind. "What song should I play?"

I said it as if I was thinking out loud, softly. But there was no one in the room except us and no other noises, so I knew Ana and Jesse heard me. I was rewarded with urgent whispering as I tapped my finger to my chin, pretending to be deep in thought. I sneaked a glance. Jesse covered his mouth and Ana's ear as he spoke to her. When he was done, he sank back down behind the table, gripping it with his tiny fingers and revealing nothing below his eyes.

Ana cleared her throat. "Please play the spider song."

I smiled at her bossy tone. I placed the violin on my shoulder and under my chin. I thought about the song. Instead of using the bow, I played it pizzicato, plucking at the strings. I played it softly, so as not to disturb any of the sessions happening down the hallway.

When I was done, I looked at them.

The gray-haired woman said, "What do you say?" to the children.

Jesse whispered again into his sister's ear. She nodded.

"Twinkle, twinkle, little star," she said.

The woman rolled her eyes. She definitely had her work cut out for her. I didn't let her give the lesson right now, though. These kids had been through hell. I could stand getting bossed around a little. I pulled the bow over the strings and let the song breathe to life. After the first round, I did it again and threw in a few new notes, letting the song trip through moonbeams and star shine before it found its way into the here and now. I did it once more, complicating the melody with sixteenth notes that slid and climbed through the heavens before they cascaded back to Earth. I ended the last note long and drawn out, letting the wonder hang in the air.

Jesse's eyes were like saucers; his chin had risen above the table and his mouth hung slack. Ana's face was flat and immutable. I listened for a moment. What would the song be for Ana? Her spirit was strong. She was a fighter. She'd fought and gotten her brother to safety. She'd do anything and everything for him. No one else mattered as much.

Like Liz.

Ana had seen so much sorrow and so much anger and darkness. And at such a tender age, she'd had to do what no one else would do for them. She'd had to be more of a protector, have more heart and more courage than anyone she'd ever known.

"I think she deserves her own song, don't you?" said Liz.

Indeed, I did.

I quieted my soul and let the universe wrap around me.

There I called them. I barely thought of their presence before they were there with me. Beautiful light reflecting rainbows encased in something that was humanoid. One of them stepped forward in front of the others. Androgynous, giant and seemingly made of crystals and stardust. She woke in me a deep love that wove its own song. Her crown was tall and pointed, and in her hand she held a staff so bright it was as if it held its own star.

Golden beings of similar shape gathered. On some I could see their faces, bright and smiling. If anything dark were about, it would flee from the presence of these mighty five who stormed into my other vision. I blinked back tears. This girl. She was so loved and so protected. She had not broken, and this was why. Because in her presence was a whole flock of angels so mighty there was no way she would not be able to accomplish whatever it was she intended.

The giant crowned angel raised its staff and bowed its head toward me. With the motion, the light from the staff burst forth, washing my vision in light and love. I was cleansed, washed of everything but absolute grace and compassion. Love was the only thing permeating through me when I drew the bow across the strings and began to play Ana's song.

The angel quickly showed me pictures, flashes of the things Ana loved. She'd tried cotton candy once. Just once. And it had tasted so sweet. She loved the way it melted in her mouth and tickled her nose. My bow and fingers found the notes that called forward those sensations, the flavors, the sugar-sweet fun of eating cotton candy. The angel was back but then just as quickly showed me how Ana loved to play in the dirt, making mud pies and pretending to cook a full meal for just her and Jesse. She made the best mud food. She could even smell the pizza she pretended to cook. And the salad she chopped and put into a mud bowl.

My bow chopped along the notes, heated the oven for the pizza, rolled out dough. And then I was shown that Ana loved to color. No. She loved to make art with colors. She created from every shade and tint of the rainbow. She tried making her own colors. Once her favorite purple crayon had run out, and she had taken the red and blue and had carefully blended the two colors with hashmarks to make the color she so loved. She was talented. More talented than any eight-year-old I'd ever seen. The angel showed me a man finding her stash of colorful pieces of scrap paper, her art. Her masterpieces. And in a fit of rage, he'd burned them with a blue Bic lighter in a barbeque pit in their empty, muddy back yard.

I didn't give notes to that.

I gave her art a song. First the notes were slow and full and deep, like the depth of the ocean colors she'd strewn together. I could taste the salt in the air, feel the moist breeze on my face. The angels turned, skipped, danced along in the open space of the eternity, their bodies whirling and sparkling. I swear I could hear them singing along. No words, all notes. A perfect harmony was bobbing along right in rhythm to Ana's song.

The notes took a soft turn and then tickled in pinks. The angels spread wings so bright and vibrant I could barely contain the flood of tears at their beauty and utter strength. I sobbed once, tasting the salt of tears as they swooped about me, flushing away the sorrow and hurt with every downward thrust of their mighty wings. And with every note, their voices rose, filling in the harmony to my melody.

The song warmed to orange. The brightness of it sent the beings of light twisting and twirling higher into the ether, leaving streamers of glittering light in their wake. And then the song built into a crescendo of a mighty, burning red that blazed into the majesty and splendor of purple, her favorite color.

What does purple sound like? Purple is strong and regal.

Purple gets things done, while being beautiful and graceful with every stroke. The giant angel took over the song. The voice was as androgynous as the way he/she looked... somewhere between an alto and a tenor, and when she sang, I understood her meaning. The song was no longer an expression; it was a prophesy. She was prophesying the child's life.

It was a good thing I was sitting. The song and prophesy rattled me to the bone. I saw in her the string of perpetrators of child abuse who would be stopped in their tracks because of the work she would accomplish in her lifetime. In her would live the fire of justice. She would set the trend. There would be no anonymity for the horror they tried to get away with. She would ensure to shout it from the rooftops. And finally, finally, we would no longer accept these things as normal and okay. Or something tragic that no one can speak of.

But first she would have to find her voice and her heart and her compassion.

Just like I had had to find them.

The realization dawned on me in a flood of light and truth. The song held its last note, and the angels gathered to me. The biggest and brightest one stood behind me, placing its hands on my shoulder blades, on either side of my spine. I felt the tingling, almost uncomfortable pricking in the muscle that made my flesh want to jump. The four other beings gathered. One hand rested on my head, one other on my forehead, two more on my throat, one on my chest, two in different places on my stomach and the other on my pubic bone, which would have been really weird and uncomfortable if it hadn't been a being of pure light.

Somewhere in my distant memory banks, I recalled these were the locations of chakras. That was really all I knew. I knew they existed, and they affected the body and behavior.

Light flowed through me. The intense love filling me was

almost unbearable. It spread like fire down from the crown of my head, tripping through my spine down the entire length of my body. At certain points within me, an intense sensation like a door opening consumed me. Warm and freeing, the pleasure spread through my limbs, filling every fiber of my being with golden light. My soul shivered with happiness.

Liz was so close we were practically one. I could feel her twin response to every opening and light-soaked touch of the angels. She wept inside me, sobbing as the last door opened. I was grateful her sobs were not mine. As it was, tears rolled down my cheeks as I lowered my violin to my lap. The beings of light gave me one final bow before receding into the universe.

I tried to hang on to the light and happiness that saturated my soul as I opened my eyes.

They were gathered around me. Ana and Jesse had even abandoned their little corner, and Ana had a small hand resting lightly on my knee. I looked at it and hoped that by touching me the beauty I'd just seen, the beauty that was an expression of Ana's soul could somehow be imbued onto her. She looked up at me in awe, tears gathered in the corners of her dark eyes.

"That was your song," I whispered to her, surprised my voice did not stutter despite the flow of emotion.

"For me?" she asked.

I nodded and leaned closer. "The angels tell me that you're an artist. Is that right?"

Her eyes went a little wider. I could sense other people in the room, other social workers and children and counselors. It felt as though a crowd had sprung up around me. I worked against the fear of being surrounded by focusing on Ana.

"They also told me that purple is your favorite color."

"Yes!" she said.

"Do you want to know what else they told me?"

She nodded.

"They told me that you are the bravest, strongest girl I've ever met. That you saved your brother and that you'll go on to save many other children. That you will inspire and lead a big, big change in the future. Do you believe that?"

She tilted her head to one side and squished her eyebrows down and together while she thought about it.

"What does my angel look like?" she asked.

"*Angels*," I corrected her.

"You mean I have two angels?" she asked.

I shook my head. "No. You have five."

Five, she mouthed.

"One is giant, bright white and has a crown and staff. Another is golden and lovely. The others are shades of the rainbow. They glitter and shift and dance to your song. They will inspire your art and every step you take to fulfill your highest purpose. Never forget, when you are lost and confused you are never alone. You are guided, and you will do great things. There is no reason to doubt and no reason to fear with such a throng of lovely beings at your back."

She nodded solemnly, determination setting her face in something like a stern look, even if it was rounded by youth.

"Wow!"

The spell between Ana and me was broken with the sound of a new voice. Ana backed away, holding Jesse in her arms. They retreated to the other side of their table. I peeked over my shoulder before reaching for the violin case.

"That was the most extraordinary piece of music I've ever heard."

Footsteps sounded on the carpet. Violin tucked safely away, I set the case to the floor.

A woman in nice slacks, a dress shirt and a cardigan stood in front of me. She was possibly older than Grandma, but her hair was a shock of short white spikes that lent her a daring youth. There was a slight tremor in her head and neck area. I tried hard not to read her. Now that the beings had gone, a shaking exhaustion threatened to overwhelm me.

"I am Harley," she said. "And that was amazing."

Another woman with a long set of curled light-brown hair approached me. She wiped tears from her face.

"I've never had music affect me so much. That was beyond beautiful. Where do you play?"

"Um... Uh... W-where do I...?"

A bald man, sporting a moustache and wearing a tacky sweater, approached. "Harley, you didn't tell us there was a performance today," he said in a thick southern twang. He reached forward and grabbed my hand.

I winced, shook it, but I was caught. All three of the people around me set their gaze from adoration and respect and pleasant surprise to clinical evaluation. Questions were flung at me from their minds. I backed away as I released the man's hands.

"Just take a slow, deep breath," Liz coached. *"These people are kind and caring. You're the psychic; you should be able to feel that from them."*

"There's just too many of them," I said.

"Breathe."

I did.

"Now. Curly brunette asked where you play. I think they think you're from the orchestra or something."

"Oh," I said out loud, not meaning to. I rubbed at my arm and shifted from one foot to the other. "I'm n-n-not *with* anyone. Actually, I'm on my way to audition for the orchestra."

I scooped up the pile of blue charts on the side table. I held them out to Harley. She looked from my face to the charts and back.

"Cathy—the forensic nurse examiner? —she asked me to

stop by and drop these off to you on my way out. And I just... the kids asked me to play." I shrugged.

Harley took the files from me, a puzzled look on her face, head slightly tilted.

I cleared my throat. "I th-th-think music is really healing. Could I come back and share it with other kids?"

Harley rocked back on her heels. "I think that's a great idea. Let's see what the kids think," she said.

She turned to Ana and Jesse, who had materialized without a sound next to me. Ana stood a few feet from me, with her stern look and dissecting gaze. She was weighing her next action, nodded then fell into me, wrapping my waist in a vice-like embrace. I fought back the urge to shove her away from me and adroitly patted her back. A voice in the back of my soul told me one day touches would not be so uncomfortable, and it was important for Ana to do this.

"Will you please come back and play for us?" She looked up at me.

I stroked her hair. "You're so much braver than me. Yes. I will come back and play."

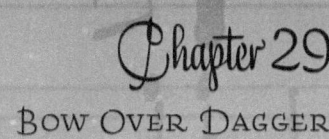

Chapter 29

BOW OVER DAGGER

I flipped the wipers on to full speed and crept down the road. Traffic was backed up. My heart was crashing into itself, causing squeezing stabs of icy pain in my neck and chest. I tapped the wheel in time to the first piece in the repertoire, even while I fought the pooling despair that I would never make it in time. I even prayed between stanzas.

The original piece I'd been writing between practicing the required repertoire, Moonlight, kept flitting into the music. My nervousness was making the pieces all sync together in an odd medley. The piece had been insistently taking my attention since all of the recent incidents, changing itself, revealing new sections to weave into the original imagining I'd had of it. I fought to regain control of my thoughts and wrestled the first piece back to my focus.

"Angels, help me get there in time," I beseeched. I checked the clock for the thousandth time. I had twenty minutes to get there, park, warm up and tune.

God, god, god, god, god! I shouldn't have stayed so long at the child abuse place. What was I thinking? I was already regretting my commitment to play for them in the afternoon on the days I worked.

"It's the right thing to do. Chill out. You'll be fine. The place is only like a mile away. Even with the traffic, you'll get there in plenty of time."

I didn't know if I believed her. I'd been staring at the same taillights in the same exit lane for five minutes. And we'd barely moved. Was there a wreck or something? I tried peeking around the cars directly in front of me, but all I saw was a sea of more cars.

"Maybe I should just give up. I'll never get there in time, and even if I do, I'm sure I'm going to mess something up. I'm going to mess it up. God! What was I thinking, even trying for something like this? I can't get into the symphony orchestra! I'm nobody. And it's been months since I played in an orchestra." I thought to Liz.

"Bits. You've got this in the bag. Don't even worry about it. They're going to hire you because you're fucking brilliant! You have the experience. You have the letters of recommendation. You have the degree. There's no reason you won't get the job. And, oh. You've got me! There's nothing we can't do together. Okay? We've got this! Besides. You know why you're doing this. It doesn't even matter if you don't think you're qualified."

It was true. My worthiness was hardly important. I'd make a fool of myself, and then some, for the chance to finally make music my career. As I resolved to fail well, the traffic inched forward, and bit by bit, the steel-gray Honda in front of me squeezed off the side to the exit. I followed suit, dropping down the off ramp and curving around into downtown Portland.

I parked. I ran. I arrived a jittery, crazy mess. My clothes were askew, and my hair was wet and frizzled from the downpour. There was only one person in the front row of chairs below a stage that was way too high and way too illuminated and way too empty. The chair and music stand beckoned me. I tried one last time to tuck a crazy strand of my curly hair behind my ear and then climbed the stairs to the stage. I wasn't sure I could do this. Most likely, I'd forget everything and just sit there like a moron with my violin clapped to my chin.

The only thing that moved my feet was the thought of Grandma lying in a hospital bed, wondering and waiting for me to get back and tell her how it went.

I tripped over a taped-down microphone cord and landed clumsily into the steel-footed chair, which squawked at me for my efforts.

"Sorry," I said into the microphone, which squealed. I hoped it didn't do that during the piece.

"That's all right," said a man's warm voice, not without a hint of amusement. "I'm Alastair and you'll be playing for me today."

He had one of those older-man hairdos. It was dark and peppered, feathered back around his face and coming down in the back over his collar. Something from the 90s he'd grown to like and had never given up. Somehow, the style looked good on him. He had an attractive air about him, a sense of knowing curiosity. A dangerous sensuality I could feel even from the stage. His face was stubbled but clean, and dark lashes framed clear eyes of the deepest crystal blue. I looked down at him and grinned.

"Just you?" I asked, surprised. I figured it would be several people.

"You might have had one of my colleagues here, but unfortunately, she was ill and had to go home early. So. Go ahead and begin the repertoire when you're ready."

I caught his accent and fell in love. Was it Scottish? Wow. He could ask me questions all night. Liz shook me.

"Hey, lover-girl. You might want to get started before he kicks you off the stage before you've played a note."

"Okay," I said quickly into the mic, which didn't squeal this time. I blushed. I knew I blushed because I could feel the heat radiating off me in a wave I was sure would cause the Scottish man in the empty crowd of chairs to strip off his blazer. A thought that warmed me even more.

"You are really naughty tonight! You need to focus."

I knew I did. I knew she was right. I didn't know what was wrong with me. I shuffled, turned and looked at the chair. I didn't want it, I decided. I circled the chair and dragged it by its plastic back a few feet away. It squealed, offended it would go unused. I went back to the mic.

"I think I'll stand," I said to Alastair. And then before I could bolt off the stage or puke, I backed away from the mic several feet so it wouldn't make that awful noise and pressed the violin between my shoulder and chin.

I finished the first piece before I really felt the sensation of playing. Every note was perfectly executed. Every crescendo well played. I nailed it and I knew it. Yet, Alastair seemed unimpressed.

"Go on to the next piece, please," he said. I played it, marveling how easily it came to me, even on stage. I had no trouble with the piece.

"That's very good," Alastair said, but really didn't sound convinced. He shifted in the seat, leaning forward. "But, you've added a little something to your music. I can't quite put my finger on what it is. Tell me, do you have any original pieces?"

I froze.

Somehow, admitting to the maestro that I had the gall to write my own pieces seemed like a confession to a childish bad habit.

"Answer the man, Bitsy!" Liz commanded.

I shuffled up to the microphone. "Y-y-yes," I said.

"I see," he said, and leaned back in his chair, long fingers on both hands found each other and formed a steeple with their tips. "Why don't you play me one o' those, then?"

"You want to he-ea-ear an original piece," I squeaked.

"I do. If you're willing to oblige my curiosity."

"Um... okay," I said.

I shuffled back to the microphone's safe zone, my stomach somersaulting around my nervousness. I'd never played an original piece for another musician, much less a maestro. I fought back a wave of dizziness, praying I wouldn't pass out or vomit. My hands shook as I tucked the violin back in place and raised the bow to hover over the strings.

The piece, Moonlight, was at my beckon call, eager to be played. Shy at first, the notes trickled out, sort of soft and sweet. They meandered through the atmosphere like lazy, fluttering butterflies with no real purpose and no real destination. But as they rose higher, they transformed, trading fluttering wings for powerful muscle and feather. My song was a phoenix on fire as it climbed up away through the atmosphere until it burst into space, a sheer, fiery rainbow of glittering song.

I was free. I closed my eyes to the stage and to the maestro in the crowd of empty chairs as the phoenix within me rose, swelled, unafraid, unabashed in its beauty. It sighed at the sight of faraway suns and winked at the sea of stars. Nothing could be so real or more right than the gentle strength of an everlasting bird's flight through the never, and the ever and the before and after and always.

My fingers shredded over the strings, my bow dancing at lightning speed as the phoenix flitted from planet to lonely planet in search, on the hunt... for something. More magic? More reality? What was it the creature sought? It was neither power nor fame nor money nor solitude.

It was love. Upon meeting its soul mate for the first time, the phoenix paused, stilled with trills of soft notes. And then more bravely, the creatures flirted, weaved and circled each other, learning the way they moved opposite their partner. The phoenix cried out, flames flowing out like a bride's veil. The mate met the phoenix's cry with a harmony so perfectly in tune the angels joined the song.

The phoenixes danced through eternity, lighting dying stars with their song. They flew through the beyond with a fleet of angels at their tail feathers. They flitted across the forever, sharing their everlasting love with the universe.

The song ended with the fading back to the Earth. The song ended with the promise of eternity. The song never ends. Instead, a bit of it was left in Alastair's soul, and I knew it would forever live there as the journey of love went on.

I opened my eyes and looked down at the man, at the maestro, the sudden realization of my little secret tendency to create my own music was no longer a secret.

The light from the stage caressed Alastair's stubbled face in a tender glow. His mouth hung open, his blue eyes wide. He looked at me with an air of adoration, surprise, awe. He inhaled, the breath catching raggedly in his throat. Then, without a word, he stood up and walked down the row of chairs to the aisle. My nerves lit on fire and sizzled through my body. I gripped the violin and bow in front of me like a shield, not sure if I was guarding against certain rejection or hiding my quivering heart. He climbed the stairs with his eyes on me. My heart swooped around in my chest. Man, was he gorgeous.

"And tall!" Liz chimed in.

I had to look up at him as he gained proximity. And then he gained too much proximity too fast. Defensively, I stepped away from him. My foot caught on the chair, and gravity curled its fingers around me. I started to fall backward, but Alastair gripped my shoulders and pulled me upright. His hands were comfortable. Warm. Big. Gentle.

"Where ya goin'?" he asked, his smile crooked under his longish nose.

"Hopefully, g-g-grace on my feet isn't required for the job," I muttered, my head buzzing with the feel of his energy so close to me.

He was a good guy. A really good guy. I could feel it all over him, and his hands on my shoulders were transmitting to me a lot of information about his kind spirit, his struggles, his loss and his deep capacity to love. It was an empathic overload, and I wished he'd let me go so I could attempt to think straight.

"Sorry," Alastair said and pulled his hands away from my shoulders.

I jerked my head up to him. Had he heard or felt my thoughts?

"And no. Performances are typically played sitting. So you'll be spared many opportunities for clumsiness." He smiled down at me and didn't say anything else.

"Oh. That's. Good?" I said.

He still stared at me.

"So..."

"We can't hire you for the open position," he said.

Smack! My heart twisted.

"*What?*" Liz shouted, and I was glad she hadn't pushed harder to voice her opinion. I might not have been able to stop her.

"Oh," I said lamely, fighting back ridiculous tears building in my eyes.

"It's not 'cause you're not good enough," he said. "It's that you're clearly a soloist. The position is second string.

"I see," I said. My stomach was somewhere in my shoes, and my heart was lodged in my throat. I couldn't quit my job. I'd have to continue working with that awful Mac truck woman until she found a really good reason to fire me, and then what would I do? With Grandma in the hospital, the bills were already starting to flow in. And they were astronomical.

I would have to get a second job to even hope to pay for it all. Which meant there would be no time for the hours of practice I needed to stay sharp for another possible career opportunity in music.

"But that song you just played. It's possibly the most beautiful piece I've ever had the privilege to hear."

"*A fat lot of good it did,*" mumbled Liz.

Inside, I could see her crossing her arms over her chest and scowling.

"You're no second string. You add a little more to the music than what I need in that position," he said, his accent growing thicker.

I looked at him while he stared at me, his blue eyes shining like a kid staring at a candy shop, wondering what on Earth he was getting at.

"Would you be willing to work with me to compose an orchestral accompaniment to that solo? It would be a freelance job. Not steady pay but our contracts with freelancers are generous."

"Really?" I asked, not sure I was understanding what he was asking. "So you want to make this piece something the orchestra will play?"

Alastair nodded. "You would perform the piece, as well. As the soloist. You'd be paid for your time composing with me. And for each performance. If the piece does well, we'll record it, and then, of course, you'd receive royalties on the sales."

He looked at me and waited, expectant, excited. I could see the music working in his mind. He was itching to write the piece, to hear it performed by the orchestra. He was already composing the bass string that would lay the foundation for the cellos, violas, violins and me. The harmony running through his head was lovely, but I had my own thoughts on how to adjust it slightly.

"Say yes! Say yes!" shouted Liz.

"And I'd be working with you?" I asked, feeling some heat rise to my cheeks as I said it.

"You'd be stuck with me through the writing process. Probably take us the better part of six months," Alastair said.

"Okay," I said. "When do we start?"

He leaned back, smiled widely to reveal his straight teeth, raised his hands to the height of his shoulders and pulled them together in a clap of excitement.

"Yes!" he said. "This is going to be amazing."

He reached forward, as if he was going to grab me by my shoulders again, and I flinched away. His arm fell awkwardly to his side.

"My apologies. I get a little overexcited sometimes."

"It's okay. I'm—" What was I? Damaged? Scarred? Sure, I was all those things, but I wouldn't let it define me. "It's just me. I'll get used to you."

I smiled at him and extended a hand while he looked at me with that worried, puzzled look people sometimes gave me when I exposed my twitches. The look that guessed why with a million scenarios.

"Let's make music together," I said.

The smile that split his face lit the room. He grabbed my hand and shook it, rattling my shoulder as if it would come out of the socket.

"Excellent. Really excellent!" He let go of my hand. "So if you're not busy, maybe we could grab a drink and chat about next steps. I can't wait for you to meet everyone. They're going to be blown away with that piece. Oh," he said, mentally changing gears. "Coincidently, what are you calling it?"

I thought about it. The piece had originally been called Moonlight, but after the last several days and all the things that had transpired, the piece had taken on a new life. Maybe not entirely altered, but infused with energy that hadn't been there before. It was as if it had evolved. That thought led me to think of what the angels had said, how we go through cycles to learn and grow. And right there, I chose for the piece a new name fitting for its evolution.

"Reborn," I told him, a sense of calm power settling into my heart.

We walked off the stage together. My mind churned. A sigh of relief was at the back of my throat, the relaxed feeling everything would really be okay.

I thought about the dagger stored safely in a box in my room. We had a choice. A choice that would alter whether we embraced our scars or erased them. But I knew if I chose to erase the scars, the music just wouldn't hold the same power.

"Can you deal with that?" I asked Liz. *"Can you hold the scars to make the music?"*

She paused and thought. *"Bow over dagger?"* she asked then sighed in resignation. *"Hey, listen. Just don't leave me again, okay? As long as we have each other, we don't need a way out."*

We would be forever scarred by the past, but for the first time ever, I embraced the idea I could allow the scars to breathe deep and rich life into my music. Unlike my past, I had the power to choose.

I had power.

I chose my new beginning and the scars shone with a beauty all their own.

To all the survivors: I hope you are finding your own way to Shine. Wading through the aftermath of abuse is not a journey for the weak. If you've survived, I pray your strength allows you to find the richness life has to offer. And after the mouthful of hurt and sorrow, I know the goodness will taste all the sweeter. If we choose to experience it.

Did you like this book?

Readers rely on reviews to decide if a book is worth their time and money. Therefore, I greatly appreciate any rating or review you're willing to give, whether it's just clicking the number of stars you believe it deserves, or writing out what you most enjoyed about the book. You can find *Bitsy* on Goodreads or Amazon.

Thank You!

Stay Connected!

www.raynalstiner.com

@rayna.stiner

@raynalstiner